ANOTHER FIRE

LYN MCCONCHIE

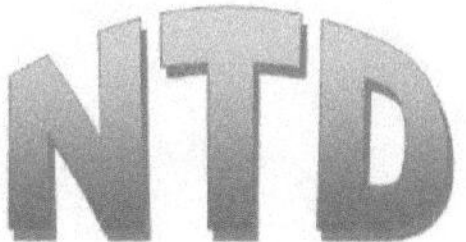

Night to Dawn Magazine & Books LLC
P. O. Box 643
Abington, PA 19001

www.bloodredshadow.com

Paperback ISBN: 978-1-937769-69-7
Ebook ISBN: 978-1-937769-70-3

Cover Artists: Constantin Opris and Muhammad Annurmal
Editor: Barbara Custer
Published in the United States of America

To those of the Blood and the People: One day, the world may turn over again as legends have foretold. If so, may you survive and thrive. And to Bryan Adams, I wrote most of this book to your music which has inspired me for some 40 years.

The fire falls into coals and ash,
But if some other traveler came,
To stir the coals he yet might find,
Some flickering vestiges of flames
But looking at the flickering light,
That lives again as flames flare higher,
It could be asked by one who sees,
"If this is the same – or another fire?"

CHAPTER ONE

The small, powerful car raced along the main highway out of Seattle, a seventeen-year-old boy at the wheel. His young face set in grim lines as he drove, his mind awash in memories that now and again struck hard enough to leave a tear crawling its slow way down his face. The car stereo was belting out Bryan Adams' "All for Love." It had been the song his parents danced to at their wedding, and he hoped it would lift his spirits. Naturally law-abiding, he was mostly keeping to the speed limit, but on a longer, straighter stretch, his foot pressed down gradually, and the speedometer needle drifted over. He was brought to notice that when from behind him, a siren sounded, and flashing lights in the rearview mirror underlined his lapse.

He pulled over obediently. Behind him, the police car halted, and an officer approached the driver's window.

"License and registration, sir?" The last word had a sudden edge to it. A kid of this age wasn't likely to own such a car, so maybe she had a thief here, someone taking advantage of the turmoil. She looked down at the registration, then her gaze went to the license. The photo matched the boy's face, and the names on both pieces of paper caught her attention. Could this be…?

"*What's* your mother's name?"

"Kerry Trevalen."

"The orthopedic specialist? This is her car?"

"Yes, Officer." Jason might be young, but he wasn't stupid. This woman knew his mother, which could buy him a break. "If it's okay, can I show you a photo?" The officer nodded. Jason dug out his wallet, opened it without quick or jerky movements, and extracted the photo of him and his mom at the zoo. Behind them, four otters reared up, paws against the glass window, looking keen to be part of the photo too. His mom was laughing, Jason had a wide grin, and her arm hugged him against her. He held it out.

The officer looked. That was Doctor Trevalen all right, and the boy in the photo and the one right here were the same. Okay, this was the doc's kid, and she owed the doc. That operation the doc had done on her arm had meant she could stay in the job instead of having to take medical retirement, and she wasn't the only officer who owed her. She handed the photo back, watched it carefully stowed away, and relaxed slightly.

"Okay, Jason Trevalen, so why are you and your mom's car heading out of town and breaking the speed limit?" She saw sudden tears well up. "The doc?" Jason nodded. "Oh, *hell!*" Officer Lefau said softly. "The virus?" Jason nodded again. Linda Lefau took in a slow deep breath. If the kid had been told to get out of town, things were only going to get worse. Likely a *lot* worse. "What about the rest of your family? Did your mom say to leave? Where are you going?"

Jason steadied his voice to reply. "Family's all gone. Grandparents went first, then Mom. The last thing she said was to take the car and anything I didn't want never to see again and go to my dad's place down in New Mexico." That was a condensation of hours of discussion. Mom had known a lot more and told him what she knew, but he wasn't sure it would be a good idea to tell the officer just how bad things were going to get. He saw the woman's face tighten and understood he wouldn't have to, that this was a woman who picked up on hints and context.

"What sort of death toll?" Linda Lefau asked quietly.

Jason shivered. His mother had once said you should never take away a person's hope completely. He doubled the figure, doubled it again, and then added a bit for luck. "Maybe five thousand per million'll make it," he said in a small quiet voice.

The officer froze, face, body, rigid, motionless, almost unbreathing. Seconds passed before she spoke again. "It's going to be *that* high? You're sure?"

"*Mom* was sure."

"And if anyone knew, she'd likely be the one," Lefau agreed. "Okay, kid. I owed her, and if she's gone, I guess any debt goes to you. So you move out now." She turned abruptly, looked back at the car, and swayed slightly. "Whoa, guess hearing that's knocked me for a bit of a loop. You get off now..."

"Officer?" The woman had been polite, and well ... maybe a debt should go both ways.

"Yeah, kid?"

"Get all your money out of the bank. There'll be power cuts, buy food that won't go bad quickly, buy ammunition, pharmacy stuff, and seeds, and do it now, then go home."

Linda Lefau straightened, meeting the serious gaze, and understood a few more things. "I will; you be on your way. I hope you make it, and – thanks." She walked back to her police car, watching as the powerful car pulled back onto the road. A momentary faintness struck, and she wavered where she stood. A wave of fear washed through her, and she knew something else. She dived into the car, drove recklessly to the nearest mall, and bolted into the bank. There she emptied the family account, crisscrossed the mall's shops buying with hasty care – particularly at the pharmacy – and with her loaded car, she headed home. She barged through the door and shouted.

A single voice answered. "Linda, that you?"

She found her husband alone in the kitchen. He, too, was a police officer but currently on leave. "Where are the kids?"

"Out, why?"

"Where?" He recognized the tone as suggestive of a dire emergency and asked no more questions.

"Steve's at the playground, Mike's next door with Scotty, and Ali's taken Tiger to the vet for his shots."

His wife nodded. "Okay, now listen, because we may not have a lot of time," her smile was a rictus of anything but genuine amusement. "I was patrolling the main route when this kid came speeding past. I pulled him over, and he's Doc Trevalen's kid." She told the story, adding deductions, and Jimmy listened in silence. He was a practical man. If what this kid said to Linda was right, and he had a feeling it was, then they didn't have a lot of time, and for once in his life, he set the law aside.

"Your granddad's cabin up in the mountains, good place for us to go. What did you buy?" He listened to the list and nodded. "Go down the road and take old Mr. Malcolm's campervan. I know where the spare keys to that and the house are. Take all the food, his guns, and ammunition, any money - he keeps a stash in a pocket behind the puppy picture - and in the cellar, he's got a portable wind generator; get that. Pack the campervan with anything else we'll need from our house."

"Where are you going?"

"Bank, mall, kids, in that order." He was grateful Alison was old enough to drive and had her license. The best thing to do would be to leave Linda's police car behind. When they left, he'd drive the campervan, Ali could drive the family car with the trailer, and Linda could sack out in the back of the campervan. He thought she was right; she had the virus. It remained to see how bad off she was, but if some of what the kid had suggested and Linda had added to was right, she should make it even if she were sick a while. The boy had said that having the virus made you immune, but you still had to survive it first, and most wouldn't. Mr. Malcolm had been taken to the hospital the previous day and, he thought, wasn't likely to make it; he could square taking the older man's stuff with his conscience. He heard the car pull into the driveway then and his daughter's cheerful voice.

"Tiger's up to date. Vet says he's a big healthy boy. I see Mom's home."

Linda Lefau took the heavy cat carrier, set it down, and looked at her daughter. "Sit down and listen, don't ask questions until I'm done, and then understand we don't have a lot of time. We act now, or we may not ... well. Just listen." Eighteen-year-old Ali listened, her eyes widening, her face going pale, but when her mother finished, she asked one question only.

"What should I do first?"

"Give Dad your PIN number and card. He'll get your money. Help me here. If you finish before Dad gets back, I'll want you to go and find Steve, bring him home, then get Mike. *Don't* say anything of this to anyone." She fixed Ali with a hard stare. "I mean it, no hints, nothing. If anyone asks, Uncle Mack is sick, and we're going to see him. Got it?" Ali nodded. "Good, go now. Dad should be back in an hour and a half at the most."

For the Lefau family, there was a concentrated effort for several hours, but by then, they had a packed car towing a packed trailer, the stolen campervan filled with supplies, gassed up and ready, and with Ali trailing the campervan, Tiger in his carrier beside her, the tiny convoy drove down their street, turned left at the end of it and headed at a little under the speed limit towards the mountains. Linda Lefau, by then, was definitely unwell. But they'd picked up items that might help, and a brief phone call to a fellow officer at the hospital told Jimmy that she'd no hope of being seen there.

They passed the outskirts of the city as he listened and relayed the information. "Gary says it's a madhouse. A lot of the staff are off sick; they're getting so many patients in the hospitals that they can't even treat them. When people find that out, they're attacking staff. He says many shops are closing early, some have been looted, the boss is calling in everyone to do overtime. I said to say I'm sorry, but I'm sick too."

Linda nodded. "The kid was right. By the time they realize I still have the car out and come to our place, it won't matter."

"No." He hoped it wouldn't. He'd taken all the police gear from it, emptied the gas tank into spare cans, and added the riot gun along with the radio. His grandfather had been a radio enthusiast, what they called a ham. His old radio was long gone, but some of the setup remained. He could hook the police radio into it so that with luck, they'd be able to sit quietly in the cabin and listen to what was happening back home.

His mind turned to the cabin. Linda's grandfather had bought the land when it was almost worthless, just over a hundred acres of plateau partway up a mountain and off along a single-car track. Her grandpa had built a cabin there, one that started as two rooms, expanded to four and then six with two sheds and a barn. The barn was currently filled with timber that'd been cut a year and a half ago and left to season after they'd had in the guys with a portable mill that made planking out of the logs. Nails were there, yes, and all the other things needed to extend the cabin further. In a few months, it was to have been a productive vacation as he and Linda did that; but now, it could be a lifeline.

They stopped at a small town halfway to their destination and raided a garden store for hand-gardening tools, a battery-powered cultivator, fruit tree seedlings, berry cuttings, and a few other things. They managed to stuff everything into the camper-van and drove on again.

Sixteen-year-old Steve was still whining that he hadn't been allowed to tell his friend's family and ask them along. Twelve-year-old Mike was silent. They kept going, and by daybreak, they turned off onto the narrow road to the cabin. Linda staggered out and looked at what could be their haven, then at Jimmy and her kids.

"If it gets as bad as I was told, this'll be our home for the rest of our lives. We're lucky to have the place and the land and be away from the city. Jimmy, sweetheart, I guess you'll have to take charge. I don't think I can do much more."

She stopped speaking abruptly, and her husband nodded. "Ali, take Tiger into your bedroom, put out his litter tray, give him food and water and let him out, and everyone's to be careful he doesn't go outside for a few days. Steve, Mike..." He gave the orders. Linda managed to reach the cabin, crawl onto their bed, and collapse there. He placed the medications they had on the cabinet beside her, left a filled carafe of water from the well, and started making lists. What they still needed, what they had, what they should - or shouldn't - do.

And that was how it went from then on. In later years, Jimmy would bless his wife for her quick thinking, and she'd bless the boy she'd stopped for speeding. Jason would never know he'd saved them, and they would never know what became of him. She only hoped that wherever he was now and whatever he did, he'd lived and was happy. He deserved it.

****

With no idea of the magnitude of the good deed he'd done for one family, Jason drove on until up ahead, he saw a sprawl of cars and trucks. He pulled a hard right, slowed to a crawl, and stopped where there was room, taking out the binoculars he had on the seat beside him. One quick look, and he knew he wasn't going to get past that lot today. There was nothing behind him, so he gambled, turned the car, and drove back in the direction he'd come from, to where, a few miles back, he'd passed a turn-off. He was watching in the rearview mirror, but no vehicles followed. He stopped some distance down the side road, picked up the map, and looked over that section.

His mom's words rang in his ears. "When things go really bad, so do some people. When there's no law, there are more outlaws. It becomes everyone for themselves, and if it's them or you, they'll kill you without hesitation. Remember that, because you may have to face the same choices, and if you do, stay alive; let them be the ones to die."

He'd never thought his kind, gentle, doctor mom could say something like that, but she had. She'd seen his astonishment and managed a smile.

"One of the things I did just before I met your father was a rotation in *Doctors Without Borders*. I saw what could happen to people who wouldn't fight back. They died, and some of them in ways that weren't pleasant. You know where the guns are; take them and all the ammunition. Keep one on you at all times, and have one to hand in the car. If someone comes for you, don't think about it. Just do it."

One hand left the wheel and crept across to touch the gun

that lay under maps and by the opera glasses. It was loaded, ready, and he would be ready, too, if he had to be – at least he hoped so. His grandpa had left the guns at Mom's place last week for checking by the gunsmith. That'd been done, and he could only be thankful for both events. He saw the indications that he'd come to a small town in another mile or two, and he slowed, went around the bend, and saw it ahead.

He stopped and used the binoculars. Nothing much moved in the hot sun; there were a few people in the main street, and he could see the banners of a used car lot. He'd remembered something else his mom had said, so he drove on cautiously and took the street that would bring him to the back of the lot. He left the car locked and entered the place from a side alleyway.

A big, jovial-looking man came walking towards him, beaming, as he thrust out a hairy-backed hand.

"How are you, young man, and what can I do for you? I know, you'd like a jeep. I've got just the one, ex-army, so it's genuine, hardly used, A1 condition, and a steal at the price I'm asking. Of course, it depends on how much you know about vehicles, but I guess a man like you would know what to look for…"

Jason did know what to look for. He'd seen that the man's eyes, above the broad smile, were like cold gray pebbles. He kept his voice low and quiet; it often paid to be underestimated. "I need a small trailer, one of the ones with an automatic release from the car. You've got one in your lot, sir. How much?"

The smile stretched. "Well, a good trailer like that doesn't come cheap, but then you'd know that. Let's go and look at it, shall we?"

He went to put an arm around the kid's shoulders and got a look that stopped the movement. The little bastard had looked dangerous for a minute for all his preppy appearance. He pasted the grin on again and led the way to where the small shabby trailer stood. Although he'd only been flattering, he was right in that Jason did know something about vehicles. Once he'd gone over it, he knew that the trailer, while shabby, was sound and the tires had decent tread still. However, Jason also knew bargaining; he looked discouraged, mentioned the worn paint, the minor rust, and made an offer. The car-lot owner gave an excellent impression of a dying duck in a thunderstorm and countered with a far higher figure.

They settled on an amount that reflected cash in hand. Jason signed papers, wheeled the small trailer down the narrow alley to where his car waited, attached the trailer, and drove off, aware that the lot owner was watching. He recalled a frequent saying of his mom's, that the easiest way to get out of trouble was not to get *into* it, and drove down the next alleyway he saw that was open at the far end. After that, he dodged about, circled, and ended up back on the side of town where he'd driven in. He consulted his map and headed off in the direction he wanted but at a tangent. He stopped twice, each time using his glasses to look all around; both times, he saw a rusty truck circling like a shark that had temporarily lost the scent of blood.

He waited until it was going the opposite way, then tramped on the accelerator, spun around a corner, and headed for the next town. No one seemed to follow. There he purchased food, filled prescriptions given him by his mother, added three pairs of comfortable boots and a good coat that made him look twenty pounds heavier. He rubbed a pinch of dirt around his chin. If he looked less like a kid, it'd be safer for him.

He circled the block, and on the way back to his car, he passed a Goodwill shop. In the window, he saw something that slowed his steps. Like the trailer, it was shabby, but he knew what it was, an earlier and simpler model of a portable wind generator. They'd been made first in 2033, they were sturdier, and that model would plod on for a decade or more before it needed maintenance. It was six years old now, so it'd been long since superseded. That didn't mean it wasn't a good piece of machinery. He drifted in through the doorway, looked at it, poked a finger into the works, shrugged elaborately, and only turned when he was directly addressed.

"It's in good working order. I can show you a certificate."

By then, Jason had noticed something else. His tone was deliberately doubtful. "Yeah? How much?" He frowned at the answer. "That's a fair amount. Old stuff, sometimes it falls apart with no warning."

He allowed the volunteer to see his gaze wander to where a small camp stove sat. It, too, was shabby, the kind that could be run on just about anything, including wood, so long as you knew what you were doing. Jason did; his grandpa had taught him. The volunteer's gaze followed his, and the man brightened.

"Tell you what. That stove goes with the generator, least ways they came from the same place. I think there's a sleeping bag, too. What say you take the generator, and I'll toss in the other couple of things?"

Jason kept his look worried, allowed the man to persuade him, and demanded the use of a trolley once he agreed to the deal. The volunteer was only too happy to oblige. He loaded the items on that, wheeled it to the car, helped Jason to load them, and grinned at him. "Have a good trip. Nice weather to camp out. Where're you going?"

"Up Seattle way." After all, the car was currently pointing in that direction, and if anyone came asking, it'd put them off.

He waited until his temporary friend left with the trolley, drove north, turned two streets down, and circled to travel south again. He was pleased with himself and still more pleased when he saw a booth by a farm gate offering fresh fruit some miles into the countryside. He stopped and bought two 40-pound boxes, one of apples, the other of loose-skinned mandarins. The sort of thing that could be eaten as he drove. To those, he added five two-liter bottles of water, just in case.

He did eat and then drank some of the water while driving, pausing any time he was on higher ground to look ahead with the glasses. It was the third time he used them that he saw the truck again. If that belonged to the man from the car lot, then he wasn't out for a Sunday drive. It wasn't Sunday, and Jason figured that seeing the same truck three times in different places suggested the driver was looking for him, and it wouldn't be to ask him to dinner. Jason dodged down another side road, found himself on the main highway again, and put his foot down. If that truck was as old as it looked, he should be able to outrun it.

He stayed, pushing his speed, on the main road for an hour before switching to side roads again, paused to scan the countryside on another rise, and said something his mother or the Grands would have scolded him for. The truck was back on his tail. He didn't *want* trouble. Why did the guy think he was worth all this? He shifted in the seat, and the explanation popped into his head. He'd emptied all the family accounts before he left the city, and he had a real wad. And … he glanced at the pocket in the door.

He was an *idiot!* Sure, he'd taken only some of it to the car lot, but he'd left the rest in there. The edge of one bill could be seen if you stood by the car at just the right angle, as the car-lot man had when insisting on helping him attach the trailer. The man must have put together that bill and the way the pocket bulged under it and come up with an idea of just how much Jason had. If Jason disappeared in some empty place and wasn't found, or if he was, but not for a while, and if the only thing missing was that wad of cash, then who were the police going to suspect if they didn't even realize what was missing? His mind pointed out that if his mother was right in what she'd believed, there probably wouldn't be any police anyhow.

He glanced back. How was he going to sleep with someone on his tail? It wouldn't be safe … his mind added something to that, and Jason's foot lifted slowly from the accelerator. The car-lot man didn't know he'd been seen. His father had had a saying for that one; he slowed further, watching the roadside. It was empty hereabouts, but an old, falling-down barn with an overgrown track to it came up. If he parked the car in there, if he left a clue…

He slowed, drove up the track, and parked his car and trailer so a corner of the car showed, just a flash of chrome bumper. He set up the stove, enjoyed hot soup and ham sandwiches, fruit for dessert, and a mug of strong, sweet coffee, then settled for the night after making preparations. Only a sliver of the moon gave light. He moved to where he was comfortable and began to sort events. It felt strange knowing he'd never see his mom or grandparents again. And he hadn't seen his dad for years. Would he even be welcome? The night was quiet, the air warm, and little by little, he slipped into a drowse.

CHAPTER TWO

In general, younger hearing is better, and Jason had excellent hearing anyhow. Half-asleep or not, he heard the brush of feet through the long, dried grass, woke completely, and froze, waiting. The steps stopped, then started again, followed by the faint squeak of his car door handle being tried, and opened. Against the moon, he saw something raised and brought down, swung again at an angle with savage force.

Jason had been coming to a slow boil for some time. He didn't like being hunted. He didn't like that some man who didn't even know him would be happy to kill him for money. His mom had worked hard to buy that car and save the cash he'd withdrawn. The car-lot man was hitting the sleeping bag again where he assumed his victim's head would be, and something burst inside Jason Waterhawk Trevalen. He brought out the gun from the holster in the small of his back, leveled it, and spoke quietly.

"That's my property you're beating to death."

There was an incoherent sound. The man turned on him, swinging up the thing he'd been using. He took a half step towards Jason, the whatever he was holding started down – and involuntarily, the boy fired. The car-lot man staggered back, snarled, and brought his weapon around. Jason stepped away and coldly, deliberately, shot again. His enemy fell, twitched, and went still in a way that said he'd never again be a threat to anyone. Jason stood there watching, uncertain if what he felt right now was horror at what he'd done or a warrior's triumph.

After a minute, he moved silently. He'd looked over the ancient barn when he drove into it, and he'd seen that in the back right corner, there was a shallow pit. He had a shovel in the car.

He got that, deepened the hole, rolled the car-lot man into it, and checked his pockets, finding a reasonable amount of cash, a bank card together with its pin number. He shoveled the earth back, leveling the top and tamped it down, taking some of the bits of rusty discarded metal and dropping them in a casual heap on top. He felt sick by now but ignored it; there was too much to do.

After another hour, he got into his car and drove away. Behind him, the barn (with a bit of encouragement) had finally fallen, something, he thought, that would surprise no one. Nor was it evident that under the collapsed building, there was a rusted truck. He drove for two hours at right angles, found the town marked on his map, and leaving the car, he slipped down the street towards the money machine. He took some of the money from the card, wiped it clean, and stuck it back in such a way the machine retained it. There, if the man had a family, they'd get it back. He'd taken only a fifth of what was there, and he thought it a reasonable payment for attempted murder. He drove off again as quietly as possible, regained the main road, and continued for another hour.

Up ahead, he saw the blinking lights that advertised a motel. He pulled in, paid at reception, and crawled into the single bed after parking the car and trailer right under his window and removing the rotor arm. He slept with the gun at hand and slept well. He left midmorning after a large breakfast, and while his stomach was at peace, his mind stayed restless.

He'd noticed no one wearing a mask, not anywhere he'd seen people. His mom had mentioned that. It wasn't any use; people had been infected long before any symptoms showed. Masks were more of a talisman than a genuine preventative, and he was immune anyhow. It looked as if the general populace had heard that masks were a waste of time and money, didn't realize how bad the pandemic was becoming, or just didn't care.

The waitress where he ate hadn't been busy, so she'd lingered by his table, telling him about her plans to travel next year.

"My sister's working in England. She can because our grandparents were English, so we have a right. She wants me to join her; it'll be great. I can see London. The prince just got engaged, and my sister says there's going to be all sorts of celebrations."

She wouldn't shut up, and Jason was too polite to be rude and ask her to go *away*. He ate quickly, however. He bought more cooked food to take with him, thanked her for the meal, left a generous tip, and got out of there. He wondered as he drove away if she'd be one of those that survived.

He drove all that day, the tires humming steadily against the road, keeping hunger at bay with the fruit. He stopped twice for gas, each time, buying a couple of extra cans that he also filled. He dared not buy too much at any one time in case people noticed, but he had no clear idea of how much time it would be before people started locking themselves away and locking up every business as well. He saw signs of it in the first small town after the motel; half the shops had been shut even though it was barely past lunchtime. He'd found a shop open and bought a good-sized pair of insulated coolers. Meat or anything uncooked, including the fruit, would last longer in those. He might have to slow down soon and didn't want to do that before he had to.

That time came as he rounded a bend towards five o'clock that evening and saw ahead a big car wedged nose first into the bank. From it came a frantic barking, and he saw a dog's head at the part-open window. Jason glanced about quickly; he saw no one, and through the partly open window, he could hear no other vehicle. He slowed, passed the crashed car, pulled in, and stopped. Far enough away that if someone hit it, he should be clear. He got out and walked, conscious of everything around him, to the vehicle where he could see inside.

The dog's a young animal was his first thought. The next that it was a breed he'd never seen before. And then he saw the occupant. A small, huddled figure, white-haired, dressed in a neat floral suit. As he stared, her eyes opened slowly, glazed with shock as they stared at each other. The dog went mad, licking her and then pawing at the window and barking, seeming to ask for help. Jason, who loved animals, couldn't ignore the desperate look and nodded.

"All right, boy, hang on, and I'll see what I can do." What he could do, was, he found, nothing helpful initially. The impact seemed to have jammed the driver's door. *Okay, what about the passenger door?* He tried that, and with protesting screeches, it opened about halfway. He heaved several times more to no effect and gave up. The dog had moved back, standing protectively over its owner, but now he'd stopped causing those strange sounds. The dog came forward. Jason scratched under the animal's chin.

"Good dog, okay, we can't get this door open any further. Let's see about your owner."

The owner spoke now in a thin, weak voice. "Thank you, young man."

Jason nodded. "I'm Jason Trevalen. Look, I'll do what I can, but you do know if I call for help, no one's going to come?"

She smiled faintly. "I know. My house is back about a mile, down the driveway on the righthand side."

Jason looked back and could see a roof in the distance. "Okay, if I help you, do you think you could get into my car, and I'll take you and the dog home?"

"I had my seatbelt on. I don't think I'm hurt; it was just such a shock. Oh, and her name is Stormy." Jason giggled involuntarily, and the old lady looked surprised. "Sorry," he told her. "It's just that my dad's name is Storm, Shandiin Storm."

"You said Trevalen?"

"That's my mom's name. I used it after her divorce. She's..." He paused and felt a flood of sorrow. "She *was* Kerry Trevalen."

There was a brief silence. Then, without speaking, the old lady raised herself slowly and slid towards the half-open door. Jason reached in to help her. Stormy bounded past him and stood on the road, wagging her tail madly and watching as little by little, the old lady came at last to sit on the end of the seat, her feet on the road, while she caught her breath. She looked up.

"I'm Mrs. Emma Hayer. Stormy's things are in the back of my car, if you could bring them, too?"

Jason nodded. He forced open the back door, finding that it was less jammed, and collected a dog's blanket, two bags of dog biscuits, several large cans of dog food, and a leash to go with the collar Stormy was already wearing. He moved them to his car, spent five minutes rearranging the contents to make room for a dog and an old lady. With anxious care, he helped Emma Hayer move the short distance to his vehicle. With her and the dog comfortable, he trotted back to the crashed vehicle, retrieved the handbag he'd seen on the floor, took the car keys, checked the trunk, and found both tools and gas. He considered that so quickly it would have looked like no time at all, and decided against taking anything.

He returned to his car, climbed into the driver's seat, and pointed to the distant roofs. "There?" Emma inclined her head. "Okay." Her seatbelt was done up, and he started the car, turning, and heading back. He drove down the indicated driveway and came out from the tree-lined avenue into a gravel circle before a large old house. "Let's get you inside. I can try calling anyhow. If no one answers, well, Mom was a doctor, and I do know a few things that may help."

Emma Hayer eyed him with some amusement. About seventeen, she judged, a well-brought-up child, respectable, decent, and besides, it was likely she had no choice. She sighed inwardly. It was bad enough to outlive all your contemporaries, worse still when you didn't like the generation after, and worst of all when you had no more choices. He would have stopped at the front door but then swung the car towards the back of the house instead. She appreciated his common sense. The front had a flight of steps up to it; the back door was more likely to be ground level – as her backdoor was.

They pulled up there; she handed him her keys, indicating which one. He got out, opened the house door, and held it open. Emma extricated herself from the car, called Stormy, and made her way into the house. Jason, she noticed, stood ready in case she faltered but kept his hands to himself when she managed alone. More and more, she appreciated who the fates had sent her. She slumped into a kitchen chair and looked up.

"The power's still working. A cup of tea would be pleasant, and there are biscuits and cake in the tins up there." She pointed. Jason started the kettle, laid out cups, saucers, and plates, fed Stormy when she nudged him and sat at the table with the items he'd gotten from the tins on a plate for each of them.

"Um, don't say if you'd rather not, Mrs. Hayer, but where were you going? Is someone expecting you?"

Emma Hayer decided to be brutally honest. There was no time to wrap things up in fancy words, and she wanted something from the boy. "Yes," she said. "I was taking Stormy to the veterinarian to be put down."

He drew one of the dog's ears through his fingers. "Is she sick?"

"No. You know there's some sort of virus out there?"

"Mom told me about it. She had a friend overseas; he knew a lot and phoned her."

"Yes. Do you know if you're immune, and if so, why?"

Jason nodded and recited the information Kerry Trevalen had been told. "Mutated virus, a form of Staph A. Long incubation period, very high mortality rate. To be immune, you have to have had a minor form of the infection and been treated by a particular antibiotic. And the intensity will depend on when that happened. If it was in the last couple of months, you'd be completely immune. The longer back in time, the worse you'll be until if it's around five to six months, you could still survive, but you'd need intensive care in a hospital."

Emma took in a long slow breath. "And there aren't any or not for much longer."

"No," Jason agreed quietly.

"That's why I was taking Stormy to the vet, to be put down."

His gaze jerked up to her face. "You've got it? You're sure?"

"Yes. I knew this morning. I can't leave Stormy or even let her go free to starve or be shot by someone. I was going to stop at a friend's home and ask if they'd take her. That's why I have her food and things. If they couldn't or wouldn't, I'd have gone on to the vet."

Jason spoke without thinking. "If *he's* still alive."

She looked up in shock, then gave a small chuckle. "You know that never even occurred to me. What about you, Jason? Where are you going?"

Over another cup of tea – he'd never really liked the stuff before, but she had an odd variety, a clear red tea that was gently tart, and he found it refreshing, the biscuits and cake were good, too – he told her his own story.

"Dad has a ranch in New Mexico. He and Mom met when she was at a hospital there doing a residency. She said it's the only time she ever did something without thinking. They were married in six weeks, and they were happy for three years. Then she needed to go elsewhere for her work. They had a row about it, but she went. She said her work was as important to her as his to him, and that was that." He could hear his mother's voice in his mind as she'd sounded when she told him the story.

"How did your father feel about that?"

Jason squirmed. He could see both sides. "I know what she was saying, but he wasn't wrong either. I mean, you can't just walk away from a ranch, and his tribe's there, too."

"Tribe?"

"Yeah, Dad's part Navajo." Jason laughed. "Mom said maybe that's why they understood each other so well to start with. Her parents were old Cornish from Cornwall, and they're sort of tribal too. Her dad – my grandpa – came over to work with

IT. Grandma was pretty good at it as well, and they had Mom quite late. They took citizenship, and she was born here, so she already was one." His face lit, remembering.

"They were great. They had this old house outside the city, and when Mom came back to live there, they built her a cottage, like a guest house. Mom hadn't even known she was pregnant when she left Dad. She told him when she had me, though, and went back a year later when she had time. By then, she'd bought a house on the other side of the city near a good school for me.

"She'd take me to Dad's ranch for a couple of weeks every year after that, but they had a big fight when I was eleven. He wanted me to live there, and she said she couldn't. He said he'd only asked me, that I should know the ranch and the people because they'd be mine one day, and she said time enough for that. I was in a good school and doing well ... anyway, it was a real fight, and after that, I didn't go to the ranch again."

"Why?"

"I'm not sure. I think Mom worried that he'd get a court order while I was there and try and keep me. She said she didn't want me to be only a ranch hand or even an owner. If Dad kept to what he said and left the place to me, I could run it with a foreman or sell it if I wanted, but it wasn't the only career choice, and she didn't want me restricted."

"What did you want?"

"The option, I guess. I wanted to keep going there every year, but, well, I liked Seattle, I had friends at school, and I didn't want to be without Mom or the Grands. I was studying. I wanted to be a doctor, and I had a head start with her being one and having friends who were, too. They'd talk to me about medical stuff. In another year, I'd have gone to a university." He looked up, sudden tears in his eyes. "I guess I can forget all that now."

"No," Emma said softly. "Now, they'll need doctors more than ever. If you make it to New Mexico, remember that. Find someone who's done the training and learn all you can. You'll be valuable, and you said it yourself, you have a head start, find books..."

Jason grinned wryly. "I have. I've got all of Mom's books in the car. She kept them from her first year of study and told me to take them, so I did."

Emma didn't ask about his mother, or what he'd called his "grands." She could guess; he was driving alone; she thought the car had been his mother's, and she'd seen the sudden tears when he spoke about his mom. She got carefully to her feet. "I'm going to go and lie down. Help yourself to food, and there are a couple of bedrooms ready. Maybe I'll see you in the morning."

"I won't leave without saying goodbye," he assured her, and she smiled.

"Good, Stormy wouldn't like that."

He grinned, patted the dog, and stood as the old lady walked slowly but steadily out of the kitchen, and he heard her climbing the stairs. She reminded him of Grandma Trevalen; he remembered how he'd spoken to her that last time and a pang of grief shot through him. To blot that out, he went looking through the house. It was big enough; it must have been something in the olden days. It had one and a half floors the top floor didn't cover the whole of the first one. She couldn't have kept it so clean by herself, and she seemed to live alone.

That set him thinking. Someone must come in every day to clean, so where were they? She'd been taking Stormy either to friends or the vet. Why hadn't someone driven her, or was she that independent? Even when she knew she was sick? And had she had the accident because she was ill? If so, she was worse off than she appeared. That sent his questions off on a tangent, and he was still thinking hard when he found a suitable bedroom and crawled into the bed.

Jason was up early the next morning, made coffee, and started breakfast. He looked up to see her coming through the kitchen door wearing a dressing gown and looking frail, with

Stormy at her heels. He'd scoped out the fridge already. "Toast, bacon, and eggs? I can do them scrambled if you'd rather?"

A brief discussion saw them sitting down to scrambled eggs with bacon and a stack of buttered toast. He had coffee, while she had more of the red tea. With the food eaten, he placed the dishes in the sink, sat down again, and asked, "Does someone usually come in to do housework?"

Emma nodded. "They did. The road here goes on and loops back to the main road. If you go down this one another two miles, there's a little farm. It belongs to the Sorensons. Maidee comes in every day to do housework, and her husband does some of the heavy work if I need him." She paused, and her voice came slower. "They just stopped coming two days ago. I phoned, and no one answered. I drove down and knocked, and no one came to the door. I went back the day after, and their animals needed to be moved to another paddock. I knocked again, and I let the animals out. They didn't have a cat or a dog, and I wouldn't break in, and so I came home. You see?"

Jason saw. "Look, I'll go there. If I have to, I can get in and see if they've just left the place. I can open other gates so their animals will be okay. At least that way, you'll know for sure. What about you? How are you?"

Her head came up proudly. "I can manage."

"Okay, I'll go now."

He drove to the Sorensons and checked. Both doors were locked, but one of the windows wasn't. He forced that up and leaned in to call. As Mrs. Hayer said, no one answered, but he could smell... He climbed in and walked through to the bedroom. They were both there, laying together, a Bible in the man's hands. A photograph in hers, their wedding photo from the look of it. He went back out of the window, shut it again, and headed for the back. There was a handful of sheep and two cows, so he opened the gates, a lot of them. He also opened the doors to the barn so they could find shelter if necessary, and there was hay they could get. He couldn't do any more. On the other hand...

He returned to check the drawers, their wallet, and purse, and found money and gold jewelry. His mother had said it could be weeks before everyone understood money and gold had little value anymore, but until everyone knew that, he could buy what he might need so long as he had money or gold. He found unopened cans and packets and took those. In the bedside cabinet, he found a gun, and on the shelf in the closet, there was ammunition for it. He took those too. Then, he looked at the silent figures, remembering something his father had told him

"Forgive me; what I've taken was taken from necessity, not from greed. I won't waste anything, I've freed your animals, and they have food and shelter. Wherever your spirits have gone, be at peace." He left, knowing Mrs. Hayer would accept what he told her. Older people knew about death, and she'd like the way they'd gone.

He drove around the back of the house again when he returned. If anyone came stealing, he'd rather it wasn't Mom's car that was taken. He entered silently to find the old lady bent over the table, her face twisted in pain. Jason jumped to support her.

"Are you okay? What is it? What can I do?"

She managed to straighten and smiled wryly. "No, I'm not okay, I'm afraid. And we both know what it is."

Jason whirled. "Sit down; I'll be back in a minute." He dived into one particular box in his car, extracted a card of pills, and went back, striding quickly. "He snapped two items out of the card and handed them to her with a glass of water. "Take them."

"What are they?"

"Painkillers. Mom gave me everything she had in the house, plus she wrote me a bunch of prescriptions. She's on any doctor list, so I've been stopping at open pharmacies and getting one of them filled out each time. I've got all sorts of stuff you need a prescription for." He saw them starting to work as the pain eased from her face.

"Thank you."

He flushed. "I should have thought of it before."

She changed the subject. "And the Sorensons?"

"I found them in their bedroom. He was holding a Bible, and she had their wedding photo. I opened the hay barn for their animals and all the gates."

"Thank you. Yes, they were married for more than thirty years and still loved each other. In many ways, they'd have been happy to go together. They never had children - nor did my husband and I - and at times like these, I'm not sure if I don't prefer it that way. It's not going to be a good world when this thing dies out."

She sighed. "My husband wouldn't have been able to deal with things here and now. He was a very rigid man, but I loved him, and he was always kind. He died five years ago, and soon I'll be with him." Stormy, hearing the note in her voice, came and thrust her head into the older woman's hand. "Yes, good girl, you're the one I'll miss."

Jason took a deep breath. He knew she wouldn't have more than another day or two, and he couldn't bear to leave the dog - or shoot Stormy either. He reached out and patted the dog and met the old lady's imploring look.

"It's okay, Mrs. Hayer, I'll take her. She likes me, and I like her. If we do make it, my dad won't mind; he's got the ranch, and he likes dogs."

He saw peace flood her eyes and knew he'd done the right thing. He was sure of it the next day when he got up early and she couldn't. But he had the pills, and he made sure they overlapped, so no pain broke through. He winced for all those that were dying without them. He made a jug of the red tea, and now and again, she drank a mouthful. It was late that night she called his name, and he came to sit by her.

"I left everything I had to charity and keepsakes to friends," she said slowly. "None of them have answered my phone calls, and after this, organized charities won't exist. When I'm gone, Jason, go through the house, take anything you want, anything you can use. There's money in my handbag, take it.

Anything of Stormy's too, and put that quilt over me," she pointed to the faded folded quilt on the window seat. "My mother made it for me when I was a child. Then set fire to the house, and don't look back. I don't want my body eaten by scavengers; I don't want my things stolen by those who take just because it's there. Will you do that for me, Jason?"

He remembered what he'd said at the Sorenson's bedside and nodded. She smiled. "I'll sleep now, and if I don't see you in the morning, I want you to know how grateful I am that you found us both. Love Stormy for me. I hope you get where you're going and that you both live long and happy lives. Good night, Jason."

He stood and walked to the door, and there he turned to look at her, giving her the only comfort he had to offer. "Good night Mrs. Hayer, and if we survive and I have a daughter, I'll call her Emma." He saw the smile, went out, and closed the door, knowing what he would find in the morning.

He woke at seven, fed Stormy, and walked step by step to the bedroom. He spread out the old faded quilt as he'd promised. Spent several hours scouring the building for what he might use, returned to the crashed car and added the gas and tools he'd seen there to his trailer, and then, as he left just after midday with the dog beside him, he looked back at the old house. Flames were rising in the still air; a promise given had been kept.

CHAPTER THREE

The next time he halted for the night, he looked at the papers he'd taken from the desk in the lounge. Stormy's papers. Somehow, he'd never got around to asking about her. Now he was surprised and interested to read them. It looked as if someone had decided to create another of the designer breeds. They'd started with a Doberman, added in a collie, and then bred back to a poodle. They ended up with a forty-pound dog that could handle both hot and cold weather. It was smart, sensible, mostly hypoallergenic, didn't bark too much, easily trained, usually okay with other animals, and – this was the kicker – with an average lifespan of twenty-five years. The papers said she was just three now.

No wonder he hadn't recognized the breed. It had been provisionally known as a Docopoo, presumable for Doberman/Collie/Poodle. If Mrs. Hayer had wanted to show Stormy, she was eligible for the "Specials" section, reserved for dogs of the designer but not yet fully established breeds. *Like the Pomshee,* he thought. He'd seen one on TV, a lovely little mix between a Pomeranian and a Shetland sheep dog. He glanced at Stormy. Shortish coat, but he thought the outer, slightly longer layer was probably shed at the start of summer, a rich pale gray with black markings, a collie's tulip ears, alert eyes that watched everything. From the list folded into the papers, she was able to recognize and obey a substantial list of commands.

"Stormy?" She cocked her head at him. "I'm sorry about Mrs. Hayer, I liked her. She wanted you to come with me and be my dog. I hope that's okay with you, too?" She whined softly, and he ran a hand gently down her head. "I'll do my best for you. We'll have something to eat, and then I'll see how good you are at what you do."

He stopped at a tiny motel a couple of hundred yards off the main road. There was no one there, no vehicle, but there was food in the fridge. He went looking further and found the safe unlocked and the cash drawer in the office. He took the notes from both; he didn't think the owners were coming back, and in the morning, he'd take some of the uncooked food. On second thought, if he started it cooking in the big crockpot he had, he could have dinner tonight, breakfast tomorrow from the lighter stuff in the fridge, and have a crockpot of cooked steak, peas, corn, and potatoes to take with him. If he found other places with the electricity still on, that pot's worth would do him several days.

He fed Stormy, ate, went out the back of the buildings where anyone driving by wouldn't see them, and ran Stormy through her commands. He wondered who'd trained her. Had she come that way, or had the old lady been good with dogs? He used the long leash he'd found with her gear, letting her get used to the idea she was with him now. He also set up a target and practiced with the gun in his back holster. Just in case.

The next day was the same: drive, find an empty motel, take food, money, anything small and useful, work with the dog, practice with his gun, stay the night, and move on in the morning. He should stop at the next town and see if anything was open. That he did, leaving Stormy in the car. The shopkeeper was surly, overcharged heavily, and looked happy to see him go. Jason was just as glad to do so. He stopped again at the next town to fill a prescription and buy things like aspirin, bandages, and cough lozenges. He was about to pay when he heard Stormy bark. There was a yell, and he sprinted for the car.

A man stood by it, scowling at Stormy. Jason arrived and the scowl transferred to him. "Should keep your dog under control."

"Why?" Jason asked reasonably.

"I come by, and she snarled. Told her to shut up, and she went mad. Stupid brute."

His mother had said that logic was a problem with some people and not to get into fights with that sort. He noticed that the man seemed to be waiting as if he hoped Jason *would* start something. Okay, don't do what was expected. Jason inclined his head to the man, looking humble.

"I'm sorry, mister. She shouldn't have fussed at you like that. I'm really sorry. I'll have to work on her more, I guess. She isn't trained yet. I sure do apologize."

He got a frustrated look and grinned inwardly. Yes, he'd been supposed to react badly so this guy would have an excuse to start a fight. Damn, he didn't want to turn his back or leave the car again. Better to go now. He hadn't paid in the shop, but then he hadn't taken the stuff he was buying either. He unlocked the door, climbed into the car, and drove away. The man stood looking after him, and Jason didn't much like that look. He remembered the car-lot man and decided to take precautions tonight.

Stormy was bright-eyed and bouncing; she'd seen off danger, a threat to her property, her territory. She beamed, waved her tail, and now and then reached over and licked Jason's bare arm while he grinned and patted her.

"Good job, girl, and we'll practice more tonight." He picked his camping spot carefully towards dusk. There was what he thought had been some sort of civic building. A reception area, an office behind that, two toilets by the back door, and several empty wire racks of the sort that usually held pamphlets. He parked at the rear where passersby couldn't see the car and trailer. The power was still working, so he plugged in the crockpot. He practiced with Stormy, then alone with the gun, shared the last of the hot stew with his dog, and afterward he looked over the building.

Somehow, he didn't feel inclined to sleep inside, but he had the sleeping bag, which had insect netting. Stormy could sleep in the car. He'd put her on the leash, so she could climb out if she needed, and if he moved the car over a bit, he could sleep just inside the line of trees. He set everything up, and around eight, when it was dark, he was peacefully asleep – until an urgent paw smacked his chest. He woke to Stormy's almost subliminal growl and came wide awake on the spot. He heard someone whispering.

"Where'd you think he is?"

"In one of the cabins."

"We could just take the car?"

"Not if he's got that ... dog in it."

"So what then?"

"I'll get the car. You find where he is, The minute the dog starts up, he'll come running. I'll give you ten minutes. There are only four cabins, and if you can't find him by then, I'll go for the car anyhow."

Jason was holding Stormy quiet with a hand on her muzzle. He grinned. He'd bet the one giving the orders was the guy who'd upset her in town. He knew from her reactions that the man was moving up and took his hand off her. Stormy cut loose. She snarled and barked until her echoes came back. There was a shout, and the opposite car door was wrenched open. Jason saw a silhouette against the moon, saw the gleam of a gun pointed towards his dog, and Jason shot. There was a yell. Stormy went completely crazy; footsteps charged towards him. Jason fired and fired again. Then there was silence.

He waited. His dad had told him never to move first. Sit tight; let a predator or the enemy get tired of waiting. Jason sat. Stormy crawled to him, draped herself across his lap. He laid a hand on her shoulder, feeling the tensed muscles. Slowly, they relaxed, until after about half an hour, she heaved a sigh and stood up. Jason dug out his small, powerful flashlight, dialed back the beam to thin and weak, then, holding it at arm's length, he scanned quickly. Two bodies were lying sprawled on the other side of the car and trailer.

He watched them long enough to be sure neither was breathing, and no one could hold their breath that long. While waiting, he'd reloaded. Now he stood, keeping light on the motionless figures. He let Stormy have the whole length of her leash and watched narrow-eyed as she went to nose them. She showed no aggression so that Jason felt more confident. He moved up until he was close enough to shine a stronger light on both men.

He picked up the long stick he had in the trailer and poked the nearest body. There was no response, and at last, he was convinced there was no danger - or not from them anyhow. He reached down, took a shoulder, and rolled the man over. Yes, that was the man. It made sense now; he hadn't just been passing in the street as he'd claimed. He'd probably been trying to get a look at how much Jason had to see if he was worth robbing. He'd seen a boy with a fancy loaded car and trailer and decided even with the dog, they could do it once they had him alone.

He rolled over the other body and stepped back as the light glimmered on the face of a boy that was probably a year or two short of his own age. He froze, horror and disgust engulfing him. A kid, he'd killed a *kid*!

He sat abruptly, turned his head to one side, and threw up. Then again. He hadn't felt much when he'd killed the car-lot man, and while he didn't like having to kill the man from the street here, well, he'd come looking for Jason and asked for it. But a kid? Stormy pressed her head against him and whined softly, scenting his distress, and absently he stroked her. She burrowed against him, and he put an arm around her.

"Yeah, I know. It's what Dad told me once. He's dead, I'm alive, and that's the way I prefer it, but it still feels bad." He forced himself to shine the light on the boy again and saw something he'd missed the first time. Still gripped in one hand, the boy held a gun. Jason allowed himself to feel better. Sure, a kid, but an armed kid is as dangerous as any adult, and with his father down, the boy would have shot Jason if Jason hadn't got him first. However, that might not weigh with any friends of the family.

Time to move, to make choices. And, he remembered Stormy's commands. He shortened her leash, took a firm grip on the end, led her to the bodies, and spoke softly but with crisp clarity. "Seek, follow."

The gray dog sniffed deeply, then, nose to the ground, began to backtrack. She followed a trail to the building, around it, pausing at each window, before moving on. It gave Jason an unpleasant picture of just how the pair had operated, and suddenly he was less sorry. She moved on to where Jason thought they'd been standing when he first heard them whispering, then circled and headed for the road past the building. A short distance down that, she turned into bushes, and there she halted and sat, her nose all but touching a vehicle, an old pickup.

Jason dialed the flashlight down again and checked it. No one inside, and no container a person could hide in. The keys were in it, and he snorted. They'd been confident. Maybe this was a long way from being the first time they'd set up an ambush. By now, he was feeling better about the whole thing. He went over the vehicle, finding several small items that indicated he'd been right. He boosted Stormy into the seat beside him, drove the vehicle back to where the owners lay and checked them. A roll of cash on the man, the boy had money as well, and a very expensive, if generic, pocket-knife.

Jason collected the cash and other items, managed, diligently, to get the original owners onto the back of the pickup, and got out his map. *If* he was on that back road where he thought he was, the map showed a small lake half a mile down the road and off along a track for another mile. It wasn't cold, it wasn't far, Jason could swim well, and if the lake was deep enough…

He spent a busy hour. The lake *was* deep enough, it wasn't that cold, and both he and Stormy found the swim refreshing. The bodies had been locked in the cab, the pickup had been sent off a small bluff and had vanished into deep water so no trace was visible, and all he'd taken had been the cash and knife, neither identifiable. However, during his actions, he'd decided that it might not be a good idea to remain where he'd camped. So once back there, he packed up the few things not in the car or trailer, fed Stormy, and drove away quietly, using only the headlights on a low-intensity dip.

By dawn, he'd seen a sign showing a campsite. Upon driving to that with watchful care, he'd found no one, just a shower and toilet block, a playground, and a concrete-block barbecue, beside which there was a large stack of suitable firewood. He grinned. The meat in the coolers was ready to be cooked or else, and he was still feeling a bit too wound up from events to sleep yet. He made Stormy's day by cooking them a barbecue and sharing it. After that, he had a long shower, used the sink to do what laundry he had and hung that on the rotary clothesline behind the block. He parked his car and trailer out of sight and removed himself, together with a blow-up mattress, to deeper cover still and slept in his clothes.

It was late afternoon when he woke. He yawned, stretched, and listened. No sound. Stormy, hearing him stir, whuffled softly, and he spoke to her.

"No one, huh? No traffic at all. I guess it's maybe getting into full stride out there. Next town, I think we will go in very carefully, buy every single thing we need or want – if there's anyone who can or will sell – and after that, we stay away from people for a while. It's a long way to go yet, and I'd rather we made it."

His washing was dry, so he folded that and placed it in the car, moved to the barbecue, and started the last of the meat. After a hearty meal for them both, he showered again, reveling in the hot water and thinking it lucky he had ample supplies of soap. He studied himself in the mirror affixed to the wall and considered what he saw. He had dark hair, brown eyes, and colorless skin (he'd never taken much of a tan, although he didn't burn easily either) and a lean, angular face.

He considered his chin; he had the beginnings of a beard. To shave or not to shave, that was the question. With his part-

Navajo blood, his beard tended to the straggly. It made him look like the popular conception of a hillbilly. With one, he looked older - just a lot less reputable. He scowled and got out the shaver. There was an outlet where he could plug it in, which reminded him of the crockpot and the last of the meat. He'd be staying tonight as well, and while there was power, he might as well use it.

He looked at his watch. It would take about six hours to cook the meat even on high. He'd gamble on no one coming by and start that now. It took only minutes, and thinking about possible callers, he plugged in the long extension cord, trailed it out of the window, and set the crockpot inside the cooled barbecue. Anyone waving a flashlight about to follow that would make themselves obvious, and if they had little light, they could miss seeing the black power cord in the dark shower block altogether.

He walked to the car, leashed Stormy, leaving her room to come and go, and retreated to his cover. The night was warm again, and he stretched out on the air mattress wearing his ordinary clothing with a loosened belt and moccasins instead of boots. Then he slept. He half-woke and heard them before he saw anything, a distant whooping, a horn blaring, and the sound of car motors. He came fully awake, glanced at his watch, noting it was just after midnight. The meat would be done. Now, if he moved fast...

Before they pulled into the site, he'd been in and out. The crockpot was back in his car, as was everything else, Stormy had been commanded to silence, and he was undercover, stretched out comfortably, watching and listening. A noisy bunch. A mix of both sexes, all teenagers, most drunk, and some belligerent. He stayed where he was. They partied for three hours until one announced he was moving on. There was disagreement, but in the end, all but three went with him. Jason watched narrow-eyed. He didn't like the look of that, two boys, one girl. She seemed sober, but they weren't. She'd wanted to go, but the boy driving had said they were staying, and that was that since everyone else had already left. He judged her to be about fifteen and the boys a year or two older. Jason had an unpleasant feeling about the trio. He thought the boys were staying for a reason, and that was confirmed as one of them made his move.

"Hey Lil, now they're gone, we can really party." He grabbed the hem of her blouse and started it upwards. The girl jumped, back-slapping at his hand.

"No."

"Aw, come on, it's just us."

"No. Take me home if that's all you've got on your mind."

"Not going anywhere, grab her, Joss."

There was a full enough moon for Jason to see something of events as well as hear them. There was a whirl of bodies before someone tripped, and they all landed on the ground. Something tore, the girl's protests changed to screams, and Jason groaned silently. What was it about him? People wanted to rob him; now a couple of would-be rapists started operations right under his nose. She'd come with them. It was clear she knew them. Was it even any of his business? But she was yelling now, a shrieking compounded of fear and rage...

"No, no, no, no, NO..." and he couldn't bear it.

He had options, but the best one was for the girl not to be raped and the boys not to be in a position to identify him. He stood up, flipped a handkerchief around his face - reflecting as he did so that it was the wrong way around, he wasn't the bandit - stepped up to the writhing tangle of bodies, leaned over, and rapped each boy's skull. A couple of years back, he'd had a discussion on that with his mom. She'd told him where to hit that'd give him the most bang for his buck without killing anyone, and now he used the knowledge. If he'd done it right, they'd wake up in an hour or so, sick, dizzy, and with one heck of a headache, but they'd live and be okay, not that he cared. Rapists deserved whatever happened.

The two collapsed. The girl stopped shrieking, and sat up, saw him standing black in the half-moonlight, and screamed again.

Jason lowered his voice a couple of tones. "S'all right. Not planning on hurting you. Can you drive?"

"W-h-h-what?"

"Can you drive? Could you take their car and go home?"

"Yes, yes, I could."

"How far away do you live?"

"About twelve miles."

"Then take the car, go home. Come back for these idiots in a few hours, or send your dad. And tell him the truth, why you have their car. Unless he'd blame you?"

She shook her head decisively. "He wouldn't. It's my fault though. I was stupid."

"Not stupid. You just thought you could trust two guys you knew. Times like these, there are times you can't."

"They aren't…?"

"No. Didn't want them dead, just didn't want you … well, you know."

Her voice was small, subdued. "Yeah, I do. Thanks."

He gave her a hand to her feet and released her as soon as she was standing. She walked to the car, checked, and spoke softly. "Keys are here. Okay if I go now?"

"Go, and don't be sorry for them. They'll survive and maybe be a bit wiser in the future. You could even let them walk home."

"Yeah." Her voice was thoughtful, laced with some amusement. "I might do that, and thanks, thanks a lot."

She seated herself and started the motor. The car moved forward, swung out onto the road, and she was gone, engine sound receding. Jason went to his vehicle, commanded Stormy to get in, and with barely a glance at the two idiots lying face-down in the grass, followed her to the edge of the main road. She'd gone back the way he'd come, so there was probably a town on one of the side roads there.

He headed south again at a comfortable speed; he'd had a good sleep, had a pot of cooked steak, clean clothing, a shower, and he was a white knight. He grinned at that, beginning to hum "I Need a Hero," one of his grandma's favorite songs. He'd bet no matter who Lil fell in love with in the future, she'd never forget *him.*

CHAPTER FOUR

The next town showed up in a couple of hours. Jason slowed down and took a back street. There were a few people out, a handful of shops open, and – there. He nosed the car into the curb, left Stormy guarding it, and headed for the shop. Once inside, he went to the shelf with fancy teas, looking for the red one he'd liked at Mrs. Hayer's. It was there, packets of it. He bought the lot and moved on, buying a large mixed bag of nuts that he put together himself. Cashews, peanuts, Brazil nuts, hazelnuts, and almonds. He found bananas and bought all the greener ones, along with a bunch of the ripe fruit, a large tin of coffee, cans of salmon and corned beef, salt, sugar, margarine, and five loaves of ciabatta bread. He added butter.

At the checkout, Jason kept his face impassive at the price asked, and paid. Making a fuss would be stupid. It wasn't as if he didn't have the cash. He was a stranger in town at a time when people were right on edge, but his mom had been right again. She'd said that before people stopped selling, prices would go sky-high. People were greedy, and until they got it through their heads that what they were selling couldn't be replaced, they'd overcharge, smirk about how much they were making, and not realize they'd be needing it themselves soon.

He wheeled the stuff to the car, stacked the food into the gap he'd made for it, and headed for the outskirts of town, where he bought and filled more gas containers at the garage there. The price was even higher, but again he paid without protest. The owner was pleasant if shifty-eyed.

"Where are you heading, son?"

"Not far, got an aunt and uncle in..." He named the town, that from his map was two hours further on and off to the south-east, and received a nod.

"What do they do?"

"Retired."

"I might know them?"

He grinned. "Probably know a lot of them, uncle's Jack Brown, and my aunt's Mary."

The garage man grinned. "Yeah. So whereabout do they live?"

"Out towards the..." He looked at his watch. "Oh, hey, I can't stand about all day. They're expecting me for lunch. Thanks, and see you."

He moved out, not in too obvious a hurry but not wasting time either. He passed the turnoff to the town he'd named to the man and kept going a short distance. There was a place to pull off the roadside there, and he did, maneuvering the car and trailer into the bushes. His hiding place was on a small rise that gave him a good look to the crossroads. Ten minutes later, three cars came up the highway, turned into the side road, and accelerated. He grinned, fired up the car, and headed south.

****

That night, he picked a place to sleep that showed no signs of civilization. Maybe with nothing to attract anyone, he could get an unbroken night's sleep. He'd paused for a couple of hours at an empty motel and got the stew heated, so that was the main course, with fruit to follow. He got the night's sleep he'd hoped for and felt rejuvenated when he drove away in the morning.

He'd spent time with Stormy, time practicing with the handgun, and had breakfast under his belt, cooked on the camp stove. Nothing like bacon, sausages, and potato cakes to set a man up for the day. Stormy had dog biscuits; he'd buy more if he had the chance, although he still had a large bag left. The fruit was half gone, as were the nuts; he had a young man's appetite, and those were useful any time he wasn't stopping. He hoped he'd find more when they were gone. Apart from anything, mandarins supplied vitamin C.

The car was running well. It should, of course; it was only a couple of years old and regularly serviced. That had just been done a week before all this blew up in his face. He was no mechanic, but he knew enough to change a tire, put in the oil, and a few things to watch for or do. He'd be careful with it and the trailer. It'd break his heart to have to leave Mom's car, let alone the trouble of trying to find another vehicle. He wondered what his dad was doing, how was it in New Mexico, how were the Diné, the people, surviving?

The tires hummed on the empty road. He stopped for the night again, saw some loose chickens, and followed them where they went through a line of trees. A farmhouse. There was no one about, so he advanced, moving slowly and silently, then halted. What was he doing? He was fully loaded, he couldn't take hens, they were messy and noisy. Driving them around would probably put them off laying anyhow, and they'd draw attention. Stormy probably wouldn't appreciate them either.

But curiosity drew him, and he surrendered with the resolution that he wouldn't take anything he didn't need. He'd just look the place over, but first, he opened the gates. Livestock whisked past him moving from eaten-out fields to greener pastures, and he thought he could guess where he'd find the owners. He was right as he saw once he'd entered the house. He glanced through the door, only slightly ajar, and moved on, finding books in a living room bookcase and taking half a dozen by authors he knew but where he hadn't read those particular volumes.

He took unopened cans and packets from the kitchen cupboard and went back to the bedroom with a handkerchief over his mouth. They'd been dead a week or so, he concluded. He took ammunition from the bedside cabinet, and in the top drawer of a dresser, he found an old pocket watch, silver, the sort you wound up. He tried it, and it worked, so he took that. His watch was a good one, given for his sixteenth birthday, but eventually, batteries would be no longer available, and it wouldn't work.

Well, he hadn't taken much, a few groceries and books, and a watch. He didn't think they'd mind, but he turned to them before he left the room. "What I've taken, I count as gifts, and I think you for them. They are taken from necessity, not for greed. May your spirits be at peace."

He departed the house, climbed into the car, and drove away. That night he read the first of the books and enjoyed it until he found he was falling asleep. He put it to one side for the night, resolving that he'd keep the books he really enjoyed. If they didn't have ones where he was going, he could reread them. His last thought was that if a book was good enough, he could read that book many times. He should also look out for nonfiction that he could learn from, even diagrams or blueprints if he could understand what they'd do or make.

He spent that night at a small house off the road. It was empty of people. From the furnishings, it had belonged to a family who'd had a dog. No dog was there either, and Jason thought that one of the owners might have fallen ill and that the other had taken them to a hospital, dropping their dog off with friends, as old Mrs. Hayer had intended to do. He hoped that wherever the dog was, it had a good home still. There were photos, and he admired those he found when he entered the sitting room to see if there were books.

Although they were nothing he wanted, he studied the photos, seeing a middle-aged couple, in most cases with what he assumed to be their dog. It was an amiable-looking Rottweiler wearing a plaited red-leather collar with a silver nameplate. In every photo, the animal was beaming, clearly happy with its humans, and getting good care. The night was quiet, electricity was still working in the house, and he found a considerable amount of food in the freezer. He cooked items for himself and Stormy and started the crockpot again. He'd leave that simmering all night so they'd have cooked food for the following evening in case their next stopping place had no electricity. At last, fed, clean, and sleepy, he locked up the house - the back door had been open - and retired for the night with Stormy on the mat beside the spare room bed.

Twice during the night, he dimly heard a dog bark, but Stormy barely stirred, and he slept again. Having resolved to shower or bath every time there was hot water, he did so again in the morning, cooked more food and ate, placed the full, hot, towel-wrapped crockpot in the back seat, and walked out to the car which he'd backed, together with the trailer, into the spacious garage. He turned to climb in and call Stormy to join him when she let out a cross between a roar and a yell. A dozen dogs streamed around the house, heading for them and acting without hesitation.

All were large, all had the attitude of animals on the attack, and he was into the driver's seat in a leap, yelling for Stormy, who joined him half a second later. He slammed the door, clicked the locks, and sat panting and gaping at the animals that were swirling around the car, standing up against it at intervals to snarl at the occupants. He glared, and one of them shouldered the others aside to smash into the car window. Jason shied back. If it did that again it could break in, and he was under no illusions about their motive. He started the car and let it idle.

Stormy was growling defiance. The big dog jumped at the window again, and Jason touched the pedal, moving the car forward. The dog hit the post between windows and bounced back, yelping. Jason looked at it, and something caught his attention. He looked more closely, and a pang of sorrow caught in his throat. The dog was a Rottweiler wearing a plaited red-leather collar with a silver nameplate. So - it hadn't been left with friends.

He drove further forward for a clear view, stopped, and rummaged in the nearest cooler to produce a single steak and a dozen chops. He cracked the window, and flipped them one by one in a semi-circle and as far from the car as he could. The Rottweiler was the largest, heaviest dog and had gained ascendancy.

It took the steak as of right and settled to tear that apart, gulping down mouthfuls. Jason sighted carefully, and as it swallowed the final mouthful, he shot. The big dog fell silently, and the rest were gone. He got out, picked up the warm body, and moving without wasting time, he buried it in the loose garden earth, placing a stake in the ground and hooking the collar to that.

It was the Navajo way to acknowledge gifts given. His father had told him that many times and he'd taken from the people that had lived here. He had frozen bread, butter, a crockpot with several evening meals, vegetables from their garden, and fruit from the trees, and this was something he could do for them. See to it that their beloved dog did not wander, starving and dying slowly, bereft of its loved humans, and without comfort. He got back in the car and drove onto the highway. And for the rest of the day, he drove silently, without singing and only occasionally speaking to Stormy, who also seemed subdued.

****

The main highway was sometimes blocked after that. Several times massive trucks had slewed across several lanes, and more than once, Jason could see they'd caused an accident. No one living was in any of the vehicles, but now and again, he could see bodies. He maneuvered around any barriers, not stopping and keeping his speed reasonable. Once two men appeared by the roadside, waving and calling. Another time, it was a woman alone. Both times he ignored them.

Stormy barked at them, and he nodded. "I see them, girl, but it's once bitten, twice shy. There's nothing I can do, they all looked healthy enough, and if as many are dying as Mom thought, they can find supplies just by hunting about."

He looked back at the woman before he rounded the bend and grinned. She was standing there, making a very well-known sign after him, and several people were joining her. "Sorry, lady, I wasn't as dumb as you hoped." She was gone behind the bend, and he made a mental note he should remember the incident. Although, he couldn't understand why they'd bother when all they had to do was search for empty houses, shops, malls, or even cafeterias in businesses where they had one of those for the staff.

Shortly before dusk, he crossed into Oregon, found a group of trucks at a truck stop, and worked car and trailer between two of them, where no one would notice. Wearily, he stepped out of the car and checked the trucks. Two had spare gas cans which he filled from their tanks and added to his stash. One was carrying wood; another had furniture. Three were locked, and he didn't care enough to look for keys, while the last one, when opened, released a stench he found almost unbelievable.

Carcasses for a butcher shop or supermarket, he thought, and with the refrigeration off, they hadn't survived. He shut the door on them and went to the café to look around. No one there, and no electricity. He did find a dozen lighters ready fueled, plus boxes of matches, and he took them all. Eventually, there'd be no electricity anywhere. His food supply was down. He'd eaten most of what he'd got from the Rottweiler house, so he checked and was cheered to find that the power must have died very recently in this area. The freezer was still cold, and the food within safely edible. He made a good dinner using the camp stove, and afterward, he sat drinking a mug of the red tea. In case of another dog pack, he kept near shelter, listening for unexpected noises.

Once he finished, he practiced Stormy's commands, worked out with his handgun, and decided to sleep in the back of the nearest truck, leaving Stormy in the car as sentry.

He woke early, jumped casually from the truck, and as his foot landed on a small pebble, his ankle turned, and he fell heavily. He sat holding it and cursing his clumsiness. In the car, Stormy whimpered, her head turning to stare up the highway. Jason hushed her, rolled partway under the truck, and looked from underneath.

The roar of vehicles became louder, and he watched as a dozen passed. The men in them wore army uniforms, and they drove army trucks, but his mom had had friends in both the police and the army, and there was something off about this lot. The virus had first hit only a couple of weeks ago, but some men had hair down to their shoulders. And, as one turned to speak to someone while they passed, Jason saw that he was wearing a non-army t-shirt under his open jacket. It was red with black lettering, and he had a sinking feeling that he knew what it embodied. It wasn't likely the army would have fallen apart that fast, so whoever these guys were, they weren't army, and he was disinclined to rush out assuming he'd been saved.

He lay motionless, watching as the convoy disappeared in the distance and decided that for the next few days, he'd keep to the back roads. The maps he had were good ones, they showed even minor roads, and right now, he still had his in-car system as backup. He found an elastic bandage, strapped his ankle, ate the hot food, and cleared out what he could use from the café freezers. It took him three hours, and he decided to take the back roads right now, and for another day or two, in case that lot would stop up ahead or return. He checked the map, decided which way to go, and hoped they wouldn't be coming back too soon.

He heard them doing just that as he got rolling, but by the time they were where they might have seen him, he was in the shadow of an old billboard, and they passed without slowing. Once they were out of earshot again, Jason moved onto the road without wasting time. He thought this was the original road that'd been replaced by the larger one he'd been on, and if so, it was probably still in reasonable shape, with a scattering of towns or villages. His ankle was hurting, and he wanted a place he could hole up in for a few days to let that mend. He drove at a steady thirty miles an hour watching for somewhere suitable, saw a spot, and pulled into a driveway that was rapidly falling to weeds.

CHAPTER FIVE

As was becoming a habit, he opened gates, allowing starving stock a chance to feed or even leave the farm altogether, and most did so at speed. At the farm's back door, he found kennels housing two dead dogs and one barely alive. In mercy, he shot her, dragged the dogs by the chains to the back of the sheds, and left them there. Poor brutes, couldn't their people at least have set them free when they knew they were dying? But on exploration, he found no bodies. Stormy was eating dog biscuits he'd put out for her in the kitchen when he returned, and he stroked her ears.

"Looks as if they went to the hospital and never got back. Come to think of it too, girl, three dogs, there must be dog biscuits or dog food somewhere here. He checked the sheds and found a fair supply. After some shifting of items, he made room for the four unopened sacks of biscuits. The fifth, half-used sack he ran fingers though, sniffed a handful, and decided they were stale. With that, he returned to the house and walked through, opening drawers, looking, and hoping for books he hadn't read.

He found a bookcase and raided that, taking a set of animal books by an English author of whom he'd heard his grandparents speak, several Science Fiction anthologies, and half a shelf of Sherlock Holmes pastiches by a single author. He'd liked the original stories, and these looked to have the same background, and while these books had been written from 2013 to 2030, it wouldn't matter. He grinned happily as he carried them out to the car, leaving out the first one, *Repeat Business,* a collection of Holmes short stories, and tucked them in wherever he could find space. It looked as if the people here had bought them as they were published, and there was a fair number.

The freezer had food in it, and he considered that. His ankle was really hurting. There was still power on here, they had a bath and a shower, and the house was behind a solid screen of trees that should prevent anyone on the road from seeing a light here. He'd gamble. It wouldn't be dark for a couple of hours, and if he got everything done, he could bed down before he needed lights anyhow. He took a pain pill, sat and read one of the short Holmes stories, and after thirty minutes, the pill was working, and he'd finished the story – confirmed in his hope that he'd like the books.

He made dinner for them both, ate, washed up, changed the bed linen in the spare room, and then luxuriated in a long hot bath. He climbed into bed, the book in one hand, a jug of water on the bedside cabinet, and started reading. Three stories later, the light was becoming too poor to read, and he found his eyes kept closing anyway, so he bookmarked the page, placed the book on the cabinet top, took another pain pill, and slept without moving until morning.

Stormy woke him then demanding to go out, and he found when he stood up that his ankle, while still sore, did feel slightly better. That changed after working with Stormy, cooking breakfast for them, and refilling the car's gas tank. He stayed a day at a time, each morning evaluating if the ankle felt well enough to move on and, for almost a week, deciding it didn't. However, by that time, he'd exhausted all the food in the house, had read other books beside the Holmes ones since he knew he wanted to keep those, and had decided to leave the anthologies behind. They had a few good stories, but not enough to make worthwhile the room they took up.

Six days after he'd driven down the long winding drive, he drove back up and turned south. His ankle was fine, both he and Stormy had had a bath the previous night, and he'd showered that morning. He felt clean, renewed, and more than ready to hit the road. It was a fine, clear morning. He noticed that the road edges were starting to overgrow, weeds were taking over front lawns of houses he passed, and he needed to keep a lookout for wandering stock. He smiled at a resting cow and calf as he drove by and thought that, considering what had happened, things could be a lot worse.

Later he thought he'd jinxed himself. Any time you considered things were fine, they stopped being. He was rolling down a narrow back road early that afternoon when he noticed that the car seemed to be driving unevenly. He stopped, got out, and walked around it. Nope, everything looked all right. He glanced at the trailer, froze, took a second look, and groaned. He was looking at a flat tire on the left side. It could be worse though. He had a spare and a jack, so all he had to do was change the tire.

Jason changed the tire, got in, and started again to pull up and recite a few words he knew. Then he got out and looked further back. Sure enough, the other tire on that side was also flat. He'd looked at the first one and decided he must have driven over something sharp-edged without seeing it. Maybe back there where he'd passed a crashed vehicle and swerved around it. And with his only spare used, what did he do now?

He decided that he couldn't do the back tire much more damage if he drove carefully and only a short distance. He could get under cover then think about this. He got back in the car and followed his decision. Fortunately, he hadn't been far from a farmhouse, and he drove around the buildings, parked in an empty barn, and got out, releasing Stormy with the command to stay close.

He was thinking that he should look at trailers with an eye to either taking a tire if he could find one that'd fit or even swapping the small trailer he had for one a bit larger when a second lot of bad luck clouded up and rained all over him. He heard Stormy making the sort of sounds she made when she played with him, called, wondering what she'd found, and she trotted back with a companion. Jason looked, suppressed a groan, and dropped to one knee to make himself less tall and possibly less threatening.

"Hello, who are you?"

"Janey, who are you?"

"Jason."

The small girl giggled. "That's funny, Janey and Jason."

"Yes. Are your mommy and daddy around?"

"No."

"Do you know where they are?"

"They're in their bedroom, and they won't come out."

Oh, dear Lord. "Is there anybody else?"

"No."

He studied her unobtrusively. She was dirty, her clothing hung on her and her eyes seemed large for her face.

"Are you hungry?"

"Yes ... *please?"*

"Okay, let's see what we can find." Now that he thought of it, he still had fruit from one of his last stops. He produced a banana from the cooler. "Do you like these"

Judging by the speed with which it vanished, she did. He gave her another and headed for the house, Janey trotting along beside him. Inside he found the bench round the sink and the kitchen table covered in fly-attended dirty dishes, an empty fridge, and - as she'd said - a bedroom door that was either locked or jammed. He left that alone for the time being and investigated the freezer he found in a locked pantry off the kitchen.

To Jason's relief, that was loaded with food. Since power was still working in the house, the contents were all edible. In a high cupboard, he found a row of cans of soup. Apparently, Janey couldn't reach them or hadn't known they were there, but they were a good brand and concentrated. He took one and started it heating at once while removing a loaf of sliced bread from the freezer and fetching margarine from the car. In twenty minutes, he had the child sitting at the table eating buttered toast and chicken soup. She would have accepted more, but he'd read that it wasn't good to overeat after a period of starvation and said that she could have another meal in a while.

It was a wasted assurance as her eyelids were already drooping. He waited as she fell asleep. Picking her up, he carried her to what he'd seen to be her bedroom. The sheets were filthy, so he laid her gently on the sitting room sofa instead, changed the sheets and other bedding, and stood looking down at her. She was out like a light, and he thought her unlikely to wake without minor violence.

Good. He could get the basics done without frightening her. He found clean pajamas in a drawer, collected a basin of warm water and soap, stripped her, washed her gently, dressed her in the pajamas, and tucked her into bed, placing the teddy bear that lay on the floor in her arms. She turned to one side, clutched the bear tighter, stretched out, and he thought her unlikely to wake for hours. Now to see about her family, she seemed to be a friendly child, but he was a bit young to adopt her … if he could avoid it. He switched a light on reluctantly, he hoped it wouldn't attract trouble, but it was getting dark.

The desk in the sitting room held bills, legal documents, an address book, and photos. The computer wouldn't connect to the internet, but he got into the email folder and learned that Janey had an aunt and uncle outside Portland, in one of the small towns on the far side. It looked as if that was where most of her family lived since another aunt and uncle were nearby, grandparents were only a few miles away, and emails from friends suggested that several of those were in the same vicinity.

He tried to connect to the internet again, failed, and sat there wondering why one of Janey's family hadn't come looking for her. He dug into the papers and concluded her parents had only this old farmhouse, not any of the surrounding land or livestock. Her father had worked from home, her mother had been a stay-at-home mom, and from some of the emails, they'd moved here to look after the mother's invalid father. He noted that address, checked his maps, and smiled. It was within walking distance.

All right. He looked in on Janey, who was sleeping like the dead. With Stormy at his heels, he took his flashlight and went to the address. The situation there was as he'd thought likely. Grandpa was no longer with the living, and he seemed not to have had a pet either. He couldn't leave the kid alone to starve, but from the emails, she had half a hundred family or friends, and one of them would surely take her in.

He went back, found her still asleep, and started another meal. While the soup heated, he headed for the parent's bedroom, tightened the flashlight lens to a thin beam, and peered into the keyhole. Ah ha. It was obstructed, almost certainly by the key, and - old house - he knew how to fix that. He found a large sheet of paper, slipped that under the door, and poked at the key until it fell out. Withdrawing the paper with the key on that, he opened the door.

The parents looked as if they'd washed, dressed in loose, comfortable but suitable, clothing, then lay down together and died. Jason scowled to himself. Had they left the kid to starve and die alone? What kind of parents were they? Or had they known or assumed the family was on the way? His gaze fell on a suitcase, and he opened that. Yup. There was a letter addressed to Grace and Simon. It occurred to him that something must have happened to Grace and Simon. They hadn't got here after all. Great, so if he took Janey to the family, he'd be bringing bad news twice over.

But he couldn't leave her here. She'd be a time-consuming, supply-consuming nuisance, but she was a friendly little kid, and he could *not* leave her behind. When the time came that he saw Mom again, he'd never be able to face her if he'd done that. He went out to put the packed suitcase and letter in his car. While he was thinking of that, he added the legal papers, the cash he'd found, jewelry, and several expensive items of her mom's clothing and footwear.

Janey woke three hours later. He fed her more soup and toast, made lemonade, adding a mild sleeping pill to that, and casually asked her questions. Yes, she had an Aunt Grace and

Uncle Simon. And yes, Mom had said Aunt Grace was coming here before they shut the bedroom door.

That made it more likely Grace and Simon had died on the trip up here or some other way after they'd left home. Phones often weren't working, so the family probably assumed that Grace and Simon were here, that maybe Janey's parents were sick, and their cousins had stayed with them, and that sooner or later, some or all of them would be back with news. Instead, it'd be him, if there was anyone left around to receive it.

Janey was asleep again. He returned her to her bed and remembered the reason he'd come here in the first place. That damn trailer. He left Stormy on guard and went out again. An hour later, he was back in the house and preparing to bunk down on the sofa in his sleeping bag. The house was secured, Stormy was with him, and in the morning, he'd have to look further afield. He had a peaceful dreamless night and woke to a clatter in the kitchen. For a moment, he was lost until he remembered Janey.

She was making toast and beamed when he came in. "Would you like honey?"

"Thanks."

"I feel lots better."

He'd bet she did. Two good meals, a night's sleep, friendly company, and most things would look better to the recipient.

"What are we doing today?"

"Looking for a trailer tire." That necessitated explanations; he was revising either her age or her intelligence upwards the more she talked. "Janey, how old are you?"

"Seven in April."

"Last April?"

"Yes." Okay, so she was seven and a half, and bright for that age, just small.

"Do you want to help me look for a trailer tire?"

"Stormy too?" He nodded, and her agreement was definite. He'd left items to thaw overnight, and now he removed them from the fridge, started the crockpot with a casserole. Once they finished eating, they set out. Not as he'd planned, but on electric bicycles. One hers, and the other, larger one, her father's, which he borrowed with Janey's permission. He made sure they weren't obvious, but Janey knew where neighbors lived, and at the third house, they found a trailer with matching tires.

"Will they fit?"

"I think so. Good job spotting them."

She danced around the trailer. "How will you get them off?"

He was checking the car there. Keys on the hook, and yes, it started, the gas gauge showed half-full. He could hitch up the trailer and drive it back. Use the jack to get the tires off. If they fitted, he was fine, and even if they didn't, he thought the car's towbar would take this trailer coupling. It wouldn't be a bad idea to use this one anyhow. It was bigger, and he could see a pair of spare tires for it, too.

In the end, he added the tires and drove them home, the bikes in the trailer. It was work transferring trailer contents, but it was larger than the one he had, it had higher sides, and with careful packing, he had extra room. Meanwhile, they'd stay tonight again. In his opinion, Janey needed more good meals and another night's sleep before she'd be fit to travel.

They had that time, and he roused himself early the following morning. By the time he called Janey, he had breakfast waiting, the crockpot was full of cooked food and stowed in the car. The gas tank was filled, tires checked, and all they had to do was eat, shower, wash up, and they could go. Janey was quiet until she came back from her shower.

"Jason?"

"Ah-huh?"

"Will I ever come back?"

"That'll be up to your family, or to you once you're old enough."

"But Mommy and Daddy. They aren't coming with us," her lip trembled. "I want Mommy and Daddy." She sat on the kitchen floor and burst into tears.

Jason knew he should have been expecting this. He went with his instincts. "Janey, you said to me they went into the bedroom and stayed there?"

"Y-y-yes."

"Did you think they were still alive in there?"

There was silence, then… "N-n-no."

"They can't come with us, but maybe one day you can come back and see they're put somewhere nice, somewhere you can remember them." He wasn't sure how much she understood, but it seemed to be sufficient.

"One day, they'll have a nice place like Ronny's mom got when the truck hit her?"

"Yes."

"Okay, we can go now."

He took her small hand and led her to the car, tucking her into the front seat while Stormy took the seat behind, and leaning forward, licked Janey across the back of her neck. Janey giggled as Jason put the car into gear, and in minutes the old farmhouse was behind them. Jason speeded up, hoping to make it before dark with enough time to get through the city and find the small town. However, he had to admit, if only to himself, that he'd miss Janey.

CHAPTER SIX

It was no more than fifty miles to the city, but as they neared that, the roads became clogged with stationery vehicles until Jason was driving no faster than he could have jogged. He threaded their way through clots and clumps of cars, and it took longer and longer. He kept at it, while in the seat beside him, Janey went to sleep. He was grateful for that. It seemed to take forever, and by his watch, while it wasn't that long, it *was* almost four hours. Finally, he made it, took a side road to the left, circled the latter part of the city, and took the narrower road again where the signs pointed, one to West Slope township, the other to the East Slope where two of the kid's family lived.

Janey half-woke. "Are we there yet?"

"You look out of the window and tell me."

She sat up and stared through the glass. "Nearly," then "Turn here, Jason. Grandma and Gramps live in that big white house there," she said, pointing. He halted at the curb, and before he could stop her, she was out of the car yelling, running up the path. "Gran, Gramps, I'm here, I'm here, Jason brought me … *Gran*!" The door opened, and Jason sat watching the ecstatic family reunion. Oh, yes, he wasn't going to be lumbered with a kid; he forced down the knowledge that he'd have quite liked to be and got out of the car as Janey came dancing back to get him.

She tugged him forward to meet an elderly couple. *Sixties,* Jason thought, the sort that, like his own grandparents, would live into their nineties if nothing got them first. Janey was introducing him.

"Grandma, Gramps, this is Jason. He found me and brought me here in his car. That's Stormy. She's a *good* dog."

The woman was looking bewildered. "Who is Jason? How come he bought you? What about Grace and Simon? Janey, what about your parents? What's going on?"

The man stepped forward. "Sweetheart, we can sort it out. Let's just offer Jason a cup of coffee and a slice of your good cake. He brought our Janey to us. Let's be polite."

Jason nodded to him gratefully. He didn't want to say some of what he knew or guessed in front of the kid, and he saw that the older man understood. What was their name in the address book? Oh yes, Braddon. He turned to collect Janey's things and offered them. "Her parents had a suitcase packed for her, and I brought some other stuff I thought shouldn't be left there. There are people who would take it."

The man passed the case and bag on. "Here, Mother, you take Janey to her bedroom. We'll be in the sitting room when you're ready." He ushered Jason in, accepted Stormy at their heels, shut the door, and spoke quietly. "I don't know who you are, son, but I think we owe you. Can you talk fast?"

Jason found a grin. "Mom always said I did. Okay, Mr. Braddon, I'm on the way from Seattle to New Mexico to my dad's ranch. Most people are dead, and I'd just go up to a house, and if there were no sign of anyone, I'd stay the night. In a house the other side of Portland, I found Janey, or rather she found Stormy, then me."

"What about her parents?"

"Dead in the bedroom behind a locked door. They left a note in her packed suitcase to a Grace and Simon, cousins I gather. They seemed to be expecting them, but they never arrived. Janey was starving. I fed her. She was filthy, and her clothes were worse, so I washed those and her. I looked though your son's papers, sorry, but I found emails and an address book, and they brought me here. There are looters about. I didn't want her to lose everything, so I brought her suitcase, any money in the house, her mom's jewelry, and some of her mom's nicest clothes and shoes so she'd have those, and the three electric bicycles her family had as well."

He took a deep breath. "I did the best I could."

The older man looked at him, then reached out, took his hand, and wrung it. "Son, you did a helluva job. You found a starving grubby kid that was no relation, you took care of her, saved her stuff, got her to her family, and I see she trusts you. That's more than I'd expect from some. I guess you had a good family. Tell me something about yourself."

Jason talked. In the middle of it, Mrs. Braddon came in and offered coffee and cake. The cake was as good as her husband had claimed. "Janey's asleep. I've put her things away in her room, all but the money and jewelry. That's quite a lot of money."

Something in the way she said that made Jason blush. "I've got enough. I don't need to steal a kid's money," he muttered, and both Braddon's exchanged looks.

"I don't know if my husband introduced us properly," she said. "I'm Eloise Braddon, and he's Jackson, Jack for short."

Jason nodded. "I'm Jason Trevalen. Mom and I lived in Seattle. She was an orthopedic surgeon. She died," he added tersely, hoping they'd leave it there. "They're divorced. My dad's Shandiin Storm. He's got a ranch in New Mexico. I'm heading there."

"And if there'd been nobody here for Janey," Jack Braddon said quietly. "You'd have taken her with you."

"Yes."

Eloise Braddon sobbed once, a slight sound. "You're a wonderful, kind boy, and we'll owe you for the rest of our lives."

Jason reddened. "She's a nice kid. I couldn't leave her where she was."

"A lot of people would have," Jack Braddon said grimly. "Same as they'd have taken the money and the jewelry. No, we thank you, son, and maybe you'll stay a day or two."

He did. During those two days, more of the family arrived, thanked him, wondered what could have happened to Grace and Simon, and some of them went looking. Jason stayed an extra day to see if there were any results. Jack Braddon came in early the third morning. "They found them."

Jason read the expression. "Dead?"

"Yes, the car was burned out, bodies in it. Bullet holes all over. You said you'd run into trouble on the way; looks as if they did, too."

"I'm sorry about that. I was lucky in a way." Braddon gave a questioning look. "Mom liked science fiction; I like some of it too. She had half a shelf of what they used to call post-holocaust, all about what happens when civilization falls apart. When she was dying, she said I should remember those books. They had a lot of things right, that when things went wrong, so did a lot of people, I should be careful, not trust too many, stay undercover, and get by as much as I could on my own."

"Your ma was a smart lady, seems to me."

"She was," Jason said quietly, "And I miss her. I will so long as I live."

"I know what you mean. Well, now we know about Grace and Simon, we'll say goodbye to them in an hour or so. Boys are digging graves now. Stay tonight, and we'll see you off in the morning."

Jason watched the farewell to Janey's aunt and uncle that morning. He went over the car and trailer and made sure everything was washed, dried, and folded away somewhere in the car. He showered that morning and came down to breakfast with Janey and the Braddons, hair slightly damp and smelling of soap. Stormy lay at his feet, accepting the occasional piece of bacon. With the meal over, he stood, Stormy looking up at him.

"Guess it's time we left. Mr. and Mrs. Braddon, Janey, you take care of yourselves."

He accepted a powerful handshake, hugs, and half-tearful goodbyes. He was walked to the car. Stormy was patted a final time. He got into the driver's seat and put the car in gear, almost unable to see the road ahead. Then the figures were diminishing in the rearview mirror, and it was just him and Stormy again heading south and hoping.

****

He drove late, right into almost dark; it helped keep his mind off things, and when he came to a crossroads, he turned down the gravel road to the left. That led to a small farmhouse and, about three miles after that, to a dead end. He turned car and trailer and drove slowly back. There were no signs of life - none human anyhow - and he halted at the farmhouse. Sitting there, he got out his maps and looked them over. If he went straight ahead at the crossroad next morning, he could stay on back roads for several days.

He approached the farmhouse carefully, finding it silent. He drove into the carport to one side and got out, scanning his surroundings, and almost immediately noticed two sleeping dogs. Stormy danced up to the nearest then backed away, whining. A second, closer look, and he realized they weren't sleeping. Someone had shot them both in the head, and from the lack of major damage, they probably used a small caliber handgun.

He guessed from that what he'd find inside, and he was right. Father, mother, and two small kids between them. Empty glasses on each bedside cabinet. So, they'd given the children sleeping pills, and once they were asleep, one of the parents had shot the kids, spouse, and themselves. Probably the dogs had gone as soon as the kids were asleep. Jason sighed. He guessed he was going to see a lot of this sort of thing, but if they'd had dogs, they probably had dog food somewhere, and he could use that. He found cans of it in the kitchen, fed Stormy, heated the stew in the crockpot, and ate a good dinner.

He was making a policy of not leaving lights on in a house while it was dark. It could tell the wrong people someone was here, so he went to bed as soon as he'd eaten. He slept soundly, woke at first light, and lay there thinking. Mom had felt it wouldn't take long before even the dimmest bulb would get the message that it was counterproductive to sell stuff that couldn't be replaced. Right now, he had a real wad of cash, and a fair amount of gold jewelry. Best if he made a list of everything he'd like to have and started seeing what he could still buy or find.

He spent an hour and a half on that after a fair breakfast – whoever the owners had been, they'd kept their cupboards full, and they'd had a house that, while it still looked like a very well-kept farmhouse from the outside, inside it was almost a show-place. They'd clearly had money. He'd noticed something else as he drove into the carport too. He took his list and went out to check, where he found the item sitting under a tarpaulin he could tie down. Jason groaned. He looked at the larger trailer and then reconsidered. No, he wouldn't take that size. The car might have trouble towing it once he filled it, and he wanted to keep Mom's car. But the trailer cover and its lashing were good. It was a fitted waterproof cover, and with it was a bundle of lengths of woven elastic, with hooks at each end. The cover had four sections that he could roll down to cover all four sides, and those lashed down, too. It'd keep everything in the trailer dry, and while he'd been lucky so far, it was fall, and that sort of luck wouldn't continue.

He unhooked the cover, added lashings – one set was longer, probably so you could pile the contents up beyond the top and use the cover to hold them in place – and added them to his current trailer. Not bad. He dragged out the dog food and biscuits he'd found, found several of the red, white, and blue airline bags, the big soft, zippered ones, and filled them with cans and packets from the cupboards, folding a beautiful handmade quilt into one bag. Into the car went pieces of gold jewelry, and another roll of cash. He grinned at that. In the past two or three years, the power grid had gone out now and then in some rural areas, and sometimes for days at a time, so people had begun carrying cash again. Those events had been usefully in the right order.

With that done, he poked through the sheds, opened a door into what looked like it might be a workshop and gasped in delight. Three – *three* – of the newest small portable wind generators. Developed by the army, they'd only been for sale to the public about eighteen months. They were beautifully engineered, truly portable, the fan blades folding into the top, ports so two or three-pin plugs could connect them, or via USB ports of the two most common shapes, and folding into the bottom, three repositionable clamps.

He'd seen the generators advertised. You positioned the clamps and clamped the generator onto a fence, a branch, or anything that allowed the wind to get to it. Then you unfolded the blades, pulled out the stalk they were on, angled that to the wind, set switches and dials, and as the wind blew, so the generator would recharge any rechargeable battery. Or you could hook a cord into it, attach a multi-plug board in the house, and run lights or other items directly from that.

The three of them were riches. They weighed fifteen pounds each and measured fourteen inches to each side. his guy, whoever he'd been, had the lot, everything that went with them - powerboards, long extension cords - and the carry straps were woven synthetic that wouldn't break or fray. On top of that, there was a small trolley, with which he could move the lot.

Jason considered the windfall, beaming until it occurred to him there could be something wrong with any or all the generators. Better to check before packing everything up, stashing it on the trailer, and later finding he'd been relying on something that turned out to be faulty. He took one generator outside, positioned it, set it going, and hooked all three lanterns into the powerboard. He'd stay another night, recharge the lanterns, the car battery, and his spare, and go around the place while that was happening in case the owner had other wonders.

If he did, Jason didn't find them, but he and Stormy had a pleasant day. He ran through her training, played ball with her, did some handgun practice, and had two long luxurious baths - one before anything else and the other after dinner. He bathed Stormy, washed the soiled clothes, put them in the dryer, and then kicked back with a book for the evening while devouring a tasty dinner culled from the freezer. What he could fit into his coolers from that, he'd stow in the trailer right before they left along with bags of frozen gel to keep it cold longer still.

Jason was up early, and once he'd showered and dressed, he went to stand in the bedroom doorway where the silent shapes lay. "I've taken from need," he said quietly, "not from greed. I'll lock up the house when I go. Be at peace. May those you loved who have gone before have already welcomed you in joy."

He went to the kitchen, washed the breakfast dishes, and put everything away tidily. After that, he went back to the outside generator, where he checked, holding his breath. *Yes*, the lanterns, the car batteries had charged fully despite that there'd been only a breeze all night. That answered that. He moved the trolley into position, stacked the recharged lanterns, and wheeled the load to the trailer, where he wrapped everything in a thick blanket and stowed it.

Right, final items. Jason went upstairs, locked the bedroom door, checked the doors and windows everywhere, locking those, and came last to the kitchen again. He moved the coolers from the freezer, one each to car and trailer. Last of all, he locked the door behind him, opened the door for Stormy to get into the passenger seat, and climbed into the driver's seat. He sat looking at the road before putting the car in motion. Ahead were the crossroads where he could stop and look around there. He'd seen a sign saying "H*oney*" as he came by. He remembered his mom on the subject and grinned.

They'd been in the supermarket – he'd have been about ten. His mom had picked up a jar of honey, looked at something on the label, and snorted.

"What's wrong?"

"Not wrong exactly. Just silly."

"What?"

"There's a '*use by*' date on this."

"Why's that silly?"

"Because they've found edible honey in Egyptian tombs over three thousand years old."

"*Really*?"

"Really. Honey doesn't go off. It has antibiotic properties."

"Then why's there a '*use by*' date on it?"

From behind them, the supermarket manager had spoken. "FDA regs. You're right, it is silly, Doctor Trevalen, but it's the law, and if they don't have that on the honey, what if somebody didn't put the date on other items, you'd assume they didn't go bad either, and you could be wrong. It's better to have it on honey, so there's no confusion."

Mom had agreed. And later, Jason had looked up what she'd said. It was true, and he'd never forgotten it. If that stall at the crossroads had honey, he'd buy all they had. He slowed as he came up to the corners, pulled into one side, and looked over the buildings. There was a small shabby church, a shop with a gas pump outside, a community hall, and a complex of five open-fronted stalls. It was solidly built, and he thought they had probably used it to hold a weekly or monthly fresh-produce market.

A man was lying back comfortably in a recliner, his face in shadow, while on a table in front of him were about a dozen two-pound jars of honey, *real* honey. The kind his mom had always bought if she saw it. Honey where the apiarist had just taken the honeycomb out of the hive, strained it though a muslin bag and into the jars, and that was it. Well, if the guy would sell, he'd buy it all.

He got out of the car, Stormy at his heels, approached the stall and started. "How much for a jar…" his words trailed off.

The stallholder was dead, sightless eyes staring ahead, and from the look of it, he'd been dead for two or three days. Jason hesitated. Should he take the honey and go, or should he put down money? He picked up a jar. The real deal all right. And properly strained too; he couldn't see anything but honey, he allowed it to roll over the lid and back, but there was no sign of anything in it like a bee-leg or wing. He wanted it…

"Are you planning to pay for that, young man?" asked an elderly, slightly shaky voice.

Jason thought later that the expression about leaping out of your skin had developed a whole new resonance for him because if it had been possible, that's what he'd have done.

CHAPTER SEVEN

He glanced down at Stormy wagging her tail a little. Okay, whoever that was didn't have a gun pointed, and the voice sounded quite old, so hopefully, the guy wouldn't attack him. He turned slowly, still holding the jar and speaking as he moved.

"Yes, I was just checking; it's been properly strained. You know some apiarists don't do much of a job at that when it's raw honey." Hopefully, that burst of information would reassure the guy that Jason was a genuine buyer.

In front of him was a dark-skinned man who looked to be eighty if he was a day. He was about five and a half feet, wore a black suit with a minister's collar, and his hands were empty. Jason allowed himself to relax. The older man smiled.

"Sorry if I startled you. I'm the Reverend Williams. That's my church across the road there. I keep an eye on a stall if someone is open for business. Joe put his honey out then went to sleep, I imagine he's been working hard, but I know what he charges. If you want to buy some, I'll take your money and pass it on to him when he wakes up." Jason was temporarily speechless, and before he could say anything, the minister was continuing. "I saw your car going down and back a day or two ago. Staying with the Wards, were you? I haven't seen them about lately, but I'm sure they're just busy. Do you know them?"

Jason's tongue took over. "Not to say 'know' as in knowing them well; we're slight acquaintances, that's all. And there's that bug going around; they haven't been too well recently, but I think they should be up and about tomorrow or the day after anyhow."

The minister nodded. "Yes, nothing gets people down for long, does it? Now, the honey…" He quoted a price, and Jason nodded.

"I'd like all of the jars at that. If you think that would be all right with Joe?"

"Oh, it will be," he was assured. "He's always pleased when he's sold out so he can go home again. Now, I hope you have change?"

"I think I can find the exact amount."

He dug notes out of his pockets. He'd spread the cash around them, so it didn't look as if he had so much. With the loose change he had, he produced the right amount, handed it over, and went back to the car for a bag. With the jars safely stowed, he turned to say goodbye to find the older man standing there.

"I don't want to impose, young man, but if you would care for a cup of coffee, and I have chocolate cake? I don't get to see many people I don't know. It would be pleasant to chat for a little while if you aren't in a hurry?"

Jason couldn't say no. He and Stormy followed the old man over the road to the small church, where he found that there were living quarters attached around the back. Through an open door, he could see a motionless form on a single bed. The old man saw the direction of his glance and nodded.

"My wife, she's sleeping, she hasn't been well. I'll just close the door."

He did so while Jason kept his mouth firmly shut. He enjoyed the coffee, it was hot, strong, well-made, and the chocolate cake was excellent. A bony slow-moving cat came in and looked at the dog on its territory, Stormy touched noses, and the cat, accepting that the visitor meant no harm, hauled itself onto the sofa and curled up. Jason listened as the minister talked about the church, his parishioners, the local area, and local politics.

"Yes, much of the traffic passes us; the freeway is up there. In a way, it suits most of us. We're only a mile or two away, but ever since it was opened, we haven't had all the noise and the fumes. Nor the accidents."

"It's delightful here," Jason said, striving to stay on a neutral topic.

"Oh, it is, it is. And they're good people. Not that they all come to church, but I don't discriminate, you know. If there's anything I can do to help, well, Christ ministered to anyone that needed him, I can do no less."

"How long have you been here?"

The old man sat back thinking. "You know, it has to be almost fifty years."

"Has there been less traffic this way of late?" That was as close as he wanted to go.

The minister looked blank. "Yes, I suppose there has." He glanced at the sleeping cat. "I'll need more cat food for Tommy soon. I meant to ask one of my people if they'd get some next time they went into town. He's almost seventeen, and he needs that special type for old cats."

Jason could see it. The older man was nearly over the edge of reality as it was. If he went into a larger town and tried to buy cat food, he could fall off the edge. And the cat - Tommy - had been gracious to Stormy as the minister had been to Jason. An hour or two out of his day wouldn't make any difference. He looked at the curled-up cat, the old minister with his slightly shaking hands, his parish dead around him, and made the offer.

"My car and trailer are all packed, but I could go back to the Wards and borrow their car. I'm sure they agree."

"Would you, that'd be very kind. Stop here, and I'll have money for you. There's cat food, and if you wouldn't mind getting me an item or two as well, I'd be grateful."

Jason drove back, collected the Wards' car and trailer, and returned, accepted a handful of small bills, and drove off. In half an hour, he was in town. He chose a strip of shops where there was no one and approached from the service alley behind them. There was a grocery store. He quietly tried the door, found it unlocked, walked in, and stepped over the body of what had probably been the owner. In some cases, as he'd seen, people died in minutes; they just seemed to collapse at once. He collected boxes full of items on the minister's list. Stormy stood guard as he did so, and he added more dog biscuits.

Two doors down was a veterinary clinic. That was empty, and the back door was locked. He broke that open as quietly as possible and took all the cat food that fitted the stipulated category. If Tommy was seventeen and lived as much as another five years on X number of cat food tins a year, the stack of filled boxes Jason had dumped into the trailer should see the cat out. And Jason knew medical terminology; he went to the back where the vet would keep expensive or dangerous medication and took much of it.

He looked over the shelves, considered his dog, added flea and worm treatments, vitamins, and a sprinkling of other useful items, and they returned to the car. He drove back to the crossroads, unloaded everything to sincere thanks, and nodded.

"I was happy to help. One thing more, Reverend Williams. You know, sometimes when cats get very old, they get sick, can't get up to go out, and maybe they're in pain." The old man nodded. "Well, there's a special medication. The vet gave me this." He handed over the card of tiny pills. "Dissolve one in a spoonful of warm water, suck the mixture into this eyedropper, and put that in the front of Tommy's mouth, tilt his head up and let it run down his throat. He'll fall asleep, and he won't be sick or in pain anymore."

The minister accepted the eyedropper and card. "A good thing perhaps that people don't have pills like this."

Jason nodded. "Yes. But if someone ever needed them, these would work for people as well, twenty in a card, that'd be one for Tommy and seven or eight for a person depending on weight. That would be all it'd take." He moved to the door. "Well, it's been an enjoyable visit, but I have to get moving. Thank Joe for me for the honey. I'll take the Wards' car and trailer back, get my things, and I won't stop on the way back if you don't mind."

The old man patted his shoulder. "It's no problem. I've held you up already. Thank you for your help, and safe driving." Jason walked to the car, opened the door for Stormy, and then climbed into the driver's seat. He was moving away when the Minister spoke as if to himself. "Only for Tommy, I can wait, and then I'll be with her."

Jason glanced up startled and saw for a brief flash in time the vague look vanish from the old man's eyes. For that second, there was a terrible agonized knowledge. Then the veil came down again, and he smiled gently at Jason. "What was I saying? Oh, yes, drive safely, and look after your lovely dog."

"I will."

He drove by the crossroads and honked once as he passed. He knew what he'd seen. The older man knew the reality but determined not to acknowledge it; he'd blanked it out. He'd taken the pills so the animal he loved wouldn't suffer when the time came. That was the responsibility of any human who loved an animal. But he knew he'd be with those he loved soon enough, and that was sufficient. The car hummed while Jason sang. Every so often he laid his hand on his dog's fur, feeling the warmth and life. It was a long road to New Mexico, and he wondered who else he'd meet on the way.

****

Jason met no one more than in passing for some days, however. Twice while checking out shops or malls for small items to add to his survival outfit, he ran into someone. The first time to his surprise, it was a family who seemed casual about everything. Jason came out of a footwear shop wearing the new boots he'd gotten, to be met by two kids patting a happy Stormy.

"Hi, is she yours?"

"Her name's Stormy."

"She's pretty," the girl told him. "Isn't she one of those designer breeds?"

"Yes. You two aren't here on your own, are you?"

"No, Mom and Dad are around somewhere."

Two adults appeared from different shops, one carrying a bolt of fabric, the other with bags of something that rattled from the pharmacy. "Hi, nice dog," the male commented.

Jason couldn't help but smile. "Thanks, she is. I'm Jason."

"Eve and Kim Nolan, the kids are Mo and Jo." She saw the look and laughed. "Maureen and Jonathon. Want to get a coke or something?"

Bemused, Jason spent most of the day scavenging with them, listening to their story and hoping they'd survive. Yet, gradually he came to understand that under the laidback smiles, the four of them were intelligent, knowledgeable, and more capable than he'd initially thought.

"We're survivalists. We just don't make a religion of it," Kim said. "We live a long day's drive from here in a place where there's no obvious road. We used to come here to shop every three months. The last time was about seven weeks back, and Mo picked up a sore throat. Then we all caught it and came back to see a doctor. He gave us allodaxin. A few weeks later, most people in the nearest town started getting sick, then dying, but we were fine. I figured it was either the sore throats we had that had immunized us, or that new antibiotic, or maybe it was both together."

"My mom was told it was both," Jason said. "I had the sore throat and allodaxin weeks before the worse sickness started. I'm fine. Everyone else I knew that didn't get sick and have that medication too, they mostly died."

Eve reached over and patted his hand. "It's tough to lose people. But they'd want you to survive and keep going."

"I know. That's what Mom said."

"Well, nice to meet you, Jason. We're heading for a hotel tonight and starting home in the morning."

"Do you know a good place?"

Kim nodded. "Yeah, come on, you can follow us, and I don't see any harm in sharing the place - for a night." There was the faintest emphasis on the last three words.

Jason met his look squarely. "It's okay; I don't want to come home with you. I'm heading south to my dad's ranch."

"Good, you need family at a time like this."

The evening at the hotel was a time to relax, sing, laugh, and talk. With the family knowing this was a one-night thing, they felt safe to discuss some things. Jason told them about the Reverend Williams while they told him about the Mayor.

"Got all the police together and told them they should take over any survivalist homes, that we'd have stuff people could use to make it through. I don't think he *got* it that just about everyone was dying. He sure didn't understand that most of the police were. All they wanted was to go home and be with their kinfolk. One of my friends was there. He said it would have been funny if it wasn't so sad. The police listened to the mayor, then they went to their cars and drove off, leaving him standing there."

Eve's faced twisted into sorrowful lines. "He went back into his office, and when no one saw him next day, someone went to look. He'd shot himself. They went to his house to tell his wife and kids and found them all dead. Looked as if they died earlier. Like your minister, I think he shut it out for a while."

Kim sighed. "Yeah, when this is all over, there's a good chance, seems to me, that some of those left will be crazy. Maybe only on one subject, but crazy. Watch for it. Crazy people can add two and two and get six; then act on that six."

Jason understood. "Yeah. I'm heading for bed. See you in the morning if I wake up before you leave. If I don't, have a good trip home, and I hope you have a good life."

They said goodbye at seven the next morning, then they were gone, and Jason was back on the road after eating breakfast. The afternoon of the day following that, someone took a shot at him. He had no idea who or why, but the bullet ricocheted off the trailer and whined into the distance. He'd been driving with the window down, now he slapped the control to shoot it up while stamping on the accelerator. He whipped around a corner left, a block, then right, and back on track again, the car bulleted down the main road. There were no other shots, and he slowed. Perhaps that'd been one of Kim's crazies.

So when after two days, he ran into a small group in a strip of shops, he was wary. They stayed back watching him, having both walked around and into the main road from opposite directions. It was an impasse, neither prepared to turn their backs on the other and not keen to come forward either. Stormy broke the deadlock, beaming and trotting toward them. One of the women laughed.

"*Good* dog, good *girl!*" Stormy was rolling over to be petted, and Jason drifted closer.

"Her name's Stormy. I'm Jason. Going south to my dad's place."

It was enough for them to feel they knew him and, as his mom had said, you aren't so bothered if you know a person. Besides, there was one of him and a dozen of them. They shared names, mentioned some of their shopping list, and Jason nodded.

"I can tell you where you'll find that. I passed a store three blocks back on a side road. I can show you, if you like?" They did, he did, and he helped them haul out the sacks of poultry feed, the seed corn, and potatoes. "Farm, huh? My dad has a ranch."

That made him still more acceptable. "Yeah? We've got a little place off east. When this came down, there was half a dozen of us with small outfits who survived. Mostly we had a nine to five job, and the few acres were for fun. But now we've decided to get serious. Just about everyone our way is dead, all the guys with big farms, so we're amalgamating, picking what we like to do best and what we're best at, and doing that. We're forting up, too. There was a group that came through in army trucks, not a real army, though. We think they raided an army camp or depot, somewhere like that. They hit a farm thirty miles from our places and wiped it out. Took everything, the family that had it must have guessed how they'd be treated if they surrendered – so they didn't."

Jason whistled softy. "Kids and all?"

"Yeah. We saw the smoke, scouted after five days, made sure they weren't still around, and had a look up close. Cows were gone. They'd shot the goats, just left them to rot. Dogs too. They'd burned the buildings. We couldn't say for sure, but one of our people knows some sign, he said from what it looked like, they'd set the buildings on fire, first two out of the house - an old lady with a kid - they shot, so the rest inside shot the kids and then themselves."

Jason stared. "Who *are* these guys?"

"Dunno for sure, but we think they could be what's left of a couple of gangs. No law, no police anymore, they can do what they like - and they are. So we're going to fort up. Pretty sure they don't know about us or where we live. We keep scouts a half-day out watching, made our main homestead look natural, just like a hill from a distance, surrounded it with a wall of sandbags with turf on top. We plan to take in more people and get some good guns and other stuff. Could use you, if you're interested?"

Jason sighed. "Like I said, going to my dad's ranch. But thanks, if I weren't, I'd grab that like a shot. Oh, and could I tell you something you might find useful?"

They listened. "From a vet, huh, and that's the name, a lot of pills per person. What about the larger animals? Do they use something different?"

Jason's grin was hard. "They do, and I can tell you what. Make a suggestion or two there as well."

They parted after an extended time at the nearest vet's office. The woman who'd been the first to pet Stormy and who'd introduced herself as Rose, smiled at him.

"Thanks for all that."

Jason looked at her. "The way I see it, people who behave the way that lot did need to be stopped. If we ever want a civilization again, we won't get it with them around."

She leaned forward and kissed him while Jason went red. "You're a smart guy, pity you aren't coming back with us, but if what you taught us saves anyone, I'll make sure they remember your name."

Jason laughed. "Thanks to you, too."

They parted with mutual good wishes an hour later, and Jason sat watching from his car as they peeled off along the freeway. Then he keyed the engine and headed out; it was time to find a place for the night. He found one, a mansion just out of town, set in its own grounds, and Jason couldn't resist. He drove up the graveled driveway, parked around the back – fancy places could draw looters even faster – and found a window he could open.

Once inside, he stood motionless, Stormy silent, all their senses extended. There was no movement and no sound. Jason relaxed and cat-footed; he moved first to the kitchen. The power was off here. He didn't open the gigantic freezers; he could just imagine what that would be like, but the cupboards, when opened, showed long lines of top-shelf items. He grinned happily; he'd take as much of that as he could when he left in the morning.

Upstairs, there was no one. Probably the owners, being rich, had gone to the hospital the minute they felt sick. He found the master bedroom and investigated an enormous walk-in closet and various cabinets. In one, he found a safe, which, to his surprise, was unlocked. In that, he found a handgun with ammunition, a stack of cash, and trays of jewelry. He took the money. If he saw anyone else selling something he wanted and who would take money, the cash would be useful. He sifted through the jewelry and took the eighteen caret items with few or no stones. The gun was a .22, but the bullets were hollow-point. They'd pack a real punch for their size. It came with a holster and detachable harness so it could be worn on a belt or as a shoulder holster, which looked good to him, so he added it to his haul, along with a few books.

He slept well that night. Stormy sprawled with him on the huge bed, and after a gourmet breakfast, he sorted out five sacks of tins and packets, many of them luxury items he was going to enjoy. He beamed as he hauled the sacks to his trailer. As always, he left everything tidy behind him with no sign he'd been there. He had just turned onto the road when through his open window, he heard the roar of motors.

Jason had always had good reactions, and he employed them now. He had car and trailer half a block away, around a corner, and backed into a short alley before the convoy would have come in sight. Then he slipped out of the car, padded to the corner, and watched as seven army trucks took the drive down to the mansion. He got back in the car and went the other way, slowly and very quietly, keeping engine sounds to a minimum. And all the while thanking his stars that they'd find no recent traces of anyone there.

CHAPTER EIGHT

Not wanting to have anything to do with the pseudo army and keen to be sure he was out of any territory they might claim, Jason drove all day, pausing only for the odd necessary break. Once dusk began to close in, he hesitated. Should he stop or keep going? Something occurred to him, and he got out the almanac he'd found and checked. Yes, an almost full moon. He'd find a place, sleep a few hours, then go on again with enough light to drive using dipped lights. He moved on, watching both sides of the road.

Out in the country again, he saw a house and drove into the carport there. He didn't waste time doing more than a fast walk-through. The original owners were there; he shut the door on them and chose to sleep on the couch in the room by the carport. He had a fully charged battery, plugged the frying pan into that, and ate a steak and chips dinner. He wanted to sleep, so he chased that with hot chocolate rather than coffee, and once the dishes were washed, dried, and replaced in the cupboard, he settled in his sleeping bag, Stormy on the floor beside him.

His watch had an alarm, one that, on the right setting, silently flicked a small bar back and forth against his wrist, and it began the flicking four hours later. In half an hour, they were on the road again, and again Jason drove with few breaks. He wanted to be as far away as possible, and he'd rather be tired for a day or two than trapped in any burning buildings by those without mercy.

He kept going, driving past sunrise, but beginning by late afternoon to watch for a possible stopping place that would hold few attractions for the pseudo-army. He found it down a side road, a road that, from his map, looped and wandered for miles before coming back to the major road again. The building was now a secondary house. It looked to Jason as if it had been the main house until either another generation or new owners built a larger home in front of it, added a line of trees between them, and probably relegated the old place to be a guest house at need.

He inspected it quickly. Small, two bedrooms, old, it had a woodstove still in place and useable. There was firewood in a lean-to by the kitchen door, but it held nothing other than the wood and basic furniture. No food, no cleaning supplies, and with the drawers, wardrobes, and cupboards all empty. Jason shrugged.

"Guess we use our stuff tonight, girl. And I'm too tired to mess around."

He opened tins, ate sardines from one and canned peaches from the other. He then crawled into the sleeping bag on the blow-up mattress and slept the sleep of – if not the righteous – the genuinely exhausted. He slept well into the next day, woke, decided to stay the rest of the day and the night and move on the morning after that. It was chilly, although the day was clear. Winter was getting close, and he should find a place to stay. Once it hit, he could be slowed by anything from floods to snow banks, and in winter, a car accident could be lethal. The charged battery provided power for cooking breakfast again, and he ate while reading. He cleaned up and found Stormy looking at him pathetically.

He grinned. "I see. You're owed a few runs, and I shouldn't get out of practice with the handgun either." He looked out of the kitchen window. The older, smaller house was well back from the road, and with both the hedge and the bigger house between them, any noise he made would be inaudible to someone driving by. He clipped the handgun holster to the small of his back, dropped ammunition into his vest pockets, and with Stormy's dumbbell in hand, went out to make his dog happy.

He started with her commands and, with that done, tossed her dumbbell repeatedly while she ran in circles, bringing it back and racing out to leap for it once more. Once she slowed, he took a break, thinking that a shower would be good and wondering about the main house's possibilities when a shrill voice slashed open the silence.

"What do you think you're doing? Who are you? Get out, get off my property..." Jason turned. About twenty feet away stood a woman, late-twenties, he thought, and in a designer dress, high heels, and with full make-up, she looked ridiculous. Her face was twisted into an expression of acid disapproval and contempt as she stared at him. Stormy stood up, wagging her tail, and the woman took a step back.

"Keep that thing away from me. What are you doing here, stealing, I suppose?"

Jason spoke quietly. "I spent the night in the old house. You should know there's nothing to steal in there. I ate my own food, used my sleeping bag, and fed my dog from my own supplies. If these houses are yours, I'll go. I didn't know anyone was here..."

She cut in. "I'm sure you didn't, and if you didn't steal, it was because there was nothing there." She waved her hand toward the old house. "And you hadn't got to the other house yet. Where's your car?"

He realized she'd come by on the other side of the old house and hadn't seen a car or trailer. He walked, not directly to her but obliquely, to make her feel less threatened. "It's okay. I'll leave." He'd be happy to go. But he wasn't going without the battery, frying pan, sleeping bag, and Stormy's water bowl.

He circled the house while she followed at a distance, like a dog shepherding him off her territory. It amused him, she was hardly that intimidating, and he couldn't see a gun on her. If he decided to stay, what was she going to do, screech him to death? He was out of her sight as he came around the front corner, and he ran quickly along the end of the old house, reached the kitchen door, and had everything back into the car before she found him again. She gaped at the car and the loaded trailer.

"You *are* a thief! You didn't get a car like that by paying for it..."

"It was my mother's car," Jason said softly.

"Your mother? *Really*? And I suppose she just went out one day and bought it?" *You could saw wood with that tone,* he thought and managed to keep his voice polite with an enormous effort.

"Yes, she was an orthopedic surgeon, and nothing in the trailer's stolen either." *Well, not exactly,* his mind added. Some he'd been given, and some hadn't had an existing owner, but none had been taken from a person who was there and protesting it.

She sneered. "So you say, have you got receipts for any of it?"

He hadn't, no, and while he could prove his mother's ownership of the car and show his driver's license - matching surnames and the same address - he didn't feel inclined to make her a present of that information. He could ask about proof she owned this property, but he couldn't be bothered.

"Answer me. Can you prove any of this is yours? If not, you can leave it right here."

Jason ignored her, clipped down the trailer cover, and opened the door for Stormy. Once she was in, he shut that door and climbed into the driver's seat. He let the window down about an inch, locked it there, and locked the doors. He started the engine and moved forward at a walking pace. She was marching to one side of the car.

"I warn you, if you take that car and trailer away, you'll be in trouble. I've got friends. Do you hear me? Come back right now..."

He circled the main house and went north, her protests fading behind him. He didn't know about her friends, but in case they were real, he wouldn't leave tracks. He followed the loop road back to the freeway, crossed that, and circled south again. By that time, he'd be out of her sight and hearing, and if she really did have friends and sent them after him, she'd tell them he'd gone north. At least he'd had a good night's sleep. All that, and he didn't even know her name - or she his, which was a good thing.

Jason left the window down that small amount, the breeze was pleasant, and he found he was singing again - a song of Ed Sheeran's that his mom had liked this time. It was a way of keeping her with him. He drove until it was almost dark - the land rising slowly towards mountains - staying on the back roads, so when he saw a dirt road leading off behind trees, he followed it. He found a solitary farmhouse, dark windows, no car visible, and he decided to stop there for the night. If it was like the last place and empty of anything, he had what he needed to be comfortable enough, and he'd make do. He pulled up by the back door, got out with Stormy, and looked across the land.

There was a cow in the small paddock by the house ... a cow, small paddock, she'd have eaten that out long since. Someone must be moving her ... he heard the door behind him open and spun. His hand, moving involuntarily from long practice by now, reaching for the gun. The woman in the doorway snorted.

"Waste of time. If I'd wanted you dead, you would have been." She was on crutches, a rifle under one arm. He guessed her to be in her fifties, with a face that showed long-time pain or illness. "Well, don't stand there, come in. I've got coffee on." Numbly he followed her in, sat where she pointed, accepted a cup of coffee, drank a mouthful, and looked around. Framed photos standing on an ancient piano, china in a sideboard, old, polished, dark wooden furniture, and lace doilies *everywhere*.

She saw him looking at those and grinned. "My grandmother's work, she loved to tat. I inherited the house when she died twenty years ago, and I haven't altered a thing." She hobbled to a cupboard, which he now saw to be an old-fashioned meat safe, opened that and tossed a large mutton bone to Stormy, who snapped it up eagerly. "Pretty dog, never seen one like her before."

"Designer breed. The breeder wanted the perfect family dog."

"Is she?"

Jason found he was smiling. "I don't have a family, but we suit each other okay."

"I'm Janet Pentreath…"

Without thinking, he recited the ancient Cornish rhyme he'd learned as a toddler. "Tre, Pol, and Pen be the Cornish men."

Her eyes narrowed. "You aren't likely to know that without being one…"

"Jason Trevalen, my mom's parents were Cornish."

She looked surprised and pleased. "As were mine. Well met, Jason Trevalen. I've food in the oven. Will you stay for dinner?"

He paused. "I should find a place to stay for the night before it's too dark."

"I've got a spare bedroom," Janet Pentreath said simply.

"You don't mind?"

"Wouldn't have offered if I did."

"Then, thanks."

They talked. He stayed that night, then another and another. He learned to hand-milk the cow and make butter in a hand-churn. She told him why she needed the crutches.

"There was a car accident. I don't know what happened; I was asleep in the back seat; we were coming here to visit my grandparents, and they said my father must not have seen the train coming. He drove over the rails right in front of it. I was twelve, they both died, and I was hurt. My grandparents took me in. I went on to the university and had a good job for years, then the old injuries got worse. Now I have to use these," she thumped a crutch on the floor.

"Five years back, the doctors said that I'll manage here for a few more years, then I'd need to go into a home of some sort. Once that time comes, I'll be staying right here." She took in a breath. "Truth is, it's getting hard to manage now, but I won't complain. It hasn't been a bad life." She chuckled. "With what happened recently, it's been my good fortune against other people's bad luck. I lived, they didn't, and down the road, there are houses, a shop, and a timber and coal merchant. Other places, too, and all of them stocked up. I get by."

He understood. She could scavenge, and she must be able to drive and have a vehicle. She'd lived here for decades, knowing all the places within miles, and if she was almost the only person left, then she could survive about as long as she wanted to. On the third morning, she asked for help with some of her salvaging, and Jason nodded.

"Sure."

"Won't bother you?"

His gaze met hers, and she grinned. "Of course, It's how you've been managing."

"Only where there's no one there, or if it's offered," Jason told her – and saw she believed him.

They came back with a load of firewood and coal, cattle food, books, a stack of sheet music, an instruction manual, and a guitar.

"Music," Janet said thoughtfully, "is a comfort and a joy. You said you can pick out a tune or two. Let's see." That night she played the piano while he strummed, and she was right. It was a joy. She knew many of the songs his grandparents had sung, and it was late before the impromptu concert stopped and he went to bed.

Jason had planned to stay a night and go. A week later, he was still there. Janet told stories of her family, and Jason told her about the Reverend Williams and his cat. Then the storm came. There was little warning. The evening was overcast, nothing new, but in the early hours – while no one was awake to see; temperatures dropped, snow started silently – and continued. And by the time Jason woke, it was a foot deep. Looking out the window, he thought it was as well they'd brought back cattle feed and wood, there'd already been cords of firewood and hay in the barn, but Janet had said she liked to be well supplied, so he'd hauled everything to the truck and loaded it. Now he was glad he had.

Janet's voice came to his ears. "Breakfast. Come and get it!"

Stormy was already on the way, and he grinned. It hadn't taken her long to know what those words meant. He joined them in the kitchen, sat, and accepted the loaded plate. He looked at it and blinked.

"Eggs? Where'd you get eggs? I never saw hens."

Janet laughed. "And you won't. These came out of a packet."

"Huh?"

She reached behind her to a cupboard and produced a packet that proclaimed to contain egg powder. "Small place southwest started doing this a couple of years back. I saw it on TV, bought a pack, and found the stuff's fine for scrambled eggs or baking; does a fair omelet too. The ham's out of a can. What do you think?"

Jason forked the last of the scrambled eggs and ham into his mouth, swallowed, and grinned. "I'd say the guy who did this knew what he was doing."

"Hope you feel that way in an hour."

"Why then?"

"Snow should stop any minute, so it'd be a good time to head back where we were and get another load. I have enough here to do me all winter, but more wouldn't hurt."

Jason simply nodded. He could afford another day, but tomorrow he should get out of here and head south. "Does it often snow here?"

Janet pursed her lips. "Depends on the year. Some years it's late; some years, it comes early. A bad year is when it comes early and heavy. Finished?"

He had, and left Stormy with her while he dived for the bedroom and donned cold-weather gear, thinking it was fortunate he'd gotten that – while her words rang a bell somewhere in the back of his head. He came back looking twice the width to find that she'd done the same. The truck had been left under cover, but plowing by foot to it was surprisingly tiring. They climbed aboard,

Stormy in the middle, and drove to the small group of buildings three miles away. That, too, was hard work, Janet knew every inch of the road, but Jason worried about how he'd manage when he left tomorrow.

They collected food from the shop, and other items, topping them off with more fuel, and once they had it all loaded, Janet went to one of the barns and took up an armload of hay. Then, rifle under one arm - a different gun, he noticed - she began to call. Jason understood her intentions as the first steer came trotting into view. Four had arrived and were eating hay when Janet stepped to one side, screwing something onto the rifle barrel. She raised it, there was an odd flat thump, and the steer nearest the truck, a solid beast of around two, fell. The others glanced at him, finished the hay, and ambled away, leaving the red and white beast prone on the snow-covered ground.

"Never seen that before," Jason said. "Silencer, I guess?"

"Yes. One of my neighbors was a collector; he and his didn't make it. The advantage of a silencer is, it doesn't sound like a rifle, quieter, different sound entirely, and I've dropped two goats before now while the rest stayed watching me."

Jason looked at the steer. "Where'd you want him?"

"Do the job in the barn. There's a pulley there and a tarp to drag him to it." The job proved messy but fairly simple, and in less than two hours, they were on the way back to Janet's farmhouse with the steer, headed, skinned, gutted, and divided into joints with those portions wanted neatly piled onto the truck. Janet had separated the organs and put them in a sack.

"Stormy, she'll like them. Once we're back, we have to make sure the meat's all put away where nothing can get at it."

Jason had a mental picture of strolling out to get a streak and finding himself face to face with a bear - or a cougar - and agreed fervently. The work after that wasn't nearly so quick. They had to finish cutting up the beast and the results packaged so they could be placed in a huge old freezer in a solid concrete room off the house.

"Will the meat be okay in there? There's no power."

"Be fine. Snow drifts there, concrete is freezing, the meat will be solid in a few hours and stay that way until we take some out and let it thaw inside."

Jason felt reassured. If he left tomorrow as he intended, she'd be okay, she had wood and coal, a ton of food, including about a hundred pounds of meat now, and with the wood range going, the house was warm and dry, she had new books, he didn't need to feel guilty. They played the piano and guitar again that night, and she sang a song matching her earlier comment. He recognized it as she sang, a gentle aching regret in the words –

And some days, it don't come easy.

Her voice touched him, as did the sorrow in her eyes.

And these are the days that never end …"

Yes, that had been another of his mother's favorite songs, along with others by the singer whose videos he remembered now. Jason hinted he was tired and went to bed by nine o'clock. He didn't even read and was asleep in minutes, so that he woke early, wandered to the kitchen and made porridge, put the kettle on, and noticed only vaguely that the kitchen seemed darker than usual.

He was enlightened on that when Janet came into the kitchen, glanced around, nodded, and went to the outer door. She opened it with slow care, and he was about to ask what she was expecting when he saw snow begin to tumble through the crack.

"What…?"

"Real snowstorm during the night. Must be four or five feet out there now."

Jason leaped for the window, hauled the thick curtains apart, and looked out into a white world, one that came partway up the windows. He stood, taking in the information and the unwanted knowledge it carried. Janet had shut the door again and was stirring the porridge. Jason spoke slowly, knowing he was trapped, that he'd trapped himself.

"I can't get out."

"Not in that car. No chains."

"The other houses?"

"They'll have a set or two, but they're for different vehicles, and you'd need them on the trailer as well, I'd think."

He didn't know, but it was possible. And could Mom's car even tow the trailer with chains on it, let alone on both? Janet ladled the porridge into two warmed plates waiting on the old wooden table, poured coffee into the mugs, and sat.

"Sorry, I wasn't expecting snow this early and not a snowstorm at all."

He sat, ate his porridge, drank the coffee, and came to an acceptance of it. He'd thought he might have to overwinter somewhere; he just hadn't planned for it to be here, or not so early in the trip. But it wasn't Janet's fault he was stuck, and he could think of worse people to be stuck with. That awful woman in the last place, for example. He stood up, reached for the bread, cut slices, and set them in the toaster. *Make the best of it,* his mom used to say. *Pouting and whining makes it that much worse.*

"No one's fault. I only hope you don't get so fed up with us here you've killed Stormy or me by the time this lot thaws," he said casually.

Janet chuckled, "Cabin fever, they call it, and no, I don't think so. Let's hope for an early thaw anyway," and on that note, she started the dishes.

CHAPTER NINE

Despite anyone's hopes, there was another fall of snow that night, and Jason remembered the meat in the concrete shed by the house. Right now, they had beef for a month or more, and the organs and trimmings saved would keep Stormy happy when added to her dog biscuits. But the meat would run out.

"We'll want some more beef. How do we get it?" He thought of trying to shovel his way through that snow and shivered.

"Quite easily," was Janet's response. "At the end of the hall, there's a ladder into the attic. You can run a plank from the attic window out to the shed. The trapdoor there lets you in and down another ladder to the meat."

Jason looked at her, tracing the procedure out in his mind. "Who on earth came up with that idea?"

"My great-grandfather, the year he had problems with a bear that wasn't in hibernation."

Jason looked at her. "Who won?"

"Great-grandpa, he got away with it."

"Got away?"

"Yes, they never found out he put a bullet in the bear."

Oh, right, probably a law. "Did he get the meat?"

"That, too."

"Sounds like a tough man."

That reminded Janet of a family tale that proved it. Between chores that day, she told him tales of her grandparents ... and their parents ... and theirs. In return, about five days later, he told her about his family; some of that surprised her.

"I said Mom was Cornish. She was an orthopedic surgeon; Dad's about thirty-five percent Navajo. Makes me about seventeen-eighteen percent. He and Mom got divorced, and I never got to see him after I was about eleven. No bad blood, not really. They had different plans, wanted different things, they never bad-mouthed each other to me. Mom told him I needed an education if I wanted to be a doctor. She told him I couldn't spend too much time on a ranch out in nowhere when I needed to study. Dad asked me around then if it was true I wanted to be a doctor, and I said I did. Maybe that made him think Mom was right."

"Did you email?"

"No internet where the ranch is. We write - wrote - a few times a year. He phoned me last birthday, sent me a gift card." Jason remembered that. It had been for five hundred dollars, and Jason had been pleased and surprised, but the best gift had been the phone call placed from the town where they had a connection. They'd talked for an hour. He'd told Dad about how well he was doing at school, his plans for his last year of high school and heard in turn that the ranch was doing well. Jason had grinned at the phone. That explained the gift card. He hadn't liked that his father might have spent more than he could afford.

"I'll be able to tell him that gift card helped me make it there," he said softly. "I had it in my wallet in case I saw something I liked, but as soon as the virus started up, Mom told me to cash in everything, clear my bank account, and hers, too."

"Do you think he'll be expecting you?"

"It may sound dumb, but yeah, I think he will. He just won't know about Mom. Wish I could have got word to him about her dying and me being on the way, but phones and the internet are down in a lot of places. I never managed to talk to him."

Janet sounded practical. "Then it'll be a nice surprise for him when you walk in."

Jason imagined that meeting, and a brilliant smile lit his face. "Yeah."

His companion shut her lips firmly. That had cheered the boy up, better it didn't occur to him that his mother had died, his grandparents, and most of the people he'd known in that city had died. His father *could* have survived, but the odds were against it.

****

It snowed on and off all day, and Janet was up early to make a list. She put the chains on her truck, got down the low flat sledge, greased the runners, and added it to the truck's gear. They'd need another beast, more wood and coal, more fuel for the lanterns, and more of anything else they could get back to her place before the raised section of road became impassable. She made breakfast, called Jason down, and while he ate, she talked.

"I don't know if you noticed, but the road from this house to the village is raised above the land around it." Jason, his mouth full of toast, nodded. "That was my grandfather's doing. Before, it used to flood, and when that happened, you couldn't get to the village, so if you wanted supplies, you had to drive out and back to the town twenty miles away - if you could make it *there*. Same for the people in the village. If they couldn't get to here, they couldn't make it out to the town. Grandpa talked to everyone, and they built the road higher."

"Smart," Jason commented.

"Yup, and convenient." She snickered. "Smart, too, because they never said anything about it. No permit, and no one outside of around here knowing about it. Made things easier for everyone for years, and now it may be what saves us."

Jason sat up. "How?"

Grandpa used a surface that's a sort of tar mix. It picks up heat, so once the sun's high - if it's a fine day today and I think it will be - the snow on the road will melt. Just that length of road, mind you, but that lets us go to the village."

Jason remembered the butchered steer in the meat room, the stacks of fuel and supplies. "Do we really need more?"

Janet's face drew into hard lines. "We do. I've lived here on and off all my life, Jason, and I know something. I know that when snow is this heavy and this early, it's going to be high and stay frozen. So long as we can get in more supplies, we need to do that."

"How high?"

"About halfway up the house. Won't affect the chimneys, but I've got steel shutters for the windows. We'll put those up as soon as we've got in all the supplies we can." She looked at him. "There isn't that much dangerous wildlife around here nowadays, but there may be animals getting together to hunt. Big animal smelling our food, they could come right through a window, double glazing only keeps out the cold, something that's a fifty pounds or more will go through that as if it isn't there."

"Maybe we should put up the shutters first?"

Janet sat, considering it. "Let's gamble. No use if the place is safe while we're starving inside it. Supply run today, shutters tomorrow, then if we can, we do another run and keep doing them until we can't get through. But one more load of meat and fuel should be just about right even if we have to change things around."

"Like what?"

"Shut off the rooms we don't need and keep the fire a bit lower. We had a winter like this when my grandpa was still alive. Towards the end of it, we had to bunk down in the drawing room. Just kept that, the kitchen/ dining room, and the bathroom open."

"I see." He did too, he thought. And yes. More supplies would be a good idea.

They had a busy day after that, while Stormy enjoyed it thoroughly. Jason hauled hay to the corner of a heavy fence. The steers came eagerly, and Janet sat quietly watching. Once they'd eaten the hay and began to drift away, she shot twice, and two yearling steers dropped. The others spooked a little but quietened and wandered away when nothing more happened. They managed to get a steer at a time onto the sledge and tow that to the other side of the house with the fence. There they dressed out the animals, and, placing the tarp on the sledge, they hauled the meat to the truck, leaving no trail.

"Dogs and other critters'll come to that," Janet said, looking at the pile of steaming entrails. "I just want them to come somewhere they'll be away from where we'll be coming and going. We've got the meat and the organs. Three steers' worth should do us no matter how long the snow lasts."

They added still more wood and coal to the meat, and Janet disappeared into one of the houses to come out with a huge armful of what looked like fur. She loaded that into the sledge, and Jason came to help.

"What's that?"

"Bedspreads. Maisie Garret's husband used to shoot rabbits for their dog. When he did, he'd skin the rabbits and tan the skins. Maisie sent them to town, had them made into a pair of lined and padded bedspreads. Weigh a ton, but she used to brag they were so warm you could have slept under one in winter and stayed fine even if the fire went out. She had lanterns, fuel for them, a big chest of candles, and she had a storeroom."

"What's in that?"

"Go and see." She added directions, and Jason, Stormy at his heels, found it. He opened the door, looked at the filled shelves, and blinked. The lady was a pessimist; either that or she'd expected what happened. He began moving everything that he thought they'd like, want, or use out to the back doorstep. Once he had that done, he moved the truck as close as possible and used the sledge to move the cartons he'd filled the rest of the way. By the time the storeroom was empty, the truck was full, and they drove back, unloaded, and returned.

"We won't get more than another load before dark."

Janet agreed. "No, that's food, bedding, and light, now let's get wood and coal. If we can't return, we should have enough to manage, although I'd like another day's worth, better sure than sorry."

"Yeah, look, you've put up the shutters before? Can you still do that on your own?"

Janet hesitated, her mind racing. She'd felt her body weakening all summer, and she'd guessed she might not make it through winter on her own, but if she said she couldn't deal with the shutters, the boy might realize.

She snorted. "I can manage. You thinking of coming back here for more stuff tomorrow while I stay and do the shutters?" He nodded. "Good thought," she said judiciously. "Get us a good dinner, early night, and if you can get at least one full truckload tomorrow, that should take us well over the line of making it."

The load of wood, coal and further gleanings from the houses were stacked on the truck, and they were back before dark. It was night by the time they had unloaded everything and stored it where it would be on hand. Janet had used an iron pot left on the range, and now she had only to divide the contents before they sat to enjoy a hot casserole with apple pie from the oven for dessert. Stormy ate cooked trimmings that had been left in a second pot on the range.

They went to their beds shortly after dinner; Jason read a while then fell asleep, Stormy on the rug beside the bed. Janet, in her bedroom, looked through her stock of drugs, some salvaged from the village. She'd known who would have what and had cleared them long before Jason arrived. Others she'd quietly taken from the town pharmacy nearest her before anyone else realized what was happening. She was a realist; she knew that her health was failing, everyone was dead in the village, and it looked as if most of the town – other towns and cities too – would be almost depopulated within months.

She'd have no one to care for her when her strength ran out. It was something Grandpa had said to her over and over in his last months. That he thanked God he had her, that he would not, did not, die alone. And – before Jason arrived – that had been her great fear, too. She'd quietly stalled his staying on, waiting. The omens had been for an early and hard winter, and if she could keep him here, she wouldn't die alone nor starve to death if she became too weak to work.

She sorted out a line of pills and considered them. That should be sufficient to get her through the hard work tomorrow. She'd take one at a time so that they overlapped effect. She left them in a compartmented container, put that ready in a coat pocket, and climbing back into bed, fell asleep within minutes.

Jason was first into the kitchen, started breakfast, and fed Stormy the other half of the pot of trimmings. Janet came in with a half-bucket of milk, poured that into the setting pan, joined him, and started a saucepan of scrambled eggs. They ate, and once done and the dishes washed and put away, he left in the truck, Janet's list in his pocket. She opened the side door into the garage and began to haul out the steel plates that would cover the windows. She could simply mount them in brackets, but they could be made safer and more secure by bolting them to the window frames.

The windows were of the sash type, so they were raised and lowered and would not be affected by having shutters placed outside of them. Her grandpa had pierced each plate with half a dozen holes, each just large enough to place a rifle to one and shoot anything trying to smash its way into the house. The plates were heavy, but she had a small hand-wound hoist on wheels that allowed her to move them into position. Nonetheless, it was exhausting, and by the time Jason was back, she'd had to take two pain pills and rest an hour, choosing the time to do that before her best estimate of when he'd return. She said nothing of either thing, however, and helped him unload.

He drove off again, and she went back to placing the shutters in position. The pain broke through the medication, and she took the third pill, reflecting that it was a good thing she had so many and that this too was probably the last major physical exertion she'd have to make before spring. In the barn, Pansy lowed, and Janet's face went white. She hadn't even thought of that. Mechanically, she hoisted a shutter into place, bolted it on, and moved to the next window. She sighed, a soft resigned sound. Humans were given animals to care for, and in the end, to do the right thing by them.

Jason came back right on dark with the second load to find all the shutters in place and securely bolted down. "I checked that house right at the far end of the place," he announced. "Did you ever go there?"

"No. The owner was away, and he'd told a couple of people he was leaving it cleared out because he was going to sell it when he came back."

Jason was momentarily distracted. "Where'd he go?"

"Canada. He had an old school friend in a small place in B.C. That's why he was selling; he planned to move there. He was staying with the friend's family while he looked for a suitable house, and he should have been back a couple of weeks ago."

"And he wasn't?"

"No. Why?"

"Because he had a funny idea of what 'leaving a place cleared out' meant."

"Oh?" Janet said. Not that it mattered. What would he have had there that was of any real value to them?

"Yeah, like I said, I checked the place. He had a real electric bike. You know the kind; it's almost a moped, doesn't *have* to be pedaled but can be if you want to. Rechargeable batteries, it'll do about 20 miles an hour and as much as a hundred miles without recharging depending on the weight carried and how flat the roads are. That was hanging on a rack with spare batteries and all the gear for it. There was even a set of solar panels that can be mounted on the bike. And he had a complete set of portable electric media in the house, and he had books."

"*Books*, what sort?"

Jason grinned. "I thought you'd like that." He reeled off several author names, and Janet's eyes widened. "That's not all. He must have known someone. Some of those were recent review galleys. A couple were still in wrapping in the porch mailbox. I opened them, looked at the dates. They must have arrived about the same time this thing started."

"Who?"

Jason recited names, titles and then smiled. "I didn't leave them there, you know. They came with me. I bought the media and the bike too. Unless you want that, I'd like have it."

She beamed at him. "It's all yours so long as I can have the books."

"And we can share the media; it's a good thing for winter." He beamed back. "And I don't know if I ever told you, but I've got a portable wind generator on the trailer, along with storage batteries and other stuff for it. I can hook the TV, music player, and all of that to the storage batteries, and he had cartons and cartons of movies, TV series, and music. I took the lot. If you like even half of it, there's enough to watch all winter. And once it's spring, maybe we could go to the town nearest you and find another lot, so you'd never be short of entertainment after I'm gone."

Janet managed a smile of agreement, forced her voice to remain casual, and nodded. "Yes, that'd be wonderful. I had no idea; he said he'd cleared the place out."

"Well, I suppose he had, sort of. Just the bike and its gear in the garage, and the books and media in his bedroom, at least I suppose it was his. There was a bed, cabinet, and a chest of drawers there too. The rest of the place had no furniture, no nothing. Curtains, carpets, yeah, but they were pretty shabby. Would the place have even sold?"

"Probably, if the price was low. The son of one of the families there was getting married, and they both had jobs in town and wanted to stay near their parents. They'd have bought…"

If they'd lived, she thought sadly. She'd liked them. She'd gone to the Kiley place first, once she'd seen no one around for days and heard on the radio before that some of what was happening. They'd been dead, all of them, and Mara's parents in their house along from the Kileys. After that, she'd checked almost all the homes, businesses, sheds, and outbuildings and found only bodies. The outside animals had been set free, but she found all the house pets she knew about dead with their owners. With some, they'd been shot. Others had no indication how they'd died.

Jason had been bringing in books as she sat and remembered. He stacked them around the walls and went out for the media. Janet stared at the growing heaps. He'd certainly been right about the amount of entertainment; she estimated two hundred books and four times that in media entertainment hours. Well, she wouldn't die bored.

"There are a couple of empty bookcases in the back room. If you bring them into here, they could go against the wall; they'd take about half that lot. And there's planking and nails in the barn?"

Jason thought. "I could put up bookshelves with that. Maybe be enough to shelve all the other stuff as well. Better for it than stacked like that. Will tomorrow do?" Janet nodded. "Okay then. I'll make a start after breakfast."

He did, and by evening, everything was on shelves he'd put up, so there was barely room to take the media items off the shelves and replace them. That way, they added insulation. He'd done something similar with the books. And, as it hadn't snowed that night, and he'd only got half the books, he'd go back. He explained to Janet, who nodded.

"That'd be good, and check his place again. I went over everywhere else, but I never even looked at his house. I think there's a small storeroom in a corner off the garage."

There was. Jason found it and came back, white with snow as it had started snowing again, and more heavily. This time he had not only the books he hadn't had room to bring on the earlier trip but also with still more. Cartons of older ones that Janet tentatively identified as "belonged to his parents. What else was there?"

"Two tin trunks, a moth-eaten fur coat, and this." He handed her a box. It was about fifteen inches long, twelve inches wide, and eight inches deep, made from small pieces of wood of several colors put together in elaborate patterns. He placed it in her hands, catching it in support, something she understood as she felt the weight of it.

"What's *in* the thing? It weighs a ton." She detached one hand and lifted the lid to stare transfixed at the contents. "What ... where on *Earth* could he have got that lot?"

"I dunno," Jason told her as they gaped at some two hundred small gold coins. "Maybe he had a relative that collected them - either that or he robbed a bank."

Janet's laughter ceased. "Or," she said slowly. "*Someone* robbed somewhere, stashed it where they knew the owner wasn't going to be back for ages." Her voice squeaked as the rest of that thought struck her. "And if they're alive, they'll probably come looking for it."

"I can take it back tomorrow..." Jason started.

Janet pointed to the window where snow was now whiting out everything. "No, you can't. And if they come back and it isn't there, they'll see smoke. They'll come straight here." They looked at each other, and neither of them found anything to say.

CHAPTER TEN

Each, in their own way, spent a restless night. Jason cursed himself for staying here. He could have gone before the snow began, could have been into the next state by now. It was his own fault, and so was finding the box and bringing it back here. Janet was right; the guy that owned the house wouldn't have left that kind of money lying around while he was gone for more than half a year. It didn't make sense. It wasn't as if someone had hidden it. It was just sitting there. On the other hand, how much sense did it make that someone had stolen it, dumped it where they thought it'd be safe, and without really hiding it either? If you had something like that, why wouldn't you just hang on to it?

****

In her bedroom, Janet, too, wasn't sleeping. That gold made her think of all the things she could do with it. She could have gone to specialists, had her old injuries fixed, maybe got her nerves numbed so she wasn't in pain. She could have gone on a cruise, got a good car, or bought books. She could have afforded all the new books she'd ever wanted. But the gold wasn't hers, and what if whoever had left it came demanding they give it back?

They could, but would the person be content with that? It had to have been stolen, and once they asked for it back and got it, well, then Jason and Janet knew what they looked like. She moved and felt pain slash down her leg. She sucked in a breath and held it. That hurt. And things were worse every week. She likely wasn't going to make it to the other side of winter. She fell asleep in the early hours, still trying to think what to do.

****

By morning Jason had made up his mind. He started breakfast, waiting until Janet was at the table, dished up the food, sat, and began. "We found skis, and there's the sledge. It's stopped snowing. If I ski on the road to the village with the box on the sledge, I should be able to get there and back before dark. I'll put it back where I found it, and if anyone comes looking, as far as they know, it never moved. They won't have a clue we know, and with it right there, they'll have no reason to look for us. What do you think?"

Janet heaved a long sigh. "I think you make sense. Finish breakfast and go. I'll do the dishes. The longer you have to get there and back in daylight, the better. Leave Stormy. If she gets into trouble out there, you could end up stuck somewhere there's no fire or food."

"Yeah." He drunk off the dregs of the coffee and got up. "Ten minutes."

And in that time, he was at the door, clad for cold weather, the skis and sledge on the porch, Janet watching as he strapped them on and picked up the sledge rope. Stormy whined as Janet held her collar.

"No, girl, you stay here. He'll be back."

Jason grinned wryly. "I sure hope so."

And with that, he glided away. He'd used skis before, his mother had been a good skier, and she'd taught him during several Christmas holidays in the mountains. Fortunately, the road to the village very slightly sloped down to that. It made it easier to tow the sledge and its contents. He pushed things a bit; he wanted the box stowed back where he'd found it and him clear of the village again. There'd be marks, but the next snowfall would take care of that. He reached the empty house, hauled the box inside, and put it down carefully, just where it had been.

He backed out of the shed and noticed a flake of snow drifting down. Jason used an expression he'd heard a coach use once and grabbed the sledge rope. The faster he was back, the better it'd be for all of them. By the time he was on the raised road, the snowflakes were falling fast, and suddenly he was afraid. If he stayed in the village, he probably wouldn't have time to get enough fuel into a house to keep a fire going all night. If he headed back and the snow got heavier...

He gambled. He'd have a better chance, he thought, if he could make it back to food, a fire, his dog, and Janet. That way, if the snow had really set in, he'd be in a place where he could survive – as he probably wouldn't in the empty village.

Janet had already seen the first flakes, that there was only a slight breeze, and she had an idea. She shut the indignant dog in Jason's room and snatched up a bundle of long bamboo stakes she used in the garden. In her room, she had a length of red material, which she'd bought some time ago to make a summer dress.

She grabbed scissors, started a cut, and ripped a length of the material free, then doubled that several times and cut and cut again. She now had a couple of dozen pieces of red cloth, long enough to tie to a stake top and flutter in the breeze. She flung on her heaviest coat, stuffed the material strips into a pocket, and with the stakes in a bundle on her back and crutches under her arms, she plodded out into the snow, walking to where her drive met the raised road and then a moderate distance towards the village.

After that, it was basic. Start back, sticking a stake into the snow until it hit the road, tie the material on top, walk five paces, stick in a stake, tie the material, walk again. The snow was moderately heavy by the time Janet made it back, and her leg was aching fiercely, but she had a good opinion of the boy's common sense. He'd have started back the moment he saw the snow coming down again.

He had, and he was using all his strength to move along as fast as he could without falling. The snow was coming down more heavily, and he was having trouble staying on the road – but then ahead, he saw the first little flag waving valiantly in the center of the road. He collected it and continued, deeply grateful that they were only about ten feet apart, and so far, the snow hadn't yet begun to obscure them at that distance. The last two were somewhat obscured, but he could dimly see the bulk of the house to the left and made directly for that.

He reached it and sagged against the door. His finger fumbled for the handle, the door opened, and he stumbled inside, catching the door with an elbow so that it swung shut. He'd left the sledge on the porch but under cover, and right now, he didn't care if a bear ate it. Janet appeared with a mug in one hand.

"Drink this."

He drank and groaned his appreciation. Hot chocolate, with a dash of brandy, he thought, and so sweet he could feel each mouthful warming him down to his toes. Janet was asking something. He listened and managed to make sense of the words. She wanted to know if he'd put the box back. He nodded. With a nod of approval, she left and came back with a large thick towel. She rubbed his face gently until he took the towel from her.

Janet watched. She'd had another worrying thought while making that drink for him. Once she saw he was recovering, she sat, waited until he looked at her and voiced it.

"You said the old books were in the shed too. Would it be noticeable they're gone?"

Jason found a weary grin. "No, remember I said there were a couple of old tin trunks there? Well, they were in those. They had a blanket over them in each trunk, so once I put the box back, I found a few chunks of wood and put those in the trunks with the blankets over them. I guess if the robber knew what was in them to start with, and if he *does* come back, and if he checks inside them again, he'll know someone was there. But that's a few 'ifs,' and I'd say there's a good chance he won't do all that."

Janet leaned back and relaxed slightly. "No guarantees, but I can add that 'if' he even makes it through to snow to the shed, and 'if' he can make it away again, he could well be too tired to put everything together and come looking for us anyway. How about dinner, and I should let Stormy out before she knocks the door down anyhow."

Dinner was, he thought, one of the best meals he'd ever eaten, and his reunion with Stormy warmed him in another way. He went to bed right after he'd eaten, let the dog join him, and slept like the proverbial bear. It snowed again that night, and next morning, he looked at the result and felt that even if there was a robber, he was unlikely to make it here, and if he did, he'd be keener to get out again than to go looking for someone who might - or might not - know anything about that box. He hauled in the supplies from the sledge and settled to eat, sleep, read and watch movies between long discussions.

They had a brief thaw three days later. The snow sank inch by inch as the air warmed, but it never disappeared, and on the fourth night, it snowed again. Janet considered events and turned to him over dinner that fifth night.

"That's it. We're here until spring." Jason said nothing but nodded in agreement.

****

It was peaceful, Jason thought, waking up a month later, warm under the rabbitskin bedspread. He rolled over, shot into clothes hastily, and went out to the barn to give Pansy hay, Stormy following. They'd fed the cow, put the bar down across the door, and were on the way back when the dog's head came up alertly. She turned, orienting on whatever she'd heard, and growled. Jason turned to look – then he was moving. Pansy was inside with the barn door secure.

In seconds, he made the house, tore open the door, dived in, and grabbed Stormy, who would have stayed. He slammed the door, added the section of steel that reinforced it, and yelled, "Janet. Don't go out."

She'd been cooking breakfast, and now she came hurriedly. "What is it? What's wrong?" Before Jason could reply, anything he might have said was drowned out by the sounds from the other side of the door and Stormy's angry challenge.

He looked at her, with the noise he not only couldn't be heard, he hardly needed to explain. Outside, more than a dozen dogs were making it clear they wanted in, and not to greet the humans with love and affection. A look of understanding spread over Janet's face, and she nodded, drew him away from the door and into the kitchen where the barking was muffled.

"How many?"

Jason grinned dourly. "I didn't stop to count; it was pretty plain what they had in mind. I just dived for the door, got us in, and shut it. The steel panel is up as well. Oh, and I was on the way back when Stormy heard them. Pansy's in the barn with the door barred and plenty of hay."

"How many would you guess?"

"Maybe fourteen or fifteen, and they're all big dogs."

Janet nodded, her mouth set in a hard line. "Right, I'll give them something to eat."

She was gone while Jason was still looking surprised. Feed them? With what, why? And why would she want to keep them around? The dogs would stay if they were fed, and how would they reach Pansy to feed her? He heard the window go up in her room, heard the rasp as the shutter panel was moved; then the shots came, and he understood. They were measured. One, two, three … he knew Janet to be a good shot, and that'd be a kill for each. She stopped after the fifth shot, he heard the shutter panel moved back, and she returned to where he stood in the kitchen.

"Right, let's us have breakfast as well."

She dished out the hot food, and they ate. Outside there was the occasional yip as one dog disputed with another. Jason ignored that and enjoyed the meal. Once he was done eating and washing the dishes, he went to the sitting room and peered through the shutter panel. The dogs were eating still, and he was able to count them. Nine standing, and other remains ... Janet spoke.

"How many?"

"Nine now. What about them?"

"Leave them. It's cold outside. They'll use up the food they've eaten, and they'll stay around. I'll get two-three more in the morning again, and if they stay, I'll try for another couple later. Pansy'll be all right 'til then. If they try for her, I've got a clear shot at the barn door. If they stay after that, I'll let them see me."

Jason calculated. Nine still, and if she got five or six over two days, the pack would be down to four or so. Let them see her, they'd come running, and so long as they'd been far enough away when they started for her, she could get all or most of those left.

"I can shoot," he offered. "If they go for you, I can shoot from the attic. No chance of hitting you, and I can aim for the ones at the back, so they don't realize at first."

"It's a plan. Let's see what they do."

What the pack did was clean up everything down to bloodstains on the snow and vanish. It was assumed they'd not gone far, maybe to the lee of the barn where they'd have some shelter. What was certain was that they were back at first light, sniffing at the barn door and scratching at the wood.

"Can they dig under that?" Jason asked.

Janet smiled. "No, there's a concrete lip. That's so people and animals going in and out don't wear a hollow in the ground. That sort of thing fills with water, and you have a mud hole getting deeper and deeper. So Great-grandpa concreted a strip that overlaps the door width. It starts about two feet under the door edge and comes forward about six feet. They can try digging if they like. It'll put them right in my sights."

Three of the dogs did try. They dug and - easily within range, and almost motionless - they fell to three well-aimed bullets - leaving their comrades to feast again. The smell of Pansy and her restless movements tolled in two more that evening, and again those remaining feasted. Jason looked at the carnage with disbelief.

"How can they be so dumb?"

"They're dogs, not wild animals. A wild animal, a coyote or a wolf, would leave the place if they kept dying here. Dogs have mostly lost that sort of instinct."

"Only four left. Do you think they'd be around tomorrow?"

"Likely," was the laconic reply, which, as both saw in the early morning light the next day, was right.

The dogs were there, looking up at Janet's window, growling softly, as inside the barn, Pansy lowed. Janet walked to the door and moved the panel that allowed her to see and talk to someone on the porch without opening the door. She lined up the rifle, and the dogs, now wary of the window but not yet of the door, stood usefully silhouetted. She shot three times. Two dogs fell over thrashing while the third howled and ran, the fourth at his side. Janet muttered something.

"Drat!" She opened the door and screamed, the rifle held down at one side, half-hidden. Both dogs stopped, turned, and she waved, sagged dramatically to one side, and wailed. They started back cautiously. Janet whimpered loudly, staggered against the doorframe, and that was sufficient. The dogs broke into a run, splitting to either side, as she waited, and Stormy, who had been forgotten, went past her in a single snarling rush, taking the wounded dog by the throat even as Janet shot the uninjured beast.

Jason was right behind his dog. He hovered, but Stormy did not need any help. Powerful jaws clamped down, the wounded animal's struggles became weaker, then ceased, and at length, the winner released him to trot back smugly to Jason, expecting praise - and receiving it.

Jason looked up from hugging his dog. "What do we do about the bodies?"

"Get them onto the sledge and take them as far away as you can. I'll take hay to Pansy." It wasn't easy hauling the sledge, but Jason made it behind the small copse of scrubby trees and dumped them there. Stormy came with him, prancing and showing off, and he grinned at her.

"Good girl, who's a warrior then?" She barked. "Oh, you are? Yes, you are." She barked again, bouncing into the air and landing up to her belly in the snow while Jason laughed. That was the pack and good riddance to them. He ate breakfast, and once he finished, he turned toward Janet.

"That's it, that was all of them, and the snow's packed down a bit. I could take the sledge to the village if there's anything you'd like. I wouldn't mind stretching my legs."

Janet spoke thoughtfully. "I don't think that would be a good idea."

"Why not? You got all the pack, we only ever saw fourteen, and you shot thirteen. Stormy got the last one. "

She looked at him. "Think how many people had dogs, they're out there, starving, forming packs to take down bigger animals, and if a human doesn't have a gun, or isn't a good shot, or runs out of ammunition, how dangerous are they? Yes, we got all of *this* pack; but what makes you think they're the only pack around?"

Jason felt like an idiot. "Yeah, right, okay."

"We've got everything we need in here. If you need to stretch, do it in the barn."

That wasn't a bad idea, he thought, and when he took hay to Pansy the next day, he looked over the building. Yes, there were ropes here, he could make a sort of assault course, and so, a day later, he swung from the rafters, enjoying the pull of muscles, while Pansy eyed him from below. Jason ignored her; he was having too much fun.

CHAPTER ELEVEN

Jason was unaware that inside the house, Janet was taking yet another pill. She swallowed that, put the water glass down, and counted. There should be sufficient to last her until spring if things didn't get worse, and then she'd have a decision to make. If she let Jason leave without him knowing how bad the pain was becoming, she'd die alone. Once it got bad enough, she wouldn't be able to cook, clean, care for Pansy, and would she even want to eat? She thought that unlikely. Pain destroyed the appetite.

If she told him, would he stay, or would he leave, and all she'd have done was lay a burden of guilt on him. If he did stay, would he hate her for holding him here? She knew he wanted to make it to his father's ranch; he talked of it, along with tales of those he'd met so far on his journey. One of those stories came to mind, and she settled to consider it. If he knew, he might try to stop her, and would he be right? The pain was worse, movement hurt unless she was drugged, and the more pills she used, the fewer remained. She was using both crutches more often, but he hadn't noticed yet. And then there was Pansy…

It was close to spring when she made up her mind. Jason had been talking over dinner about the ranch, his father, his fear that something might kill him on the journey, and that his father would never know what had happened. He gave no indication of considering that his father might not be alive. Could she point that out? But even if he accepted that possibility, would it make him stay? She knew it wouldn't.

She waited until next morning when he went out to feed the cow. Then, silently, she went to Jason's trailer and looked over the bags where he kept some of the items salvaged during his trip here. She found what she wanted and padded back. If she timed things right, she'd have what she wanted and backup too. She knew from the story he'd told he didn't know how many pills he had, and she had that now in case.

The days and nights came and went, and clear signs showed it was spring. Trees greened up, the snow level dropped inches at a time, and the wind was warmer. Jason drove the old truck to the village and checked the box he'd returned. It was there – and so was something else. He came back to tell Janet.

"I think we know the robber."

"Robber?"

"Box … gold … robber."

"Oh, right. We know him? How?"

"Because he's there by the shed where the box was." He looked at her. "And you were right. There was another pack." She waited for the explanation. "I saw a car there, so I checked it. There's a body inside. The face is a cherry-color. He died from carbon monoxide poisoning, is my guess."

"Why would he die from that?" Janet cursed the pills; they were making her slow, stupid. She knew what he was saying should make sense.

Jason sat down and explained. "I'd say it was like this. He made it back to the village, went to get the box, and while he was there, a pack came. He dived into the car. He could have shot a couple, but we know what they'd have done then, and they'd stay. He may have only had a couple of bullets, or he may have been a bad shot. He ended up trapped in the car with an empty gun anyhow. The car was stuck in a ditch, and I'd say he couldn't get it out, and he couldn't go outside of it to dig. He got cold, so he started the heater."

Janet got it now. "The exhaust was plugged with snow. He went to sleep in the nice warm car, and the carbon monoxide got him."

"Yeah. I looked in his wallet."

He laid out papers. A parole notice with the conditions. A clipping about a man who'd raided a coin shop and taken gold coins and a parquet box that had belonged to the owner's French great-great-grandmother. Another clipping that said the thief had been tentatively identified as Vincent Marrisen - criminal history - and a driver's canceled license in that name with a second license, different name, identical photo.

Jason watched until she'd read them all and looked up. "Him, yes?"

"I'd say so. What did you do with - things?"

"I got the car out with the truck, towed it past the village, and left it in that big dip behind the wood and coal place. I noticed it when we were there before winter. That's filled up with water and iced over still. Once it's summer, it'll thaw, the car will drop. The windows are open, so in a year or two, he'll be gone, and it's deep enough the car won't show unless you get a drought and who'd care if they *do* find it? I brought the box back."

"Let's see." He got it, opened it gently, and they admired the contents.

Janet smiled. "Leave it in the sitting room. There's plenty of time for us to decide what to do with it. It'll be another two, three weeks before you can drive out of here, and we'll have sorted it out before that."

He hefted it into the corner where she pointed and went to his room to think. She was right. It wouldn't be longer than three weeks now, and he could be on his way. What was he going to do about her? He didn't want to leave her on her own, but he was pretty sure she wouldn't leave her home and Pansy. And no matter how much he liked her, how guilty it'd make him feel, he couldn't stay either. How did he tell her any of that? Three weeks later, he found she already understood.

The road was clear. He'd driven the truck up to the main road and back again. Pansy had had a week in her paddock, retiring to the barn at night, and the mad cavorting had died down. Jason quietly made preparations. He still didn't know what he was going to say or if she'd ask him to stay. He was living day to day and hoping a solution would come to them. He didn't need the gold if she asked to keep it.

He was packed ready, and he waited. Janet watched his guilt and counted pills. Yes, the last of the pain pills would be gone by tomorrow night. She made a delicious dinner and told silly jokes. She'd read every one of the books they'd found, all she'd wanted to read, watched all the TV series and movies over winter. It was time.

"Jason. We should talk."

She saw the pain in his eyes as he nodded. "I know."

"No," she said gently. "You don't. You think I'll refuse to leave here, and that's true. But you're afraid I'll ask you to stay, and that's wrong. I'm dying, Jason. Just before this all started, I filled a prescription. My doctor knows I'm sensible, and he knows that in the winter, I sometimes can't get out to his office to get a new prescription, so he gave me one that lasts longer than the usual time. That medication's almost gone, and without it, I'll still die, but it'll be a slow excruciating death, and there's no guarantee I could find more of it if I went looking. With me gone, who will look after Pansy? She's an old cow, the hay's gone, and she couldn't survive if she was let out where there are dog packs and people with guns. I wanted her to have one week of spring, a week of being free in her paddock and eating the new grass. She's had that."

"What do you want me to do?"

"You told me about the Reverend Williams and his cat. Do the same for Pansy and me. Once I'm gone, drive away and don't look back. I know you have the pills, please, give us both a clean painless death." Her hands went out to take his. "A friend does that for a friend. A human does it for an animal. Do it for us both. And if you can't, then give them to Pansy, and leave some with me. I'll take them once you're gone."

He sat, her hands warm on his, and knew the only decision he could make.

"I'll go out to Pansy now." He found the waterproof bag in the trailer and took out two of the large-animal pills – two would make sure. He went into the barn with a saucepan of warm sugar water, dissolved the pills, added the mix to her water bucket, and watched as Pansy eagerly drank the sweetness. Once it was gone, he set her free in the barn with the last hay. Then he turned and left.

He found Janet was in the bath when he called. "I'll be out soon." She was as good as her word, appearing in her jade houserobe, hair brushed out, feet bare, and her face calm. "Pansy?"

"I'll check tomorrow, but it's done. I gave her two of them."

"Good, come into the bedroom." She placed her crutches against the wall, climbed into the bed, arranged the bedclothes comfortably, and looked at him. "I want you to have Maisie's rabbitskin bedspreads; you'll need them next winter. Take the box; it won't be of any use to me where I'm going. Open the top drawer there." She pointed, and he found a shabby leather jewelry box. "Before you leave, take anything from that you may want. Take any of the food left, any tools or gear. Before you go, set fire to the barn, I don't like to think of dogs eating Pansy. That's all."

He looked at her helplessly. "Okay ..."

"How long is it likely to be once I take the pills?"

"An hour. You'll probably go to sleep in fifteen or twenty minutes."

She looked at the small windup alarm clock on her bedside cabinet. "It's seven o'clock now. If I take one soon, I'll be gone in time for you to get a good night's sleep and leave first thing. Will you get them for me now?"

Mutely he went and came back with the small pills in one hand, a bottle of wine in the other. "You said you didn't mind a glass of wine now and then. I found this in one of the houses and saved it for you."

"You can leave them with me, or you can stay. I'd like to have Stormy here."

He called, and the dog padded in, looked from face to face, and for the first time, climbed onto the bed and lay down beside the woman. Janet stroked her, picked up the wine, and drank a mouthful, maneuvering so that he would not see the other larger pills that dropped from her left hand into the glass and dissolved in seconds behind her shielding hand.

"A good wine, something suitable for a final drink and a toast." She raised the glass to each in turn. "Wherever you go, whatever you find, may your lives be long and happy, may you find what you wish for, and may your deaths be as peaceful and painless as mine. *Vyaj salow*!" She picked up the pills, placed them in her mouth, and washed them down with the wine.

Jason knew what the phrase meant; his Cornish grandparents had often used it. "And a good journey to you, Janet Pentreath. Smooth traveling, bright sky, and those you love to meet you at the end of the road."

He took her hand and held it, watching as her eyes closed. In ten minutes, her breathing evened out, and he knew she was unconscious. It was much faster than he'd expected, but then she was older and weakened by the pain she finally admitted to. He got up, leaving the dog beside her, and went to gather up the rabbitskin bedspreads. They went into the car trunk wrapped around the box of coins. He opened the jewelry casket and sorted through, taking plain gold or silver items. There was a chased silver locket, and he flicked the catch open to find a photo of a young smiling girl. The face was half-familiar, and he knew why when he saw the inscription. *"Janet Pentreath, aged 11, on her birthday."* It would have been taken just before the accident.

Carefully he closed the locket and placed it in his pocket. He'd keep that, and one day maybe he'd have a daughter to give it to. He salvaged the unopened tins and packets in the kitchen. Hours earlier, Janet had set the crockpot to cooking the last of the steak, adding slices of potato, so that should be well done by the time he wanted to leave. There was a set of "unbreakable" mugs, hand-painted and each showing a different animal. He took those, moved to the sitting room where he took down the crossed knives over the mantlepiece. Both were real, not ornamental, and old. He set to work at various arrangements for another hour, and once he completed them, he went back to the bedroom where the occupant lay under the dog's gaze. He spoke formally.

"I have the things you gave me to take. The night is clear and fine, the moon bright, the road's open, and I would rather go now," he said quietly. "A long sleep and a joyous waking when that time comes, *ak'is* - friend."

He laid his fingers against the side of her throat for a long moment. There was nothing, and he thought her skin was cooling. He straightened the bedclothes, bent and kissed her forehead, called the dog, and went out to the packed car and trailer. Leaving Stormy sitting in her usual seat, he walked to the barn. Pansy lay there as if she had settled in the straw and fallen asleep. Jason patted her shoulder, feeling the death that had claimed her.

"You were a good cow and had a long life. Now you've a peaceful death and let you lie undisturbed." There was a loft filled with straw bedding still, and he'd made a fuse that trailed across the floor to the barn entrance. He lit that, watched the fire race upwards, and stepped out of the barn, leaving the door ajar for oxygen.

He went back to the house and paused on the porch, where he lit another fuse. The house was old, all dry wood, and it would burn like a torch. Janet hadn't wanted Pansy's body gnawed by dogs. He didn't want Janet's body to go that way either. He'd left a window open on each side of the house, and it would be a bonfire. He stepped into the driver's seat, shut the car door, and drove away slowly. The road wound, and at a bend that rose a little, he looked back over the land. Twin towers of flame rose against the starred night sky. Scavengers would find nothing there, not of what had lived there or their belongings. He drove on under a bright moon until the car lights were gone into the dark, and had anyone stood by the rising flames, they would have seen them no more.

****

It was a long night; he drove into the day and only stopped in the early afternoon when he saw a small motel. He checked through that, finding it empty of food and most smaller items. He parked the car under a back window, took a bed in the room overlooking that, and left Stormy on guard in the car. He had a quiet night and woke feeling a little sad but accepting events. His mother used to say that it was better to look forward than back. The past couldn't be changed, but you could make whatever of the future you wished.

With that in mind, should he stay on the freeway or take to the back roads again? He decided on the highway for a day to let him see how it was holding up and who might be traveling on it as well. *Moderately well* and *no one* seemed to be the answers to that. He saw no other traffic, and while some of the minor side roads he saw from higher sections of the freeway looked to be degrading, the main road itself wasn't falling apart yet. The road was straight, he could see far ahead, and he drove fast. He spent the night under an overpass in his sleeping bag, got back on the main road in the morning, and continued south at speed.

Now and again, he saw a figure walking into shops near the overpasses, a dog pack once, and several wandering cattle. He didn't need anything, so he stayed on the freeway, driving now at a steadier speed but always watchful. Once, in the distance, he saw a small convoy of the army trucks going the other way, and he whipped the car off down a ramp, zig-zagged along back roads half a day, and only resumed the freeway once he was sure they hadn't circled back hunting him. He didn't know more than he'd been told, but from that alone, he didn't want to meet them.

He stopped in secluded spots every day to run Stormy, play ball, remind her of her commands, and practice with his handgun. Four days into his journey, he remembered the rifle and silencer he'd taken from Janet and started to practice with that as well. It was a semi-automatic, and he liked it. Nothing fancy, just an excellent, workmanlike tool. He ran out of edible meat save what he had in cans, and when he saw a young bull, he stopped, shot from cover, and practiced what he'd learned from Janet, remembering her affectionately.

Nights he laid out the wind generator and recharged the portable batteries for minor things like a heater, a power unit he could cook on, or heat water, and he had taken the small player on which he could watch movies. Those he picked up at various places, watching them and leaving those watched - which he didn't want to see again - at the next area while he looked for more. There was a limit to what he could carry in the car and trailer, and other things were more important than minor entertainment. He crossed the border into California and stopped for the night to think.

If he stayed on the main road past San Francisco to Los Angeles, there was likely to be more people around. By the law of averages, that meant that some would be predators, and he didn't want - or need - that sort of trouble. He stayed on back roads after that and passed San Francisco a month later. He would have taken the road to the east then, but a massive gridlock of vehicles spilled over the road on both sides. He checked cautiously on his electric bike and found the blockage extended too far in width and depth for him to circumvent.

He took it as an omen and drove on towards Los Angeles, getting partway to San Diego before he halted for a night to consider his direction and go over the maps. When should he turn east to cross Arizona and head for the ranch? He was near the Santa Ysabel Reservation and was tossing a ball for Stormy with no indication that anyone was around where there was a shot.

Jason felt the burn as it plowed diagonally across the front edge of his left shoulder, and he yelled in pain and fright. Another shot whined off somewhere, but he'd already gone flat with his handgun out. He moved and groaned at the slicing pain. Stormy was gone at the first shot, running low to the ground. He heard the scream seconds later as he fell, the thrashing, and he too was up again and running for the commotion. He hadn't known what he intended, but if he'd wanted to save the shooter, he'd been a bit too late. Stormy had killed the man.

He lay, sprawled, his throat ripped out, filthy clothes, an old gun dropped to one side, and the stubble on his slack face showing a gray that suggested he and the gun had aged together. Stormy sat as he ran his hand down her head. "Good girl." What else could he say? By her lights, she'd done the right thing, and anyhow, if she hadn't, he could have taken another bullet. His shoulder was bleeding, a steady seeping, and he staggered back to the car to find dressings. With the injury cleaned, a dressing on, a pain pill taken, and Stormy reassured, loaded gun in hand he looked for his attacker's base.

He found nothing, and after a while, he gave up. He didn't think the man could have walked that far, but judging by his clothing and the gun, he'd have nothing worth finding anyhow. He returned to the body and checked the pockets. Just a penknife, the old gun, and a handful of loose bullets. He studied the face; not Navajo, not any tribe, he thought and was thankful for it. He called Stormy, climbed into the car with her, and drove away.

What he needed now was a refuge because while he didn't have a bullet in him, infection was a possibility, and he was drifting into shock. He could feel that starting, and he knew enough to know it could be dangerous in itself. He followed a road that angled east - wincing at the pain as he drove - saw an old barn, and behind it a farmhouse. He'd seen no other building for miles, so if this place was empty…

He drove up and got out, encouraging Stormy to scout. He could see no recent signs of tire-tracks or footprints, she gave no indication of anyone, and he entered the house in silent caution. The smell told him no one living was here. If there had been, they'd have removed the dead, and they hadn't. If a stranger had come later, they'd have left tracks. He circled the building to find a guest cottage, and he made for that. Scavengers would go to the main house first, and if anyone came prowling, Stormy would let him know.

The cottage had a single large bedroom, a king-sized bed, and side cabinets took up most of that, with a bathroom off one corner, while the other room was a composite of sitting room, dining room, and kitchen. No power, well, half the country was off-grid by now, and Jason had the generator. He set that up, hooked in the heater, aimed it at the bed at a low setting that would allow it to run for hours, fed Stormy, left out more food - in an automatic dispenser he'd found - and a large container of water for her, crawled into his sleeping bag, and collapsed, shaking. He took another pain pill and relaxed. Blackness overwhelmed him, and he gratefully slipped into it.

CHAPTER TWELVE

He woke when the heater used the last of the battery power, beeped a warning, and switched off. He'd set up the generator so all he had to do was roll off the bed and recharge the heater. He did that before reaching for a bottle of coke and a fruit bar. He ate, drank, felt weakness flow over him again and surrendered to it. He'd left the door blocked half-open so Stormy could come and go, and she used that while watching her master with worried eyes.

It was a week before Jason felt better, still not a hundred percent, but on the way to it. The wound was healing, but he was weak, and he knew it. He sat there eight days after the attack, considered every aspect, and decided that the idea of staying here wasn't wrong. Not forever, or even not more than a few weeks, but he needed to be fit again, and if he moved on and ran into trouble, his weakness could end up getting him killed.

He looked out of the window and remembered the big old house in front; he could explore that for a start. He'd used up supplies in the past days; if they had something to replenish those, it would be good. He stood up and called.

"Stormy?" She came running, "Yes, good girl, good girl, let's go and see what's around." She barked softly, her tail swirling, mouth open in a happy grin. "Yes, I know, you've been worried, well, we'll stay a while, and we can work on your commands, play ball, and I can practice too." He laughed when she raced back to him, the ball in her mouth as she thrust it at him. "All right, ball first."

He played for almost an hour behind the cottage and found he was still weaker than he'd thought. He worked the left shoulder cautiously. The pain was much less. He'd do without painkillers during the day now and take only a half at nights. He counted the cards of allodaxin too and grunted. Lucky he'd replenished that supply any time he'd seen even a card with only a single pill left. They'd become available to the general public a bare year before the virus struck, and they were very effective.

He remembered his mom talking in her last days. "We can't be sure, but you remember Joe Singer, the researcher? Came here to dinner a couple of times?"

Jason had nodded. "Tall, dark," he'd grinned. "And not at all handsome." Singer had the scar that was what remained when a bad hare lip had been corrected, and he was a homely, craggy-faced man anyhow.

Kerry Trevalen laughed. "A good man, and that's better than looks any day. A good researcher too. He says he can't be sure yet, but his tests suggest those that caught the recent sore throat and were specifically treated with the new antibiotic are the immune ones. How recently that happened anchors just how immune they are."

Jason's look had met hers. "I had that sore throat only last month..."

"So you should be completely okay."

He felt a wave of sickness turn him faint. "Mom? You never got it? Now you're ... you mean you have..."

Her eyes on him were accepting. "Yes, love. Joe's given me a couple of things that should retard the full effect briefly, but we don't have the time for me to lie. I'll be dead in about three or four days. I talked to your grandparents yesterday after you did, and they would have died late that night. The last thing they said was to tell you they loved you, they were proud of you, and you should live and remember them."

Jason choked. "Mom, what do I do?" Her face was calm and a little stern.

"You take my car. You empty our accounts. Take the gas cans and fill those, and fill the car. Look over what food we have.

When you buy, get dried food as much as possible, it's lighter to carry, doesn't spoil as easily or as quickly, and all you need for it is water. Other food, get cans, mainly meat, ham, corned beef, fish. Get a trailer as soon as you can find one. Take your good clothing, not just the expensive stuff. Aim for warmth and durability. Take footwear that's durable and comfortable and all the socks and underwear you have. Take my handgun and ammunition and buy, or pick up more ammunition as and where you can. Make sure you have a spread of guns."

She listed items and things to be done, and he'd sat there and written it all down. Every item, the suggestions, the sayings - dropped in with a smile - the orders. He'd gone out and obeyed those, coming back with everything she'd said - and a few ideas of his own; approved when he told her.

"Now, it's a long way to the ranch. You'll meet people here and there, some good, some bad, some just looking out for themselves. But remember one thing, Jase, Kipling said it best, 'he travels fastest who travels alone.' If you have someone with you, you expect them to do some of the watching, some of the work, and if they fail, then it won't only get them killed, it can get you dead too."

She'd smiled. "You're the best kind of loner. You like people. You make friends easily; people like and trust you. But in a pinch, you can do without them. It's a long trip you'll make, but any time you want to take someone along with you, think hard about it. If they distract you, if they halve your resources without giving back, if their attitudes, their character, impedes or endangers you, they're a liability, leave them! If you have only yourself to lean on, you're likely to be more careful, a lot safer, and more likely to get where you're going."

"Mom, you aren't like that."

"No," she sighed quietly. "Your father is, though. You got that trait from him but with my sociability. It's a good combination. People don't realize that if push comes to shove, you can walk away from them. I took a while to see that with your father, but when I did, I couldn't live with it. But, the fact is that it may be just that which will keep him alive. He can make the hard choices without breaking his heart, and he will. He built that ranch up from little, but even then, love it as he did, he could have walked away from it if that was what was needed to survive. And I think you have that in you as well."

She'd fallen asleep abruptly then, and he'd gone to his room and cried. He didn't cry much anymore, he thought, his hand playing with Stormy's ears. Maybe because he'd come to know Mom had been right. He did like people, he'd always had a bunch of friends, but when the dying started, he'd walked away from the city, from them, without looking back. He hadn't phoned any of them. He'd just gone.

He'd liked Janey, but in the end, he'd been happy enough to leave her with her family, and truthfully, he'd never wanted to take Janet along. A survival trait Mom had called it, and he'd survived. He felt the need for sleep growing, crawled into the sleeping bag, and drifted. His last thought as he fell into sleep was to wonder if his survival was - or would be - worth it in the end?

He woke stronger, made breakfast, fed himself and the dog, and played ball with her. He still had some energy left after that, so he ran through her commands, shot at a piece of paper on a tree truck a score of times, went in and put his feet up to read a while, then made lunch. After that, he decided to go to the main house. If there was anything there to add to his outfit, he might as well have it. That was something else Mom had told him.

"People will die, Jase. Most of them. If Joe's right - and myself I think that he may be - then by the time it's all over, the population could be culled as low as a tenth of a percent of what it is now. But you remember something and don't ever forget it. All those old post-apocalypse books of mine that you've read, they suggest that only the decent, or mostly decent people will make it and that in the end, it's the righteous that triumph." Her smile had been grim. "In reality, it won't work that way. It'll be the lucky, the cautious, the smart, the prepared, yes. But nothing says they'll also be nice, kind, decent people. Carry a gun, better still, carry two, neither of them where they can be easily noticed, and if you need to use one, don't hesitate!"

He hadn't. It tied into another of her sayings, a line, he thought, from one of her favorite authors. Something about not wanting it on his tombstone that he was a nice guy, and that got him killed. So when they'd come at him, he'd shot to kill and survived.

And she'd talked about scavenging.

"With the amount of those that'll die, you're likely to come to house after house, maybe entire small townships or suburbs where there's no one left. If there are no survivors, it isn't theft. It's theft if you ambush a man to take what he has. It isn't if you walk into a house and everyone there's dead. Or if someone gives you what's there and they have the right to do it. You'll have to find the line you're comfortable with and stay back of it. But in the end, if it comes down to your survival, Jase. You do whatever you have to." She'd taken his hand. "You're my son, and I love you with all my heart. I want you to live, to find someone you love, and have children."

He'd felt the tears back of his throat. "I will, Mom, and I'll name a girl after you."

She'd laughed. "Make it Kerry, though, not Kerenza."

Jason belted the handgun to the small of his back, added the little .22 in its holster to his ankle, and shook his jean's leg over it. One day, yes, if he made it, if he found someone, if they had kids – then there'd be a Kerry, he smiled, an Emma too, maybe a Jan, Keren if it was a boy. He padded around the cottage, Stormy fell in behind him, and they approached the main house alert to everything around them.

It was a large place, maybe built shortly before the first World War. Through the windows, he could see it had a dozen bedrooms, a huge kitchen, and living rooms. He grinned; it could even have a library, and that'd be great. He saw no sign that anyone had been there since he'd driven up. He entered, making no sound and pausing to breathe in once the door shut behind him. The smell of decay was there, and he sighed. A year ago, he'd never have dreamed that he'd be walking uninvited into houses not his own, to the stink of dead bodies – and know what he was smelling.

But that was then, and this was now. He saw a half-open door and beyond that a bench top. Absent-mindedly he flicked on a switch and almost leaped out of his skin when the light came on. Odd, the cottage didn't have power. Had that been shut off since there was no one living there when the virus hit? He circuited the room, finding fridges, freezers, lights, and appliances, all working. Food in the fridge, despite the cold, was long since inedible, but the freezers were both partly full, and contained a mix of luxury items – in which he had little interest, he'd never liked caviar – and hearty steaks, pork chops, roasts, vegetables, fruit, and packs of bacon and ham – all of the best quality.

There was a large crockpot in a cupboard. Jason hauled that out, plugged it in, and watched as it heated. He put in pork chops, some of the vegetables, and added a potato and bacon soup-mix into it. With dinner started, he felt free to continue his prowling. He did find a library and snorted at the shelves. Matched books, all in fancy binding, all the classics, but once he'd opened several; and found them uncut, he knew they were for show and nothing more. His mother had always despised those that had books for show only, and so did he. Books were for reading.

Off from the kitchen, he found what he thought had been the staff quarters. Bodies, each in a separate room, with the rooms well furnished but with chain store furnishings, and the pictures were generic prints. The residents had mostly magazines, although one had a shelf of books, mostly romances, and another had a stack of textbooks on horticulture. He gleaned through them; paper money almost certainly wouldn't be accepted by now, and he had plenty anyway, so he took nothing from the rooms.

The upstairs gave him the fright of his life as he mounted the stairs, turned left, and came face to face with a man. Tall, dark hair that straggled down over his shoulder, a sparse beard, faded jeans, a startled look on his face as he grabbed for what was a weapon. Jason grabbed for his gun … saw Stormy was not reacting, and froze, then relaxed, letting out a slow sigh of relief. A mirror. A wretched full-length mirror. He leaned on the stair railing and laughed while Stormy wrinkled her brow at him.

Then he studied the image again. He'd better start shaving again. His father's people didn't develop facial hair, but he was enough his mother's blood to have done so; and he thought, as he'd earlier decided, that it made him look disreputable rather than adult. If he had to have something, he could grow a mustache. And while he always brushed and combed his hair, he hadn't quite realized how long it was growing. He chuckled and spoke to the image.

"Warrior of the Diné, you should have a braid with an eagle feather. A braid anyhow, I think, and I remember one of Dad's tales. I'll see if I can find something to match that."

He found the bodies, a man, a woman, and two children and looked at them. Strange, the human impulse at the last is to leave notes, to die together, or both. They'd been one of the 'do both' types. They lay in each others' arms, empty glasses to either side of the huge bed, and he could guess how they'd chosen to go. On the bedside cabinet by the man's side lay a letter, neatly addressed 'to whom it may concern.' He left that and went looking into rooms, walk-in closets, and storerooms. He took a bag and gleaned.

Fur coats – his mother had told him about those. They could be separated into the component skins and resewn to fit a new owner once relined. Or they could be used as bedcovers and for other purposes where warmth was required. He found four and gathered them into a heap where he could take them later. Jewelry, they had gold, silver, and platinum. He took only the items where there were few jewels and more metal. He found a tray of gold coins and added those to the parquet box, taking too a beautifully engraved bone-handled knife and a black leather coat.

He grinned at that, flung it over his shoulders, and looked down as it fell to his ankles. It fit quite well, it was of the duster type, and he felt as if he should be walking down a Wild West town street to meet a shooter. He laughed at the fantasy. Still, the coat was of a quality that would last and last and could be worn by a rider. He'd take it. He added it to the fur coat pile and moved on.

He found two items that fitted what he wanted. One was a leather case, probably kept as an heirloom, he thought, when he opened it and found an ivory-handled folding razor in its leather pouch, a mirror ditto, two shaving brushes, and a large - very dried out - cake of quality soap between them. There was also a whetstone and a strop. He dropped that into his bag with a pleased grin. And in the woman's bag, he found something odd. He opened that up to find a knife about two inches long, the blade a little longer than the handle. The sheath over it had a thin metal V shape that covered the blade edge, which, as he discovered, was an excellent idea since it was razor-sharp. That went into his pocket; he knew what he would do with it.

Finally, he checked the linen closets. Here he found soft wool blankets of the sort that cost hundreds of dollars, bed linen, and magnificent quilts. Jason groaned to himself. He'd like to take the lot – and couldn't possibly fit them in. On the other hand, he had an idea, and he'd leave them for later, now; he picked up the envelope and opened it. It was handwritten in a neat copperplate.

"To whoever reads this.

We were Paul and Diana Redding; our children were Chloe and Martyn. We got sick about the same time, and when we called for an ambulance, no one came. I went to check, and all the servants were too ill to help. I phoned our doctor, and he said he was dying, the whole world was dying, and he couldn't be bothered with rich idiots anymore. I said I'd report him, and he laughed. So if he did survive, he is Doctor Peter Rasmussen, of 13 Treaston Lane and he isn't fit to be a doctor.

The staff died last night, and it was very unpleasant to see. I told my wife that we will die with dignity, and we aren't leaving the children to die like that. They will; they're too sick to get out of bed now. So I got my mother's pills, she died of cancer a year ago, and at the last, she had powerful painkillers, which I never returned. I made orangeade from real oranges, the way the children like it, and they drank that, then they went to sleep, and I know they won't wake up.

Diana and I have talked. I've said all the things I ever wanted to say to her, and she's done the same for me. We've always understood each other. But to you, whoever you are. Take whatever you want, and pay us for it this way. We want to be decently buried in the cemetery with a headstone. We have the right to be remembered. Bury my wife and me side by side, with my boy by my side, and the girl with my wife.

Paul David Greer Redding.

Jason stood there and laughed until he cried. Paul David Greer Redding, so entitled that he wanted a dying doctor to be sanctioned by the Medical Council for being rude. So entitled that he thought he could make demands even after death; right down to the placement of the bodies and a headstone. Who did he think *would* remember them? Or care? On the other hand, Mom had always said what goes around comes around. No headstone. And he wasn't carting bodies to a cemetery he didn't even know where to find or – if there were more than one locally – which one had been meant.

Jason whistled Stormy and went outside, walking the area and looking for some place where he could partly fulfill what was wanted. He found it. In an out-building, he found a trolley, and past the cottage, there were signs one of the gardeners had been doing tree work. There was a large hole, a woodchipper near that, and a stack of branches by the chipper. Presumably, the pruned or trimmed branches went into the chipper and then into the hole to rot down. Very well. When he went to check, the crock-pot had produced a delectable meal which he shared with Stormy. He wasn't going to empty those freezers before he moved on unless he stayed half a year.

He spent the next day sorting bedding to take only the best of what he'd already had and what was in the main house – ending up mostly with bedding from the house plus Janet's rabbitskin bedspreads. With that done, he took a day to play with Stormy, practice her commands, and his marksmanship. Early the morning after that, he brought the trolley into the house and, one by one, wrapped the bodies in the bedding on which they lay, then added an outer wrapping of something bright and pretty from the bedding left over, anchoring it with pillow cases torn into strips.

He took three older quilts and laid them at the bottom of the hole, bringing the bodies there on the trolley, two at a time, placing them as Redding had demanded. Over them, he laid a final pair of matched quilts, overlapping, and on those, he dropped branches until the quilts showed only an occasional flash of color. Then he used a shovel to fill the gaps. With one of the small diesel-powered machines in the shed, he pushed dirt over that, then larger stones and finally a dozen pieces of old concrete laid flat in a sort of crazy-paving.

With that accomplished, he went back to the shed, found the sheet of marine-ply that he'd already given two costs of white enamel paint, and painted in black with the names of those he'd buried. Once that was dry, he laid several coats of clear varnish over it. He parked the small machine at the head of the grave and wired the ply to that so it looked over those below. He stood at the foot of the grave and looked down.

"I couldn't take you to the cemetery. I don't know which or where. I couldn't carve a headstone, but you've got the best I could manage. You're together the way you wanted. I'll leave the house and the cottage cleaned up when I go, and I'm not going to take more than I need or can use. You said to pay you this way, and I've done my best."

He nodded to the grave and walked back to the guest cottage. He'd feel more relaxed staying there until the time came to move on, but he'd make it comfortable with items from the house. That took the next day, and he lay back on the bed afterward. The memory of the razor and the tiny knife reminded him of his plan, and he started on that. He shaved with care. Admired his smooth cheeks in the mirror, brushed his hair out, and plaited it carefully, tying off the braid. Then with a black thread he fastened the knife up under the braid. It was an old story, and *that* knife had been stone, but it had been what the Diné had then. This was better, and if he ever needed it, it would be there. He smiled at the mirror, and thought a warrior smiled back. As soon as he regained his full strength, it would be time to take the road again – and that, he hoped, would be soon.

CHAPTER THIRTEEN

Hopes are something that hasn't happened yet, and don't count on them, his mom said. Jason found that truer than he'd expected. He woke the next day feeling weak and sick again. His shoulder hurt, and panicked, he pulled his shirt down and looked at the wound. It had been healing; now it was swollen, red, hot to the touch, and he bit back a yell of rage. The earth he'd tossed about as he filled in the grave, could there have been something in that? He'd brought his mom's medical books and thanked the stars for that. He read his way through every relevant passage he could find and was none the wiser. Maybe he'd just strained the wound by working so hard.

In the end, he decided to go for common sense. The next morning, the wound had swollen to where the skin had thinned over it. He took the braid-knife, sterilized it, and flicked the blade across the hot swelling. Pus spurted, and carefully he swabbed that away, wincing at every touch. Once the wound was clean, he washed it out with antiseptic, dressed it with a soothing ointment, topped it off with a sterile wound dressing, took an allodaxin, and swore. It looked as if he wouldn't be moving on now. Oh, well, that'd please Stormy. More time to play ball.

Each morning, he cleaned the injury, took another allodaxin, ate well, and took vitamins from his stash in the trailer. Once he was stronger - a month of being careful - he started checking other places he could reach on the e-bike. It was silent. If it ran out of power, he could pedal, and Stormy enjoyed trotting along just ahead or beside it if the road was wide enough. He found a second house some two miles away, further back from the road, down a thread of narrow dirt road, and investigated.

It was smaller than the place he'd taken over, and there were no bodies. But there were books, and he spent that day reading, choosing, and finding a bag to carry them safely. Some were paperbacks, others were hardcover. He chose sixty, knowing he'd be overloading the trailer but unable to let any of the books remain behind, and anyway, every time he ate from his supply, the load would diminish. He took the volumes home, then, realizing that he wasn't planning on leaving yet, and he could read others before he went, he returned, brought home another thirty, and started reading those.

****

He'd been at the cottage or house almost three months, and it was time he moved on. He should double-check everything and set a day, so he moved outside to consider the car. Gas? Yes. Water? Yes. Oil? Yes. Okay, he climbed in to start the car. The starter motor ground, whirred, and Jason felt a shudder run down his back. He tried again with the same result. He felt so scared he was sick to his stomach. Wait; the battery? He found the charged spare, swapped them over, and the car growled happily into life. Jason collapsed, sitting on the ground. His mother had said that you could scare you more than most other people could. How right she'd been. Now, when should he go? By what road, and his shoulder still hurt if he overused it? Should he wait a while longer?

The knowledge that he couldn't take all the books he'd found and wanted to read decided him. There was food here, the power was still working, he could stay a couple more weeks, read the books that were too many to bring, and it might be a good idea too, to hide his presence. That extra time here would be a present to himself.

Then, too, Stormy had woken him two nights ago growing softly. In the distance, when he opened the window, he thought he'd heard a vehicle engine. He hesitated, but in the end, he stayed, compromising by loading almost everything onto the trailer, cleaning both places so they looked uninhabited, and moving the car and trailer to a well-built hide on a downward sloping track that angled off to one side of the main road, the shelter made of tied branches with a large dark brown tarpaulin lashed under them so no sunlight would sparkle on chrome.

He read, ate, exercised, roughhoused with the dog, worked on his gun skill, and slept late. And in that extra two weeks, he felt himself come back to normal, to full strength and energy and knew he'd made the right decision. Each morning he made sure there was no trace of his presence, and it was as well he did so. It was one day short of the time he'd planned to leave when Stormy woke him again after he'd gone to bed at dusk so no lights would show.

"What is it, girl?" He listened, and the sound came clearer. Engines, not cars but trucks, a growl that said there could be as many as half a dozen, and the convoy he'd seen months ago came to mind. He'd been sleeping at the cottage this past time, and the main house would show no signs of recent occupation. The engines seemed to be getting closer, and he moved with lithe speed. His mom's saying came to mind, "that the easiest way to get out of trouble was not to get into it." If that lot were coming this way, and it sounded as if they were, then he'd do better to be gone before they got here.

He commanded the dog to silence. Scooped up everything in the cottage and ran for the hide. Once there, he loaded the items into the car and left Stormy to guard that while he returned to sit ten feet up in a tree behind the cottage, binoculars in hand. He heard the trucks arrive before he saw anything. The engines snarled into the front of the main house and, one by one, parked and stopped. He heard voices, not enough to know what was said, but he knew the sound of a man giving orders when he heard the tone.

Jason swore quietly. The real army, some of them, or those fake-army guys he'd been told about. Either way, he wasn't keen on being found. Footsteps approached, and someone spoke.

"Big house's empty, power's working, and there's food. Barres reckons to sweep the area." He heard someone enter the cottage, and the voice asked. "Anyone there?"

Another voice answered that. "Nah, no sign of anyone, place's empty."

"Okay, I'll tell Barres, good enough headquarters for us."

"How long do you think he'll want to stick around?"

"Month maybe, longer if there's anyone worth it we can find."

"Yeah," the voice became explicit about who he'd like to find and what he'd do then, and Jason clamped his lips together. Not real army, unless the military had gone a long way downhill in less than a year. This had to be that bunch, or something like them, that Rose had told him about and who'd killed all those people back in California. The sooner he got out, the better, just do it so quietly they never knew he'd been around.

He stayed on his tree perch listening, watching through the binoculars whenever a light was shown, and after several hours, it looked as if everyone had gone to bed. He didn't think they'd even bothered with guards unless they were sticking close to the main house. He moved away, a few steps at a time. People didn't register a brief sound; it was the longer, continuing sounds they noticed.

It took half an hour before he was back at the car, and once he was there, he reassured Stormy, put the car into neutral, and pushed it until it began to move downhill. He slid hastily into the driver's seat and guided it along the track to where that began to circle back to the road. A slight wind had gotten up blowing away from the house, that should give the car's engine cover. He started the vehicle and inched out to the main road.

There was no reaction from back there, but he kept the speed and the noise down until he was several miles away. Then he swung in and halted, brought out his maps, and studied them. He had to go broadly east if he wanted his father's ranch. He didn't want to be seen by anyone who'll tell that lot whatever they'd seen, and he didn't want to take any dead-end roads or ones where the car might break down. He traced road after road on the map, decided that the best things he could do now was get out of the immediate area and move southeast on a better road.

He drove all night, using only the sidelights, and moving at no more than twenty-five miles an hour. By the time the sun was starting to light some of the land, he estimated he traveled two hundred miles, and he turned more to the east. He accelerated, driving fast for an hour on a mostly straight road, then turned back southeast and went more slowly. If he were right, he would be on the further fringe of the area they'd talked about sweeping. If he picked the right place to lie up, he'd know if they headed his way and he should find somewhere with a second exit.

He found that at a small ranch lying back well off the main road in a valley. It was a complete accident, but he pulled off the road to take a break and have something to eat. Stormy chased a rabbit; he followed her, gun in hand in case of any predators. They zigzagged and broke out of a stand of trees and bushes to find a narrow dirt road, which he followed, out of nothing more than mild interest.

There, slightly below, were buildings. Jason approached carefully, leaving the car and trailer parked under cover. The buildings were well-maintained, the yards clean, but some distance away, there was a large black patch as if something had burned there, something hot. He saw no one and no signs of an occupant so that he was about to enter when a dog came around the corner. It took one look and hurled itself at him, whimpering, panting, and pushing the long collie nose into his knees. Jason laughed and petted the animal while Stormy eyed it suspiciously.

"Good boy, good dog, where'd you come from? Hungry?" The dog assured him that it was starving, and he dug a couple of dog biscuits from his pocket, giving one to each dog. He checked the braided leather collar, noting that it had been handmade. The small engraved metal plate stated that the dog was Laddie. Property of Mr. and Mrs. Tim Crispin of the Crispin Ranch.

"Laddie?" The dog barked happily. "Yes, that's you, isn't it? Have another biscuit. Okay, what happened to your people, boy? Did they die?"

A voice spoke dryly. "No, we didn't."

Jason straightened abruptly, and his gaze flickered around. No one. Whoever it was, knew to stay out of sight. He nodded in the general direction of the voice.

"No harm intended. Looking for a safe place to stay a while, that's all. You're Mr. Crispin, I expect. You've got a good dog there. I'd have taken him with me if he was alone."

"He isn't."

"No," Jason agreed. "I got that. Well, if it's all right by you, I'll move along."

A woman's voice spoke quietly. "You fed Laddie."

"He looked as if he was a bit hungry."

"What's your dog's name?" the woman asked.

"Stormy."

"I've never seen one like her before. What is she?"

Jason grinned. "Believe it or not, she's one of those new designer breeds."

"I thought so; I saw something on them on TV last year. Tim, let the boy come in and have a meal." There was an indistinct mutter. "Look at his dog, no cringe to her, and he fed Laddie. If we were dead, he'd have taken him, so he didn't starve. Let him come in."

There was a put-upon-sounding male grumble, then a man appeared from a slightly different direction that Jason had thought him to be.

"Annie thinks you're all right, boy. You'd better be."

Jason followed as the man walked away, and as he did so, he evaluated his unwilling host. In his sixties at least, average height, lean, hawk-faced, gray hair, faded blue eyes, the slightly bowed legs of a man who'd ridden almost from birth, and dressed in relatively clean jeans, checked shirt, and leather vest. He carried a very well-used rifle and wore a holstered gun on one hip with a sheathed knife on the other. Loaded for bear, as the saying was. A man who'd taken one clear-eyed look at what the world had become and reverted to the ways of his ancestors.

He wondered how far the woman had gone in that direction and found she hadn't, or not exactly. She was waiting by the door, smiled at him as he rounded the corner, and looked pointedly at his boots. He dropped to the ground, tugged them off, placed them neatly by the door, and entered the house as she indicated.

"What's your name, son?"

"Jason. Jason Trevalen."

"Where are you from?"

"Seattle when the virus hit. My dad has a ranch in New Mexico. I'm heading there."

Stormy was making overtures, and the woman smiled. "Good girl. Sit." Stormy sat. "Well-trained too. Did you buy her?"

Waved to a chair, Jason sat and recounted the story of an old lady and her dog. "I couldn't leave her. All Mrs. Hayer wanted was for me to either kill her clean or take her with me. I couldn't kill Stormy, so we've been together ever since."

Mrs. Crispin was bustling around, bringing out food, lemonade and setting the table. He looked her over unobtrusively. Tall for a woman, gray hair and blue eyes like her husband, lean too, and wearing jeans, comfortable moccasins, a similar shirt, and a loose hand-knitted vest in two shades of blue with black buttons. Her long hair was tied back with a blue ribbon. Her clothing was clean, her manner confident, and her hands, while they were worn and calloused, were also clean, with short scrubbed nails. Whatever had happened in this area, neither were letting their standards go.

The food was placed on the table. The Crispins sat and bowed their heads briefly, although neither spoke aloud. The food was dished up onto Jason's plate, and he ate, finding it well-cooked and much to his liking.

"You've still got power?"

Annie Crispin smiled. "We have a double-generator system. The power company, when we set up years back, wanted far too much to bring lines out here, so we invested in our own."

"I bet that's been a blessing since this started. Half the country I've seen hasn't got power anymore."

"It's been a blessing, all right," Tim Crispin agreed. "We began with an ordinary generator. Gas one. Mother said when this new type came out, that we should get them. Solar and wind power and cross-linked. We only bought it two years back."

"Spares?"

Tim Crispin smiled complacently. "Living out here, we know better'n that, we got us a good lot, big discount too for it all. Spare panels, blades, and a real clear manual for everything. I'm handy enough. If it quits, I can fix it. Got a lathe. If one of the main parts goes, there's a fair chance I can make a replacement."

Jason was slightly awed. "Wow, I wish I knew that much."

Annie spoke casually. "Yes, having a car's a worry these days if you aren't a mechanic. Is it a big car?"

Jason spoke without thinking. "No, it was Mom's car, sports type, but it's a good one. She'd only had it a couple of years when this started."

Her tone was gentle. "She didn't make it, your mom?"

Jason felt heat behind his eyes. "No, her parents went too, right before her." Then he realized how much he'd given away and stiffened.

His gaze met Annie's, and she nodded. "No need to worry about us." She sighed softly. "We had a daughter and a son-in-law. They had a baby. Baby got sick a few weeks before all this started. They didn't, though. They were in Colorado Springs a month later, visiting friends. Then the sickness began, and it hit them both. Woman they were staying with, she could fly, had a little single-engine plane. Twin-seater. She started getting sick as well, but her baby, she was all right. We talked on the phone; she said everyone was dying there, even the doctors and nurses, so she would try for here. Bring the babies. We said we'd look after them both if she could. We were fine."

Jason remembered the black burned-out patch. "She crashed?"

Annie bowed her head. "Yes. Plane just sort of folded up around her. She threw the babies. Ours was nearest, so she threw her first, then her baby. Tim caught them. Plane started burning…"

"An' I shot her," the man said, his voice gruff. "Couldn't get her out, wasn't going to watch her burn alive. She saw me line up the gun and said thanks afore I shot. Once it cooled, we got her out, buried her with the baby out back in the old cemetery."

"Her baby died?"

He saw tears in the woman's eyes. "I was glad she didn't know, but it must have happened in the crash. Baby's skull was broken. She died that night. We buried her in her mother's arms. Dressed them both nice, wrapped them in my grandma's quilt. She died saving our blood; we owed them all we could do. They've got a headstone. Says that from the Bible about 'Greater love.' We go there every week and pray for them. What about your mom?"

"I buried her before I left. She said to leave my grandparents, said it was too far to their place and in the opposite direction. That she'd rather I made it out, and so would they have." He met her look. "One day, if I can, I want to go back there. If I can find anything, I'll bury them."

"All you can do is try," Tim Crispin said heavily. "That's what the plane lady did. She tried, and died knowing she'd done her best. Died believing she'd saved her own blood, died with a smile on her face seeing Mother here holding the babies."

Jason felt the slow heat behind his eyes again and allowed the tears to come, a slow stream as they welled up. Annie left her chair and stooped to lay an arm around his shoulders. "Cry for them we've lost," she said. "Cry for them, mourn them, remember them, then move on. That's what my dad always said. He said we owe it to them that their loss makes us stronger, not weaker. That's how they'd want it."

Jason straightened. "Yeah, that's how my mom thought." He stood up and started to clear the table of dirty plates. "Let me do the dishes, and then I'd better get going."

Annie exchanged looks with her husband, who spoke. "If you'd like to stay here a while, we'd be pleased, son. You and Stormy too."

Jason hesitated, but they wouldn't have asked if they weren't sure, and it was dark now, finding some other place would be difficult. He'd probably have to sleep in the car, uncomfortable at best, cold, cramped, and he'd have to shift stuff about to make room.

"Thank you. I'd be grateful."

"No need, planning on doing the dishes, weren't you?" Tim Crispin said with a teasing tone. "Call it square."

In the end, they did the dishes together, Jason washing, Annie drying, and Tim putting everything away neatly into the cupboards. They'd just finished when there was a sleepy cry. Annie vanished to return with a child of about a year, wearing bunny pajamas, her wisps of fair hair tousled from sleep, and with wide blue eyes fixed on the stranger.

"This's Allie."

Jason grinned, while Stormy who'd been lying quietly out of the way, stood and went up, poking her nose into the small waving hands. The baby chuckled, patting, while the dog's tail went mad.

"She likes kids," Jason commented. "Looks as if Allie likes dogs too."

"She's a real Crispin, likes all animals," Allie's grandfather said proudly. "She'll run the place once she's old enough."

There was a hiatus while the baby was fed and taken back to bed. Annie reappeared and took Jason and Stormy to a room with a single bed, indicated the amenities, and left him. He stripped to his underwear, crawled into the bed, and slept, with

Stormy on the mat beside him, neither rousing until they heard sounds of life in the kitchen. Jason stretched, groaned, and stretched again, dropping a hand to the dog.

"Best night's sleep I've had in a while, girl. I wonder if they could use a hand for a week or two. I wouldn't mind a break in a place like this. Off the beaten track, no one's likely to find it that doesn't already know it's here. It feels safe."

He dressed, walked out to the kitchen, and was greeted by Annie, who spoke.

"Jason, if you'd like to stay for a week or two, we'd be happy with that. There's a few things Tim could use a hand with; that'd pay your bed and board, and we'd feed Stormy." She said no more, merely waiting for him to speak. Jason thought that it was ideal; here, he'd just been thinking he wanted to stay for a week or so, and then that was offered.

"I'd appreciate it," he said honestly.

Annie smiled. "Then that's settled," she said comfortably. "Breakfast, then you can find Tim, tell him what I said, and ask what he'd like a hand with."

This schedule carried out saw Jason helping to put a new roof on the chicken house. As Tim explained, "It isn't that it's so heavy, as it's awkward. Needs someone on either side, and I'm not keen on Annie doing it. Needs a ladder, and she isn't good with them."

The next day Tim saddled two horses. "Gotta bring the herd in to drench them, check they're all okay. You ride?"

"Some." He wasn't going to boast, although his dad had always said he had the makings of a good rider. He swung aboard the stocky gelding, found that its neck reined well, and while it didn't usually exert itself, when cued, it had a fair turn of speed. To his surprise, they weren't bringing in horses but a herd of around thirty goats. They were large animals, the biggest goats he'd ever seen, and Tim noticed his surprise.

"Crossbreeds. Chap years back bought in a dozen Boer goats, South African animals. Not as hardy as they should be, wrong climate for them. He was spending too much on the vet and decided to get out of them, so I bought the lot, crossed them with Nubians I had from a friend. It's taken a few years, but I've ended up with a multi-purpose goat, grows fast, ends up big, good taste to the meat, and gives a fair amount of milk."

"How do you milk them?"

"By hand. We keep about seven or eight does in milk and more in kid, rest are bucks, or wethers, and those does that aren't the best, we have them growing on for meat. Big advantage to the milk is that people aren't allergic to it the way some are to cow's milk."

"What's it taste like?"

Tim Crispin laughed. "Some love it; some can't stand it. Personal taste, I guess. I like it myself, and so does Annie. Allie's being raised on it."

The goats were ambling towards the distant buildings, and Jason relaxed in the saddle. It was good to be riding again, good to be out in the sun, good to be able to forget all the things that had happened. Maybe when he made it to the ranch, he should suggest to his father that they come back and buy a few of Tim's goats. And if his horses were as good - well, there could be a chance there too. He was starting to doze on the smooth-paced gelding when Stormy growled quietly. Jason knew that sound and came alert between one breath and the next.

CHAPTER FOURTEEN

He spoke softly, not in a whisper, the hiss could carry, but in a low voice. "Tim, something out there, Stormy says so."

Tim said nothing but turned his head so that he could see the dog out of the corner of an eye. "Human?"

"Don't think so."

"Okay, you armed?"

"Yes."

Jason wasn't going to particularize, but he had the handgun in his back holster under the vest. It was a .38 revolver, but once he found some of the hollow-point ammunition in an empty house - whose original owner had been a gun devotee - he'd taken all he could find and loaded that in preference. There was a snarl that didn't come from the dog, and a large black form came out of the brush. It was right behind Tim's horse. A paw shot out and hit the animal's haunch, leaving long red streaks, and the horse emitted a shrill scream of pain and fright before it bucked.

Tim catapulted off over one shoulder, and the horse fled, taking the rifle. Jason's animal was backing and sidling, the smell of blood upsetting it, and Tim, dazed, tried to get to his feet. The black figure roared and reached for the man. Jason acted without thinking. He dropped lightly from his mount, letting it go free. His hand flickered, came out holding the .38, and dropping into stance, he fired. In a roll like thunder, he emptied the gun; a hand dived into a pocket and came out with loose bullets which he thumbed into the gun to reload while watching the black form.

Tim Crispin had made it to his feet and looked at the boy. "Son, I don't think you'll need those right now. That bear just isn't going anywhere."

Jason finished reloading anyhow. His father had told him that an empty gun made a good club if you needed one, but that wasn't why they were made. With his weapon ready, he shuffled a step closer at a time. The thing on the ground stayed motionless, and without looking up from it, he asked.

"How sure are you it's dead?"

"Pretty sure. Hold on." Tim retired to find a long stick and poked the heap of fur. There was no sound, no movement, and he poked again, and again, with no reaction. "Looks as if it's done. Good shooting."

The words were laconic, but the tone was one of deep approval. Jason flushed and then laughed, quoting, "Man does what a man's gotta do."

"And you done it," Tim chuckled. "Wonder what made him look for trouble. Bears around here are usually quiet enough unless they're real hungry, or..."

Jason had turned the animal over and pulled back an arm. He looked up. "Or wounded," he said quietly. "Look at this."

They looked. A long, shallow wound showed all along the bear's flank just under the arm. It would have given the animal a bright flash of pain any time that side or arm moved, and bears tend to the short-tempered.

Tim was calculating. "He must have been either just starting to stand up or sit down. He was at an angle anyways. Wouldn't kill him, it'd heal up in time, but it'd sting, keep him feeling it every time he moved. He was probably after a goat, and we got in the way, not surprised he took a crack at me. Wonder what happened to whoever did it?"

"Stormy can track a bit."

Tim looked up. "Right, put her on this 'un's backtrail, and let's see." It took time and considerable squirming through the brush, but they came to a spot where there was a single shell casing. There was also a lot of blood, and their gazes met.

"Ran into one another by accident, I'd say," Tim muttered. "Looks as if they were close too. From the blood that bear got in a swipe, then they went in opposite directions. Which way would you run?" He was moving, orienting himself the way the shooter might have stood when he shot, and Jason considered before pointing.

"That way."

Tim started walking, and spoke softly. "Gun out, son, this here's a man that shoots first when he's surprised."

Jason nodded, drew his gun, and moved cautiously forward while Tim moved out to flank him. They heard nothing and finally broke clear of the brush into a small clearing. It was a complete circle, except for a narrow opening on the far side. Standing by that was a motorcycle with a small three-wheeled trailer of the type that was being sold with them of late. Sprawled half under that was a man.

"Hold up and watch for me," Tim ordered, and Jason obeyed, understanding the command. If the man attacked, he'd die before he could reach Tim; but the man didn't move as he was gently pulled from under the trailer. They saw his face then and both men shuddered. He had little of that remaining. Something had torn off the jaw, obliterated most of the face below the eyes, and there was only a red ruin left. The whole of a heavy woolen jacket was saturated with blood, explaining why there'd been no blood trail, and Jason felt sick.

Tim looked at the body as he stood up. "Wouldn't have thought he'd have made it this far, not like that. Must have been real determined. Wonder why?"

Jason, who was looking over the trailer, spoke, his voice constricted. "I can tell you that." He thrust both hands into the stacked contents and lifted them free. In his arms lay a blue-clad toddler, looking up sleepily and without apparent fear. The boy would have been a year or so old. He was well-dressed, clearly cared for, and, like Allie, fair-haired and blue-eyed

Tim nodded. "Yeah. He was trying to get back to the kid, went under the trailer, so if the bear came after him, he had a chance to shoot it before it got either of them." He sighed. "I loved my daughter, but I wouldn't have minded a son as well. Guess I got one."

"What about Annie?" Jason asked

Tim glanced at him and grinned. "She'd jump faster'n me to take the kid. Now," he turned around, looking at the sun. "From here, the road should be that way. Can you ride one of these things?" Jason nodded. "Okay, then let's all get aboard and head home."

Jason pointed mutely to the body.

"Leave him. We can come back tomorrow and bury him and take the bearskin as well. Right now, I'd like to get out of here in case that bear had a friend or someone else heard the fussing and comes around."

That, thought Jason, *was good sense,* and he allowed Tim to tuck the baby back in the bedding. While Jason climbed onto the motorcycle, Tim climbed on behind him, and Jason turned the key, hoping it worked. It did, and they rode slowly for home, arriving just as Annie was about to start looking to see what had become of them.

"Horses came home without you," she snapped. "Pat's got gouges all down one haunch, and Mike's stepped on a rein and torn the stitching. You go off on two horses, and come back on a motorbike. What in the world were you doing?"

Tim mutely removed the child from his bedding and passed him to Annie. "Saving this." He hugged her while she held the child and crooned. "You always said you wouldn't have minded a son too. Now it looks like you got one."

****

The goats were all well, and when they walked to the bear carcass the next day, one kid was bouncing on top of it, playing king of the castle with the other. The men laughed and gently shooed the small creatures away before skinning the bear. Jason looked over the skin once it came free.

"That was a fair size, should make a good rug."

Tim nodded. "Yes, they stretch when they're tanned, too, so once it's down, it'll look more like a grizzly-size skin. I'll take it to the barn and hang it on the far wall to work on. After that, we can have something to eat, then go look at whatever's in the trailer we brought home with the baby."

Jason went over the motorbike and trailer contents a few hours later with Tim. To Annie's delight, they found the child's birth certificate, which named him Geoffrey John McDonald, son of Angus McDonald, and Maree Griffith of Los Angeles. It gave his date of birth, showing him to be now thirteen months old, and another certificate listed his mother as having died four months later of a cerebral hemorrhage. The certificates were together in a small lacquer box, along with a small amount of jewelry, none expensive but all in good taste. And there were several photos. Annie picked those out and looked at the smiling faces, then at the handwriting on the back.

"His mom, dad, and grandparents on each side." Jason wondered what they'd call him, and after a moment, inquired. Annie considered it. "Geoff Crispin," she said decisively. "We'll tell him the truth when he's old enough. He deserves to know his father died protecting him."

"Besides," Tim said thoughtfully. "You know the sort of thing that can happen. Him and Allie aren't blood relatives. You grow up with someone, mostly you aren't interested, you see them as family, but it can happen, and I don't want them thinking we'd be upset if it did."

Jason said nothing but nodded. His mom had told him a story once about a boy in her class at school who'd fallen in love with someone like that. Not kin, but the family saw it that way, and once they found out about it, the kids were tossed out, and the family wouldn't have anything to do with them. Annie saw a remembering look on his face and asked. Haltingly he told the story, and she nodded.

"Exactly. They lost two children they loved, and for what? It was legal, and so far as I'm concerned, it was moral too. The law in many places lets first cousins marry, so what's wrong with two children who aren't any relation to each other? No, if later on, it happens that way, we'll be happy they love someone we already know and love too."

Tim grinned. "And if it should happen, it'd save us worrying about how we'd split this place." He looked at Annie, and they laughed.

Geoff turned out to be a good child, placid, happy, and apparently very pleased to have another child of around his age with whom to play. Meanwhile, Jason was out with Tim every day, working on the land, learning to milk a goat, digging post holes for a new fence, and twice going hunting.

"There's deer around. You don't see them unless you look, and I only shoot yearlings. That way, none of the meat's wasted, an' there's no orphan fawns."

"What about rabbits?"

"None much on this place, but there's a good few down by the stream a couple of miles away. Why?"

"Stormy likes them, and there's no waste there either."

Tim chuckled. "Up to you, son. But if you bring back more than the dogs can eat, I'm sure Mother will know what to do with them. By the way, you aren't tied down here. If you want to take that motorcycle and look a bit further out, you're welcome."

Jason did – finding a house thirty miles to the east where the front lawn was alive with rabbits. He was lining up the .22 when something tiny and tabby scrambled across the property with a raccoon after it. Jason shot involuntarily, and the raccoon dropped. The kitten sat down and wailed. A slight pathetic sound. Jason walked towards it, making reassuring sounds, and the kitten watched. He reached it, scooped it up, and after a hiss or two, it settled against him, and he smiled. Where it had come from, he had no idea, but he could guess who'd love it.

In that he was right, Annie cuddled the kitten, fed it, and it slept in her lap, small stomach bulging, and throat vibrating with a faint contented purr. She looked earnestly at Jason. "It isn't feral. Maybe you should go back there and look around."

"I could. If there's nothing Tim wants me for tomorrow?"

"I don't. You go and see what else is there. And if there's anything we could use and nobody around, bring whatever you find back here. No owner, it's not stealing."

A conclusion Jason had long since come to, but he was cautious when he reached the house. It might be his belief, but it wasn't necessarily the belief of anyone living here.

Instead of people, he found a note pinned to the back door and read it.

Josie,

Willie's sick, but not the virus, we don't think. We're going to the hospital in San Diego. When you get here, don't worry, we should be back in a day or two. Help yourself. Please look after Miss Chat; she's just had kittens in the shed, her cat food's there on a shelf along with a can opener. See you when we get home,

Karen.

So the kitten he'd rescued had been domestic as Annie had thought. *All right, the shed. Let's see about the rest of the family there.* He opened the door slowly and saw at once that any precautions were wasted. The raccoon had come here first. Miss Chat – he thought it must be her – lay dead, two bloodstained kittens with her. She was a big cat, and her tabby pattern was lines of spots rather than stripes. She'd died fighting, and Jason felt a wash of sadness.

"You were a warrior, girl. I'll bury you all together; you deserve it." He went to pick up the body, and something stirred. He stepped back hastily; you got snakes in sheds, but no. A live kit stared up at him from where it had nestled against its mother's body, and a small pink mouth opened in a demanding cry. Jason scooped up the baby, and like its predecessor, it huddled trustingly against him, then wailed again.

"Hungry?" Let's see, cat food on the shelf, the note said."

It was there, along with the promised can opener, and in seconds, the kitten was eating. Jason hunted around, found a sack, and dumped all the cat food in that. It had a "use by" date of almost three years in the future still and would be good insurance if Tim and Annie ran short of meat. A further thought occurred to him, and he went looking. The shed door had been shut, but one kitten had got out, so there must be a gap somewhere. He found it in a corner, where a board rotted at the bottom would allow the exit of a small kitten, and he blocked that off. Leaving the kitten, he went to the house to reconnoiter, finding a cat carrier, and, in a cupboard, bags of cat biscuits.

"Useful." There was a soft fluffy folded blanket on top of it, and he tucked that into the carrier; clearly, they belonged together. He went out to collect the kitten, which settled into the carrier and fell asleep. Jason inserted a finger through the wire and stroked it, eliciting a small rusty purr. "Yes, you sleep, not long, and I'll have you back with the other bit of family you've got left, but I want to look around here first, and I'll bury your mom and the others."

He did that first. It felt right. But with them gone, he looked through the shed, noting several good-quality tools, a hand lathe, and a large box. He read the print on that and felt a wide smile stretching his face. A wind generator, an expensive brand, unused, probably only just acquired, then "Willie' got sick, and no one got around to putting it up. With it was a four-pack of the storage batteries. He put both boxes to one side, added the lathe, tools, and containers of nails and screws. Then he moved on to the house.

The owners had been comfortable from the look of things, he concluded as he wandered the rooms. Luckily, he and Tim had emptied the motorbike trailer, he could take the pick of items, and if for some reason he couldn't return, well, he'd had the cream. He went back to the bike, ran it to the shed, loaded his selection, and parked it by the back door. Over the next few hours, he was busy choosing, packing, and pausing at intervals to pet the kitten, who watched the activity wide-eyed.

He came back to the main bedroom at last. There was a photo there, two middle-aged people, arms around each other. Willie and Karen, he assumed. There was a jewelry box in the dresser's top drawer, and he loaded that without looking inside. In the bedside cabinet on what, from some of the stuff on it, had been the man's side, he found a handgun and a box of matching ammunition and added them to his gleanings. He grinned wryly, speaking to those who'd lived here. "A pity what killed you wasn't something you could shoot." He found a gun-cleaning kit in the dresser and took that too.

He surveyed the wardrobe and selected a wool coat he knew to be expensive and looked unworn. There was underwear in unopened packets, both male and female, and he took them, as well as packages of socks. They were unlikely to be for sale any time soon. He added a few good clothing items, finished putting them in the trailer, and then, with a suitable niche created for the cat carrier, he added that last of all and ran a rope through the top and fastened it to either side of the trailer.

"That should do it. If they want anything else that's here, we can always come back." He turned the key, the bike rumbled into life, and he headed back to the Crispins. The roads were empty and silent, but he stayed alert. Twice he saw a fleeting glimpse of deer, and the birds seemed less worried about a human riding by.

He wondered how long it would be until the wildlife forgot to fear people. How long before there were no guns that worked, no ammunition left, no gas for vehicles, and even the new generators had broken down, so electricity became a thing of legend. He guessed that could be the last thing to go. The most recent solar and wind generators were designed to have any single part replaced, and there would be a ton of those around. There were electric lathes like the one Tim had, and the hand lathe he was bringing back, you could make single parts with either of those if you knew what you were doing. It'd be a lack of batteries that could bring everything to a halt.

He reached the ranch, and while they unloaded his salvage, he said as much. Tim shook his head. "Maybe, maybe not. The generators don't have to store power; they can just be run and use it directly. Then, too, you know people, there'll always be someone who works out a new way to do something, some way to keep the luxuries." He looked over the stack of items brought back. "Was there anything else there you'd have brought but couldn't fit in?"

Jason considered the question, remembering the rooms, the closets, the cupboards in his mind. "Can't think of anything. But I'll tell you what, it struck me when I was loading all those packets of underwear and socks and stuff. No one'll be making any of that any more. Won't be able to buy it either. Now could be the time to stock up on all of it you can find."

Annie, who'd been listening, put in a comment on that. "And knitting wool, fabric, needles, and thread. If you run across a handheld sewing machine, that'd be good. It isn't just going to be the big things we miss; it'll be the small ones. Brushes, combs, hair clips, all sorts of stuff."

Tim was looking thoughtful. "Barns."

Annie and Jason stared. "What?" That was Annie.

"Barns," Tim repeated. "If we do collect a stack of things, we'd need somewhere to put it. Last time we were in Calexico," he added thoughtfully. "There was a new franchise. Flatpak farm buildings. Rancher could put in the foundation, set anchor bolts in that, then buy a flatpak and bolt it down."

Jason looked at him. "Your truck, would it carry one?"

"It would."

"Do you think…?"

"I do. Have to be careful. Other people could have the same idea, and I've no mind to get into a war. But it'd be useful. Could go to Gerry's down the road a ways first. He was planning on putting in a couple 'a new sheds, got in the cement and stuff to do it. Haven't been there since and heard nothing from him. Could be the virus got him."

"And," Annie added in a flat voice. "If so, the cement'll likely still be there. Tomorrow, we can go and see."

It proved to be a busy day. The cement was there, as were a stack of the flatpaks, designed to be a line of five small barns for storage and housing livestock. There was boxing for the cement, reinforcing rods, and in addition - on hire as the papers they found stated - Gerry had two electric cement mixers. They hauled everything home, laid out stakes and string, and determined where the barns would be best placed. Gerry had also had a larger newer truck that'd been added to their haul, and with it, two days after that, they headed for Calexico, all three: Tim, Annie, and Jason, locked, loaded, and alert to danger. The two toddlers were left shut in a room. It was a risk, but now and again, they'd have to take one.

CHAPTER FIFTEEN

They drove into the town around 8:00 a.m. with both trucks, the ranch one driven by Annie and the newer one by Tim. Jason was with Annie. There was no one on the streets, no one they could see in any building's windows, and Tim nodded.

"All commercial places around here, and we've come in the back way. Only trucks come that way, so we aren't unusual. No one getting paid, so no one's working. If we don't make much noise, we might get clear with a load and no one seeing."

It worked. Tim knew the franchise place he'd seen, and they went there. Jason could drive a forklift, and they'd brought charged batteries with them that would allow several hours of running time. Being electric, the small vehicles were silent, and Tim found padding that could be placed on the truck bed and then between each layer, so the items made little sound as they were loaded. With the larger truck filled, Annie drove it out of town and parked behind a billboard. There she would wait.

The men went looking further, watching every step. Twice they saw someone, and each time they were unseen themselves. They found more cement, reinforcing rods, another mixer, boxing for concrete, and various tools intended for that work. They loaded them in silence, being careful not to allow even a clink if it could be avoided. With that ready, they looked at each other, and Tim spoke in a low voice.

"We may not get back here again safely. Question is, while we're here, do we look over a few more places or quit while we're ahead?"

"You made a list?"

"Yeah, for all the stuff we've got, I did add a few things we could use if we found them. Axes for one, more ammunition, boots, kid's clothes, Allie's growing out of hers, and Geoff needs things too. Toys for them maybe, if we see anything we can get without trouble. More canned or packet food, spices, salt, sugar, coffee, hot chocolate, you know the sort of thing." He looked at Jason, who nodded.

"Do it like the army. Advance one up at a time. You know what you need. Go ahead, and I'll cover you."

They ended up on the fringe of houses, and still, there were few people about. Jason spoke quietly as they loaded a trolley with items from a shop empty of people and half-empty of supplies.

"There's been looting here, but they may have died before they emptied the place."

Tim chuckled almost inaudibly. "Looting? You mean what we call salvage?"

Jason grinned. "Yeah, okay. Now, where can we salvage boots?"

They'd parked the smaller truck half inside the open back doors of the shop, where the loading bay was, and out of sight of the street. Tim stood, a hand on the open door, looking around.

"If I recall it right, shoe shop's just on the other side of that alley. If we go down that, we can get the back door open and not be easily seen."

He was right. They pried the back door open. Jason slipped towards the front of the shop, saw no one, and silently shut the open front door. He placed a seat for trying on shoes in front of it and wedged that there. If someone saw them and tried to get in, that'd slow any attacker long enough for them to get away.

He picked out a line of boots, chose a pair in his size, and then went down the rows and shelves, taking any pair that would fit and looked durable. To those, once he had everything suitable, he added sandals, moccasins, sneakers, and then joined Tim, taking the full sack he had.

"I'll put this lot in the truck while you get the kid's shoes."

He reached the truck, loaded the sacks, and saw a flash of color. He drifted in that direction to find a spilled line of jewelry stretching almost six feet along the pavement. He stopped. That could be a trap, and was the sparkling line worth the chance? No, he decided, it was all jewels, little metal, and what metal he could see was the paler shade of nine carets, which probably meant the "jewels" were semi-precious only. No, it could be a trap, and what was there wasn't worth the chance, on the other hand…

If he'd set a trap like this, where would he be waiting? From a corner to the rear, he heard a tiny hiss and looked back to see Tim gesturing. He joined him to hear the question. "What are you doing?"

Jason grinned. "Putting myself in the head of someone waiting in ambush out there."

"Huh?"

Jason explained the jewelry, and his conclusions. Tim shook his head. "Don't stick your face in a bear's den to see if it's home. You say the jewelry's worthless, so what do you get out of finding if it's trap, where they are, or what they're after?"

"I guess so."

Tim looked at him. "Other hand, there's useful things in a jewelers, Clocks, watches, maybe a few pretty ornaments for Annie, metal cups that won't break. Don't know where they got their bait, but I know where there's a jeweler."

They went there, collected a hoard of valuable items as Tim had said, including to their pleasure, two e-bikes that could be altered in size, that were in a lean-to at the back of the shop. Each of those had a matching trailer, the long-life batteries, and solar panels. Tim scooped them up.

"Perfect for the kids in a few years. I'm taking the engraver as well. Kids like names on their things. I always did."

They made it to where Annie waited, and the trucks left the town again, unseen, unheard, and their raid unknown to any there. And as Annie pointed out once they were home and unloading, having let the children out of their room.

"It may get safer over time, fewer people left; some may go to Los Angeles or San Diego, better pickings, more people they can work with. They don't know we were there this time. Maybe we go again and stop if we're ever seen."

That wasn't going to be tomorrow, Jason thought as they sketched plans. They had the entire line of five smaller barns to do foundations for and then set up the ones from Gerry's. After that, they had the two large barns they'd got from town. Some of the barns had to go up before it rained, and the salvage they had was damaged or ruined. It took a week. They did the smaller ones, with all three of them working dawn to dusk on getting the foundations in and waiting for the concrete to set.

While they waited for that, Jason worked on Stormy's training and his own gun-handling and went with Tim to look over the horses. "M' granddad started with an Appaloosa/Morgan cross stallion and a bunch of yearlings he got cheap. Mostly fillies an' weedy even for their age. He gelded, broke, and trained the colts and sold those, put the fillies to the stallion once they were old enough. Turned out to be a good mix. Ended up with ponies just over fourteen hands, smart, sensible, good-looking, and strong. We sold them mostly as broken to saddle for horse-trekking, some for harness work, and now and again, if we had a real good one, we'd get one of the local kids to ride it in shows and sell to someone that wanted to move up in the games section."

Jason was looking at the horses. "My dad breeds them too. Along with cattle and a few buffalo."

"Buffalo?"

"Yeah, they make a good cross - called beefalo - and he says he likes to see them."

Tim glanced at him. "You don't say much about your dad?"

"Guess not. I haven't seen him since I was eleven or so. He and Mom divorced, and she said it'd been bad for my studies to spend too much time on the ranch. She was right, I suppose. But looking at things now, it wouldn't have mattered."

"You didn't know then and nor did she," Tim pointed out. "Didn't you say your dad's part Navajo?"

"About a third. He doesn't push it much, though. Goes to some of the tribal events, but he owns his ranch, it's well off-reservation land, and about half his cowboys are part-Navajo, but he won't keep anyone who doesn't do the job just because they're of the blood. I've never been sure how he feels about it."

"Where'd the blood come from?"

"His mom, she was around three-quarter. I don't remember her. Dad says she got flu and died when he was in his teens. His father sold the ranch they had and moved further towards the mountains then. Got a high price, and the new place was bigger and affordable because it was a lot further from town." He fell silent briefly. "I think maybe he blamed the reservation for her dying. A lot of them were ill that year."

"Happens," Tim agreed. "I've got family diaries from the early nineteen-hundreds. One of them was by a chap that fought in the war then and was on leave afterward. Where he was, they had a real epidemic of flu, hundreds dying, and they weren't Navajo."

"No."

Tim changed the subject. They moved the horse herd and returned to the ranch house for dinner. Afterward, Jason lay sprawled on his bed thinking. His mind wandered to his dad. He knew his parents had loved each other; it was just that they wanted different things. And him, what did *he* want? He'd known before this all started; now, he was adrift. He'd wanted to be an ordinary doctor, living somewhere he'd know almost all his patients, their histories, their troubles, and he could help. Make a difference.

His mom had been a specialist, and she'd made a difference, but she'd never really known her patients either. Her skill had made that cop she'd helped help Jason in turn, though. But being a specialist was probably something no one would be again for decades, maybe hundreds of years. But a plain doctor, he could still be that if he could find a teacher. Would his dad mind if Jason didn't want to be a rancher? Or could he be both, have a ranch with someone to run it, while he doctored? He fell asleep thinking.

****

The two larger barns went up a week later. After that, all three of them started filling the storage space, with Tim and Jason taking quiet drives around several of the main road ranches Tim knew to see if anyone lived there still and if not, what could be salvaged. One of the things they saw was livestock, some in pitiful condition.

Tim was rounding up cattle from a ranch that was quite near as the crows flew, and if you took a track over the land behind his ranch. Jason was riding along and looking at the number of moving beasts.

"Can you graze all these?" asked Jason.

"You never rode to the back of my place. Looks like it ends if you don't go all the way there, trees, scrub, rocks, and nothing more. Isn't like that. You go through the scrub, and there's another valley beyond, fair bit bigger than mine. I always wanted to buy that and could never afford it. Government wanted a fool price, you can't get into it 'cept across my land, but they expected me to pay as if there were public roads in." He looked at Jason. "I don't have to pay now. Room to spare, and I'm taking only good stock."

That he was, the boy mused, watching the cattle ambling ahead. They'd quietly salvaged from half a dozen ranches where only the dead inhabited the houses, and Tim had skimmed the best stock from each. They'd driven to them later by truck and brought back the best of gear and items from the houses as well. They'd buried the dead, that was fair, and they'd put up wooden markers with the names.

The two kittens he'd found were girls; they'd found a boy in one of the houses, crying piteously by a dead mother, and

Annie had taken him in happily. But no dogs, only here and there, a body, unfound by scavengers. He said so.

Tim nodded. "The way people think. Most shot their dogs rather than imagine them starving slow, but they figured cats would manage, there's small animals to catch, water in ponds."

"Cats don't like to live that way, really," Jason said.

"Maybe not, but they tend to survive where dogs are likely to die. So most shot their dogs, let the cats out."

They rode on, Jason thinking of dogs - loving, trusting their owners - what had they felt when their human raised the gun? And cats, expecting to be fed, loved, and cared for, finding the door shut, the voice they ran to never heard again. He'd taken Stormy, and her owner had died in peace. He wished there could have been someone for all the other dogs and cats. How many would survive? Come to that, what about the cattle, horses, sheep, goats? How many would fall to predators, how many would die because there was nobody to rescue them? His mood was grim as he realized that in a time of death, it wasn't only people who died.

****

That night, he let Stormy sleep on the bed with him. The following day, he went to take Tim aside by the line of barns.

"If you want my help with the rest of the storage units, we need to do them now. You said you wanted to make one more trip to Calexico and get another line of barns, so you've still got storage room."

"You've decided to move on then?"

"Once that's done, yeah. If it's okay with you and Annie."

Tim looked at him, amusement glimmering in the faded blue eyes. "And if I said no, you have to stay on; you're going to do that, aren't you?" Gaze met gaze, and Tim shook his head. "You aren't, and we both know it. We've been happy you stayed so long. Annie and I appreciate the work you've done, and we hope that if you make it to your dad's ranch, sometime you'll come back and see us again. Now, let's get to this work."

"Now? Today?"

"Might as well. It won't get done for sitting around talking about it."

"Just the big truck then?"

"Nope, you drive the smaller one fine, isn't as if there's a traffic cop out there looking for drivers without the right license."

They both laughed, and Tim headed for the barn where the trucks sat side by side under cover. He tossed Jason the keys and started the larger truck, pulled out at a steady speed, and headed for the town.

It was quieter still there; no people on the streets, the shops where items had been taken seemed to have lost little more in the weeks since. They went first to the franchise and stacked every one of the smaller barns they could find, of the sort that locked together, topping the load off with the only large barn remaining of the big single ones.

Tim looked at what remained. "We've got enough of the foundation materials left at the ranch to do these. What d'you think?"

"Take what's here," Jason said. "Once I'm gone, you may find another place with the barns. If you do and you can only make one trip, you won't have a problem." He walked over to the stack of cement bags, activated the forklift, and filled the bed of the truck he was driving, adding other materials once he had the bags loaded. With the warehouse empty, he stepped off the forklift and walked over to Tim.

"Shops? We cleaned out most of what we could use from the shoe shop, but a while back, Annie said she'd like knitting wool and fabric. Is there a shop selling that sort of thing near here?"

"Yeah. Get the trucks out of sight, and we can go there. Good thing you brought the e-bikes, we can get around without being heard, and with those trailers, they'll carry a lot more than we can on foot."

They unloaded the electric bicycles, both of which had been painted a dark brown, and slipped silently through back alleys to the shops Tim knew. They loaded both trailers, emptied them into the trucks, and returned for load after load until they had everything they thought would please Annie. Then they dropped the bikes onto the side hooks and drove out of town, watching behind them and ahead to every side road.

Once back they called Annie. She came, the three kittens and the dogs at her heels and gaped at what they presented. "That's wonderful. I'll store most of it. So long as we can salvage clothes that fit the children, it's fine, but that won't last forever. A few years and ready-made clothing will be gone, but I can still knit things and make clothes for them. I'm so pleased you thought of it. Thank you." She kissed Tim, hugged Jason, and patted the excited dogs.

They strolled back to the house together, and they were almost there when she said something that stopped Jason between one step and the next. "You know, I thought it was you two coming back half an hour ago. I must be going deaf in my old age. But I could have sworn I heard trucks." They both realized that Jason had stopped dead.

Tim turned to look. "Jason? What's wrong?"

"Trucks," Jason said quietly, looking at Annie. "You thought you heard trucks going by on the main road. Which way was the wind blowing?"

"Same as it is now."

"From the road to here?" Annie nodded, watching him with a slow burn of fear starting in her chest. "Then the sound faded. Could you tell which direction it was when it did that?" She pointed, and Jason took in a deep breath. "Okay. If it's the similar people, I saw their type first in Oregon, then in California, and I heard more about them there. They probably raided an army depot and got trucks and some boots and uniforms. They aren't soldiers. The person who told me about them thought they could be what was left of a gang. There's about thirty or so that she knew about, and they aren't nice people."

He recounted the story about the group burned alive – or shot if they ran out – the slaughter that had included small children. The Crispins listened, horrified. Tim considered possible angles once the story was done.

"We came home by the back road, only crossed the main highway once and for a couple'a seconds. So if Annie heard the direction right, they went by before we crossed the road. We crossed about ten minutes later, but the wind would've been blowing the sound away from us by then. Using the main road, they'd have been going through the town not long after we got back. Question is, would they bother with the place?"

Jason heaved a sigh. "From what the girl who told me about them said, they're looters plain and simple. It won't be the bunch I saw near home, but if they're the same kind, they're dangerous. They'll take anything that strikes their fancy – alcohol, women, chocolate, expensive gear, new vehicles, jewelry – if it catches their eye, they'll grab, and if anyone tries to stop them, they'll get a beating at the least, and it can get a whole lot worse than that."

Tim's face tightened. "*Women*?"

"So long as they're female, she never came right out and said, but I got the impression they don't care how old a girl is, and some won't care if it's a boy either."

Annie glanced up at something and spoke in a shaking voice. "There's a lot of smoke from the direction of town. That's some big building burning."

Both men spun to look, and Tim's voice was savage, a tone Jason had never heard from him before. "Not a building, Annie, love. That's a half a town burning, and may heaven help them."

The smoke billowed up, drifted towards them, caught another breeze, and went higher. Now and again, it turned black as it found something different. Jason watched, sickened by what it probably meant.

Annie spoke quietly. "When danger comes, you have choices. You can hide, run, make a treaty, or fight. If those men are what Jason says, then they won't even consider a treaty. If we run, we lose everything; we couldn't carry that much. If they don't stay in the area long, we could hide with a good chance they'd never find us. Before this happened, we mostly shopped in Brawley, and we took home what we bought. We never had it delivered, and no one much has even an idea of where the ranch is."

Tim nodded. "So, we could hide, particularly if they don't stay around. The only other chance is to fight." He looked at her. "I'm good, love, but I'm not that good, fact is I never was. Jason says about thirty. That's a few too many."

"Not if we play guerrilla," his wife said. "If they've burned out the town, there'll be people got away or survived, and they'll have one thing on their mind, getting even."

"I'm not making the ranch into some guerrilla stronghold. It's easy to invite people in, lot harder if they don't want to leave."

"I was thinking of the Gila River. Do you remember the Jacksons? Long time back now, when we were young, they bought land in the bend there, set up a chicken ranch. Idiots were city folk and planned to rear free-range birds. Coyotes got them. Jacksons went broke and walked away."

Tim whistled quietly. "I remember. Buildings are still there, place isn't that easy to find, cirque, and they had it walled off."

"And what no one left hereabouts knows," Annie said softly, "apart from me that is, who grew up playing with the Jackson kid over the five years, there's another exit."

Tim snorted. "Yeah, into a desert. Try strolling across that and end up like one of those old Egyptian mummies. There's stories."

"And there's one you never heard because only my grandpa knew it," Annie retorted. "I'm not talking about the desert. Let *them* try that. There's another way out besides."

Tim looked up at the rolling smoke, "I'd rather not run," he said, thinking it through. "We can hide, but if they stay, they could find us anyhow. So we wait until the smoke dies down and maybe go looking to see who survived and if they'd like their own back. Fact is, we could do without that sort around. Depends on the town, too; they might have fought. If they did a decent job, they might have cleared out some of that lot, and that'd make it easier." He nodded. "Yeah, leave it 'til we've got some of the barns up, and I'll scout, see if the trucks are still around. If so, we can see who might like to join us." He looked at Jason. "You were thinking of moving on. You don't live here. It's not your fight."

Jason met the look hard-faced. "You're friends. I'm in," he said briefly.

CHAPTER SIXTEEN

Tim, Annie, and Jason sorted out everything they'd brought back, put it where it would be conveniently at hand, and started on the large barn and half of the smaller ones. This took a week with all three adults involved, but once they were finished and when on that last evening, they were sitting down to eat dinner, Tim spoke.

"No sight nor sound of those trucks. I scouted down the road a ways. Tomorrow we take the spare barns and foundations to the cirque. Get them up, and we have a place we can suggest people go."

Annie looked up. "Food for them?"

That started a debate which Tim ended. "There were places nearer than us. We can get the barns done, see how the old house is, and maybe do a round-up from those places."

Most of that program worked. Annie stayed to watch the children and do the usual chores. Tim and Jason took the trucks and worked three days getting the spare link-barns up. They remained in the old house while they did that and were considerably reassured.

"I'm surprised it's in this good a shape after so long," Jason said, watching the flames in the old fireplace.

Tim chuckled. "I'm not. You didn't see them, but there's cattle on the far side of the stream. They've been lying up in the scrub there. Didn't get close enough to see if they're branded, but I'd say one of the places close to here has been using the cirque's grazing."

Jason nodded, remembering something he *had* noticed. "The gates."

"Ah huh. Yeah, they were shut, and I had to open them for us to drive in. That means someone left here and shut the gates behind them. Why, if there was nothing here that was theirs? No, I'd say somebody moved cattle here to have options, and while they were here, they fixed up the house."

Jason could understand. If someone had survived, even for only a while, they might have thought that shifting some cattle to where they wouldn't be easily found would see to it that even if their home place was attacked or taken over, they had something left.

They slept peacefully that night, Stormy on guard, and with morning they hunted out the cattle. Tim looked at the brands.

"They were moved here since the start of the virus all right, although not long after, I'd guess. Half of them aren't marked. All the young 'uns and some of them are yearlings, so it was before then. I know where they came from, RVT, that's Robert Vargas Thompson, his ranch is the nearest to here."

Jason was counting. "Twelve cows, a bull, ten yearlings, and eleven calves at foot."

"Yeah, and this place'd take fifty times that, particularly if you were eating the spare yearling bulls."

"Better to add a few horses and maybe goats for milking," Jason commented. "I had a thought before too." His companion raised eyebrows in a query. "Brawley and maybe Calexico again. If you put two-three link-barns together, added a self-contained fire, furniture, kitchen items like a sink and so on, and wired it with a wind or solar generator, you'd have a good house."

Tim Crispin looked interested. "That's a bright idea, son. Yeah, I know places in both towns that carried the gear. And there's people might be happy to get away from a town that's on all the maps. We're done here. Let's go look at Thompson's place."

That was something both had half-expected. Dead bodies on the beds, with what was left of a shot dog lying by them. Tim eyed the bodies sadly. "That's everybody, and the dog was hers. Well, now we know. Let's take a look around the rest of the place."

It was depressing. Jason got the impression that the family had dusted, vacuumed, polished, and tidied everything before they lay down. The dresser's top drawer contained all their legal papers, with a jewelry box on top of them. He opened that. Nothing of use, save a big old silver wind-up watch. He took that and passed it to Tim.

"Someone should have that. It doesn't even need batteries."

Tim took it. "That was Bob's grandfather's watch. Yes. It should go to someone who'll look after and value it. Now, let's check the livestock."

That was much less depressing. They had been left to wander the entire property, all internal gates opened. Two barns had been left open, and it could be seen that the cattle used them for shelter when that was required. A third barn held fodder, hay, and hard feed, a lot of it, and Tim eyed that with approval.

"We can use that, handy we have the trucks, we'll take it all back home." He heaved open the smaller door to the side of the next barn, revealing two e-motorbikes with wide deep-tread tires. "Off-road, useful." A small electric car, that'll be good for Annie; we'll have power available long after gas mostly runs out." And a wall of tools neatly hung up with an army jeep close by the wall. Tim grinned at that. "Bob got that when he was in San Diego, and the army were selling some off. Now, what's in the side room?"

Jason whooped when the door was pried open. "Power generators, spares, cables, and for both sorts, great."

His companion was checking over the neat piles. "Yeah. I don't know what he had in mind, his place already had all this, but there are two more portables for both kinds, plus spares. Hang on…" he ruminated. "Yeah, that'll be it. I recall him saying a year or two back that he was thinking of adding a few camper-vans parks and maybe a cottage or two. Some relative of his'd done that up past L.A., and they were earning a lot of money."

Jason seized on that. "So he'd got in generators. Could he have bought cottages too?"

Behind the barns, they found that Robert Thompson had. They were four kitset homes there; two had one very spacious bedroom, while two had two double bedrooms.

Tim looked at them. "So, those two with the one big bedroom'd be ideal with a couple. The other pair would do for a family. You could put a double bed in one room, and two sets of bunks in the other. Let you house parents and up to four kids."

Jason nodded. "If I had to guess, I'd say he planned to double-wire them too," he saw Tim's puzzled look and elaborated. "Solar power one, wind power the other but cross-wire them in pairs. That way, if one sort of power goes out, the other one keeps the basics going."

"Clever, didn't know you could do that," was the comment.

"Yeah, friends of mine had two beach places. They did it."

Tim nodded. "Right, let's take the power generators and the spares; we can just about get them on the trucks." He cast a regretful look at the cottages. "We'll come back for those. Right now, let's get everything home, and we can come back tomorrow."

Jason would have liked to ask what Tim wanted with four cottages but decided to mind his own business. In any case, he discovered the answer to that once they'd hauled everything back to the Crispin Ranch, unloaded it, and were sitting down to a very late dinner. Tim was describing the cottage, and Annie nodded.

"You're thinking of maybe a place for the kids when they grow up."

"Yeah. Put one of the larger cottages together with a smaller one, and they'd make a good-sized three-bedroom place. If they get together, we'd have one spare. If they don't, they've got one each, and both with double power. I saw the water tanks to go with them out the back of the barns as well. Bob had a powered forklift. It won't take more'n a day's work to get everything loaded and back here."

"After that, you might go look at the town, too, now," Annie suggested, and the men nodded.

Jason had duplicated many of his music files for Tim and Annie, now as they drove home, he flicked on a switch in the truck, and Bryan Adams started singing "Last Night on Earth."

Tim began to singing along, and Jason joined in with enthusiasm.

"Got the top down, can't stop me now

Let's burn down a one-way highway"

It seemed appropriate to both of them."

The day after that provided a very early start, a day of hard labor, and a late return, but Tim already knew where he wanted the cottages, and they placed them there. There'd been a small, long barn they'd managed to add on the larger truck, and that was placed lengthways behind the cottages as storage for them. Tim studied the sky.

"Fine day tomorrow. We'll put that barn's foundation up and move all the generators and gear into it as soon as we have it done. Day after, we can go take a look to see about those towns." He scowled. "Mind you, after seeing that much smoke, I'd say at least one of them took a fair hammering. Question is, did they hand some of it back?"

****

When they drove into Calexico two days later, using only the bigger of the trucks, they found that the people had. On two streets, they saw burned-out army trucks, and in one, as they passed, they glimpsed the gruesome sight of the driver, who hadn't escaped when the truck burned. Tim smiled in grim approval.

They turned the corner and found a line of armed men watching them. Tim halted his truck, leaned out of the window, and nodded politely. "Tim Crispin from the Crispin Ranch. I see you had trouble."

One of the men lounged forward. "The name's Major Kayne, you ask if there's trouble? Guess you might say that. Crispin, huh? Did you know Sam Connell?"

"Yeah, bought his big Boer buck when he was selling some of his goats."

"Didn't you have another breed?"

"Nubians."

"Yeah, that's it." He turned and nodded to another man, and Jason saw they were accepted. Locals, not the enemy. Half an hour later, Jason was describing what he knew or had heard of the fake army, Tim mentioned the old Jackson place in the cirque, and the retired Major Kayne, whom they'd just met, and who'd taken on the town's defense, was listening.

"So there was only around thirty of them most of the time? That was all we had here." His smile was feral. "Now there's fewer. We know we killed seven, and from the reports I've collated, possible kills go to another four, and severe injuries may run about nine-ten. I doubt they'll be back…."

Jason spoke quietly. "They're doing what they do because they don't want to work. They like being able to take whatever they want, including women. I saw a group in army trucks more than once; no guarantee they were the same bunch each time. And the girl that told me about them said that they had fifty members at one stage."

Kayne scowled. "Could be they split into two groups to cover more ground."

Jason, who'd seen some of the biker types where he came from, and who'd heard his mom, other doctors, and a psychiatrist friend talk for hours on the subject, nodded at the major. "If they were part of a gang originally, they won't take losing and just walk away. They'll regroup, come back, fire the place, kill everything they see. They have to."

The major eyed him. "Why?"

Jason did his best to explain. "It's pride. If they back down, any other gang will walk all over them. They'd be known as cowards. It's an honor thing."

"There probably aren't any other gangs left around here."

"Doesn't matter," Jason told him earnestly. "It's how they'll *feel*."

The major shrugged. "We'll watch for them. They came

stomping in here, and we handed their heads to them. We can do it again if they're stupid enough to try it a second time. Now, what can we do for you?"

Tim caught the boy's eye and signaled him to silence. "We worried about the town, saw all the smoke a while back, and Jason said about that bunch, so we thought we should come take a look. How bad were you hit by the virus?"

The major's mouth tightened. "Bad enough. About fifty percent of the population died, Lot of others went to relatives. Some holed up in their places and don't come into town. We're about out of food, and they won't share…" a man muttered in the background, and he turned to look. The voice shut off abruptly, and the major turned back to Tim. "What can you do for us?"

Tim pursed his lips. "What about Mexicali?"

"Closed to us. What can you…?"

"Beef," Tim cut in. "We can bring you back a truckload of fresh killed beef. Have to do the rest of the butchering yourself, but that should help?"

The major sat back in his chair. "It would. Truckload a week, let's say. Be a big help. Means we don't have to go looking." A cold shiver slid down Jason's spine. The discussion after that was brief. Speaking deferentially, Tim disengaged them, and an hour later, they were driving out of town. Jason watched their back-trail and spoke softly. "We're being followed."

"Guessed we would be," Tim agreed. "That's why I'm not going home. We'll cut back towards Brawley and off to the east. Was at a ranch there a few years back." He grinned. "Conference on goats. If the owner's gone, I'd like his goats, but he had cattle too. We'll kill a truckload, bring them straight back, they'll think they know where we are, and if no one follows us back there a second time, we can salvage there and take what we get to our ranch once we're sure they're gone."

They *were* followed to the place east of Brawley, and when Jason scouted silently back towards the road, he saw a burly man sitting, looking bored on an electric motorcycle. He reported back to where Tim had the cattle in a yard and was shooting. Jason guessed from that there was no one alive in the house. The cattle milled and bellowed but fell one by one, too packed in to escape. Once they were dead and silence fell, Jason spoke, keeping his voice down and his movements casual.

"One man, electric motorcycle, I suppose they thought that if we couldn't hear it, we couldn't see it either."

Tim snorted. "Can he see us from there he is?"

"No, I think he's just watching to see where our place is and make sure we come back as we said we would."

"Good. Use the hoist, get them onto the truck, I'll go and take a look around."

He vanished towards the house and was back in an hour. "Goats are all in a couple of big paddocks out the back. They've got shelters."

"How come they've survived?"

"Bucks can be pretty nasty if they want to be, and Boers are the biggest breed there is. 'Sides, most of the larger predators around here were killed, although that could start to change in a few more years. So we'll get the major off our necks and come right back. I don't like what he's got in mind for us; he's a liar as well." And on Jason's questioning glance. "Let's get this done. Tell you about it later."

Jason noticed the flash of silver as the 'bike cornered into town after them. Right, he'd come back when they did, now if only he didn't follow them back out again. The mountain of beef was well-received. Men started butchering, several starved-looking dogs arrived for the offal, and the major nodded approval.

"No wastage, men. They can have whatever's useless, but nothing edible."

Tim waited until a brief dissension arose to take the Mayor's attention and then nodded to him. "See you in a few days, sir. Me'n the boy have to go. We've got chores to do." They climbed into the truck – left parked around a corner out of the way once unloaded - and headed back to the goat ranch, Jason watching every yard of the journey. Once back, Tim looked at him.

"Anything?"

"Nothing I saw. Let me go scout while you..."

"See if he watches me, yeah."

Jason was back quickly. "No sign of anyone. Okay, now what about the major?"

"Goats first." They walked those into the corrals, Tim selected all the best animals, and they loaded them quickly. After that, they filled the truck with other items, food for people and animals, the best bedding, several guns and their ammunition, gas in cans, a skimming of the best adult clothing, and a trunk of children's clothing, probably outgrown and put away.

There was still no sign of a watcher. Nevertheless, they detoured, turning back, overrunning their trail, and vigilant, but after several twists and turns, Tim headed home while Jason asked again.

"You said the major's a liar. Why? What was said that bothered you?"

Tim sobered. "It was when he was saying what had happened to the people there. He said that some holed up in their places and didn't come into town. Said they were about out of food in town, and those outside wouldn't share... Then this man started talking behind us, he looked, the man shut up as if he'd been gagged, and the major started talking to me again. He assumed I didn't hear. I did. The guy said that "they'd be fixing that. They shared or died." He drew in a deep breath. "It sounds to me as if the major's running groups to take food from anyone that has it, even if they're alive and it's their place and their food." Jason stared at him and said nothing for a long moment. Then finally, he spoke, his tone incredulous.

"But, Tim, there's food everywhere still."

"I know. What I thought was that maybe the people outside of town are planting vegetables - sort you have to plant every year. The major's lot are going out and taking half. That way, they come back and get some every year while the people do the work. They could have fruit trees, too, and he'd taking half the fruit and maybe making them do the picking as well. But even if I misunderstood, he's likely a liar. He said that about fifty percent of the people in town died. Not what your mother said, was it?"

Jason shook his head. "No, she said about a thousand per million would survive."

"Yeah, and Calexico population was about sixty thousand. If only half died, that would have left around thirty thousand. Even with people going to relatives' places and some holing up outside of town, I can't see that as less than twenty thousand. Did anywhere you saw look to be that many people?"

Jason didn't even have to think. "No."

"Okay, look at it the other way. Say twice her estimate is about twelve hundred. Say a couple of hundred left, and another hundred are holed up. That would mean the population is around a thousand plus or minus. What would you say about that?"

He thought, called into mind pictures of everything he'd seen whenever they were in the town, and very slowly, he nodded. "Sounds more or less right."

"Could be, if the major culled out those that were too old, too sick, uncooperative, or that he thought were wrong in some way, maybe known thieves or something. And then there's what he said to me. Remember?"

Jason did. "He said you should bring a truckload of beef a week. It'd be a big help. Then he said that if you did, they wouldn't have to go looking." He shivered again. "I thought it was a threat, that if you didn't, he'd find you anyway."

"That was how I read it," Tim agreed. "You'd have noticed that I talked about the Jackson place but never said where it was. Just that it was a cirque. None of them seemed to have heard of it, and that suggests he doesn't know our area down here. Now, let's get this lot home, unloaded, have an early night, and tomorrow we can take animals over to the Jackson land. I'd like a few there, so if we have to run, we've somewhere to go."

"I can think of a better place," Jason volunteered, and Tim glanced at him.

"Where?"

"That valley back of your ranch. The one I didn't see even when you were saying where it was."

"Yeeeesss," Tim said slowly. "Not a bad idea, easier to get a barn to, move animals there, and something I never told you, there are caves as well there."

"Look at it tomorrow then?" Tim nodded.

As promised, they had an early night and left the ranch at first light heading for the back valley. *There certainly are caves,* Jason thought, peering into the depths. Ideal for storage, anything bulky that couldn't easily be damaged but that they wanted to stay dry could go here. They spent a hard-working three days moving items there and building doors to block off the caves. With that done, they drove under cover of the dark before dawn - and via back roads that were little more than tracks - to the goat ranch, killed and loaded cattle, arrived in town almost before anyone was awake, unloaded the carcasses, and were gone.

"Anyone following?"

Jason grinned. "I don't think anyone was awake enough."

"Right, we'll take the rest of the goats to Jackson's with their gear. That way, if the major goes where we were, all he'll get are cattle, and there are enough of those all over. While we're at it, there was a ranch down east from Jackson's. They had some odd breed of cattle, French I think, big meaty beasts. Could run a few to Jacksons too." That took care of that day and the next, after which Annie decreed a day off.

"You've been working without a break for weeks. It's almost fall, so we'll have a picnic while the weather holds."

It was a wonderful day, Jason thought as he lay in bed later that night. The kids had rolled giggling in the grass. The dogs had played fetch. The kittens had cornered a mouse. He, Annie, and Tim had lain back on the warm, sweet-smelling turf and talked when they weren't teasing the kids, throwing things for the dogs, or rubbing the tummies of purring cats. If only there could be more days like it, but then you had to work if you wanted to eat. He fell asleep smiling.

The day after that, they raided the goat ranch and delivered another load of beef – this time arriving in town right on dusk and again managing to leave without seeing the major or being detained. Jason laughed as they cleared the jumble of buildings.

"I bet he isn't going to be pleased to hear he missed us again."

"Likely," Tim said, taking a left-hand road and then another. "And before you ask, I'm planning on finding someone that'll maybe tell me something about the major and what he does. First time we were here, I was asked if I knew Connell. I did, he died a few years back, but he had family well out of town. They'll talk to me I reckon, and they're a big family. If they survived, the major probably hasn't got around to them yet; easier to hit the small places." After an hour of driving, he headed down a narrow road for five miles before turning into a driveway with a massive gate across it.

An elderly man drifted out from the side of that, and Tim grinned at him. "Tim Crispin, knew your brother, and I thought if anyone knew something, you would."

"Something about what?"

"Man that's running Calexico, calls himself Major Kayne."

"What do *you* know?"

"That he's a liar, may be making people work for him that don't want to."

The older man eyed him sourly. "Got that right so far as it goes. He's not a major, got a dishonorable discharge, and no right to call himself that. He's a thief and a trouble-maker, and we told him if he comes here again, we'll do what they used to do in the olden days and hang him from a tree over the gates. He hasn't been back. But I heard of you. My brother said you were a good man. Get down, come in, and we'll talk."

CHAPTER SEVENTEEN

They talked. Jason learned the old man was Alec Connell and that he owned the ranch - a large one - he lived there with two sons, a daughter, their families, and an elderly sister who'd never married. A total of fifteen people who were family. In addition, they'd taken in nine people who'd been friends of someone of them and who'd lost their own kin. They had power systems and were armed to the teeth.

"You were asking about Kayne. He arrived here not long before the virus did. Called himself Major, and I can't tell you why, but he smelled phony to me. Too much the honest soldier, I guess. A caricature. Thing is, he never knew I had friends in the military. I got them looking around and had the information only a week before things went sideways. Yeah, he *was* Major Kayne, but he got a dishonorable discharge, and when that happens, a soldier loses any rank."

Tim leaned back in the chair. "Can you say why he was dumped?"

Connell sighed. "He was feeding information to half a dozen companies that gave them an advantage when tendering for gear they were selling the army. They didn't know how long it'd been going on. One of my friends thinks he'd been doing it for years, though, and he'd likely made millions. He was discharged, fined the last two payments they could prove, and that was that. I think my friend was right, though. Kayne bought a place in Calexico. Paid the sort of money for it that he shouldn't have had otherwise."

Jason spoke thoughtfully. "Everything aside, what sort of soldier was he? Did he ever do anything but sit at a desk?"

Connell shook his head. "Desk-jockey I heard, and his subordinates didn't like him much. He took credit for any good idea they had."

Jason sat back. Okay, that probably summed it up. *The only things the major's been good at were taking bribes and credit for other people's work.*

They had a meal and left. Tim was quiet on the way back to the ranch, but just before they pulled into the road leading there, he spoke. "We'll stay away from Kayne. Right now, he's got what he wants. Respect, people in that town think he's a genuine, retired soldier, and they listen to him. If you try telling them the truth, most won't believe you, and they may go further."

Jason nodded. "But you heard, he was a desk-jockey; if there's real trouble there, he probably won't know what to do."

"Maybe not, but they're acting together. Break that up, and it could do more damage than finding out what he really is. Promise me, Jason, you won't say anything."

"Okay." He was reluctant, but Tim could be right. Chaos was rarely better than cohesion. And anyway, he remembered something Mom had said. Even the worst man may have a good spot, or even if he doesn't, he may do something terrible that ends up being for good. He only hoped it'd work that way with Major Kayne.

****

A week later, they went to Jackson's again. The animals were doing well, the house was water-tight, and they were pleased with their work. They circled to a small ranch Tim knew, which was empty. From there, they salvaged a complete camping set of tents, sleeping bags, solar stove and heater, pots and pans, cutlery, and an extendable awning, all of which they found neatly packed in the garage.

Tim took everything. "Come in handy if we need to house a family beyond the buildings at Jacksons or the ranch."

They were on the way back when a woman stumbled into the road. She had splashes of blood on her clothing and stood waving desperately.

Tim hissed. "Gun out, get ready. I think she's fake. Watch all around." He'd did not need to tell Jason, who already had a handgun out and held below the edge of the window. Tim spoke through the microphone on the truck as they came to a stop by her, engine idling in gear, with Tim more alert than he appeared.

"Problem, miss?"

She flung herself at the door. "Please, help me. I was abducted, I got away."

"They're after you?"

"No, no, I got clear a couple of hours ago, but I can't walk any further. Give me a ride into town...."

To Jason's eyes, Tim concentrated on the poor woman, but he'd come to know the man by now. Tim rarely lost focus on what was around him as well, and Jason certainly hadn't. That blood was fresh. If she'd gotten clear two hours ago, it would have started drying. Then, too, the small, low bushes by the road were moving slightly – against the wind. He tensed. From the bushes, three men leaped at the truck, trying to haul the doors open. On Tim's side, the woman had the handle and was dragging down on it, screaming.

"Shoot now," Tim spoke clearly, and Jason shot. The small triangular window in the corner of the frame had been wedged. Now he jabbed the wedge out with his left hand, leveled the revolver, fired three times, and – Tim had the truck in gear and they were building up speed. One man clung to the side, Jason shot a fourth time, and the man fell away, rolling and tumbling. Tim flicked through a couple of gears, stopped, and spun the truck into reverse. The bandits didn't even realize he was on the way back until he rolled into them.

Two of the downed men went under the wheels; the third bounced off the side and went sprawling. The woman ran without a backward look, the fallen man howling curses after her. She disappeared into the brush, and Tim halted the vehicle.

"Gun on him. Shoot if he even looks at me sideways." He bent over the man and took him by the shoulder, eliciting a yell of pain. "Where's your camp, and how many of you are there? She the only one left, or do you have friends? The truth, or you're a dead man."

The man glared up. *He'd been good-looking,* Jason thought. In his twenties, good clothing, and expensive boots - although maybe he hadn't paid for them - but he had fair hair, blue eyes, and an innocent look. Or he would have had if his face wasn't twisted with a combination of pain and hate. Tim shook him.

"Talk or hurt worse."

"All right, okay. Just us three guys and the bitch, picked her up a week ago, her idea to get the truck. Damn, I can't believe she got Dan and Ed killed. You want the camp; she'll be cleaning that out in a few minutes." He gave directions, basic, but Jason could see his companion knew the place.

Tim nodded. "Okay, on your way."

"I can't move."

"Then die here," Tim said, putting the truck in gear again and heading back the way they'd come. Once at an apparent bay in the scrub, he pointed the vehicle and drove forward. Behind a curtain of bushes, Jason saw a tent, a fire-pit, various scattered pieces of gear, and the woman, just coming into the open part by the tent. She looked at the truck and bolted. Tim went after her until she was staggering with exhaustion, then he broke off the chase and left her to reel on.

"Why?" Jason, who had followed, too, was bothered at the pursuit.

Tim glanced at him. "I never wanted to catch her, just get her gone. That way, she won't be sneaking back to ambush us. Go through everything, take unopened food containers, ammunition, anything we can use. She can have whatever's left when she gets back. That's her payment for the ambush. She could have just stopped us and asked for help, offered to work. She figured it was easier to kill us and steal anything we had."

As he checked through the camp, Jason came to the same conclusion. She'd had three "friends," now two were dead, and she'd left the last without hesitation to whatever Tim and Jason might do. He took down the tent, folded that onto the truck, added the sleeping bags - expensive brands as he saw - collected ammunition, and rejoined Tim.

"That's everything worth having."

"Okay, get on board."

Looking back, Jason thought there was little left at the site. He watched ahead and saw the two bodies where they'd left them. The third man was gone, and there was no sign of the woman. They were an hour still from home, and he settled to watch the road.

Annie was waiting for them as they arrived. She came running out and eyed what they had. "Who got hurt?"

Tim looked at her. "Why?"

"Look," she pointed at the truck side, and they both saw the long smear of blood.

Tim nodded. "Bandits on the road. We're okay; they aren't."

"Good, that's the way 'round I like it." She helped them unload while Stormy capered about them. Jason ate dinner, slept like a log that night, and woke, wondering where the woman was. Then he decided he didn't care. He was sorry for old Mrs. Hayer, who'd loved Stormy. For Janet, who'd done her best and hurt no one. For his mom and grandparents and the friends he'd lost. But he couldn't feel sorry for *her*.

Tim called him for breakfast.

"What are we doing today?"

"Talking to a few friends. If you'll tell them what you know of the fake army?"

Jason nodded. "I don't know that much, but I'll tell them what I can."

They came in ones, two, and small groups. *Mostly family,* he thought, watching them arrive. A father with his sons, brothers, maybe cousins, but that seemed to be how they'd survived, and now they stayed together. Blood was thicker than water, his dad had said, and in this new fractured land, it looked as if that was how it had realigned. From brief comments, he realized most were from old families as Tim and Annie were, farm people, and they had come to the call from one of their own. Once they were there and settled, Tim looked at them.

"Two things you need to know about current dangers. One is about Major Kayne." He retold all they'd heard from Connell, and Jason saw the thoughtful looks and nods.

"The other is what my friend here can tell you about the type of gang that hit Calexico. It isn't certain they're a single gang. They may be two or three that combine against a larger place. Which means," he said over the muttering. "The assumption, they took a beating and won't be back because they lost a lot of people, may be wrong."

The muttering went up a level. "When the virus started killing people, Jason here lived in Seattle with his mom and her parents. They all died, and he headed south to join his dad in New Mexico. On the way, he saw and heard things about this bunch or their type that you should hear too."

He sat down, and Jason stood. "I saw their kind in Oregon and again several times as I came down through California." He told them his experiences, adding. "I can tell you they aren't a genuine army. One time, only weeks after the virus, I saw them close enough to see two things. One was that at least half of them had hair past their shoulders. Hair doesn't grow that fast, and even in today's army, soldiers aren't allowed to have hair anywhere near that long. And while they wore army uniforms, under them, they had t-shirts that were anarchist, or supremacist, or black rock."

A man stood, middle-aged and with a straight back. "If he saw that, then he's right. They aren't army," he agreed. "You know me; I was in the reserves until five years ago. A plain t-shirt if you can't find an army one. Solid color, no slogans, and nothing endorsing anything or anyone." He made a scoffing sound.

"Can you see any decent man wearing something that endorses terrorism anyhow? As for black rock, some of you may not be familiar with the term. It means the rock bands that sing about rape and murder, about torturing and cruelty and makes them out to be good things. They're underground bands. In 2036 and last year, two killing sprees were committed by stupid kids that followed them. Bands got smarter when the government cracked down. They still sell merchandise, but now it's all coded. Initials or artwork that means something to their followers but isn't so readily noticed by those that don't know them. If this young man saw so-called army personnel wearing them, I can tell you they weren't real army. Oh, and he's likely right about the hair too."

He sat down. Jason had a chilling thought and decided he'd hold that until the end of the discussion. Tim nudged him, speaking from where he sat.

"That's what Jason saw, but he heard something from people he met. He believes that what they told him was true, and I think it likely. Jason?"

Jason stood up again. "I was in Oregon, and I got off the freeway to see if I could find supplies at a strip of shops along a main road. I ran into a group of people there. They were wary. I was being careful, but," he grinned. "I had my dog with me, and one of them liked dogs. I introduced ourselves, and we started talking. They were looking for poultry feed. I'd passed a shop where I'd seen a lot of that, so I took them there, helped them load it, and I found out they came from east of where we were. Bunch of small farms mostly, and with my dad having a ranch, they decided I was okay."

They had, he thought, and he'd liked them. "The woman that liked my dog started telling me stuff – her name was Rose – she said that when the virus came down, there were half a dozen of them with small outfits who survived. Mostly someone in the family had a proper job, and the few acres were for fun. But now they'd seen what it was going to be like, and they'd decided to get serious. She told me that just about everyone their way was dead, all the guys with big farms, so they were amalgamating, picking what they liked to do best, what they were best at, and doing that. Doubling their acreage and taking in wandering stock."

He was giving them the background so they'd get a sense of what the people he'd met had been like, and he saw them absorbing the information. "Rose said they'd started forting up, too, that there'd been a group came through in army trucks. Her friends didn't think they were real army. They believed they'd raided an army supply depot, somewhere like that. The group hit a farm thirty miles from her place and wiped it out. They took everything." His voice unconsciously deepened, signaling grim news. "She told me that the family that had the farm must have guessed how they'd be treated if they surrendered - so they didn't."

The ex-reservist spoke. "What happened?"

"Her group saw the smoke. After five days, they made sure that lot weren't still around, scouted to make certain, then had a look up close. Cows were gone. They'd shot the goats, just left them to rot. Dogs too. They'd burned the buildings. She told me they couldn't say for sure, but one of their people knew some sign, he said from what it looked like, they'd set the buildings on fire, first two out of the house - an old lady with a kid - they shot, so the rest inside shot the kids and then themselves."

The ex-reservist growled. "Who *were* these guys? Did they have any ideas?"

"I asked that. Rose said they didn't know for sure, but her people thought they were what was left of a couple of motorcycle gangs. No law, no police, they could do what they liked, and they were. So her bunch had come west to forage. They were going to fort up really hard in case they came back. She was pretty sure that lot didn't know about her people or where they lived, they were going to keep scouts a half-day out watching, make their main homestead look like a hill from a distance, surround it with a wall of sandbags and turf the outside of those. Dig a couple of escape tunnels.

"It could be helpful here too. Rose said they were going to get in more people and get some good guns and other stuff. That bunch weren't the only ones that knew where to find a supply depot. They had livestock, good fertile land, and they weren't being chased off it. I asked if anyone at all had got a close-up look at the killers, and she said no, but one of the scouts had a look at them through binoculars. She said lots of them had long hair and red t-shirts with black writing under their uniform jackets."

He held up a hand as discussion broke out. "Yeah, it sounds just like the ones I saw, which made us think it probably was. I asked how many there'd been, and she said one time one of their people had seen least seventy; it could be eighty or even more. Any time I saw them, there were only about twenty-thirty, which is why I thought they might split up to scavenge and come together again at an agreed time and place."

He took in a breath. "One last thing. The main black rock band was called Death's Army. Their supporters wore red t-shirts with black printing. The band preached that the end of the world was coming, and when it did, their followers should sanctify themselves by the blood, pain, and death of unbelievers."

There was an uproar. The ex-reservist got silence by shouting the loudest. "You think this lot are Death's Army followers?" Jason nodded. "And even if they aren't, there could be near a hundred of them?" Jason nodded again. "Then I don't give a damn *who* they are. We're in trouble, we hang together, or they'll hang us separately." He shouted down another outburst. "How many of you like the idea of being surrounded by dozens of maniacs and having your family burn alive?"

The consensus was that *no one* liked that idea.

"Then we stick together. Never mind Kayne, whether he's genuine or not – and I reckon he's not – he's city. We set up scouts. We watch the roads, we know every inch of the country between us. We get at least half of our animals away somewhere where that lot won't find them, and we set up escape routes."

Jason caught Tim's satisfied look and spoke under the noise. "You expected this?"

"Lived here all my life, and my dad an' granddad and his dad, before me." Tim's low voice didn't carry. "Major Kayne be damned. That's John Arren, army family, farm family, knows what's what on both sides. And everyone that knows him'll listen."

Jason sat quietly, doing some of that himself and hearing that John Arren did indeed know what he was doing. By the end of the meeting, he had scouts organized with a roster. He had an agreement to pool a percentage of gas and diesel and start creating underground escape routes from all farmhouses. They'd pool basic farm machinery too and move a portion of livestock to Jackson's cirque.

"And weapons. Who has guns? All of you, right. Anyone short of ammunition for them? Five of you, okay, we can see about that. Hands up who has any really heavy gun or sniper-stuff? Oh, your great-great-granddad's, I suppose? And you've got ammunition for it too? Good."

Jason's looked at Tim. "His great-great-granddad?"

Tim grinned unpleasantly. "Big game hunter back in the early nineteen-hundreds. Mike doesn't use the guns, but he keeps them in good shape. If they'd stop an elephant in its tracks, I'd say they'd do some damage to a truck too."

Jason thought that likely, and grinned back.

The meeting broke up near dusk, and the members left, all but John Arren, who was staying for dinner. Once they'd eaten, he pushed his chair back and looked at Jason. "Tell me something about yourself."

It was politely spoken, but Jason understood it as an order, and that was fair enough. If many people were relying on the information he gave, they had a right to know how reliable he was. He started with Seattle, keeping it as brief as possible.

"My mother was an orthopedic surgeon. Her parents, my grandparents lived there. She went to New Mexico to do post-graduate study, met my dad, and they got married. But she couldn't keep doing what she wanted there, so she moved to Seattle; they got divorced. I stayed with her. Mom and the grands died when the virus hit, but she told me to get out, go to my dad. Told me what she knew, told me where to get some supplies."

"The dog?"

"I found an old lady in a crashed car. Stormy was hers. She asked me to take her; she had the virus." Jason was terse.

"What did your mother know about the virus?"

"Doctors talk to doctors, and some of her friends were researchers." He explained the combination of allodaxin plus a minor earlier infection, and John Arren nodded slowly.

"So if you had them in the right order, you were immune. In other words, everyone still alive now is likely to stay alive, at least so far as the virus is concerned?" Jason nodded. "You've been staying, helping the Crispins. Why?"

"Mom, she said it's better to travel slow and safe than in a rush. Said it's a long way, and I should grow into the journey, walk in beauty." He found a sad smile curving his mouth, and Arren was onto it.

"What did that remind you about?"

"A song my dad used to sing. It's a blessing."

Arren looked at him sharply. "Your father's Navajo?"

Jason nodded. "About a third. He doesn't follow a lot of their beliefs, and I didn't learn that much, a couple chants, a few words. But I know the song; he always sang it to me when I left."

"And he has a ranch in New Mexico; do you think he's alive?"

Jason winced. "I don't know," he said honestly. "I'll find out, I guess."

"You plan to stay here a while longer?" Jason indicated agreement.

"Why?"

Jason fumbled. "Uh, Tim and Annie are friends."

Arren looked at Tim, who nodded. Arren nodded back. "All right then. You'll tell us when you do decide to leave. Now, you don't have anyone here, and you're free. I know an army depot. It's small, it isn't regularly staffed, and there's a good chance no one has run across it yet. Would you be willing to come with me to salvage it?"

"Just me?"

"No, it probably has trucks there; we could use more drivers, any suggestions? His glance encompassed them all, and Annie smiled.

"Talk to Alec Connell. Tim can tell you who he is if you don't know. Other than that..." she gave several more names, two of which Arren registered.

"Good thought, yes. And I'll talk to this Connell. He sounds useful."

****

John Arren, Jason thought two days later, didn't allow any grass to grow under his feet. Tim had gotten a message just before dinner to say that Jason would be collected in Arren's truck mid-morning tomorrow. So he was waiting when the expected salvage party arrived and parked at the Crispin gate. Arren got down, waved at his passengers to join them, and made introductions. Jason had been expecting something to be said about bringing Stormy with him, but Arren merely waved the men towards them.

"Alec Connell, Jason Trevalen." The older man looked Jason over.

"You were with Crispin when he came calling a while back, weren't you?"

"I was."

"Good man, if he's okay with you, I guess I am too."

Arren had been waiting. "Right. And these are Mark and Gordy - and Fred. He's Mark's brother." He didn't need to hear that, Jason reflected. Fred looked a few years younger, but otherwise, they were two peas in a pod. "Now, let's hit the road."

They did, driving nor-nor-east on a well-made narrow road until they topped out on a slight rise and saw buildings below. Around them was a high concrete wall and several warning signs affixed to that. Arren put the truck into gear and rolled down the slope, watching the road ahead with the air of a man who expects an ambush and plans to outguess it. It made Jason jumpy, and he, too, was watching when something leaped into the air by the roadside. He yelled a warning, the truck swerved away, and there was an explosion. Jason found himself unharmed, sitting in the front seat by Arren, both covered in fragments of glass from the window, and the truck stalled.

CHAPTER EIGHTEEN

Arren swore, got the truck into gear again, and they raced forward. Jason was shaking.

"What was that? It looked like it jumped out at us?"

"Yes. Form of grenade, triggered by proximity and a lot of metal approaching."

The men behind them were calling questions, and Arren motioned them to silence as he swung from the seat, stood leaning out, feet on the truck's floor, and raised his voice. "Listen, and you'll hear what I know. That was a form of proximity grenade. The truck triggered it. I'm not sure it was meant to hurt us. It was more likely to have been a warning to stay away, or to whoever's at the depot to say someone's coming."

He waved down more questions. "What makes you think I know more than you do? What I *do* know, and some of that's thanks to Jason here, is that it can take days or now and then weeks, for some that got the virus to die. They'd have had time to set booby-traps, and if they thought they might be too sick to fight for a while, but that they'd recover, they'd have had the incentive to keep people out. We move in slow and careful. Don't take chances, don't act too quickly, and keep under cover as much as you can."

He allowed the truck to roll down the last of the slope and stopped in front of a pair of heavy gates. Arren got down and walked to them. He called out his name, rank, and serial number. His voice echoed to no response. He called the information again, adding what Jason thought to be a password. Again, there was silence. Arren spoke again.

"I'm coming in. If anyone shoots, you'll be shooting at a superior officer, and I'll have you court-martialed. This is a legitimate order. I have the gate code." He reached for the gates, touched a keypad there, and both gate halves drew back until the truck could pass. When there was no response, Arren returned to the truck and drove through the gates. He parked in front of the sign saying "Reception" and got out.

There was still no indication of life, and he nodded to Jason. "Come with me and bring the dog. She'll hear or smell anyone here before we do."

Jason moved ahead of him, opened the door, and spoke a soft command. Stormy vanished down the passage, and Arren halted, waiting. She was back in minutes. Jason looked at him.

"No one. Not alive anyway."

"Split up, I go right, you go left, note anything useful or interesting."

There was nothing useful, Jason found, but interesting was another matter. He found messages. They'd come over a printer in code, and someone had written the translations underneath. They said the staff was to stay where they were, not to admit anyone to the depot, further orders would arrive, and until then, they should contact no one. If the depot was approached, identification of those coming was to be verified. If none was forthcoming, anyone attempting to enter the depot might be met with as much force as was required to prevent a breach. The messages were all neatly attached to a clipboard in order, and it looked as if they were duplicates. He said as much to Arren.

"I'd agree. These were the file copies. The originals would have gone to whoever commanded here."

"You said sometimes there was no one here?"

"I meant no operational soldiers. There was always a commander, clerks, checkers, and a coder."

"How many?"

"Twelve normally, sometimes fourteen or fifteen." Arren glanced about. "It's the sort of position they give to men finishing a career. The kind of soldier who's conscientious, hard-working, and reliable, but without leadership qualities. Plodders.

Usually single, no close family. Putting in their time until they retire with a pension."

Jason turned slowly, looking all around. "So, where are they? I'd think conscientious, hard-working, and reliable staff would be right here asking who we are, demanding to see I.D. cards, and telling me to get the dog out of the office."

John Arren grinned and considered him. "I do like a man with common sense. Either the staff isn't here, or they are, but in no condition to say that. Let's start looking."

They did, but Mark's arrival provided an explanation. He came in looking sick. "Found everybody. They're dead, looks like they've been dead since this started. No sign of anything but the virus." He waved a hand towards the door. "Come and see if you want. But I'd say it's all of them."

Arren, once he was at the small barracks, counted. "Yes, that's the commander's rooms. Coder's next to them. Clerks have a room each, five there, rooms for the checkers, and yes, there's five bodies. So that's all the regular staff I'd expect."

Jason, with his experience, had been quietly going through the coder and commander's rooms and found something he'd half-expected. "John, the commander left a letter."

"Where was it? What made you look for that?"

Jason looked wry. "Too much experience. It seems to be a human thing; we want someone to know, so read this. Just be grateful they didn't set fire to the place."

"Many do that?"

"A number of them."

"Okay." Arren put a hand out, and Jason passed him the letter. He waited until everyone was with him, listening, and read the letter aloud.

To my Superiors,

We were ordered to remain in the depot, to admit no one without clearance, to make no further contact, and to await orders. This we did until some of my staff became ill. I isolated them in their rooms. They died. No local medical staff answered when I called them. The television said that the illness was widespread, perhaps worldwide. More of the team died. Sergeant Michaelson went out and placed a booby-trap by the road so we would know if an approach was made in force. He died two days later, and I am the only one left. I have become ill. To whoever finds this letter, I commend my staff, they remained at their posts until they could no longer work and died in their country's service. I could not have served with better people. Please see that they are respectfully interred and their long service acknowledged.

Commander Virgil P. Harrington.

Arren looked at what was left of the letter's writer and saluted. "We'll obey that request, sir. So far as we're able." Jason stirred, and he glanced at him. "You can deal with this?"

"I can."

"Very well, choose a man to help you, and the rest of us will go and see what we can use from here."

Alec Connell spoke. "I'll help if that'll suit you, young man?"

Jason acknowledged that and moved to the bed. "The best way is to wrap all the bedding around them." The other four men tramped out, and Alec and Jason started their work.

It was an unpleasant job, but one by one, they wrapped all twelve of the depot staff in their bedding, secured that, and carried the bodies to a section behind the buildings that looked to have been a garden once. There were still a straggling rose bush, a camellia, and several tiger lilies and irises. Once the bodies were lined up, Alec searched for a digger or at least shovels. He returned with a small digger. It ran silently, so Jason assumed it was electrically powered.

Alec confirmed that. "Yup, still plugged into a charger when I found it."

"A charger? Solar power?"

"Wind generator cross-wired with solar. No one says different, and I'll take that. It's a major rig, and we can use it. We've got people trickling in still. We were a big family, and some lived a fair distance. Those that lived came home, we're up to fifty plus now, and some're bringing friends. Taken in an orphan or two as well, and we need that rig if no one objects."

"Doesn't take two to run the digger," Jason commented. "I'll go have a word with Arren."

Before that, he detoured, slipped by buildings, looking in the windows, and found what he'd expected. A stack of the portable wind and solar generators, all neatly bundled complete with sets of spares. They weren't the very latest, but they could be cross-wired, and any duo would run for some forty to fifty years with the extras and provide power to several buildings. He'd watched as Arren had opened the gate, and now he used that number to see if the doors would open. They did, and he entered silently, Stormy at his heels. He counted the generators on their pallets and grinned in delight. He could work with that. Then he went in search of Arren and drew him aside.

"We have all the bodies out back where there was a garden. Alec found a digger, and he's seeing to the graves. Once we have them in those, you might want to say a few words. I checked the rooms; there's flags, enough for one each. And flowers we can lay."

"Good, what else?"

"Alec wants the main generator system. He has a widespread family, and they're all coming home, those that lived. They've passed fifty, and they've taken in family friends and orphans too. They need it." Arren frowned, and Jason shook his head. "Hear me out, sir. There's a whole stack of portable generators with spares in one of the storage sheds. You may not have seen it. It's a single huge shed right behind the main buildings. I looked at the generators. They're not the newest type, but they can all be cross-wired, solar and wind. If you want a suggestion, get Mark to drive back right now, he goes to pick up one person as a driver from any outfit you think is okay and comes back with them. How many trucks have you found?"

Arren considered. "Fifteen and the ones we came in make nineteen." He smiled abruptly. "As you say, not the newest, but fit for purpose. I'll tell Mark. His brother can go with him as shotgun just in case. That many generators, huh? Looks as if what I thought was right."

"What was that?"

"Someone saw this coming. I wonder how many other small depots around the country were stuffed full of emergency supplies at the last minute."

"Full?"

"Yes. Usually most of the warehouses are empty or nearly so. The ones we've checked have all been filled to the doorways. Food, tools, weapons and ammunition, powered or manual items like cultivators and farm equipment, and there's a smallish one filled with first-aid packs. And you say there's a whole warehouse full of cross-useable generators and spares packs with each?"

"There are." Jason was fascinated. "So someone thought that if whatever was starting got really bad, it'd save more people if depots like this had it all rather than it being in some major city."

Arren looked at him. "Yes, I guess some army brass used his head for something other than a spot to hang a hat. This place will save a lot of people, Jason. And if I knew who he or she was, I'd put up a memorial."

Jason grinned. "The office has copies of all the incoming messages. It shouldn't be too hard to find out. Now, do I tell Alec he can have the big generators?"

"Yes. Say he can take a truck back to his place with them as soon as the funerals are done, and you can help him get the generators down if you will." Jason nodded. "And after that, too, we'll start shuttling everything out from here. It may take a week, but we'll strip the place. One thing on that, we need to watch for the fake army on the road and for anything Kayne may do. I'll make sure every truck leaving has at least two people. They'll have orders to shoot first and ask questions after." His grin was dangerous. "And to add to that, we also found five dozen grenades. Now, go and see how Connell's doing and come back once you're ready."

Jason trotted away, concluding that this depot and its possibilities were something he should remember. If Arren was right, there could be others of them - all equally well supplied - and it was not impossible that one could be near the ranch in New Mexico, and no one knowing about it.

He was back looking for Arren in a couple of hours, Arren called everyone in, and they stood at the foot of the grave, a long trench, now with bundles spaced down the depths, each bundle with a flag across it. The commander had his from his office. It had been found, a full-size one, folded on a shelf. But there'd been others, and Jason had, as he'd said, found enough for each staff member to have one. Flower petals were sprinkled over the flags and the bodies. The sweet scent drifted up to those that stood there.

Arren stepped forward. "You were good soldiers," he said quietly. "You stood your ground, stayed faithful to your orders and your trust. You died at your posts like many soldiers before you, and we honor you for it. As the highest ranking soldier in this area, I commend you; let you lie in peace, knowing you never did less than your duty." He looked around at the silent line. "Does anyone else wish to speak?"

Alec Connell stepped forward and softly recited the Twenty-Third Psalm. No one else moved until Jason, remembering something he'd learned from his father, stepped forward and sang. He had a good voice, untrained but on pitch, and the tune was one his father had taught him, both music and lyrics. He'd learned to play and sing it, all the while wondering why his father had taught him a death song. Now he wondered if his father had known that something lay in the future where it might be needed. He changed the words a little as he sang, but he knew the old ones would not have minded.

Once he was finished, he stepped back, and Alec, who had moved to the digger, spoke. "Let each cast earth on those who died. Let it fall kindly on those that kept faith."

One by one, they obeyed. Alec started the digger, pushing the hills of raw earth over the bodies until the trench was full.

Then Arren, who had made a cross, thrust it deep into the earth. There was no room to list names, and as all knew, the weather would have seen to it that whatever materials they used would have been gone in months. But he'd done better in a way, Jason believed. He'd used a length of plank as the crosspiece, and along that was deeply engraved, "They kept their trust." He felt tears burn at the back of his eyes. What better memorial could any warrior have?

Arren cleared his throat, gave orders, and the assemblage broke up. Mark and Fred headed for the truck. They would stay the night at their homes before returning with people while Alec and Jason headed back to the offices to search for any helpful information, leaving Arren and Gordy to begin the heroic task of listing stored supplies.

****

Mark and Fred arrived the following day; the back of their truck filled with people. Tim had come, two more from Alec Connell's family and those from other farms in ones, twos, and threes, wherever adults could be spared.

Arren wasted no time. "We have nineteen trucks, we'll load double generators on each, and after that, we'll add food, ammunition, first aid kits, and tools until the truck's full. Depending on where that's going, eventually, we want an even distribution to each farm or family. Line up, write down who you are, how many on your place, if there's any particular item you need, and directions to your farm."

A line formed quickly, but as Arren had started the day by having Jason, himself, and others filling the first four trucks with basics, it took little time before the first of them was rolling out of the depot gates. Jason caught up with him mid-morning when he was briefly alone.

"I found something."

"What?"

"This," he passed over a message copy, then a second. Each detailed nearby depots. "I think they sent them so that if any of the staff survived, they knew where the other ones were that could be close enough to reach."

Arren studied the lists. "One for this end of California, one for this side of Arizona." He looked as if a considerable weight had been lifted. "Four here, three there. Considering what's in this one, it's a bonanza. Who else knows?"

"No one. I found them in the commander's bedroom when I was moving his body. He had them taped under the desk."

Arren stared. "What made you look there?"

"You said to search for interesting or useful information. I figured some of that might have been hidden, and I looked."

Aran's hand went out and clenched briefly on Jason's shoulder. "Good man. This could save a lot of lives, give us a chance at a future. Say nothing, I'll tell Tim and Connell, but we need to clear these places carefully if we don't want to be attacked."

He left Jason to load trucks while he went in search of Alec, and Jason lightly brushed his fingers over another set of maps and messages tucked into the large pocket sewn into the inside front of his jacket. He didn't know if they'd been sent, if the commander had asked, or if they'd come by mistake, but he had all the information needed to find and access seven depots in New Mexico. If he made it home, he'd be coming with something guaranteeing a welcome; the more so as two of them bracketed the area of the ranch, both only fifty or sixty miles away from the ranch house. He turned his mind to loading and got on with it.

The trucks shuttled back and forth for the prophesied week. In the end, they did as Arren had said and left stripped buildings. They had even managed to dismantle three of the smaller ones, and they had gone to house people on ranches where more family had made it home. Mark and Fred had contributed solidly in another way when they were sitting in the depot's staff canteen reminiscing.

"Remember that year we went to the beach down the coast from San Diego."

Fred laughed. "I was only four. I don't remember much, just the sand and the water, and that funny place we had. You were, what, eleven, what was it, Mark?"

"Called it a challey or something. Bunch of them, and caravans too."

Alec Connell stiffened, although only Jason and Arren noticed. "Where was it?" Alec asked casually.

"Dunno," Mark shrugged. "Not Imperial Beach. Dad said that was too crowded and too expensive. It was a smaller place south from there."

"How far down from Imperial Beach? Couldn't have been that far. That's almost at the border as it is." Alec questioned.

"Far enough it didn't count as that; far enough we couldn't hear the racket they made all night." Mark laughed. "Far enough that no one was giving orders about everything. Few signs up, that was all. Real dead in winter, I'd think. It was a summer place. I seem to remember Dad saying that once fall arrived, everyone left until summer."

He turned to teasing his brother about another vacation, and Arren, Jason, and Alec exchanged thoughtful looks.

Alec spoke in a low tone that only the other two heard. "Caravans'd be moveable and some of the chalets too maybe, depending on the type and size. Dunno about you two, but I plan on going there and seeing what can be moved – right along to our ranch."

Arren pursed his lips. "Yes. Back when some of this started, I had a driver come into my place. Sick, then he died. He was running empty, dropped off farm machinery at the border, going up to L.A. to collect a load there, then over to Vegas." He looked at them. "Want to guess what he was driving?"

Jason got it first. "A flatbed."

"Yes, massive thing, one of those that can be configured as a single wider level or two levels. And depending on how wide or high any chalet is, I'd say you could maybe fit six on it, four anyhow, and it has a towbar on back. Power those things have, it'd haul even the biggest caravan." He grinned. "Wonder how many chalets and caravans there are down at this beach of Mark 'n Fred's."

Arren nodded slowly. "Have to be careful, lot of other people between us and them would like some of those. The fake army for a start, not that they'd necessarily want them to use, but it'd amuse them to burn the lot so we didn't get them."

Both his listeners nodded. Arren rose and stretched. "Last load tomorrow. After that, we might take a run up the coast once we've had a couple of days to catch up at home."

The final load left the stripped depot the next afternoon. A convoy of more than twenty trucks, they'd added several over the week, and all loaded down with supplies that would improve the lives of those that received them. Arren had taken everyone involved to one side at some time or another and warned them.

"People talk. Others listen. Then you get people who'd like something for nothing. So keep supplies under cover where they won't be noticed."

Gordy had nodded hard. "Yeah, we got neighbors that borrow. Anything we got, they're right there asking for a loan. *Loan* – that's when you give it back, an' they don't. We got into the habit of putting stuff in places they don't see. And now, with things tight, we don't loan nor give, and we twice had someone try to break into a shed. Dad's started letting the dogs run loose of a night. That stopped it."

"And nobody knowing what you got's another method," Alec agreed. "They're less likely to come hunting if they don't know you've anything worth looking for."

Jason was in the second to last truck as it pulled out, Tim driving, Stormy with her paws on the windscreen. Tim smiled at her. "She's been a good dog?"

Jason thought of how she'd been the one to find those maps and messages the commander had hidden. She'd sniffed at the desk, tried to get her nose under it, and he'd realized it was a fair hiding place. That hadn't been all. The coder, a small woman whose papers said she'd been a year short of retirement, had had her own cache. Maps and information on five more depots in the part of Texas that bordered New Mexico – they'd been in a packet, along with duplicates of the California and Arizona information. And in another, larger cache, made under a floorboard, and which Stormy had also indicated, he'd found some handy – and interesting – items. He'd stashed those and said nothing. Now he smiled at Stormy.

"Yes, she's been a very good dog. Her owner had her on a contraceptive implant. I found more in a vet's place. If I ever get where I'm going, I'll let her implant run out and find her a boyfriend. I'd like to see her puppies."

"What sort of dog?"

"Doberman, Malamute maybe, or one of those gold collies."

Tim dissented. "Not one of them. I read about those, and they're brainless."

"Collies are smart," Jason objected.

"Not that sort. Bred the brains out of them, getting the head narrower for showing. Vet in Scotland did an article on it. Shetland Sheepdogs are fine though, use one of them maybe?"

Jason nodded. Stormy was smart, and if she had puppies, he wanted them to be smart too. So, not a gold collie, and maybe not a Malamute either. A Sheltie sounded fine, though. Yes, perhaps one of them – if he could find one and it hadn't been neutered, if not, then a Doberman would do.

The truck pulled into the Crispin Ranch, and Annie was there with the kids. Jason helped unload, ate his dinner, almost falling asleep in it, and stumbled to bed. It was ten the next morning before he woke, and then it was to Annie's worried voice.

"I'm telling you, Tim, it's smoke. No, not from Calexico. It's more northwest."

Jason rolled out of bed, thankful he slept in a t-shirt and boxers. Once outside with Tim and Annie, he, too, looked and agreed. "That's smoke, and it's thickening up."

CHAPTER NINETEEN

The smoke started turning color as they watched, and both Annie and Tim relaxed.

"Vegetation," Annie said, seconded by a grunt from Tim. "Been a dry summer, no fire brigades, only hope the wind stays southeast, that'll see it doesn't come this way."

"How far away, do you think?"

Annie looked at Jason. "Thirty, forty miles. Not enough if the wind changes."

"Should we do something about it?"

"Keep watch on the wind direction, about all we can do at the moment."

The wind stayed where it was and even died down to a minor breeze. By late that afternoon, no more smoke showed, so Jason went to bed and slept comfortably. He was woken the second morning in a row by worried voices and rolled out of bed to find several people conferring with Tom and Annie.

"Yeah, it died down, but it was going again this morning. I don't like it, Tim. Yeah, it's been a bit dry this year. An' no, I know we got no fire brigades now, but you know as well's me what could happen if the wind changes and strengthens. And it's funny, starting and stopping like that. It's not natural." The speaker was a man Jason vaguely recognized as living further away along the highway in the fires' direction. He was red-faced and blustering, but this time Jason thought he was genuinely concerned.

Tim looked at him. "So what do you want me to do, Ray?"

"Someone should take a look, see what's going on."

"Why don't you?"

The red-faced man looked uneasy. "Got the ranch, women are nervous, could be trouble wherever that is."

"And you don't want trouble," Annie said softly.

"No, well, no, I don't. But someone should take a look."

Jason had come to that conclusion already. A loudmouth the man might be, but he'd know the country. If he was bothered, it could be for a good reason. Jason slipped quietly back to his bedroom, donned suitable clothing, grabbed his emergency backpack, and rejoined the discussion, Stormy at his heels.

"I think Mr. Lucas is right. Someone should take a look. I can go. I've got an electric bike ready charged, and I can take a spare pack of batteries. That way I won't be easily heard, and if something is going on, I can find out what."

From his left, he heard agreement and a question. "Makes sense. You got another bike?" Jason did and said so as Fred joined him.

"Mark said to come here, he thought someone would go, and I'm spare, so he thought I could go along with them. Okay?" Jason agreed. Fred might be only sixteen, but like his brother, he was sensible and level-headed.

"Yeah, there's another bike, and you're welcome."

It took only a few minutes before Stormy was on the small bike-trailer behind him, and they were gliding silently off along the highway. Fred grinned at the speed. "Had a bicycle for years but not one of these, didn't know they could go so fast."

"We can afford to speed until we get nearer the smoke," Jason informed him. "Once we get closer, we leave the bikes somewhere we can find them and go in on foot."

"*That's* why the dog."

"Yes, she's trained, she can scout, and if someone sees a glimpse of her, they're less likely to start yelling about it than they are if they see one of us."

They cruised for an hour until they were into the area where the smoke loomed and billowed. Fred spied a fallen tree. "Hay, Jase, look, you could leave the bikes there."

Jason halted his bike, rode to the tree, and looked down. "Yeah, a good spot for one of them."

"Why one?"

"Because it won't be a lot of help if someone runs across them both and takes them. If we put them in two different places, that gives us a better chance."

Fred thought about it. "Yeah, guess so."

Jason was riding in a circle around the tree, spiraling further and further out. He saw a slab of concrete on one circle and lying down, he peered underneath.

Fred joined him. "What cha' got?"

Jason was looking over the ground. "I think there were buildings here, and I think this was a cellar, or maybe storage of some sort. We'll leave it now, and I don't want to hide the bike here. That way, if someone finds the bike, they may find whatever's here too." He walked further out and looked down. "Here would do. See, thick grass, but it's covering a ditch. Hold the grass back." Fred did, and his companion placed the e-bike at the bottom of the shallow ditch. Fred let the grass fall back into position and beamed.

"That works. Look, you can't see a thing."

"Right, nip back and tuck your bike under cover, then come back. From here on, we're on foot, and Stormy goes ahead."

They moved with slow caution, the gray dog flitting before them, all her senses alert. They were near to the fire now, they could feel the heat, and it was hard not to cough loudly when wisps of smoke blew over them. Then the dog returned, lip lifted in a soundless snarl. Fred, signaled by Jason to stay, looked mutinous; his mouth tightening, but a second, more vigorous signal sent him to crouch, waiting. Jason and Stormy moved on, watching, listening, both knowing that somewhere there was an enemy.

Jason could see that ahead the trees thinned, and stopped to consider. If he moved into clear land, he could be seen, but he'd know nothing if he didn't have a better view of what was there.

He remembered something he'd read – that man tends not to look up – and moved back some distance. Then, with Stormy waiting below, he climbed a tall well-branched tree. The foliage was thick, and once Jason had reached a good height, he could see over to the cleared area, and what he saw almost sent him off his branch.

"That lot," he muttered. "What are they *doing*?" He poised motionless, and after ten minutes, he climbed down and found Fred, signaling him to stay silent and follow.

Once they were out of range, he sent the dog to scout and sat. Fred dropped to sit beside him. "Okay, the fires aren't natural. They're being lit by that fake army bunch."

"Why?" Fred asked, quite reasonably.

Jason grimaced. "Because they're nuts. So far as I could see, it's their version of a barbecue. They light a patch of ground, someone runs up with a stick of marshmallows, grills that, shares it, and then lights more land."

Fred stared. "They … you … they really *are* doing that?"

"Yeah. I know it sounds crazy. That's what I said, they're nuts. They're laughing their heads off every time they light more stuff, then one of them pushed someone else into the burning bits, and everyone thought it was hilarious."

Fred's eyes narrowed. "You know, it's like Ray said, after a dry summer, things burn. So what if they did?"

"They?"

"Their cars, trucks, all their stuff."

They looked at each other, and slowly two huge smiles blossomed. "Yeah," Jason said. "We'd have to be careful, don't want them guessing it was a person."

"If they lost all their gear, they might go somewhere else…"

"Or head our way to steal what they lost," Jason said. "Don't want that either."

Fred picked up a stick and sketched. "They're here right now. Town's here, our ranches, most of them, are over here. Why should they go that way?"

"Those distances aren't as far apart as they look," Jason added, frowning as he came to his senses. "Too dangerous. It's not a bad idea, but if they lose everything, it's likely to be our places they raid to gear up again." Fred had a protesting look in his eyes, but Jason was adamant. "We're here to see what's happening, not to make things worse. Let's go."

They regained the bikes and set off for home, Fred's ranch was closer, and once he reached the ranch gate, he looked hopeful. "Um, could I keep the bike tonight, bring it back in the morning? It'd be great to ride it first thing."

"Yeah, okay. And, Fred, you did a great job." They shook hands solemnly while Stormy sat behind her owner. Jason rode home, grateful he didn't have to do that with a second bike balanced beside him. Although, came to think of it, Fred must have gotten to the Crispin ranch on some transport, or had he caught a lift with one of the others? That question was settled when he wheeled into the yard and found an unattended vehicle he didn't know still sitting there.

Annie came out to meet him. "How'd it go?"

He explained, then waved at the vehicle. "Whose is that?"

"Fred's. Hang on, why didn't he come back with you?"

"Said he wanted to ride the e-bike back in the morning," Jason replied, looking at the tiny runabout.

Annie shrugged. "Probably tired and didn't want to admit it. That way, he got home without having to ride on to here and drive back again. Never mind that, there's roast pork, baked potatoes, gravy, and peas for dinner."

Dinner was pleasant. He talked, explained what he'd seen, and marveled at the fake-army's enjoyment of burning things and being idiots. Tim listened and commented tartly. "All one to them, isn't it? That was the black rock anthem. Do whatever you want. If that's burning grass to roast marshmallows, fine. If it's burning down a house with kids inside, fine. Just so long as you enjoy doing it, it's your right."

Jason went to bed thinking about that. The fake army were

dangerous, they needed to be stopped, but so far as he'd seen, it was a case of "let someone else do it." That was why they'd come to Tim, to get someone to go and see why there was smoke. So he'd gone. His report of that bunch burning up bits of land as a barbecue probably wouldn't make anybody take action. They'd groan, say the people were idiots, and then sit back and hope said idiots didn't overrun them. It'd need a real outrage to get the locals to unite.

Mark arrived the next morning when it was only an hour past first light. He was hammering on the door, yelling for Fred, Jason, anyone to answer him. Annie got there first and yelled back.

"What do you think you're doing, waking people at this hour? What are you yelling for? Can't you knock like other people, and why're you here anyhow?"

Mark, outshouted, stepped back. "Look, I'm sorry, Mrs. Crispin, but is Fred here?" Jason, hastily dressing, could hear the conversation. Annie snorted. "No, he isn't. He asked Jason if he could keep the e-bike for the night and bring it back in the morning. He said it was fun to ride. I can tell you that Jason came home alone and told me that. I was outside when he got back."

Jason joined them and nodded agreement. Mark stared. "Where'd you leave him?"

"Right at your ranch gate," Jason snapped. "It wasn't until I got back and saw his jeep I wondered. I didn't know how he got here before that. Annie thought he might have been tired and not wanted to say. It's miles from your ranch to the Crispins, and then he'd have to go back again. It made sense to me he'd skip that if he could. What're you saying, that I left him at his gate, and he never came home?"

Mark stood still. "I believe you, but look at it; you left Fred with the e-bike at our gate. He didn't come in; he hasn't come home at all. What *did* he do? Where'd he go?"

A terrible suspicion struck Jason. "I can't believe he'd be so silly," he said numbly. "I told him it was too dangerous. He said he understood. We rode back to your ranch and shook hands when I left."

Mark grabbed his arm. "What are you talking about?"

Jason drew on all his strength and told of what they'd found, of Fred's idea, how Jason had thought it too dangerous, and, after some discussion, brought Fred safely back to his gate and left him there. "I told him," his voice was anguished. "He agreed with me. He shook hands when I said he'd done great. He asked for the bike then. He must have had that in mind all along."

Mark's gaze met his. "Yeah. Ninety-nine percent of the time, he's smart and as sensible as all get out. That one percent, though… Last time, he tried to ride an unbroken horse Dad had just bought. That was two years ago. The horse was completely wild, and it tried so hard to get rid of him it lost its balance and went down. It broke a leg, and Dad had to shoot it. Fred broke both legs, and I thought for a bit Dad would shoot him too. Can you take me where you were last night?"

"He can in half an hour," Annie said flatly. "He eats breakfast before he does, and so do you if you haven't eaten yet. And listen, Tim'll go around the neighbors as soon as he's eaten. We'll round up a bunch of people who can come and help you look, and in case they've got him. Tim'll pick people that'll fight."

They ate quickly. Jason took the motorcycle. He might need the speed rather than complete silence - although for that, his e-bike went in Mark's jeep - a match to the one Fred had used. They reached the scene of the barbecue and found nothing but scorched earth, tire tracks, and discarded rubbish.

Mark groaned. "Where can the stupid little bastard have got to?"

Jason stared about and could see nothing, no indication the boy had ever been there. "They were over there. If he was caught, there could be some sign this way." He signaled Stormy, who had inhaled scent from the shirt left in Fred's small car. She ran along the burned edges of the land and halted, whimpering. Mark went white.

"What's she mean?"

Jason dropped to one knee, sifting the loose earth in his fingers, raising it to his nose. He looked up. "I'm sorry, Mark. There's blood here."

"Not Fred's. It doesn't have to be Fred..."

"That's the scent I gave her. I told her to seek out Fred. There doesn't seem to be a lot. He could just have a flesh wound."

Mark looked at him, his eyes bleak. "No, if it was something minor and he was free, he'd have come home. It's his blood, and he's not home, so either he's bad hurt, or they're holding him. And if he was bad hurt but around here somewhere, the dog would have found him, wouldn't she? She stopped here. That means his trail does too."

Jason met that bleak look. "Yeah." He heard breaking twigs and spun. Tim was coming towards him, a tail of more than twenty other people following, each armed.

Tim came up with them and tilted a questioning eyebrow. Jason explained, and there was a quiet muttering among the group. One of them, a scruffy old man with a look of wire and whipcord, grunted. "They got him. Only reason the dog couldn't follow. Got him in a vehicle. So what do we do about it?"

Mark's voice was quiet, with a deadly edge. "I'm going to find them, save him if he's alive, bury him if he'd dead - and a lot of them with him if that's so."

The old man grunted. "Where you gonna look?"

Mark turned slowly, looking about him while they watched. Stormy came alert, her ears up, while she pointed. Mark halted, and his whole body seemed to lean towards something. Involuntarily everyone went still, and far in the distance, they heard the same thing that dog and man had heard. The opening shots of a battle. Mark was gone, running for his jeep. He vaulted in and was accelerating even as it lined out for the town. Tim snapped two words at Jason and dived for his own vehicle, Jason right behind him. No one was standing still by now, Mark led a line of racing vehicles, but once on the town's outskirts, Tim veered, swinging the vehicle half across the road.

He raised his voice in a clarity that carried to them but no further as the cars halted and drivers leaned out to hear. "We don't go charging in. Just get us killed."

John Arren stepped out of his land cruiser. "Circle, and come in behind the defenders. That way, we're shooting in the right direction, and they know we're with them. Tim and I go ahead. We'll find out what we can and pass it on. No one shoot before we're in position. Watch out for Mark."

He and Tim started their cars and led off while two by two the vehicles followed, more sedately now, as they part-circled the town, edging closer to the sounds of war. An erect figure appeared from behind a building as they closed in.

"Major Kayne, you're Arren, aren't you?"

"I am. What's happening?"

The major was no longer a dapper figure. He was grimy, sweaty - and looking more like a real soldier than he ever had. He nodded acknowledgment at the line of listeners. "They hit us about an hour ago. I had guards, so we had a few minutes warning, but they set fire to houses, shot the people when they ran. They looted a couple of shops." His laugh was bitter. "Did them no good. They were pretty much empty already. We thought we'd taught them to stay away, but they've found friends. There's sixty or seventy of them this time, and they have everything. Guns, grenades, Molotovs, we're dying out there."

Arren nodded. "We're here as reinforcements. Where do you need us?"

The major straightened. *"If the center cannot hold,"* he quoted. And Arren smiled, finishing it.

"Then anarchy is loosed upon the world, The blood-dimmed tide is loosed, and everywhere the ceremony of innocence is drowned. Very well, we'll hold the center. If you have men good enough, have them circle the enemy, take them from the rear, even if only as

snipers staying back. That lot aren't real army, enough die and they'll run."

Jason, listening, wondered if that was so, one of the things he'd picked up amid the trash was several empty packets. He knew about the drug they'd held. It made the user fearless, impervious to pain, and still able to think, to some extent anyway. The Major, a phony or not, was doing well, and it would be wrong to say nothing.

"Excuse me, Mr. Arren, Major, my dog found the site where they'd been. I picked up drug packets there." He fished one out of his pocket and offered it. The Major took it, showed it to Arren, and both men winced.

"I see," Major Kayne said slowly. "That explains a lot." And to John Arren. "Your men have a right to know about this. They should be told, and then if they stay, it's their choice."

Arren took a second packet Jason produced and walked down the line, talking, showing the packet, and explaining what it meant. Two cars pulled out of the line and drove away before he returned.

"They're the only men in their family. They're needed; the others will stay. Now, Major, your orders?"

Jason knew that there was a minute there when the major almost told the truth, but he saw this was no time to sit about confessing and watching his town fall apart. He nodded. "Thank you, Mr. Arren. Take the center of defense if you will." He pointed. "That way, and I'll see you get more ammunition as it's required."

There was no sign of Mark that Jason could see. He'd swung off, to come around behind the enemy probably, find Fred and get away with him, and, thought Jason; if he succeeded, he'd be one of the luckiest guys ever known. He got back into the car and sat there with Stormy half across his lap, Arren led, and they drove slowly through town to where the greatest volume of shots, cries, and shouts sounded. Tim halted the car short of the worst of it and signaled everyone to join him. John Arren spoke when they were ready, all eyes on him.

"Don't shoot in a hurry. Take your time. Never waste ammunition. Find a target and aim for the center mass. Better two shots two men than twenty that miss. This lot won't scare, won't run until they've lost half their number or more. Even then, they may not run. Don't show yourself to make the shot that means you may die right along with your target. The idea here isn't to die for your side but to see the other sons of bitches die for theirs. Now, follow me, stay under cover. I'll allocate your stands."

Jason and Stormy got an old house; the porch's front wall was solid stone blocks mortared together. In three places, there were pillars, one each end and in the middle. He inspected those and saw they too were stone blocks, sheathed in wood, and he grinned. The fake army wouldn't expect that. He could stand up using them as cover and drop down behind the front wall, and in both places, it was unlikely anything they had would come through. He settled in, Stormy sighed, went to sleep by him, and Jason waited.

CHAPTER TWENTY

It wasn't that long a wait, although it seemed like it to Jason. After fifteen minutes, he saw a movement, a flash of color. He forced himself to relax, mind in neutral, and then it came again. His smile showed white teeth as he led the figure … held … held … and as it paused, he shot. Forcing down the desire to shout as the figure fell; he kept an eye on it.

There was no further movement, and he allowed his gaze to drift away, waiting for someone else to move, to show. The figure stirred. Jason moved his position, shot again - carefully - and it slumped. Definitely a kill this time. He sat back and patted Stormy, who eyed him sleepily.

"Okay, girl. That's one; let's see how many more we can get while this picnic lasts."

He had two kills and a possible when someone decided to hit back hard. A fusillade smashed into the pillars and wall, and a flying chip of stone slashed diagonally across the corner of his face by his left eyebrow. He dropped down behind the wall and touched where the pain bit in. *Ouch.* Not deep, though it was bleeding freely. He took the bandana from around his neck, tied it across the injury, and sighed. That'd keep blood out of his eyes anyhow. Something he'd read once struck him, and his smile anticipated. Now, if they followed that…

He looked carefully at the wall; it had some crenulations where every second block had an extra one atop it. Like a castle, and while they were only eight or nine inches above their companions, that should do nicely. He dug into his pocket and found something he'd picked up a couple of days back from the bedroom of a deserted ranch. That would help. He sat there, placing his position, grooving it into his head, into his body, practicing the planned moves in his mind.

Then he waited, staying silent, under cover, not shooting again, and shots started from the other side. Searching fire, designed to seek out a defender. Jason sat quietly, and the fire died away, there was a pause, and it started again. He remained motionless. It took almost a quarter of an hour, but the attackers were impatient - and hadn't read the same book, Jason reflected as he listened to faint sounds in front of him. A muttering, the graunch of a step, a brush of clothing against wood. He poised, ready.

Men burst out from the buildings slightly to his left, running, guns in hands, teeth bared in anticipation. Here was where planning paid off. Jason had long since been ready. He moved to where he could aim between the low crenulations, and shot, once to the body mass, switched aim, fired again, then again. The targets returned fire, but he was unseen and the fire unconcentrated. He shot twice more, a miss and a peripheral hit. But they'd had enough. Six had come running, two were running back, a third limping but moving fast, a fourth staggering behind them, to go down before he reached cover.

That one rolled, groaning and then yelling, "Hey, hey, you bastards, come'n help me." "The bastards" appeared disinclined to do anything of the sort. His target was holding one hand pressed hard against his waist, but Jason could see blood running through the fingers. He contemplated that. If he shot, he revealed where he was. If he didn't, the man would die, whether he got to cover or not. However, while he was in the open, one of the others might take the risk.

Jason sat. The man screamed curses, his voice weakening. The shouting trailed into silence as he coughed. Blood came in a gush from his mouth, his hand fell away, and his body slumped, twitched, and stretched out. There was a burst of angry yells from where the others had gone to cover, and Jason smiled tightly. A flicker of movement showed as someone, enraged, moved carelessly. Jason shot. There was a howl, and he sat back. As his dad had told him, *don't lose your temper when you fight. It makes you do silly things.*

He breathed in deeply, held it, and breathed out, feeling his heartbeat slow. A soft whistle came from his right, and he glanced there. Mark eyed him.

"John wants to know how you're doing."

Jason pointed in silence, and Mark edged around to where he could see. He looked, and there was a surprising respect on his face when he turned to look at Jason. "Five, huh?"

"They're *fake* army, remember."

Mark nodded. "Yeah?"

"They're used to going five or six to one. Right now, they're spread out, so they don't see the beating they're taking. My bet, once they see how many they're losing, they'll run. Tell Mr. Arren that. We should get as many as we can before they know."

It might have been true, he thought a time later, but most attackers appeared high on something, and they seemed to think it made them invincible. It didn't, and after half a day, word came to close in where possible. Jason moved to find the fight concentrated now along the main street, attackers to the north, and his side to the south. And, watching up and down the line, he thought the attacking numbers had shrunk to under half.

Stormy had moved with him and was asleep at his feet again. Jason took a drink from his water bottle, gave some to his dog, and watched the street. It was quiet, hot, still, and he grinned as it reminded him of a string of the old John Wayne westerns he'd enjoyed watching with Grandpa. A movement to his right attracted his attention, and he stared. There was a burbling sound, not understandable words but the noise a toddler makes when they're intent on their pursuits, and abruptly a small figure trotted out into the street after a rolling ball.

Jason hesitated. How the … *who* the *hell*…? He slid along the wall to where he could sprint for her, and another figure was before him. It wore army camouflage, and while the hair was graying it moved fast and lithely, scooping up the child and spinning to race for cover again. A barrage of shots peppered the surroundings. The figure jolted but barely slowed, vanishing behind a building, to the whoops of Jason's side. He looked after it, had that been who he thought? Nah, couldn't have been.

He went back to watching, and a short time after that word came again: "Advance."

Jason obeyed, dodging from cover to cover, shooting where he saw a target but not unless it was a good shot. Then, in front of him, a building seemed to explode, and he jumped back. That'd been a rocket-propelled grenade. He'd heard the Fakes had some of the launchers; he looked to either side, making sure he was well separated from anyone else on his side. Another grenade landed, and there was a thin scream. His heart was pounding. He breathed in, forced calm, and moved forward again, zigzagging, eyes and ears alert. At his heels, Stormy snarled savagely.

Jason turned to the sound, his gun leveled. Something moved, and he shot, a sudden horror taking him even as his finger tightened. That hadn't been a friend? Had it? He saw the figure clearly then and felt his body relax. No friend. The sagging body wore the army uniform, but under the loose tunic, the "Death's Army" t-shirt showed. It was filthy, the red background half obliterated by ominous stains, but he could recognize it. The lead band of the Black Rock brigade and no one who wore *that* would be a friend.

The man must have been half-bright; he'd waited for Jason's line to pass him and planned an ambush - not counting on a keen-eared dog.

Jason reached down to pat her. "Good girl, nice work. Let me know if there's any more like that, okay." A muscular tail whacked his leg, and he smiled, speaking under his breath to whoever might perhaps be still around to hear. "Thanks for her, Mrs. Hayer."

Jason moved towards the prone figure. Dimming eyes studied him, and teeth showed red. "Don't bother, kid, I'm done. Got it high in the back an' can't move."

Jason let the dying Death's Army follower see him relax, but unobtrusively he remained alert. A dying wolf had one priority: take your enemy with you. Jason would, and he doubted this one was different. "What's your name?"

"Why?"

"Don't you have a family?"

The man choked, laughing. "Not anymore, and they wouldn't have cared anyway." He fumbled a hand into his pocket. "Got something I can pass on though. You might as well have it, pretty bit of sparkle, here..."

Jason knew the moment the shape showed against the fabric. He shot, and with only seven feet between them, all his practice paid off, saving two lives. The grenade rolled free, pin still firmly in place, and the dying man smiled as blood poured from his ruined hand. "Smart kid. What's *your* name?"

"Jason Waterhawk Trevalen."

"Indian?"

"Diné" He saw the man didn't know the word and added. "Navajo."

"Well, kid, gonna take my scalp?"

Jason snorted. This had to be the oddest conversation he'd ever been part of. "No use to me." He hesitated, wanting to say something and not knowing what.

The man looked back, smiled, a rictus more than amusement, spoke two words then, "Gye Spencer," and Jason saw the life die out in his eyes.

He stepped over to the body and looked down. "You died well, Gye Spencer. May those wherever you go, know that." He stooped and collected the gun, checked it, empty, and patted lightly over the clothing. That grenade had been the only one, the jacket lying beside him was a fine one though, soft leather, with silver buttons. He took it carefully. It'd been cared for, and didn't fit too poorly. He nodded to the prone figure and signaled the dog to move out.

A thought came to him then, and he spun, looking around

for someone on his line. Finally, he saw one and called softly. "Mr. Connell, Mr. Connell?"

"What is it?"

"The enemy. I just found one who was mostly paralyzed. He tried for me with a grenade. I got him before he pulled the pin but warn the others. They could have passed them around, so most could have one. He said he'd got jewelry to give me. He could have pulled the pin and lain on it to die too. Move him and get it."

From where he crouched, Jason could see Alec Connell's face harden. "Likely. I'll pass it on. Good thought." He was gone, and Jason shifted position, pacing forward.

About three minutes later, he heard the blast of a grenade and wondered, but not for long. Connell slipped towards him. "You were right. One of them was lying on a grenade. Everyone should be warned by now, though. How are you doing, son?"

"Stormy and I are in one piece still. What's happening?"

"We've taken out more than half, and we've people circling to catch them from behind. If we can, we'll wipe out the lot. They're too dangerous to let run."

He was gone again, and Jason nodded after him. That was true and while in the world that had been, it would have horrified most, this was a new world, and practicality ruled.

****

The battle lasted all night. John Arren was right, and they had drawn all of the Fakes into a circle. By dawn, the Black Rockers realized it, and their only battle now was to break out and flee. However, word had gone out to all the nearby ranchers, and they released those they could afford to have gone a day or two. This reinforced the circle, which, hourly tightened until finally, only a dozen Fakes were remaining in a single building that was completely surrounded.

Jason hissed as he saw someone waving a white rag from a window there. Mark had joined him and snorted. "They've got a nerve, after some of what they pulled. Arren isn't going to agree to that."

Jason agreed. "Their word's no good anyhow. He knows that. Let them go, they promise to go away or be good, and that'll hold right up to the minute they recruit more and come back."

John Arren spoke from behind them. "And as you say, I know that."

"So, what do we do?" Mark queried, looking at the building. "That place is built like a rock. It was the town hall back in the nineteen hundreds. We'd get a lot of people killed trying to break in."

Jason had been remembering, and he spoke now. "Told you about them and what that girl said to me. Grenades might not take the building down, but it'd break the windows and with them open…"

Arren's smile bore all the chill of a hard winter. "Do unto others," he quoted. "Yes. And we can. Even so, there's a fair distance between these buildings and that one, and anyone running into the firing zone won't run back."

Jason started talking. With a circle of men keeping the Fakes occupied, they set out to collect grenades. With sufficient found to break every window in the building, and Jason with his supplies, they took time out to eat, drink, and rest two hours, then assemble again. Alec Connell had contributed Jason's supplies, and now John Arren was looking him over.

"You can do this?"

"It's no more than a hundred feet. Less from a couple of places. Mark knows how to help me, and I was pretty good when I was a kid."

The man opposite him shut his mouth on an instinctive comment. No, this wasn't a kid any longer. He saw the eyes, the blood-encrusted wound that slanted along one side of the face, the light tread, and the alert, balanced movements. The dog at his side was a fighter too. No kid, and the plan was a fair one – if it worked. And if so, it could save many lives, or save him from the bitter choice of letting this marauding bunch walk free.

"Okay," he turned to those awaiting his word. "Start the

music and see if they dance."

Grenades hit the building walls. The place was stone, and they did little damage to that. The windows were glass and lasted only as long as it took for the grenade to burst. There was a concentrated minute or so when to those inside, it must have sounded like the trumpet of doom, then everything fell silent, and as they understood the walls were unharmed, those waiting heard the burst of laughter and jeers from within. Arren grinned. "Your turn, Mr. Trevalen. Play the music and make it hot."

Jason moved into position, Mark beside him, Stormy hanging back where he'd ordered her to stay. Alec Connell had had souvenirs from long ago, which he'd loaned to Jason. They'd been fine weapons in their time, and they'd still work against the enemy. He eyed the distance, the slight breeze – that'd not be a problem, but he must watch in case it grew stronger – he shifted position slightly, so he was equally between four targets, raised the bow, and shot.

The second the arrow left the bowstring, his hand went out for the next. Mark slid it into his fingers, and he shot again. A third shot and a fourth, He moved along the targets shooting, a double shot to each, and he started again. He could reliably reach six windows, and there'd been twenty arrows, all prepared for his effort. He shot until the quiver was empty, and Arren, who was watching with a good set of binoculars focused on the windows, grunted his satisfaction.

"That's started the job. Now we wait."

It didn't take that long. Smoke began drifting out of the shattered windows, and the jeers turned to shouts. The yelling increased, then the coughing began. A white rag was waved violently out of a window, and Arren shook his head at the looks toward him.

"No. This is what they've done to women and kids. If we show mercy, they'll come back with twice as many, and it'll be us needing mercy. Anyone think we'd get it?"

Heads were slowly shaken. None thought this lot knew

the meaning of the word. They understood how likely it was that sooner or later, it would be ranches and the town dying if they backed off now. It was brutal but realistic. As Connell had said when this was discussed earlier, "A dead enemy lays no second ambush."

Arren signaled, and the shooting continued. The smoke thickened, and abruptly a man burst out of the door. He had a gun in each hand and was firing wildly. He howled as he hurled himself at them. Jason saw the gun line up and shot, as did four of those by hm. The man dived face-first into the dust and stayed motionless. Another broke from the building and died when Alec Connell lined up his old rifle and put two bullets into the runner's heart.

From the building, two shots sounded, and Arren looked around. "Not prepared to die fighting, I guess. Wonder how many are left in there?"

On the other side of the building, they heard a volley sound. Shouting, then a second volley. "Maybe five or seven," Alec commented. Then, "Hey, look up there!"

They looked, to where on the roof two men hauled along a third. They dodged behind a peaked part of the roof, there was a shot, and one man tumbled almost casually down the roof's slope and landed sprawling. He made it to his feet and yelled up.

"Donny, get them, 'fore they get me."

Donny, Jason mused, was too slow, the man in the street died, and from the roof, another man toppled, landing limply in a way that indicated he wouldn't be getting up again either. The man left on the roof must have thought any chance better than none. He came into view running, a short spurt over a level section that gave him some impetus as he jumped for a roof from the old building where he was. He screamed when he saw he'd missed, flailed briefly, and crashed into the street with the sound of breaking bones. His head hung to one side, and no one bothered with a finishing shot.

Connell pursed his lips. "I make that up to three left in there."

Arren agreed. "Question is, why aren't they coming out? Could they have found some place to hide in there?"

"Nope," Connell shook his head. "Couple of places they might think'd work; they won't in the long run. Just wait a while."

They did, some sitting, others standing until smoke was sucked into the building as a door opened somewhere inside. Alec Connell yelled a warming. The last three came bolting out, guns firing, lips peeled back in snarls of hate, eyes glazed with whatever they'd taken to nerve themselves to the attack. They died as they ran, toppling forward, and the shooting died away.

The building burned all night. In the morning, the group scoured it, finding three bodies. The third, and unexpected, was that of a woman, her body dumped in a steel cupboard, but they could see she'd died before the fire once she was removed from it.

Connell swore. "Jane Deaver. Lived with her ma and pa out a ways. Old, crippled they were, she came back from L.A. to look after them. Someone should go check on the old folks."

Jason volunteered, and Mark drove since he knew the directions Alec gave. He looked at Jason as they cleared the town. "Hope they're both dead."

"What? Why?"

Then Jason understood, and sighed a little for the civilization that had seen older people cared for when there was no family to do so. There were no nursing homes for older people anymore. If you had family and they would take you in, then you could be all right. If you didn't, or they wouldn't, you'd survive on your own, or not - probably not. No more Government pensions, no more disability benefits. If you had children, you provided for them, or they died because mostly no one else would give you anything. Some kinder souls would - and find out rapidly that every loser nearby would take advantage of them. They were back to frontier society, and contrary to legends of a golden age, he was aware that it hadn't been, nor now would this one be.

They reached the house where Jane Deaver had lived. The door was open, and Mark looked at that as they stopped. "Not a good sign."

"No. Here Stormy, go seek, find people, careful now." The gray dog bounced out of the car and trotted for the door. There was no human voice to be heard, but as she passed the door, she snarled and dived forward, her war cry rising as Jason jerked upright, flung himself out of the door, and raced to join her. There was no need for that. She was coming back to meet him in a ball of whirling fur and screeches. Stormy was growling, whatever she battled was making indescribable sounds, and Jason leaped out of the way as the entire writhing confusion headed in his direction.

CHAPTER TWENTY-ONE

Mark stepped out of the car, picked up a shovel that leaned against the fence, and advanced. Briefly, the whatever-it-was was uppermost and he struck with the flat of the blade. It was a good hard smack, impacting on the hindquarters, and it screeched, broke apart from the dog, and raced for a hallway door. Stormy intercepted it, but by then, both young men had recognized her opponent.

Jason yelled his dog's name, and she reluctantly returned to him. He stared through the open door. "A lynx? That was a lynx. What's it doing here?"

Mark spoke thoughtfully. "You saw Jane's body. How long would you guess they'd had her?"

Jason pondered. "I'd say the body was maybe half a day dead, but there were a heap of bruises, and they'd been done over a while. Could be a week or so, could even have been a couple of days longer."

"And when they took her, they left the door open. Nice weather-tight den."

"Den ... kits ... you think she has babies in there?"

"Yeah, and I think she's found it useful another way too. No need to go out hunting for meat."

Jason retched once at the partly eaten bodies visible through a half open door, but the lynx was a wild animal. To her, they would have been meat, and she needed food to make milk to feed her babies. "How do we get her out of there?"

"Look through the windows, find the kits, shut her off from them, then get them out of the window and away from the house," Mark said practically.

It made sense and was a plan that should work. The two men crept around the house, found the kits parked in the lounge, a sofa rug raked into a nest for them. They looked to be about seven or eight days old, and neither man wanted to kill them. Mark managed to flick a loop of twine to catch the doorknob. They waited until the lynx settled with her kits. Jason made a noise, encouraging Stormy to bark as well, and the female came prowling out of the lounge to find the front door shut. Mark hauled on the twine, and the door between the mother and babies slammed shut, leaving her trapped in the house but away from her babies.

Mark yelled, "Quick, get them out." There was no need to tell Jason to hurry. He could hear the female attacking the door and her screams of rage. He climbed in through the lounge window, bundled the babies, and was out in less than a minute. He raced for the edge of thick shrubbery, tucked them under that, and removed himself at speed. There was a crash as the lynx soared through a previously unbroken window, she screamed again, and one of the babies answered with a tiny meow. She ran to them, and there was silence while all participants considered their positions.

Mark joined Jason, and they hastily entered the house, shut the door behind them, shut the door to the room with the broken window, and leaned against it, panting. Stormy looked up and was patted by both. Jason checked her scratches. He'd clean them out with antiseptic as soon as possible. Maybe there was something here. He said that and went in search of a bathroom cabinet, Mark at his heels.

Both passed the main bedroom and Jason shuddered. "Leave that 'til last?"

Mark nodded. "Yeah, definitely."

There was antiseptic in the cabinet. They tended to the dog's scratches and returned to the lounge where Mark opened drawers and closets. "Nothing worth whatever they did."

Jason looked at him. "That sort don't care. They got to kill someone, got the woman, I bet they found a few things to steal, and they were quite happy."

Checking the place turned up nothing of value, and only the average items of cutlery, crockery, cookware, and bedding. So wordlessly, Jason bundled what remained of the bodies into the bedding, tied it off, and he and Mark took them from the house.

"Where?" asked Mark.

Jason pointed to a dip in the land. "There. Dig that out a foot or two, and then fill it up to level." They dug, making the trench almost three-feet deep in the end and Mark hauling over several rocks from a broken wall near where they dug. Jason went into the house and came out again once that was done, with a faded quilt. "This is old; they probably valued it. Lie it down and put them on it." They did so.

From the house, he'd taken a Bible. He quietly read a verse, laid the Bible between them along with a photo he took to have been these two and Jane, produced a brighter quilt, laying it over the bodies and tucking it in around the bundles, Bible, and photo, and looked down.

"Those that killed you and took her are all dead. Sleep in peace." He took up the shovel and covered the bright quilt, Mark found a spade and helped until the dip was level, and they dragged over the stones laying them in a pattern that would make it difficult for scavengers.

Mark looked over once they were done. "No one will live here again, the house is small, the land isn't that good, and it's too far from anyone."

"What do you think then?"

"Strip any fruit and vegetables, clean out anything worth it in the sheds, and share them with our families." He looked embarrassed. "Or with your friends. If there's anything in the house they'd use, we can take that too. There's a trailer in the shed."

Jason nodded, and they started. The trailer was, to his surprise, both large and in excellent condition. Mark claimed that, and it was agreed. By the time they finished, it was filled, a tarpaulin lashed over the top, and they drove first to the Crispin Ranch where Annie met them looking surprised.

"I thought you were still in town?"

Jason explained their adventures.

"All right, put anything you earmarked for us in the end storage barn. If we don't use it, someone will. The food's good. But why's poor Stormy all scratched up?" Mark arrived in time to hear the question and grinned.

"She got into a catfight, Mrs. Crispin." Annie listened and patted the gray head thrust under her hand.

"Poor old girl, minding your own business, and that nasty cat attacked you. Never mind, I happen to have a big bone in the kitchen with your name on it. You two, where are you going now?"

"To Mark's place, we'll put my e-bike on the trailer, and I can ride back from there. I'll leave Stormy with you."

Jason returned at dusk to find Tim talking to Annie, Stormy settled at their feet. Dinner was quiet, and once they were done, dishes washed and put away, Jason asked the questions that had been with him since the battle.

"Will they take Jane Deaver back and put her with her family?"

"Yes." Tim was certain. "Arren said anyone we know where they came from goes back. Unless someone says they wouldn't want it, or their family wants it otherwise."

Jason smiled approvingly. It felt right that poor girl should lie in her own land with her kin.

"Did they find Fred?" Jason asked.

"Nope, guess it amused that bunch to hide the body, and with them all dead, there's no one to say. Sorry for the family, but not much we can do about it." Jason nodded and changed the subject slightly. "What about that man who saved the baby? The one that ran right out into the street?"

Tim's face cracked into a broad grin. "You mean Major Kayne?"

Jason gaped at him. "Major Kayne, you mean he ran right out in the middle of a battle, to get a baby under cover? I thought he was a phony, not a real soldier?"

Tim looked at him. "I guess there's times a phony comes good, son. And the major surely did. John Arren confirmed him as a major in front of everyone. Said he'd done damn good work in defending the town, and saving that little girl would have got him a medal in the old days. The major went all shades. I tell you, I thought a hell of a lot more of him after everything he'd done. I heard once, cometh the hour, cometh the man. Guess it was his hour."

He met Jason's straight look. "An' you don't need to tell us it's coming up to yours, too. We figured now that lot's done for, we're all right here, and you're rested up, you're figuring it's maybe time you were on your way. Long road to go yet, and it won't get shorter." Jason made to speak, and Annie broke in, her voice kind.

"We know, and don't worry about us. Two of the town families are moving here. Six in one family, eight in the other, along with a couple of cousins. They were worried about their old folks, and I said that if they came here, they'd have a house each, land they can fence and put in vegetables and fruit trees. The old folks can babysit, keep records, anything that's easy work. And it's sense. We don't know how long we'll be able to find gas; and when that runs out, all the work will have to be done by hand. We've got enough land here, and it's safer than many places. They're good people. I know them a bit, and so does Tim. We'll have company for us and a community for the babies to grow up in." Her gaze met his. "You've got family of your own, Jase. It's time you found your dad. If he's - gone - you'd always be welcome here if you want to return."

They talked into the night. His mom's car and the trailer had long been in one of the storage barns. Jason drove it out every two weeks, making sure the battery was charged and that anything used from his supplies was replaced. Tim got out maps and ran his fingers along some of the back roads he knew.

"Problem is that it's been getting on for two years now since the virus. No one maintaining the roads, no law, you've got bandits, plus ordinary people who'll shoot on sight because it's safer for them. The roads are crumbling, and that's far worse on back roads. They were never that good, to begin with. You could go this way." Tim indicated a route. "That'd have you skirting the bigger places. You could lie up during most of the day, drive from a couple of hours before sunset until the light's gone, or through the night if there's a good moon. It'd take longer, but even so, four or five hours of driving at a steady speed, maybe more, and you should be at your ranch well before winter sets in."

Annie touched his hand. "We'll miss you, there'll always a place here for you, but before you can settle, you need to know if your father's alive, Jase. And if he is, it'd be natural for you to stay with him. Look at it this way, once you'd found him, and after a few years on your ranch, there'd be nothing to stop you from coming back to see us. It might be that we could start a regular run between your ranch and here. Trade, buy and sell, learn things from each other. Swap animals to improve the breeds."

That thought sent Jason to bed happy. It was true. If his father wasn't - if he wasn't around - he could return, take up land nearby, work with Tim and Annie and the kids again. But now he was going to the ranch to find the truth, who'd survived, what had happened, and if there was a place for him on his father's land. And Annie was right in what else she'd said. He slept well that night, woke knowing that he would have no more than a day or two more here. The decision made, the road called to him, and he'd answer, see what lay at the end of it, and if needs be, he could make a new decision after that.

****

Almost fifty people came to see him go. Major Kayne and John Arren presented him with a small scroll, a box of seed packets, and two boxes of ammunition. *They covered almost everything,*

Jason thought, and he accepted gratefully. Four of the townspeople who could play lined up, as did twenty people wearing sashes.

"Some of our militia," Arren said as an aside. They formed a double line from the storage barn doorway out to the drive, and down it, Jason walked to his car. He climbed in, allowed Stormy a last pat from Annie, and closed both doors with his dog in the car. He looked at them, his friends, Mark was there, and Gordy, Alec Connell, and so many others he'd met over the months. He smiled, and only those closest knew that his eyes filled with tears.

Jason abruptly remembered that concrete slab he and Fred had found, and called to Tim. "One thing before I go..." He described the slab, the lid, and his thought that it could cover a cellar. Tim gripped his hand.

"Drive well, Jason, remember there's always a place here if you want one."

Jason nodded. He touched the accelerator, and slowly the car moved down inside the double line. At the same time, the four played a song that he recognized with a start as "The Leaving of Liverpool," a song his grandpa had often sung when Jason was small. Who on earth had known that one? With musicians and militia cleared, he picked up speed, turned onto the main road, and glanced in his rear-vision mirror. He'd left one home behind in Seattle. Now he was leaving another. But while if he went back to Seattle, the only thing there for him were graves, here he had something he could remember, a place that would take him back. His smile was wry. It had been a joke of his mom's that home was where, when you had to go there, they had to take you in.

He drove on, Stormy settling comfortably on the passenger seat beside him. He drove all night. If Tim and the maps were right, there was nothing but the occasional ranch on this part of the journey, and he'd make time while he could. That afternoon when he paused to take a break, he set out the wind generator. There was a good breeze, and it would charge the battery for a camp stove and the tent heater. He took to the road two hours later, and around eight that evening, he found an almost derelict barn and backed car and trailer into that, setting up the generator again. Annie had packed him food for a couple of days; he ate some for dinner, drank hot chocolate, curled into his sleeping bag, and slept, Stormy on guard.

The next day he moved on, the Crispin Ranch, and Calexico far behind him now, hope driving him, and kin – if the Great Spirit answered prayers these days – waiting ahead. That night he remembered the scroll tied with a strip of green ribbon, and found it on the floor under the back seat, where he had no memory of putting it. He brought it out, unrolling it carefully.

The lettering had been done by someone who knew calligraphy. The top and bottom of the paper had been slid into a round length of bamboo slit carefully so the paper could be inserted and then most likely, he thought since it seemed to be firm there, glued in. It wasn't parchment, but someone had pasted two sheets of paper together to give the effect, and he smiled, wondering who'd done the work. He held it flat and read the words slowly. And when he had read them, he sat for a long time, thinking, remembering, and feeling deep gratitude that of all the places he might have found, all those where he might have remained a while, he'd stayed with those who'd given him this in farewell.

"To Anyone Who Reads This,

Be it known that the bearer – Jason Trevalen – came to us when our community needed strength, common sense, and courage, and he exhibited those. He shared freely, behaved honestly, and fought for us when the need arose. We owe him the lives of some, and in return, we offer this testament. A good man carries this scroll, and let no one deny our honest appreciation. Should he ever return or send friends to us, our doors will always be open

Major Morgan Kayne
John Dalton Arren
Tim and Annie Crispin
Alec Dylan Connell.

He reread it and sniffed, rolled it up, and tucked it away before pulling out onto the highway driving northeast, watching for anything unusual. There was nothing for all of that day, but he stayed alert, reached the river, and followed that along the road beside it, crossed at the first available bridge, and cruised on slowly. He circled the old Yuma Proving Ground, and after two more days driving, he reached a main highway and cut back towards Blythe, breaking off onto another road before he got there, bringing the map out over and over to check the route. So far, it had been as if the whole country was empty. He'd seen only wandering stock and no apparent signs of people.

That fifth evening towards dusk, he looked for somewhere comfortable; spied a large white house in the distance and slowed, staring across the fields at it. Stormy whined. Jason turned to look where she was gazing and saw a small child waving wildly. He slowed further, and the dog went into a frenzy of barks, growls, and snarling as if what she saw wasn't a child but something lethal, something deadly dangerous, and involuntarily he pressed down on the accelerator. The child jumped back, Stormy, far from winding down, was more and more hysterical, and he trusted her. He didn't know what she sensed, but he wasn't taking the chance that she was wrong.

He whipped the car and trailer around three corners, looked about, saw an old barn, and drove down an overgrown drive towards that. Once there, he backed cautiously into cover and leaned back in the seat, scratching the dog's ears.

"Okay, girl, what was that all about?" Stormy whined, thrusting her head under his arm, and he hugged her. "Yeah, yeah. Okay, let's see the map again."

He must be about four miles by road from that house and the kid, a third of that straight across country. The smart thing would be to drive on, but – he grinned – his mom had always said she didn't need a cat when she had him. It was the truth; he liked to know things, and he'd never seen his dog behave like that towards a child before. He set up a camp stove, they ate, and he looked over the car and trailer.

"I don't think I should leave them here, girl. It's the obvious place if someone comes hunting me. So, I'll move on a'ways and use the e-bike. You want to come along?" Stormy made it clear she wasn't about to stay behind, and he grinned. "Okay, you can come along. Now, let's find a good place to leave the gear."

He found one another four miles further along, drove the car and trailer under cover there, and saw to it that both were secure. With Stormy behind him in the silent e-bike's trailer, he headed into dusk, until in the distance, he saw a light. He closed at a walking pace and nodded once he could see the building's silhouette against the clear night sky. That was the house. Now to find out what had spooked his dog so badly?

CHAPTER TWENTY-TWO

Jason found a track that circled the building. The light he'd seen at the front matched another at the rear. After he parked the bike by a tree, he whispered a command. Stormy ranged out; she found no one and returned, but by that time, he was at the back door and realized that the light was in the kitchen. He broke off small branches, stuck them into his hatband to break up any straight lines, and crept close enough to look into the window. Three people - two women and a man - sat there, drinking something, and he could hear their voices.

"Damn kid couldn't get him to stop."

"Wonder why, always worked before?"

"Said there was a dog in the car going crazy, barking an' growling at her."

"Yeah? Damn. And he had a full trailer and a real fancy car too. Bet there'd have been good pickings in that lot."

A chill slid down Jason's back. Those post-holocaust books of Mom's, there'd been people in those found it easier to let others do the work then plunder what they collected - and some who were even worse. He stepped back, looked around, sent Stormy on a sweep, and then moved back to listen once she reported no one was out here with him. The woman was talking.

"Yeah, and we're almost out of..." something he couldn't hear... "I wan' a good stew. Last one's on the stove now." She stood up, walked to the stove, and looked to one side of that. "Joey, get these bones out of here, drop them down the hole at the back."

There was an indistinct complaint, and the man joined her, scooped up a sack, and started for the door. Jason moved around the corner of the house and followed. There was something about this that tweaked all his nerves. He saw a flashlight bobbing down the path, heard a slithering crash as something was tossed down, and retreating footsteps. A door opened and closed, and all was quiet again.

Jason walked to where he'd heard the crash and looked back at the house. If he was right, no one there would see a flashlight, the more so if he showed a light only briefly. He turned down the light, so it was barely a glimmer, and investigated. Yes, there was a hole here. He dropped lightly down and, holding the flashlight below the lip, he opened the sack and shone it on the contents; bones, fresh, bloody - he threw up violently - and human. He'd seen enough of his mom's work to know what he was looking at. He vomited again and swiped his sleeve across his mouth, kicking loose dirt over the vomit. He vaulted out of the pit and hissed softly at Stormy. She fell in behind, and within minutes, he was back where he'd left the e-bike. He started that and went silently along the highway to where he'd parked his car and trailer. With the bike loaded, he and the dog in the front seat, he sat a while, thinking.

How much was any of this his business? If he took the tale of what he'd seen to some local, would he even be believed? Or would they turn on him instead? Jason sighed. It fell under one of his mom's maxims, he guessed. That "the only thing necessary for the triumph of evil is for good men to do nothing." And if it'd been someone he knew who disappeared, and he found out that someone had known and had shut their eyes to it, how would he feel? On the other hand, no one required him to be a martyr. He'd go take a look at the locals, and see if any of them were receptive.

He looked up the nearest town on his map. It'd had about thirty thousand people; it could be down to a few hundred. And that was odd too. Less than two years after the virus, why would those people need to do that sort of thing? There were livestock all over. Almost every empty farmhouse still held food and supplies. He spent the night locked in the car with Stormy, ate cold food from cans, and moved on at first light.

The town was barricaded. He drove around the outside, and so far as he could see, every road coming into it was blocked. Only the main street in and out was open. He hesitated. Just how much danger was he putting himself into if he went into the place and couldn't leave freely? He shrugged and decided to take the gamble. He drove in, wound the window part way down as he approached the barricade, and hailed the man standing there in what looked like a rather battered sheriff's uniform.

"Hello, sir, I'd like to buy a few things if that's acceptable?"

The man nodded. "Gold or trade. Now, what's your name?"

"Jason Trevalen."

"I'm Sheriff Ted. Where you coming from, an' where you going?"

"From Seattle, going to a ranch in New Mexico."

"Kin there?"

"Yessir, my dad's got the ranch."

The tired-looking sheriff leaned on the blockade. "You come all the way from Seattle since ever'body got sick?"

Jason decided to open up. A sympathy vote could be useful. "Mom was an orthopedic surgeon there. I was at school," he allowed his mouth to sag in sorrow. "I wanted to be a doctor. Guess that isn't likely now. Parents were divorced, school time with Mom, vacations on the ranch. She got the bug, and when she was dying, she said to take her car and trailer and get back to the ranch." He deliberately remembered her dying, and what he knew would happen did so. A fat tear rolled down his face. "I been on the road too long, but I'm going home."

The sheriff nodded. "Okay, son, you go ahead and get whatever anyone will sell you. Which reminds me, what roads did you drive to get here?" Jason detailed them, and the sheriff frowned. "Surprised you got through. We know a few folks have started out that way and not made it."

Jason smiled sadly. "Only thing I saw was a little girl waving me down. I'd have stopped, but my dog went wild, growling and snarling, barking at her. It sort of freaked me out, so I kept driving." He noticed the man straightening, a tenseness coming over him, and stayed casual. "Right outside a big white house. Huge place. Stormy's trained, so I thought maybe she knew something I didn't. Better safe than sorry."

"Yes," the sheriff agreed. "Much better these days. Tell you what, my Letty makes great doughnuts. Once you've done shopping, why don't you drop in and sample a few." He gave directions; Jason nodded and drove on. He filled up on gas and bought fresh food items, trading gold for them. Everything was overpriced, but Jason had no complaints. Fresh bread and butter were a luxury, as was the large jar of raspberry jam.

He found the sheriff's house and was greeted by a middle-aged woman who smiled at them. "Nice dog, come in. My husband says you've traveled a long way."

They were sitting over a plate of doughnuts with mugs of strong coffee when the sheriff returned. He shook hands, asked about the trades, ate a doughnut, then got down to business. "I said the way you came has been seeing a lot of folks not making it."

Jason nodded. "How do you know?"

The sheriff scowled. "At first, we didn't. But I hear things. An' I put two and two together. Anyone with a loaded trailer, anyone driving that particular stretch of road, they seem to just disappear. It's a whole long piece, near a hundred miles, and some of them who vanished, well, let's say they weren't idiots nor easily taken. I figured whoever was doing it – if someone was – was doing it clever. And a kid'd be that. With things the way they are, there aren't many'd pass by a small kid waving at them an' all desperate-looking. But your dog thought there was something off about it, and you say she's trained."

Jason nodded. "I found an old lady dying. She was upset about Stormy, so I said I'd take her, look after her. I promised. An' I have. Mrs. Hayer said she'd been trained, give me a list of commands, and we've done them together ever since. It's true she went crazy when that kid stepped out waving me down." He laughed, looking a bit embarrassed. "Reminded me of the movies when it turns out the kid's a vampire or something. Silly, really. No such thing."

He buried his face in the coffee mug, watching unobtrusively. Had that been enough? The sheriff was considering; then his gaze met Jason's. "Maybe not, son. And maybe there's worse things than vampires. Tell me, could you go straight back to that house? Do you know just where it was?" Jason nodded. "Would you mind doing it?"

Jason sighed. "No, sir, Sheriff, I think if you believe there's something going on there, it's my duty. Tell you, too, As I drove past, it looked to me as if there was a second drive, one that went in a big loop right around the place, from the road and back to it again. We could go in from the back if I'm right about it. Maybe scout the place?"

"Yes," The sheriff was considering that. "Smart idea. All right, we can give you and the dog a bed for the night, and I'll get some of my people in tomorrow. We don't have to go charging in, just scout like you say, but if we find anything..."

His face set. Jason thought he wouldn't like to be one of those in the big white house if there was something found by this man. He was confirmed in that opinion after a good night's sleep, a hearty breakfast, and the arrival of a dozen men, all of whom listened quietly to Sheriff Ted, then to Jason, and nodded agreement to the proposals. They'd circle the place at dusk when it was light enough to see things, but people looking out of the windows wouldn't see far.

The sheriff, with Jason and Stormy in the passenger seat, led off. They came to the circling road, and Jason pointed it out. "If we park the vehicles here, we can walk down the road and come in from the back if that sounds good, Sheriff?" It did, and fourteen heavily armed men crept in a half-circle to where Jason signaled a halt. The sheriff spoke in low tones.

"From the look of it, this should be in line with the back of the house. No hurry, keep your eyes open for anything. Don't start shooting, don't yell or call out, assemble at the back of the house and wait."

Jason moved off in the direction of the pit, the sheriff behind him, the others spreading out. He made a point of apparently almost walking into it then shying sideways. "What's that?" was the sheriff's demand.

"Garbage pit, I guess." He shone a light into it and shied back very obviously.

"See something?"

The other men were halting to come back. Jason dropped into the pit – neatly obliterating his original footprints – and shone his flashlight directly into the sack's mouth, showing the bloody bones. He retched, looked up, and in the glow, they could see his face was greenish-white as he looked at those around him.

"My mom was a surgeon. Those are human bones."

Sheriff Ted joined him, tipped the sack out, and looked at the bloody remnants of someone that tumbled across the earth. "He's right."

"You sure, Sheriff, it ain't a bear?"

"Nope," he stirred one with a toe. "Human. Butchered from the look of it. Guess we know why some haven't been making it through this stretch of road into town." There was an almost subliminal growl from the listeners as that sank in. The sheriff straightened. "All right, we go in, anyone fights, kill them." He looked at Jason. "You hang back, son. People get excited. I don't want them seeing you, not recognizing you for a second or two, and shooting."

Jason had no problem with that. He didn't want to be shot by mistake either. "I can watch the back for you, Sheriff. I'm a fair shot. Anyone comes running out and not calling my name; I'll shoot them in the leg."

"Do it." He turned. "Okay, everyone, listen up. I'll open the door. You go past me, either side, clear each room. Once the first floor's clear, we go up the stairs."

Jason settled himself into what looked to be a firewood shed. He noticed the house's back door had been left unlocked, silly, or had the occupants assumed they'd never be suspected? The guys weren't making much noise. With the door wide open, he could hear the odd scrape, but nothing to wake a sleeper or anyone involved in doing something. That changed abruptly.

There was an incoherent bellow of rage, and someone started shooting. Someone else screamed, a child was howling, two men shouted, and a woman screamed again and again. Jason waited. A man came scuttling around the side of the house, making for the drive behind, and Jason recognized him. The one who'd taken out the sack of bloody bones. He had a bag in one hand, and the whites of his eyes showed in the twilight - a volley of shots rang out inside, and the man spun to dive in a different direction - even as Jason shot. The man went down, rolling, clutching at his leg, and howling wordlessly.

The sheriff came out after several minutes and looked over at the boy.

"Leg?"

"Just like I said."

"Good, rest are all dead, but I'd like a few questions answered." Jason wanted to ask about the child and decided not to. If she'd survived, he'd find out soon enough. If not, he didn't need to know. The sheriff ambled over to the man who crouched, holding his leg and glaring up.

"Who're you? What right you got to attack us? I'll get me a lawyer and sue your ass, bankrupt your stupid town. "

Most of the men were outside again by now, and one of them started laughing. "Lawyer? Sue us? You vicious stupid..." He moved into a description of their captive's appearance, brains, morality, and hopes of anything whatsoever in this life or the next. The sheriff intervened.

"That'll do. We know who and what he is." He turned to the captive. "I'm going to ask you a few questions."

"Don't have to tell you anything. Gonna kill me anyhow."

The reply was almost gentle. "That's right. But there's ways an' ways of dying. Talk, and it'll be quick and clean, don't talk – and scream until you do. Don't matter about those in the house. There's no one left to call you on it. And after what we found, there's no one here who'll have any scruples about making you answer."

Jason, standing in the shadows, nodded. Sounded as if they'd been able to identify some of the belongings.

****

After that, it was an unpleasant business, but finally, they had all the information they were likely to get. Meantime, the men took turns going in and out, bringing supplies, property, papers, and valuables to be piled into the vehicles.

The sheriff looked down. "All right. If you know anything more, better tell us now."

He received a look of hatred and a snarl. "Go to hell."

Sheriff Ted nodded. "You before me, mister. Joe, get the rope."

That, too, was messy and initially noisy, but faster, and once the body swung without movement, the sheriff turned to look into the corner where Jason stood. "What do you think, son?"

"There was rain last night. Burn the house once you've got everything out you can use," Jason said quietly. "That way, it can't be a base for that again, and it clears the bodies too. Fire cleanses."

The sheriff nodded. When the convoy finally drove away into the quiet darkness – without any other person added to their number – there was a reaching pillar of fire behind them.

Jason stayed another night, and in the morning, he and the sheriff talked, the lawman asking, "You knew about them?" Jason explained. "So you weren't too sure how we'd react. Fair enough, son. Locals can be funny about some things, but they weren't any of ours. Mind you, you had no way of knowing that, and you did us a favor. No idea how many they could have killed if you hadn't gone out of your way to let us know. If you come back this way, you drop in, my Letty she does like that dog of yours. Guess I'll have to look out for one. What'd you say they are again?"

Jason grinned. "A Docopoo. Could look for a pomshee otherwise, smart, feisty, easily trained as well, and small." They parted with good wishes on both sides, the barricade was pulled back, and Jason drove into a morning of clear blue skies and a slight breeze. Somewhere during that day as he drove, he found he was singing.

"A new day's come – a new moon's risin'
I take my chances on the blue horizon."

He had, he thought as Bryan's song continued. He'd taken a chance there, but it had worked out, and there'd be no more people vanishing from the road.

****

He drove carefully all day; the road had cars or other vehicles on it. Some pulled into the side of the road, others askew across the highway. Twice he stopped to check a truck where it looked as if it could hold valuable items. The second had maps which he took back to the car and laid out on the front seat to study. Judging by them, this driver had come from a depot in his dad's area. Interesting, the truck had been empty, but documents with the maps suggested that the depot, if still unlooted, could have stock that would be useful. He took maps and papers; better no one else, other than those who already knew about the depot and its contents should get to see the information..

Stormy laid a hopeful paw on his arm and whined. "Want a run, girl? Okay. I'll pull over as soon as there's a better area." He did so, and for an hour, they played. Jason practiced with the handgun and ran Stormy through her commands. He drove on after that, beginning to watch for a place to stop overnight. That came almost at dusk when he saw a long driveway curving off to the right, and in the distance, it seemed to be leading to a sprawling house on the hillside.

He slowed and patted the gray head pushed against his arm. "Yeah, here, I think. What do you say, girl?" She barked softly, and he grinned. "I'll take that as a 'yes.' Let's go take a look." The driveway was deteriorating. *Not surprising,* Jason thought, *considering that it's about twenty months since the virus first hit.* He pulled up outside the house and looked at it. Nice, a family home most likely, and an old one; the sort of place that someone had built as four rooms and added another room every generation or so. A large garage at right angles to the house with four vintage cars visible through the open doors. And they'd been there a while; debris was blown against them.

He let Stormy out while he drove the car and trailer cautiously along the back of the garage, where it wouldn't be seen from the main road or the driveway. He stepped out of the car and paused. There, along the lea of the garage in front of him was a man standing looking at him. Jason waited. Nothing happened. The man continued to stare, no movement, no comment or greeting. It felt – off. Stormy appeared abruptly and approached the silent figure, whining. The man exploded into action. In a fraction of a second, he had a short-hafted axe in one hand and leaped for the dog, shouting something in a hoarse voice that simmered with rage.

Jason yelled in response. "Hey, it's all right, she won't hurt you. She likes people. Hey, stop that." As the man took a swing, missing the dancing dog by the length of her fur. Jason leveled his handgun and spoke slowly, in loud clear tones. "Stop where you are. Stormy, come here."

The dog obeyed – the man did not. Instead, he turned to follow Stormy's retreat, seemed to see Jason, and charged at him, axe swinging up. Jason took one look at the twisted face, filled with an unreasoning rage, and shot. The man staggered, screamed, and came on. Jason shot again, then again as it became clear this was life or death. The attacker faltered, stopped, and slowly slumped where he stood. Stormy snarled, and Jason waited. Their attacker fell over onto one side, half-curled, then straightened out, shuddered, and went limp, and Jason took what felt like his first breath in minutes. Stormy nosed the motionless body then pranced back to where Jason could drop his hand to her head. He blew out a long sigh.

"Wow, I wonder what all that was about. Let's take a look at this place. It looks good." He revised that opinion the moment he opened the door. What it looked like was one thing; what it smelled like was another. It stank of human waste, of rotting food, of unwashed human, and of death. He went looking and found the latter in a bedroom as expected and with a letter left on a bedside cabinet, which was not unexpected, although the contents were. He read and recent events became clearer.

Stormy sensed his emotions and came thrusting her nose into his hand. "Yeah, nothing we can do but bring him inside to be with them. Poor guy, brain damage, they said, couldn't bring themselves to kill him before they died. Maybe they thought the death toll would be a lot less, and some of their friends would come here, take him with them."

He remembered some of what he'd seen and shook his head. "The way things are, they wouldn't have."

He trawled through the house, using one of his lanterns as the light faded into blackness. A few items he could use, a few tins or packets, but almost everything edible was gone. He guessed the occupant had eaten first what he liked. Once he was starving, the rest would have gone - or maybe not. The power was still working; they'd had a wind generator. He turned it off, dismantled the generator, and hauled it into a place where anyone casually wandering about would be unlikely to find it. Five years old, one of the commercial types that should work for a couple of decades. If he ever came back this way, he'd know where to find it.

With his gleanings added to the car or trailer, he spent the night in a spare bedroom, woke and ate early, then found a toolshed. It had a good-sized wheelbarrow as he'd expected. With some difficulty, he loaded the body, wheeled it to the main bedroom, and heaved it onto the bed to lie with the two already there. He'd brought a blanket from the spare room, and he laid that over the still bodies.

"I'm sorry I had to kill you, it may not have been the worse way you could have died, though, and now you're together. I took some stuff. It won't be wasted." He paused, could think of nothing more, and turned away, Stormy at his heels as he traversed the long hall and walked out of the wide doorway, shutting the door behind them. He climbed into the driver's seat, Stormy hopped into the passenger side, and he started the engine. Behind him, as he departed, the house was quiet and would remain so. The bewildered raging creature who had inhabited it unwillingly alone was now at peace.

CHAPTER TWENTY-THREE

Jason drove all that day without a break. The teaching of civilization warred against his later knowledge. Someone like that was to be protected, allowances made if need be, they were not to be hurt, they were to be helped, assisted, cared for – and he'd killed the man. But then there'd been no indication he was other than simply violent, and his food had been almost gone. What would he have done then? A hand crept over to stroke his dog.

"I didn't know, girl, and I guess he didn't know we weren't doing any harm. I'm sorry I had to kill him, but it was like Dad said – better him than me." He winced at the brutality of that, rolled the tension out of his shoulders, and shrugged. If he *had* stood there and died, the guy would probably have perished in a couple more months, and Stormy would have gone as well. He drove on, stacking the event in the back of his mind, not to be remembered again unless it was for the lesson. Over-thinking it wouldn't do him any good, and brooding on it would only upset him.

The next night's place he found was an old overgrown campsite. He slept in the cabin, cooked on the barbecue, and showered in cold water. Two days more of driving, and he was – according to the still-standing signposts he saw – coming up on Phoenix. He spent the night in a bedroom in the back of a small house that was empty of life – or death – while he scanned his maps. No, he'd go around the city; he traced roads and nodded as Stormy put her paws on the table to look at the map.

"Bigger places mean more could have survived, and some would look at what we've got and see a lot of stuff worth taking. I'd rather not get into a fight I don't have to." The memory of that still figure lying ... he pushed it away and considered the map again. "No, we can go to Lordsburg, Deming, then north to Socorro. We're getting closer to home, girl." An involuntary smile lit his face. "It'll be great to see Dad and the ranch again."

A thought slipped into his mind, that while the ranch was most likely still there, there were no guarantees his father... he thrust that down too, rolled up the maps, stowed them safely, and crawled into the sleeping bag, switching off the lantern, and settling down. As one of the guys at his school used to say, *manana es otero dia* – tomorrow was also a day.

The next morning, he drove on over what seemed like endless roads over endless days. He was going mostly north now, and while the season was moving into early fall, the weather stayed warm. Each morning he woke with a feeling of anticipation. Each day was closer to Dad and the ranch. Sure, that last place had been completely empty, everyone there had died, but his dad would make it. He was tough. He knew how to manage, to survive. Jason sternly repressed the thought that his mom had been the same and she hadn't. He watched for the signposts, and at last, he saw one that said Socorro. After that, he'd reach Belen, and he could start east towards the ranch.

Socorro was a wasteland. He stopped well out of the town and stared. It had burned. He didn't know if someone had set fires, or if there'd been a natural wildfire that, with few left to fight it, had swept over the town and razed almost all of it to charred timbers and a few concrete buildings that had been strongly enough built to have stayed standing. He instantly decided not to stop there or even to drive through the place when he heard Stormy growling softly. He didn't know why, but whatever was upsetting her wasn't something – or someone – he wanted to meet.

He got out his maps and discovered there was a bypass on both sides. Good. If he waited until dusk, he could take one and drive without lights until he was past the town. In the dark, any person lying in wait wouldn't see which road he was taking and he could be past before they could cut him off.

It worked. Something was moving in the rearview mirror, and Stormy looking back with her window cracked an inch or two, snarled her disapproval of whatever it was, but he was past the town and clear, and he put his foot down for a few miles, before slowing again. It could have been animals. On the other hand, it might not have been, and he wasn't going back to check.

Fortunately, he thought, as he stopped to pour gas into the car's tank, he'd refilled the cans wherever he found gas still available, but they were emptying, and he hadn't been able to refill any for days. He started watching the roadsides. Some of the places out here would have their own gas stores, and better he looked now than after he ran out.

There was no more than a day's worth of gas remaining when he came to a signpost that sent him off a short distance at right-angles to a clump of houses with a general store. There were no signs of life but half a dozen wandering cattle, and – he let out a yelp of joy – a lone gas pump outside the store. He drove the car and trailer out of sight behind the store and sat listening. No sounds bar natural ones, but he should be careful. These days, everyone had likely learned to be quiet and not rush out to strangers. He let Stormy out and spoke to her in a voice that wouldn't carry. "Go look, girl."

She swung silently around the nearest house and vanished. He sat, waiting, hoping there was gas in that tank and maybe more food in the store or the houses. Stormy came padding back and looked at him. Okay. No one around she could find. Gas first. He checked. No power to the pump, no problem, he had a hand-pump on the trailer, and he used that to fill the car's tank, and then every can he had, finding and filling another three from the store.

The store hadn't been looted. It looked like everyone here had died from the virus around the same time and with the place being off the main road and not visible from there either, no one else had found it before he had. Jason walked around it, the store and pump, eight houses, some sheds, and a couple more houses standing alone over to the northeast with cattle nearby. He decided against going to those.

He stayed the night in one of the houses, and in the morning, he raided the store, replenished his food stacks, found sacks of dog biscuits to put in the trailer, then wandered from house to house not taking anything, just looking. He opened the door of the fourth house, and a black form hurtled towards him with a roar. Jason fell back, tripped over the step, and sprawled, rolling while his hand latched onto his gun. He ended up on his belly, his torso and head reared up, while he searched for whatever that was. He focused even as his ears informed him that the whatever-it-was had met Stormy, who wasn't happy about it. They'd ended up around the corner of the house. Jason made it to his feet and ran.

Even as he rounded the house, there was a howl of pain, another one that cut off, and he yelled his dog's name, gun lining up as the antagonist came into view. He lowered it a second later while Stormy came to him. "What in the hell is *that*?"

"That" was a large black shape that seemed to be all fur. He approached and gingerly turned it over with his foot. A dog, what kind he couldn't guess. It was black, the fur was about half a foot long, and he suspected that the dog would have been all bones under that. Someone's pet, they'd died. It had stuck around the only place it knew and resented his intrusion into its territory. The thought briefly crossed his mind to liken this to that other place, and he shut down the memory at once. But if they'd had a dog, they could have dog food still?

He checked and added a few tins to his trailer. He stalked the cattle, however, and saw a solid yearling bull that had drifted away from the small group. He went after it and shot once – blessing Janet's silencer. He only used that for meat, and with luck and care, it'd last a while yet. After that, he worked, hanging the bull to bleed out before skinning and gutting the carcass, and chopping it into steaks and other cuts of meat he could use.

By then, it was evening again, and he hauled the offal away from the house in which he'd spent the previous night while he took the meat into the kitchen there. The power was off, but he laid out a wind generator and set that up to charge. Later he cooked steaks on his portable stove and enjoyed dinner, even as Stormy enjoyed hers uncooked, ending with a large bone, and when they left the following day, he had the meat neatly stowed into one of his two big coolers. That'd last them a while.

A day later, he shot a young deer that halted to look at him from the roadside right on dusk. He stopped long enough to bleed, skin, and gut it, and that night he charged up the tiny cooler he had, and by morning, he was able to pack the second cooler with the meat, and both with frozen gel packs. There was nothing like venison, and there was sufficient to last him and Stormy several days.

The next mid-afternoon, he reached a house that he estimated to be about five miles from Belem. It was up a long winding drive he followed, looking to spend the night, and when he came to the house, it looked empty. Between the constant vigilance, the driving, and doing everything himself, he was weary to his bones, and if this house felt welcoming, he'd spend a couple of nights. He'd made good time since he left the Crispins. He could afford to have a break.

Studying it, as he was, from the circle of gravel in front of the house, he could see it was a good-sized place and attractive. It must have been repainted right before the virus because it gleamed in the sun, and everything about it was neat. Jason parked the car under cover, got out, and stretched. Stormy bounced out and wandered to the door, which, when her master followed, he found to be unlocked. Great, that meant he didn't have to do any damage. He'd never liked having to break into homes. He entered quietly, as there was no smell of death, and he opened the nearest door down the hallway.

He looked, and a gasp of delight came from him as he saw the books. Shelf after shelf, whole walls filled with them. Stormy made a slight sound, and Jason looked where she was staring to see a cat advance. It looked dignified but not aggressive, and the animals touched noses politely. Jason grinned.

"Hey cat, if this is your place, I hope you don't mind me borrowing a book to read. I've read everything I've got with me." Several things hit him then, the first, that the cat was well-fed, an abrupt remembrance that the gravel turning circle outside had been raked, and the third was a low well-bred male voice.

"Of course, young man. Come in. Your dog *is* house-trained?" The voice sounded amused. "I see she's cat-trained anyway."

Jason nodded, too stunned to react in any way but as if this was normal. "She's house-trained, sir, and she likes cats. Um- it really *is* all right if I borrow a book to read? I thought the house was empty, and I thought to stay a couple of nights, but I can go..."

A thin gentle-faced older man rose from an enveloping armchair. "No need for that. I rarely get visitors nowadays."

"I've got food," Jason offered, feeling as if he was in a dream. "I shot a deer the other day, and if you like venison...?"

"I do, I do, and that's very kind of you. I have bread to share. I baked only this morning. Oh, and I have butter as well."

Jason felt saliva flood his mouth. "I haven't had bread or real butter for weeks. You have a cow?"

"A Jersey, and a couple of milking goats as well. I can offer fruit for dessert; we've always had an excellent orchard. The kitchen's this way." He had risen from his chair and patted Stormy as he passed. "There are three spare bedrooms; you are welcome to choose one. What's your name?"

"Jason, Jason Trevalen. I lived in Seattle with my mom until things went bad. I'm on the way to my dad's ranch."

"In times of trouble, family is a great comfort. What did your mother do?"

"She was an orthopedic surgeon." Jason was still feeling bemused. It was as if none of the past couple of years had happened, and he was talking to one of his mom's elderly colleagues again.

"Ah, yes, a fine profession. And your father has a ranch?"

"Yes. I'm on the way there." They reached the kitchen, a large, well-lit room with clean counters, a breakfast island in the center, and several loaves which emitted a delightful smell of new bread from under their covers. Without asking, his host cut two thick slices of bread from a loaf, spread butter generously, placed them on a plate, and handed it to Jason. He took a bite and almost groaned at the taste, texture, and feel of the warm bread.

"That's wonderful. Thank you so much, sir."

The look he received was approving. "I'm Gareth Pearman. My friends call me Gary. As a guest, that is acceptable as well. Now, I suggest that you choose a bedroom, bring in what you would like to have at hand, with the venison first so we can get that started cooking. How would you like it?"

"Baked?"

"Ah yes, with a pastry casing perhaps? We could have a fresh fruit salad for dessert."

Feeling that he was swept up in a riptide but ready to go with the flow, Jason nodded happily. Anyhow, as he knew from his mom's colleagues, a man like this wasn't making suggestions so much as announcing what he intended and wasn't expecting you to differ.

Not that Jason intended to, but he could continue to contribute.

"I have chocolate if you'd like some, sir … Mister Gary? I found a small place down off the main road – eight or ten houses and a general store. I think everyone had died and no one had found the place afterward. The store hadn't been touched; everything there was still there, just sitting on the shelves. I took all the chocolate. There were biscuits, blocks, and loose chocolates in jars, and well, I didn't see sense in leaving it behind."

"Nor would I. Well, we could have a packet of the biscuits, if you have any that are peppermint chocolate. I do like those, I admit."

Jason grinned. "I've got some and a box of the blocks of it too. You would be welcome to have all of those. There are other types I like better."

They started the venison baking in a spirit of mutual goodwill. The meal - eaten some hours later and under the light of a small but lovely chandelier - was superb; the venison delectable in the gravy, the pastry flaky, the vegetables had been fresh-picked, and the fruit was ripe and sweet. Stormy got a slab of the raw meat cut into bite-sized pieces to prevent her from dragging it around and had finished before them. She dozed near Jason's chair while the cat - introduced as Jay– lay curled up by his human.

Replete, Jason sat back and pushed forward the biscuits he'd placed by his side of the table. Gary opened the pack, laid them on a plate, and vanished briefly into the kitchen to return with a steaming coffeepot and two mugs. He filled them, pushed one to Jason, and raised his eyebrows.

"Sugar or milk?"

"Both, if that's all right?"

"No problem," he was assured. Gary considered his words before adding. "Not yet, anyhow. I have all the milk needed, but sugar will run out at some stage. Fortunately for me, a depot was opened near here two years ago. As you may have observed, the railway runs through this area, and a transport company opened a depot just out of Belem to send items from here to Albuquerque/Santa Fe or west to Flagstaff and beyond by rail."

"A large depot?"

Gary smiled briefly. "Large enough for my friends and me." Jason fixed his eyes and the man's face and the older man smiled. "A genuine interest or politeness?"

"Genuine," Jason said flatly. "My dad used to say there's no one and nothing you can't learn from."

Gary chuckled. "Very well, you asked for this. I was a professor at the University of New Mexico until 2030, when I inherited this house and a fair amount of money from a very elderly bachelor uncle. Family home, my great-grandfather owned it before that. I decided to semi-retire at this point, took up a position working three days a week at the Central New Mexico Community College, and came home here for four days a week. Jay knew both places and didn't mind commuting.

"As you can see, this place is somewhat out of the way, so I had a comprehensive eco-power-system put in; cross-wired for a gas generator, solar panels, and wind generator. I was at the college for another six years and chose to retire completely then. I sold my other house in Albuquerque, and as I was sixty-five and still fit and healthy, I thought I'd enjoy a long retirement."

Jason nodded.

"Yes," the tone was wry. "I had all of three years before things went bad, but I have no right to complain. I've been most fortunate. In the past few years, this area has become a place where many people retired. One of the first was what I might term an amateur survivalist. He wasn't obsessed, but he was knowledgeable, and he'd come to it via roleplaying when he was younger. He created several games, made a reasonable amount of money, and chose to retire at fifty. We became friends, and the two of us together with five others who live near here met regularly to live-play and chat."

Gary sighed quietly. "I have since wondered how many other groups there were of our kind and how many survived. Seven older adults, all comfortably off, living in an area of power outages - usually at the most inconvenient times - they'd all done as I did. And under our friend, Ray's influence, we'd all laid in supplies of anything we used regularly. Velda, one of our group, had her granddaughter and her baby come to stay a couple of weeks. The baby had a sore throat. Velda picked it up, passed it on at one of our meetings before she knew, and we all arrived on our doctor's doorstep needing treatment. That was a month before whatever the illness was that struck everyone."

Jason sat up, and Gary noticed. His gaze sharpened. "You know something?'

"Yes, your doctor gave you allodaxin, didn't he?"

"He did," Gary said slowly. "That saved us?" Jason explained briefly, and Gary nodded. "I see. We needed both the minor infection and the antibiotic, that specific one, and then we were immune depending on how long we'd have had them before the virus spread." Jason agreed. "I see. We all wondered why we'd survived. We'd come to a conclusion it had to be something like that."

"What about the granddaughter? Did she have it?" Jason spoke without thinking and waited for the reply, wishing he'd kept his mouth shut.

Gary smiled. "Yes, if you're wondering what happened to them, you can stop worrying. Jess is a smart, sensible girl. She had the infection and the antibiotic, and she'd been home nearly three weeks when the virus hit. She's separated, rented her place, had just traded in her car for a bigger one because of the baby, and she didn't waste any time. Her landlady was one of the first to catch the virus. She died. Jess took one look at the situation when she took the lady to the hospital and found how bad things were getting. She emptied her bank account at a hospital ATM, went home, packed everything plus anything useful from her landlady's place, and made a run for Velda. Jess lived in Glorieta, that's a town before you get to Santa Fe, and she left in the early hours. She was here the same day, and by that time, we'd all heard things on TV, and Ray was phoning, telling us to take precautions."

"And you all did," Jason acknowledged.

"Yes. As Ray said. Buying in advance just meant that we had things we'd use anyhow if things didn't get too bad. If things went as bad as he thought they would, what we did could save our lives." Gary looked thoughtful. "I admit I was surprised at how long people here would take ordinary paper money."

"I know. Mom said even when they stopped taking that, they'd probably take gold."

"We discovered that. Velda had her husband's grandfather's coin collection – all gold. Ray said to buy necessities while they were for sale and to buy things that would - as he put it - have a prolonged use. We got fruit-tree saplings, seeds of just about anything edible - he said to buy old varieties, not hybrids, they often wouldn't have fertile seeds - and look for animals too. I took Velda's old horse float and bought the cow and goats back here. We all have chickens, and Ray has a bull for our cows." He smiled briefly. "We expect to live comfortably for the remainder of our lives. Ray's the youngest of the group, and he's in his late fifties now. I admit to being worried about Jess and Fee - Fiona. Jess is only twenty-seven, and Fee's two and a half. What sort of a world will it be for them? The seven of us will probably be all gone in twenty years, and there have been attacks on some places that have supplies already."

Jason looked at his host. "I'm going to my dad's ranch," he said slowly. "All I can say is that he's a good man, the ranch is pretty isolated, and if he's okay, I'll have a place there all my life. I can't promise anything, but if he's okay and I make it there, I can talk to him about Jess and the baby."

Their gazes met, and Gary nodded. "Thank you. Now, it's getting late, let's head for our beds, and we can talk more over breakfast. Ray's likely to be over mid-morning, and I'd like to introduce you two."

Jason helped clear the table, feeling weariness catching up with him now that he was well-fed and relaxed. He took Stormy out for a brief run, went to the bedroom chosen, took a quick shower, brushed his teeth, and crawled into bed, with Stormy curled by his feet. Sleep swept over him like a tsunami, and he sank into the wave without dreams.

CHAPTER TWENTY-FOUR

Jason woke at first light. It had become a habit, and Stormy usually asked to go out about then. He took her outside and stood a while, enjoying the crisp, clear air.

From the porch, Gary spoke quietly. "A lovely time of the day. It should be fine for a few days yet too. Now, what would you like for breakfast? There's toast if you'd prefer that to bread, and there's sausages, bacon, eggs, and you can have milk, coffee, water, a soft drink, or cordial."

Jason laughed. "I'd better not stay here too long, or I'll get fat. Toast, bacon, eggs, and sausages, please. And milk."

Stormy had dog biscuits, and the sound of her crunching happily by his chair made a perfect morning so far as Jason was concerned. Ray – Shaw – showed up at ten by Jason's old silver pocket watch. He was a lean man who didn't look his years and who greeted Gary with obvious affection. Jason had seen men like that before; a lot fitter and tougher than he appeared, he'd make an excellent friend and a much worse enemy. Ray looked the boy over in turn. *Trust Gary to pick up some stray.* Ray felt eyes on him and turned casually to glance around, that was a dog, medium-sized, gray fur, and intelligent, intensely watchful eyes.

Jason saw where he was looking and spoke. "Stormy, here." She came, sat at his feet, and waited. "Stormy, this is Ray, Ray, this is Stormy."

Ray Shaw grinned. "Hi, Stormy. You're one of those fancy breeds I'd guess. That's okay. I like a good dog. How do you feel about being friendly?"

Stormy recognized some of the words and advanced, sat, sniffed his boots, and looked up. He dropped a hand cautiously and scratched under her chin until she beamed and her tail wagged slowly. "Well-trained, too, I'd guess?" Ray offered. Jason nodded. "You planning on staying long?"

"Three or four days if that's okay with Mr. Pearman."

Gary saw that Ray was making assumptions and spoke before anything unwise could be said. "He shared his venison and chocolate for dinner last night. I haven't had either in a while. Did the dishes, made his bed, and the dog's house-trained, likes Jay too - and Jay likes her." Catching Ray's gaze, he nodded slightly and saw his friend relax.

Ray sat and looked at them. "All right, I'd bet there's a tale about how you two survived and made it this far. Be interested to hear if you don't mind telling?"

Gary left and returned with a coffeepot, mugs, milk, sugar, and teaspoons. They drank coffee, ate more of Jason's chocolate biscuits, and Ray heard the story. Jason made it fairly brief, and at the end of it, Ray nodded.

"Your mom sounds to have been a good smart lady. I do like common sense. So you're heading for your dad's ranch. What's he raise there?"

"Horses, beef cattle, goats, a few buffalo, and some of their cross-breeds."

"Big place?"

Jason considered, *how big was "big?"* "Fair size. His father started with a small place, did well out of it, and had a chance to buy elsewhere the year before Dad was born. Then, back a while, Dad decided to sell and buy further out again. Man that he knew, his father died, and he'd never wanted to ranch. The place had gone right down for years as his dad got old and didn't want to spend money or hire anyone new. His men got old and retired, until there was just him there the last year. Then he died, and Dad's friend inherited it. He offered it to Dad for the unimproved land price, and Dad's no fool. He sold his current ranch in a week and bought that one."

"Why unimproved?"

"The house was old, built the end of the eighteen-hundreds, a room at a time. Nothing modern. The land had been let go for nearly twenty years, and there was pretty much no livestock. The land's up in the hills, miles from any place. Dad ended up with a ranch that was more than twice the size of the one he'd had, and he had the livestock. He'd been thinking of culling herd, then he got this place and just moved everything there."

Jason remembered some of what his mom had said about the place. It had been the isolation that had been the deciding factor in the divorce. Jason had loved it during his visits, but his mom had been right. If he lived there, he'd have had to be driven two hours to school every day or boarded somewhere for the week. And once he got older, boarding would have been the only option. Now, he reflected, the ranch's isolation could have been the saving of those there. So he hoped, anyhow. He was about to say that the nearest towns were Milan and Blue Water when he stopped himself. Better not to say – just in case.

Ray looked thoughtful. "So you can ride?"

Jason nodded. "Well enough. Not much practice lately, but I had a friend where I lived; they had a farm just out of Seattle. I learned to milk too. Dad used to have a milk cow, chickens, half a dozen pigs. He said that if you lived a long way from buying milk, bacon, and eggs, it paid to have them on the spot. He cleaned up the orchard and the vegetable garden as well."

Ray considered that. "Sensible man." He grinned at his friend and the boy. "Good stock on both sides from the sound of it. What did you plan to do, ranch or take up something else?"

"I wanted to be a doctor," Jason said flatly.

"Fair enough. It isn't as if we can't use every one of those we get. Now, this wide place in the road you found a day or two back. You only took some of what was in the store, not all of that, and from nowhere else there?" Jason nodded. "Would you mind taking a couple of us back there – say, tomorrow?"

"No, I'd be happy to." A hint of red showed over his cheekbones. "I'd have liked to bury the store owners where I took some stuff, but I didn't know who'd kept the store."

Ray relaxed further, thinking still better of the boy. "We can do that. Less than a dozen houses, with three or four of us, wouldn't take that long. Okay, I'll come over with some of the others tomorrow about the same time as I got here today. Gary, you'll come too?"

"I will. And I'd suggest Jess. Women find things where men don't think of looking."

Ray gave a short crack of laughter. "That's the truth, and she's a good worker." He got to his feet and headed for the door, pausing in the doorway. "Bring the truck, Gary, and you know the drill."

He departed, and they heard the car sound fade as he turned onto the road. Jason spent the remainder of the day washing and drying clothes and bedding using Gary's washer and dryer, practicing commands with Stormy, reading, and eating, after which he cleared away the dishes, washed, while Gary dried them, and went to bed quite early. Tomorrow, he suspected, would be a day that would require a lot of expended energy before it was over. It was.

****

Ray arrived earlier than he'd said, but both Jason and Gary were ready. Stormy, having recognized preparations to go somewhere, had been ready since breakfast. Jason checked his guns before he joined the men. He thought Ray hadn't realized he was armed. Jason had the gun in the small of his back any time he was awake, close by when he slept, and he was so accustomed to having it, he was no longer conscious of its presence and thus showed no apparent signs of being armed to anyone watching.

It was another fine day, the sky clear and blue, a faint breeze, and Jason led the way south. He pulled up to the turnoff, halted, and when everyone joined him, he pointed.

"It's a mile that way. Eight houses with a store and a gas pump, couple more houses in sight a bit further on. I didn't see any animals except a few cattle and a dog that went for me - Stormy took that out. I did check the houses by the store in case there was anyone there. I found bodies, and I'd say the whole place died within a day or so of each other. I found it because there was an old signpost half fallen over, and I figured you didn't put one up without it showing somewhere to go. I removed it when I left."

Ray grinned. "That sounds good to me. Okay, I'll lead off. When we get there, circle and space out so we can leave fast if we have to. We'll clear the store of anything we can use first, then split up and check the houses."

He climbed back into his car, which towed a large trailer, and headed for the hamlet. Jason's quick look as he pulled up behind Ray's vehicle said that nothing had changed. He glanced over at the people. Gary, Ray, Jess, and another man he'd not been introduced to but whom he'd heard called Bill. With Jason that made five, and each of them driving a truck or car with a trailer – he'd emptied his car, left his trailer loaded, and taken a spare of Gary's – they should be able to empty the village of anything wanted.

A movement showed that some of the cattle were still around, and he decided to shoot a couple. Gary had a large freezer that was half-empty. That'd take one animal once it was butchered, and everyone could eat the other over a few days. He'd check with Ray first though, it was possible they all had freezers, and if so, they probably had meat. It wasn't as if there was any shortage of roaming cattle. Ray had the door open at the store, and as Jason arrived, he was already pointing out items that should be taken. He looked at Jason.

"You never took any of the tobacco and cigarettes?"

Jason shrugged. "Never smoked."

Ray chuckled. "Nor do I, but there's plenty that did, and they'd trade. Bill, I see they had a big shed behind this, have a look there, will you?"

Bill, a powerful-looking seventy-year-old, tromped out and tromped back minutes later, a broad smile creasing his face. "Come and take a look at this lot, will you?"

The shed, bigger even than it had appeared from outside, held pallets of cans, sacks, and boxes. They were labeled, and Jason stared at the largesse. Most were staples - sugar, tea, coffee - the instant kind - flour and salt. In the boxes, there were cans of meat - ham, corned beef, spam - cans of fish and vegetables. There were four large boxes of soup packets and two even larger containing cans of soup. There were sacks of powdered milk and a huge pile of bags against one wall, chicken feed - wheat by the look of it.

Ray whistled softly. "This lot alone'll keep us going for a couple of years. Jason, I reckon you should have the first pick. Take anything you think would be useful, and I'll help you load it."

Jason looked it over. His car and trailer were full already. He should take something, they wouldn't feel right if he didn't, but it should be light, maybe something he could lighten even further and pack into odd corners. The packets of soup would do nicely.

He pointed. "The powdered soup. It's in packs, but the packets inside probably say what's in them too. If we dump the boxes, it'll cut the weight, plus they can be fitted into any gap. Powder weighs nothing much, and I can find water almost any place."

Ray approved. "Good choice. Okay, everyone, sort out what you want. Once we've got the place empty, we may need to go home and unload it all."

They had a very busy few hours after that. They added only a little of the store's contents then headed back to unload their salvage. It was early evening when they were done, and the consensus was that they'd join up the next morning. By the time they were done, Jason and his host were ready for a quick meal and a comfortable bed. Gary had them up early, however.

"I know Ray; he won't be able to relax until we've cleaned out that place."

"I wondered about taking a few of the cattle, or do you all have enough beef?"

Gary pondered a moment. "We could. I'm almost out of it, and Velda may be too. Better to take it while it's available than run out, and there's nothing around. I'll tell Ray."

Ray agreed. "I was hoping for a deer or something else, but what Gary says is right. Better have beef than nothing. Who's going to shoot it?"

"Let the boy do it."

"Okay, three yearlings if they're around."

Jason nodded. "I'll wait until they're away from the store and get them all at once." He saw the doubtful look Ray gave him and said nothing. He had his secret weapon. He was using his mom's car for this, and his guns were always in that.

They arrived at the hamlet. Jason got out with Stormy at his heels and together, they went quietly in search of the cattle while Ray organized the others to empty the store before checking the houses. The cattle were no great distance, and yes, the yearlings he'd seen were there; two heifers, three more young bulls. He'd take the yearling bulls; there was already an adult bull with the cows, and he'd drive off the younger males any day now anyway. He could come for them once they had everything else loaded. That way he could get help with the butchering. He returned to find Gary staggering out of the store with a long carton.

"Here, I can give you a hand with that. What is it?"

"Thank you. It's tool handles; always useful. Jess found them under a stack of empty boxes. We're filling the boxes and taking them too."

They placed the carton in the trailer and went back for more boxes. The store emptied quickly enough. Everyone took a break for something to eat and drink; then they started on the houses. They looked to have mostly been built around the same time, somewhere at the end of the eighteen-hundreds, Jason thought. The first was tidy. There was a lot of dust, but clearly the owner had been house-proud until the end. The body was in bed. A note lay folded on the bedside cabinet. Ray picked it up, read, and grunted.

"To her nephew, she was expecting him to come after she told him on the phone she wasn't well. Guess he was even less well. Says he knows where to find her jewelry and papers. He's her heir, and he should give his daughter her gold bracelet and her books. Jess, you look for the stuff she mentions. Rest of you go through the place. If it's use or value, it comes with us."

Jason joined Jess, who welcomed him with a smile. They found nothing at first search, and Jason started tapping walls. Jess chuckled. "Secret panels?" Jason grinned back and continued; to find a wall section behind the bedhead in the main bedroom, giving off a softly hollow sound. He probed, prodded, pressed, and with no result, he looked at the now-wrapped body. Then he twisted himself into the position someone lying on the bed would use to reach that section of wall and pressed hard, sliding his fingers up, down, and across the area. Something shifted under the pressure, and he pushed again. A panel opened, and inside he, and Jess watching, saw a couple of small wooden boxes.

Jess whooped. "Smart boy, hey Ray, Jason found the stuff the lady was writing about." She reached in and hauled the boxes from where they rested and opened them as everyone came crowding to see. One contained papers, birth certificates, a title deed, school reports, death certificates, and wills. The other had the jewelry.

Jess turned that over, turning a necklace to see the marks. "Nine carat this one, some of the other stuff is silver, cheap, no one would trade for that."

Jason kept his mouth shut, she was right, but it seemed disrespectful, looking over things someone had loved, mentioned as she died, and dismissing them as worthless. He saw from the look on Gary's face he felt the same, but he, too, said nothing. Ray nodded.

"Not of any great value," he confirmed. "But one of you may like it. Jason, if no one else does, you take whatever of it you want; you brought us here. Now, everyone got what's useful from this place. If so, we'll look at the next one."

The next house had belonged to a quilter. She had the loom, the scraps and patterns, the reels of thread, scissors, and all the other necessary equipment. Jess fell on those with delight. "Velda quilts, she'd love all this."

"Take it," Ray gave permission. "But the gear, not the finished quilts. Share those out." Jason accepted one, a king-size single. It showed lines of dogs and cats, while in the center, a larger cat, an Ocicat from the markings, and a fluffy gold dog curled up together. A note attached to it said,

"Ordered by Myra Patenden, paid for, to be collected."

Jason smoothed the quilt, thinking the lady who'd ordered this must have been an animal lover, maybe she had the dog and cat depicted, or maybe they'd been hers when she was young, and she'd wanted to remember them. What had happened to her – and her animals – had she survived and been too far away to bother coming here to get her quilt, or were they all lying in a house like this one, slowly going to bones? He gathered and folded the quilt, took the note off, and laid it by the bed. The others had left the room, and he spoke very softly to the anonymous bundle on the bed.

"You did lovely work. I'll treasure this. Thank you." The jewelry box had been left untouched, and he moved the items carefully, looking them over. One set caught his eye. His grandmother had had something like them, and he knew what they were. Green garnets set in sterling silver. Two bracelets, a ring, a teardrop pendant on a squash blossom necklace – the blossoms each with a green garnet in the center; rather than turquoise – a curved hair comb, and a pair of earrings for pierced ears. The earrings could be separated, used as studs, or with the drops added as longer earrings. Considering all the jewelry lying about these days, they were of no value, as Jess had said, but they were lovely, and he liked the garnets and silver. It was less gaudy. He picked them up, wrapped them in a tea towel from the kitchen, added the gold bracelet, and nodded again to the figure.

"I'll treasure these too. I'll see the rest of it safe again as well." He placed the boxes back behind the panel and slid it shut. He passed empty bookshelves - they'd probably be cherished; it would be a long time before more books were published - and he could see other items had gone as well. He paused again in the kitchen to add an attractively colored biscuit container depicting ponies. It was empty, but it could be used to hold any smaller items. In the next house, he could see people moving past the windows. Ray was leaving to head for the third house, and Jason called to him.

"I thought about taking a look at the houses over there," he pointed to the furthest ones, and Ray waved acceptance and permission. Jason looked down.

"Okay, girl, let's see what we can find. Go, seek." He pointed at the houses, and Stormy trotted ahead, casting around the yards and sheds. By the time he reached the dwellings, she'd covered the ground and made no indication of anything interesting. Jason walked into the first shed, looked around, moved items, and shrugged. "More of the same. Nothing I need. Let's see what the house is like?"

It was a dump, he concluded. The owners, or perhaps renters, hadn't bothered to keep it clean and left stuff lying all over. Not as if it had been looted, but the long-standing grubby untidiness that said they'd never had a place for anything and no concept of the idea. He wandered through the rooms, found the owners dead as expected, tossed a blanket over their bodies, and moved on. Nothing of interest anywhere, so he left that house and tried the other one nearby.

That was more productive. Jason found five large sealed packets of nuts in the kitchen cupboard. *Someone here liked nuts,* he thought. He gathered up the packets - peanuts, Brazil nuts, cashews, almonds, and hazelnuts. Good supplies for traveling. He checked other cupboards but found nothing more he wanted. In the bedroom were bodies, and he eyed them sadly. A man, a woman, two children, and a baby, all cuddled together in a king-sized bed. A room next door held children's clothes, books, and toys, so he went to the door and yelled Jess's name. When she arrived, he pointed to them, and she pounced. Leaving her gathering and packing the items, he moved on.

Outside, he approached the nearest shed. It groaned as he pushed the door open. He wiped dirt from the large window at the back, and with light streaming in, he could see that it contained tools, machinery, oil, and gas cans – he hefted those noting they were full. He took a large knife in a sheath from the wall to look at it, withdrew the blade, and stared. Wow, he'd seen one of those once, a Bowie, and if it wasn't genuine, it was a fantastic copy. The sheath was genuine deerskin, fringed and ornamented. He studied that, recognizing some of the motifs. It *was* real, and while it might not be right to take it without showing the others, the motifs were Navajo and … he heard footsteps and dropped the knife and sheath into his pack.

Ray spoke from the doorway. "Anything interesting?"

Jason nodded to the cans. "Gas, oil, and diesel too. All full."

"Great, I'll get Bill to collect them." He went out calling, and Jason took the opportunity to push the sheathed Bowie under the towel at the bottom of his pack. Ray came back. "What did you get?"

Jason held up the packets of nuts. "I'll take them if no one minds; they're good for traveling, means I won't have to stop to eat if I don't want to."

"What's their date?"

He'd already checked that. "Another year to go."

"Okay, they're yours. Did you want any of those tools?"

"No." He turned and a curved shape caught his eye. "Yes. Maybe." He dug into the items and backed out, holding a bow case. He opened it, looked at the contents, then dug again to come up with a quiver stuffed with arrows. "I'd like this."

Ray shrugged. "If you can use it and you want it, fine." There was a faint note of scorn, and Jason smiled, saying nothing but adding the objects to his pack.

Bill appeared, listened, and started hauling out the full cans, walking them two at a time to his car. Ray disappeared, and Jason began looking through the chests lined along the back of the shed. His attitude remained casual when he opened the third one, and he was trying to decide how best to distract Bill when he heard the roar of an engine. Bill jumped out of the doorway, there was the sound of a shot, and he returned, his body slowly turning, collapsing as he sagged to the ground, a growing splotch of blood covering his shirtfront. Jason dived for the back window, opened it with care, and exited to circle behind the house.

CHAPTER TWENTY-FIVE

Jason moved in short bursts, smoothly, a couple of paces a time, until he dropped to lie almost flat on the ground and peer around the edge of the house. He snorted in disgust. Idiots. Four men, all in a truck, handguns, and they'd warned everyone by shooting first. They looked and sounded drunk too.

On the other hand, Bill was dead; he didn't think Jess was armed, so it was three against four. Best shave those odds down a bit. He moved to where he wouldn't be seen and smiled unpleasantly. Jason and his friends were cut off from the weapons in their vehicles, but he had something that was just as good at this range. He removed the bow from its case, strung it, and selected arrows.

Dad had taught him to shoot arrows when he was a kid, and he'd thought it fun and a way of sharing time. He'd kept it up because he enjoyed it, and because he felt that it connected him to that part of his heritage. People often didn't understand how lethal arrows could be. They were silent, too, and this was a really good bow. He watched until one of the assailants separated from his friends and went to stand, concealed, as he thought, behind a tree. Jason shot. It was less than fifty yards, and the arrow took his target in the throat. He had a second arrow in the air a second later that was a heart shot, and the enemy slid to the ground in silence.

Right, one down. Jason's side seemed to have gone to ground; at least there was no sight or sound of them. Sensible. He rose and padded around behind the house, Stormy silent at his heels. He had an arrow on the bowstring and saw one of the assailants with his back to Jason as he cleared the building. Jason shot and stepped back into cover. The man shrieked, staggering, falling to writhe as his friends came running, shouting questions.

"What the…?"

One man bent over, holding the wounded man by one shoulder. "Mike, Mikey? What happened, how…?"

The other was standing, looking around. His right hand held a large handgun which waved in all directions as he tried to look everywhere at once. Jason shot him next. He was armed, less preoccupied, more dangerous. The man went down even as the one bending over his friend spoke.

"Geeze, he's dead, Mikey's dead." He straightened. "Did you hear me, Mike's…" He realized that his companion was down as well, and before he could react, Jason shot twice. Then there was a long silence. *Never be in too much of a hurry,* Dad had told him. *In warfare, it's usually the first to move that dies.* Jason stayed motionless, listening.

Under his hand, he felt Stormy relax. Okay, she couldn't hear or smell any danger. He moved positions and called Ray's name quietly. A voice answered.

"Jason, you okay?"

"Yes. How many of them did you see?"

"Four."

"That how many I saw. So that's it."

"I can only see three?"

"Other's by the big tree," Jason called, keeping his voice low. "I shot him first."

"You got them all?" The tone was incredulous.

"Looks like it. Stormy," Jason waved to the bodies. "Go check."

She trotted over, sniffed all three bodies, obeyed his whistle to find the fourth, did so, and announced safety now prevailed. Jason grinned, sliding out of cover to join her and look over the truck that the enemy had used. It reeked of alcohol; there were bottles, cans, chocolate wrappers, bits of stale food, and stinking clothing. He wrinkled his nose in disgust as Ray joined him. Jason had unstrung the bow, and Ray looked at that and then at Jason.

"Looks as if it was useful after all. I thought you just wanted it to show off."

"No, I learned to use one for fun, but I wasn't bad."

"I can see that. Lucky for us, you found it."

"I'd like to hang on to it."

Ray grinned. "I can't see any of us trying to take it away. Let's get this bunch moved. There's still work to do, and the cattle won't come back if they smell death. Besides, this lot could have friends out there, and better they don't make any good guesses and come looking for us."

They hauled the bodies into the truck. Jason recovered his arrows, added empty gas cans to the truck, and Ray drove them down the road while Jason followed. They pushed the truck over the edge of the road, drained the gas tank, and left the truck hidden in scrub, a tomb for those who'd started something they couldn't finish.

It took all that day to finish clearing useful items. Jason took the trunk he'd found in the shed, saying nothing, and after a glance or two, none of the others asked. Bill's body went back with Ray, who commented briefly on that. "Knew him for years, not a bad guy. I'll bury him on my place, and we can clear his house later when there's time."

It's none of my business, Jason thought, and he asked no questions. The group returned the following day, Jason produced the silenced rifle, and Ray gaped at it.

"That what I think it is?"

"Got it from a nice lady I stayed with last winter. She died, said I could take anything I wanted – after. She got it from a neighbor who died from the virus."

They sat quietly in the store and waited. Jess hadn't come, but Gary was with them, and mid-morning, the cattle wandered in to find oats scattered in patches along the grass. The bull started eating eagerly. The cows and small calves joined him, and then the yearlings. Jason sighted carefully, shot once, and the yearling bull furthest from the group sank to his knees and rolled over. The others took no notice. The unrecognized *thump* made by the silenced rifle was unthreatening. Jason waited until the other two yearlings he wanted had moved to one side, then shot quickly, twice.

The first also fell quietly. The other bawled and bawled again so that the small herd took notice. The bull advanced, smelled the blood, pawing the ground, looking around him. His head dropped as he thrust one horn then the other along the ground, making an angry rumble, a sound that threatened whoever had attacked his herd. Jason sat right where he was. The bull nosed a yearling, the first shot. However, he could see and smell no enemies, and after a brief time, he did as Jason had hoped, gathered his herd, and moved off, still rumbling his anger.

Ray turned to Gary and spoke quietly. "Follow them and watch. If they start back, let us know. We don't want that bull circling back." Gary nodded and went after the small herd while Jason produced the manual hoist they'd brought. With all three yearlings strung up to tree branches, he let them bleed out before they started the butchering. Ray, to Jason's amusement, produced a small chainsaw, and the work moved swiftly. Ray knew what he was doing, and between them, they had the job done in a couple of hours.

Jason had taken an old tarp from the store and allowed the offal to stack on that. He separated the organs, dropping them in buckets brought for the purpose - Stormy would enjoy those – after which he rolled the tarp and dropped it on the back of the truck.

"I'll take the rubbish down the road and dump it," he offered.

"Do that, and I'll scatter the other half of those oats before we leave. That may keep them coming back. It means we know where to find them if we need more meat."

Jason drove the truck to where they'd left the bodies. The truck containing those couldn't be seen from the road, but the bodies would draw scavengers. It might be handy if anyone looking for the men found the tarp's contents first and stopped looking there - assuming that was why the flies. He allowed the tarp to unroll as he pushed it over the road edge. The contents scatted down the slope, and with a smile, Jason rerolled the tarp – he could wash that out at Gary's place - climbed back into the truck and returned to the hamlet. Ray glanced about as he pulled up.

"Get the truck over here. I'll load the meat and hides. You go get Gary and tell him we're going back now."

Gary watched the cattle graze in a field where the gate was open and was happy to leave them to it. Ray had most of the work done by the time they got back, and they helped with the last loads before climbing into the truck and heading home. Ray dropped them off at the big old house and grinned at Jason.

"Take what meat you want now. I'll go on and share the rest out with the others." They did so, staggered inside with full buckets and the steaks and roasts, and spent the remainder of the day wrapping, marking, and placing the parcels in the freezer. The cat was right there throughout, accepting half a diced kidney and settling to eat it by Stormy, who was enjoying another.

With the work completed and the freezer loaded to the top, Gary produced cheese sandwiches and hot chocolate, and they shared a peaceful meal, talking until Gary asked a question.

"That chest you brought back. Can I ask what's in it?"

"Blankets," Jason said without elaboration.

"Blankets, I thought you had some already?"

"I do. Thought a few more wouldn't hurt."

Gary nodded. "I suppose so. Anyhow, I could use a good night's sleep; I'll see you in the morning." He headed for his bedroom, the cat, having finished his dinner, bounding after.

Jason sighed, stood up, stretched, and followed suit, Stormy at his heels. Once in his bedroom, he shut the door, used a chair to make sure he didn't get a surprise visitor and went to the chest. It was cedar wood, of a good size, still beautifully polished, and with brass fittings. Old, he thought, probably made around the time of the contents, and it had a newer hasp so it could be padlocked. It hadn't been when he uncovered it, but he'd found padlocks in his travels, and he'd taken them. One was brass and had come with two keys. From now on, he'd lock the chest.

He raised the lid and looked down. He'd told no less than the truth; there were blankets there. However, they weren't the usual kind; both were hand-woven and hand-dyed in soft colors, the patterns composed of rounded curving lines. Long ago in the home of one of his dad's friends, he'd seen a blanket like these. They were Navajo, old, beautiful, and probably of considerable value - although that would not have mattered to the old woman who'd owned it, and it didn't matter now to Jason.

He shut the chest, walking over to pick up the bowie knife, and stood looking at the bow case. That and the contents were genuine, too, as was the knife's sheath. Had the items been bought? Probably not; few would sell things like this. It was more likely they'd been stolen or even that the dead family inherited them. He'd looked around the house; there'd been no sign of anything else that matched, and the scattered papers he'd looked at hadn't indicated the family was Navajo. So he'd reclaimed them. He unwedged the door, crawled into bed, permitted Stormy to join him, and slept.

****

Gary woke him the next morning with a tap at the door. Jason woke and called for him to come in. He was presented with a wooden tray containing a large omelet, toast, and a mug of steaming coffee. Gary pulled up a chair and sat while Jason ate.

"I thought we should talk?" Jason met Gary's serious look and nodded. "You said when you arrived that you'd meant to stay two nights or so. It's been almost a week."

Jason thought he heard an agenda there. "You want me to go?"

Gary winced. "No, if I had a choice, I'd rather you stayed, you'd be very welcome, but I know you want to find your father, and all I meant is that I think you'll move on soon, and I want to ask a favor before you do." He took in a slow breath. "You told me about that minister...."

Jason understood then and broke in. "I can leave you the same thing, a few of them if you want."

Gary sighed. "I do. Ray's a good man and tremendously tough in his own way, but he'd never do something like that. He might with an animal if he liked it, didn't want it to suffer, and there was no one else. But he wouldn't do it for a person. He'd walk away and not come back for what he'd think to be 'long enough.' I'm not like that, and I can look facts in the face and accept what I see. I come from a long-lived family, I'm not that old yet, and I'm fit and healthy, but that won't last forever. Velda's older than I am, and she's fading. She talked to me about it. She's afraid to die slowly, in pain, or unable to move, and you can guess what that'd be like with no hospitals and medical services now."

Jason could. "I'll give you twenty-five pills. The ones where one will see you don't wake up. For a big dog, you only need half, a quarter one for a cat. That should cover you for anything, even someone coming to try and take over." His smile had an edge. "Half a one will make a human sleep twenty hours or more, so you can kill them and save a half. Albuquerque is close enough for you to drive there. I can leave you a list of drug names. Look for one lot in a vet office, and the others at any hospital or hospice. They could even be in the homes for old people."

"Thank you."

Jason finished the last of his breakfast and, reflecting it was good he'd slept in his boxers, he left the bed and looked at his host. "I'll get them now. That way, you have them in case I forget later. I'll write the list tonight after dinner. Remind me if I don't." He donned pants and a t-shirt and went out, returning in a few minutes with a small plastic vial. "Here they are. If I can suggest it, break them into groups of five in some small containers, and put them around. That way, you should always have some at hand."

Gary smiled. "Good sense. I will. Now, what do you have in mind for today? "

They spent the morning doing the washing and hanging that out to dry in the sun. Jason decided to write his promised list after lunch and handed it over immediately once it was done. "Read that and let me know if you have any questions."

Gary didn't. "I'll put it away safely and make copies in case. Now, if you'd like a trip, there's a compound I know about that none of us have ever checked." Jason raised an eyebrow in query and Gary chuckled. "Small sect. They have the place barricaded to a fare-thee-well. They aren't official preppers, but they live that way. I haven't seen anything of them since the virus started, and they may all be fine, but if not...."

Jason nodded. "If not, they could have a lot of useful stuff, and maybe animals that need letting go."

"Exactly."

"How far?"

"About ten minutes north, then up a track on the right, and I happen to know - even if they didn't - that you can overlook their compound if you circle to the left where there's a small rock outcropping that can be climbed if you know how and where."

"What about Ray?"

"He never knew about them. If there's anything there he needs to hear about, I can let him know once *we* know."

"Okay."

They left five minutes later, Jay protesting abandonment while they were driving away until his meows faded in the distance. The compound was easily found if you knew where to look, Jason observed. Otherwise, he doubted anyone would come across it by accident. They left the truck in cover, circled to the rock outcropping, and yes, as Gary had said, it was climbable if you knew how and where to put your feet and hands. Once on top, they produced binoculars and contemplated the walled circle of buildings below.

"No one." Jason continued to scan. "I can't see any animals either. Do they keep any in there with them, or do they have them past the compound?"

"They have goats and cattle out in a field beyond that line of scrub. They don't have cats; they're said to think them creatures of the devil, but they had dogs, maybe half a dozen. I don't see any." Nor did Jason. The two men exchanged glances, and without discussion, they descended their lookout and approached the compound's wall. Jason considered that.

"I can climb it. If I go over by the gate, I can let you in." Jason didn't wait for agreement but went to the truck. He drove it to the gate, climbed up onto the cab, and scaled the last few feet of wall to drop over on the ground beyond it. The gate was, as he'd suspected it would be, chained and padlocked, but they'd brought heavy bolt-cutters which made short work of the chain. In minutes both stood in the silent compound. Gary moved forward, Jason a pace behind and to his right side so his line of fire was clear. Nothing moved, and the only sound was their soft footfalls.

Jason halted as they reached the main building and looked up. "That's an integrated eco-power system. It's made to be removable quite easily, and I bet they have spares for it. If you tell Ray, he could take it out and store it."

"I will." Gary tried the door handle and found the door unlocked. He opened it, and they both stepped back hastily. "I'd say we can guess what happened here."

Jason could only agree; the stench was horrific. "How many lived here?"

"No one knows exactly. I'd have said about thirty all the time; it could be as high as a hundred people came and went."

Jason produced a handkerchief; Gary found one of his own. "Let's see what's here."

What they found was sickening. Everyone in the compound was dead. Apparently, they hadn't given mercy to anything, so that babies had starved in their cradles, toddlers lay dead around the various rooms, and the dogs, shut in and left to themselves, had eaten what they could of their owners before succumbing to thirst. Jason felt tears well up and resorted to swearing instead.

"What kind of people *were* they?"

"I told you," Gary said heavily. "Some odd sect."

Stormy sniffed her way around the building in and out of rooms where the door was open. She did not indicate finding anything alive, and Jason felt sick at how the children and animals in this place must have died. He followed her, Gary circling the other way. They met up a short time later, and Gary spoke thoughtfully.

"There's s ton of items here that would be useful. And we should look for cellars. Word was that they did some digging once they got the wall up."

They hunted, turning over carpets and mats, but it wasn't until they left the main building and investigated the garage and vehicles that they found a cellar. Gary called.

"Jason, here. There's a trapdoor under this service pit." Jason came running, and together they lifted the door to find a large area below. It was filled with supplies; guns and ammunition, medicines, first aid items, and a vast array of food in every kind of container. Gary looked at this with satisfaction. "I'd say that should see us all out."

"Yes." Jason studied it. "My suggestion would be to leave most of it, just take whatever is there that you don't have. That way, if you ever get attacked where you are and have to leave, you could come here. What about their livestock?"

Gary led the way beyond the buildings and through a wide gate, halted, and waved a hand to where some animals grazed peacefully over five large paddocks, each with the gates open to the others. "That lot was theirs."

Jason surveyed the group. "Six cows, and they look like dairy cattle, a dozen goats and sheep. Do you know how much land they had here?"

"Maybe a hundred and fifty acres, but most is in trees or scrub."

"So this open land would be all that's in grass?" Gary nodded. "About twelve acres, I'd say. Just enough for the animals here."

"How do you work that out?"

"Land of this fertility should graze six stock units an acre. Roughly speaking, a cow is six units, with six sheep or goats to the acre. There are approximately sixty animal units here, so – that matches the land you said with a little over."

Gary frowned. "What does that say to you?"

Jason grinned. "That they have automatic filling for the water troughs, that there aren't many predators around this area, and that someone wasn't a true believer. The first two, because I can't see any dead animals, the last because someone opened up the whole grazing so the animals could go from paddock to paddock. That's against the 'let them live or die as they stand' bit, isn't it?"

"Yes," Gary said slowly. "They didn't shoot their dogs, but I know some of them hunted. Maybe they didn't count livestock as falling under their laws, maybe the dogs counted as members of the compound, but these creatures didn't."

Jason shrugged. "People, no accounting for them or their beliefs. But now you know what happened to the compound; you can tell Ray. Any other place we should look at while we're out?"

"None I can think of … oh, yes, there is." They returned to the truck and Gary drove back to the main road, continued north another eleven miles, and slowed to turn into a thread of unidentified road.

"I don't know if there's anyone left alive here. The family who owned this land had a vacation house right down the end of this road, bought a right of way and the house on about three acres years back from a local farmer. They come and go; we never had any idea when they were here unless one of us saw them around. I'd completely forgotten all about them until you asked." Gary's truck wound through the bends of a narrow road, becoming overgrown. "Doesn't look as if anyone's been over this since the virus."

They broke out of the trees to find a house with the rarely mistaken air of an empty dwelling. There were no visible vehicles, the curtains were all drawn, and Gary swung the truck around to halt by the back door. "Let's take a look anyhow. Just as well to know what's here in case we need anything."

There was ample bedding, Jason concluded after he'd pried open a back window and they'd entered. A few cans and packets in the kitchen, mostly sauces, spices, and stuff like that. The house was furnished, but nothing special although everything was of good quality. He said that, and Gary smiled.

"Yes, and no cellar that I know of. This was the extra house on the land; farmer's grandparents had it. And before you ask, he lives – or lived – right on the other side of this place. By road, it's a long way. If we ever need to check, we can, but between the village, the compound, and what we already had stocked, I wouldn't bother."

They drove home silently, pausing for Jason to shift to his own vehicle. He followed Gary, thinking about what he'd said. The truth was that he and his friends were simply waiting to die. They planned to live comfortably until they did, with no desire to do more than maintain what they had. It wasn't for him to criticize. However, he felt it was time he and Stormy were on their way. Gary would like him to stay, he knew. And Ray would find them helpful, but if he stayed, he'd become impatient and say something, offend someone – better to leave on friendly terms and maybe come back sometime in the future if it was possible.

CHAPTER TWENTY-SIX

He broached that subject over breakfast. "I should think about leaving."

Gary looked at him, his eyes kind. "Yes. It's one thing for us; oh, I know what you were thinking yesterday. A bunch of oldsters waiting to die and being comfortable until that happens. It's true. We don't have the energy or the need to do more, but you're young; you do. Find your father and start building something for the future. Once you settle in where you're going, maybe you can come back, gather up the compound's animals for a start, and there are others around. You told me about the Crispins; there'll be gas for the taking for years yet if it's in the rights kind of vented tankers, or tanks, you could go back to see them while it's still useable. In a generation or two, people will go back to horses." He chuckled softly. "You could make a cattle drive to them, swap animals to stop inbreeding. Mutual defense alliance."

Jason looked down at his plate, and Gary smiled. "Not your fault, any of it. But it's your world now. Make something better. One thing, I never asked. Your mother was a specialist; it's my experience specials have specialist friends. What was her idea on the final death toll?"

Jason met his gaze, decided, and gave him an honest answer. "She thought about a thousand per million still surviving after five years." For a while, he'd doubted she was right, but his journey had driven home that she had been. Gary was summing that up.

"So, in America, we'd maybe have around four hundred thousand." He considered that. "But that's everyone. People like me, and Ray, and Velda. Too old to have children or to do more than..." he left that comment. "And we won't be the only ones. There'll be some that don't see why they should work when there's so much for the taking. Some may have medical problems, are infertile, or don't want children. Others may end up alone, assume they're the last person standing, and stay where they are to die - or those that actively suicide later. Out of that four hundred thousand, if you take out my kind and all of those others, you could have halved that."

"And some in small isolated groups," Jason said, thinking of discussions with his mom. "If it never occurs to them to go looking until they find others, they'll stay where they are and inbreed until their group collapses. People have their agendas even when this happens. There'll be those who want to lead and start a war with someone else who wants to lead, even if both sides are only in the dozens. Criminals who continue to do whatever they want, and those that try to stop them - people will die that way too. And there's accidents, the sort they survived before, and won't now."

He took in a breath. "That's why I have to go. I wanted to be a doctor. I learned a fair bit, and I want to learn more. I need to find someone trained and learn from them."

Gary eyed him kindly. "Yes, I see that. You have medical books with you?" Jason nodded. "I thought you would. I can tell you something else you may find useful. There was a doctor and dental office in Grants. Normally you'd turn off before that, and you may still, but at Grants, there'd be the books, the equipment, and probably a lot of medication. Medical staff may have survived there. Even if you go straight to your father's ranch, remember Grants."

"I will. Thanks."

"When would you like to leave?"

"Morning after tomorrow," Jason said after a brief thought. "If there's anything you could use a hand with tomorrow, we can get that done. I'll go to bed early then and leave at first light."

"Sounds sensible." Gary looked at the small barometer on the wall near him. "That says fine weather. We can do a roast, and I'll bake bread tomorrow too; you can go with a stack of beef sandwiches in a cooler, a couple of bottles of real lemonade, raid the orchard, there's fruit, and keep driving all that first day. It'll be full moon by then, and you can take a break until it's up and go on half the night. It's about a hundred and fifty miles depending on the roads you take, and there may be things that slow you down. So if you get a flying start, that's a help."

"Well begun is half done," Jason recited. "That was one of Mom's sayings. I'll do that. You go, I'll get the dishes."

Gary stood, and Jason saw that he was tired. "Thank you." He walked out, and Jason heard his door open, pause for the cat, and then shut. Stormy looked up at him and whined.

"I'm sorry to leave here too," he said to her softly. "But I'm not ready to sit back and live on salvage. They may only have twenty years, but I could live another fifty or sixty. I want my time to mean something. I want to leave something behind me that's remembered. Come on, girl." He slept well that night and woke to a sunny day - with the faintest edge of chill on it when he tossed back the bedclothes

That told him his decision was right, it was moving steadily towards winter, and before then, he needed to be at the ranch. With what he knew and could tell Dad, they would have time to raid Grants for that medical and dental gear, even to come back here and take some of the compound's animals. Maybe go up to Albuquerque and see what could be found there, and then there were the army depots he knew about.

He thought of Jess and the baby, no, she wouldn't come, not until Velda was dead, and truthfully, he hadn't much liked what he'd seen of her. He dressed, breakfasted with Gary and the cat, and went out to pick fruit to take with him while Gary baked bread. They spent the remainder of the day clearing gutters, mowing the lawn, and painting the house eaves. Jason went up the long ladder where it would be a risk for Gary, and while

Gary rested later, with a roast giving off savory smells from the oven. Jason laid out some of the things he thought he could need. Stormy followed him, bouncing a little, seeming to understand they were leaving soon.

He slept that night, but only because he'd taken a pill from his stock. Otherwise, he'd have stayed awake, second-guessing his decision over and over. As it was, he woke before it was light, shared bacon and eggs with Gary, said his farewells, stroking Jay until the cat purred and turning back to hug Gary impulsively, speaking in a choked voice, "I'll come back if I can, I promise."

"Yes, and you'll be welcome any time, but the day won't get any longer."

His last view of the older man was Gary, standing by the front door, cradling Jay, his hand lifted in farewell. Then it was him and Stormy, alone again, on the road with a destination that would be there, towards a person who might not be. He did as Gary had said and drove all day, stopping only for brief needed breaks, eating the fruit and sandwiches as he went, and when dusk came, he stopped long enough to light the small stove, cook hot food, eat that, rest for a couple of hours, and move on again at moonrise.

He was halted once by trucks and cars that straddled the road, blocking it, but he managed to shift one far enough that he could squeeze by. He went on, turned west at the old dirt road that headed for the Ramah Reservation, and took the road up into the mountains, driving carefully in case there were more roadblocks. Midmorning, he found he was dozing off at the wheel, and being almost as sensible as his mother always said, he halted. It wouldn't help anyone if he crashed. He pulled the car and trailer off the road into cover. Lit the stove and ate, fed Stormy, played with her for half an hour, and crawled into his sleeping bag for an hour.

In the end, he slept solidly for three hours and woke to find it around midday, but he had only another two hours driving – more if there were any holdups, but with luck... Thinking of that, he heated water, enjoyed hot coffee, the last of the beef sandwiches and fruit, shaved, washed all over, and donned clean clothes. He brushed Stormy while she wiggled in delight and stretched hard, unkinking his back, before reclaiming the driver's seat. Now he remembered every bend in the road. Each was a step closer to the only family he had left, and he was torn between hope and wondering what things would be like now after two years of the virus and what place there'd be for him here.

****

Shandin Storm, known as Sunny to his friends and as dangerous to his enemies, was walking across the ranch's front yard when he heard something. In the last two years in particular, he'd learned to pay attention to *everything,* and he paused in mid-stride. That was a car engine, one heading his way from the sound of it, and he moved into the barn's shadow. Might be a friend, might not, he'd stay back until he knew. His hand rested lightly on the butt of the powerful handgun always at his side. Shandin had very good long sight, and from where he was, he had a clear view of the car as it labored up the last incline, slowing as it came on.

He stared, amused. Sports car – the look and color struck a memory, and he grabbed for it. Hadn't Kerry sent a photo? Yes, she had, one of a car very like this one. This had a loaded trailer covered with a tarp, a gray dog with its head out of the window, and a man driving. Shandin couldn't get a good look at him, but sufficient to see there was only one person in the car – a male.

The car halted, and the man got out cautiously, back half-turned, alertness to his stance that told the watcher this was a seasoned warrior. Young from the way he moved, but he had a handgun at his back – it had shown the shape when the breeze caught his loose shirt – and the dog – the slight breeze veered again, and Stormy barked, looking at the person she knew was there.

Jason spun, hand reaching back as a man came out of the shadows. Then – he knew that face, that man. His hand dropped away, and he spoke in a breathy voice as if the air had drained out of his lungs.

"Dad?"

They moved together, and then he was in his father's arms. He remembered the strong arms as they held him, hugging as if they would crush the two of them into one.

"Jase, you got here."

He leaned back. "Yeah." He saw the question and didn't make his father ask. "Mom didn't make it. The grands died too. She told me to take her car and anything I didn't want to lose and head here. She said if anyone would survive, it'd be you, to say she loved us both." He half laughed, half wept as he added the catchphrase that had been a joke between them all. "She said we should live long and prosper."

Shandin Storm hugged his son to him, then flung an arm about his shoulders, leading him towards the house. "We'll do that, and she'll know." Stormy barked. "Your dog?"

"Her name's Stormy. She's a great dog, a couple of times, I wouldn't have made it here without her."

"Then she's more than welcome. Come in."

****

A year later, they made an expedition to find the army depots Jason had recorded. The items in those were varied and hugely valuable. They included a vast store of gas in venting tanks to make sure it remained uncontaminated. There was food, weapons and ammunition, medical supplies, and a library of how-to books.

Jason grinned as he drove over the ranch, Stormy, head out of the window as usual, beside him. "Okay, girl. We'll stop soon. I just have to check the herd."

He did so, played for a while, worked on her training, and then sat back while she chased a rabbit. He'd slotted into the ranch as if he'd always lived there. He'd expected some of the guys here to resent him, but it hadn't worked that way. On the reservations, fewer of the People had died, infections were common, and a semi-retired doctor from Grants – married to a Navaho woman – had had access to allodaxin and treated them with it. Jason grinned. As a result, more of the People survived, and gradually, they were taking over empty ranches and homesteads. He could see the possibility that in generations to come, it could be that there's be more of them than other races.

It hadn't hurt his rep amongst the guys here that he'd come almost the length of the country alone, apart from Stormy, that he'd fought, killed where he had to, carried a battle scar, and had led them to the depots. Nor, that next summer, they were planning to go back to Belen to gather some of the abandoned cattle and sheep and return to restock the ranches here. And that his dad was talking of a much longer drive – to the Crispins, to exchange some of what was surplus here for some of their goats. With both those trips, he'd be returning to friends, and that impressed his workmates here too. He whistled Stormy, and they drove home.

Shandin was in the main room, talking to a man Jason didn't know. "Hi, son, meet Doctor Levin."

Jason beamed. "I heard of you, sir, really pleased to meet you."

The talk over dinner was of the need to start training a junior doctor or two, and Jason understood as soon as the subject rose, what his father had in mind; yet, he'd come to see he couldn't be a doctor as he'd always intended. Not full-time anyhow. When invited to contribute to the discussion, he did so.

"Yes, I wanted to be a doctor. I bought all Mom's medical books with me, stacks of medicine, all sorts of other stuff as well, and I'd still like some training, but I think we don't just need one or two new doctors. I think we need paramedics. A good number of people who know what to do in emergencies, enough that there'll always be one around. Not just a doctor that has to cover thousands of acres and once the gas runs out could take days to get to a patient." Doctor Levin looked at him and then at Shandin.

"Smart lad. Talks common sense, thinks in generations, not a year or two." And to Jason, "You'd train as a paramedic then?"

"Yes."

****

He did, part-time for five years, during which time he managed two trips to see Gary and their small group, returning with sheep, goats, cattle, and horses. Velda was dying the second time, and he sent the others home, waiting, staying with Gary until the old lady was gone. Jess took over the house and refused to leave.

"My place, she left it to me, and I'm not going. Plenty of empty houses around, I'm not short of anything."

That was true, and he wasn't going to kidnap her. He attended the funeral, saw Velda laid to rest, and went back to the ranch with a real determination to make an expedition back to the Crispins. Stormy had found her mate a year after their arrival at the Shandin Ranch, a coyote-dog mix puppy born there, smart, tough, and trainable. Jason named him Cocoa for his color, thinking that the dog half had been a chocolate poodle. They produced a steady trickle of puppies that threw to their parents, and Jason had a waiting list of those who would like one. He often looked at them and wondered what the man who'd made Stormy's designer breed would have thought.

In the fourth year, the ranchers fought off a bandit group, and in the fifth, there was influenza that killed a dozen people. And in the seventh, when he was twenty-six, Jason led the expedition he'd always hoped for. Back to the Crispin ranch, where he was greeted with tears and hugs. Mark came over a day later and wrung his hand.

"That cellar you told us about before you left. We found it, an' we found Fred there. Guess when they chased him, he remembered it, got down there somehow. He was gone when we found him. They'd beaten him pretty bad, but we had him to bury and our family's grateful. Come over to dinner tomorrow." He did.

And as a result, Jason found a mate of his own, Jaya, Mark's younger sister, who married him before everyone and returned with him. After that, both his family and the ranch prospered.

The virus had left locals who didn't carry any of the Blood more prone to other illnesses, and by the thirteenth year, more than half of the ranches were owned by the People, or at least those who carried their genes.

Gary died when Jason was thirty-seven, Ray from an unidentified sickness three years after, and Jess vanished with her by-now adult daughter. He never knew where they went, why, or what happened to them, and truthfully, he didn't much care. But the Crispin ranch – and the other lands he and his father added to the Shandin Ranch – flourished as did the whole of both areas, and soon it would be time to visit Tim and Annie, Ally and Geoff, again. It would be good to see friends and their children.

EPILOGUE

Jason rode over the slope towards the old Ramah reservation. He was aging, but not so old he couldn't handle a quiet ride. He studied the land as he went; it'd been a good year, enough rain, good growth, and a steady increase in livestock. A lot of what could be salvaged was gone now, and gas almost so. Any they found went into the depot tanks where it would stay uncontaminated, for emergency use. Ahead a dog barked, and he smiled. One of Stormy's line. He'd taken her because she looked just like his old girl had. He chuckled softly. Old men had their fancies and should indulge them.

Ahead he saw the ranch furthest out from Ramah and which was owned by a daughter. He'd had five children before his wife, Jaya, died. Emma, Janet, and Kerry - names long promised - Crispin-known-as-Cris; and the youngest, Shandin, named after Jason's father. They were all in their forties now, strong, intelligent, healthy, and - his smile widened - with solid common sense. Nice those traits had perpetuated. The ranch ahead had been taken by Emma and held her husband, two children, two elderly relatives, and four employees.

He slowed as he approached, remembering so much. It had been his eighty-first birthday last week - and a heck of a celebration *that'd* been. But clear in his memory was the trip he'd made almost sixty-five years ago. He'd found friends, defeated enemies, traveled over land that now in many places had long ago gone back to the wild - in more ways than one. Zoos, wildlife parks, and private sanctuaries had often let out their animals so that in some places, elephants roamed, zebras competed for grass with feral cattle, and were preyed upon by lions, tigers, leopards, and wolves.

In this area, they'd kept all that lot out. It was their land, for those who were born to it. And every year, the boundaries spread wider as more of the People claimed it. His father had always had good horses. It had been a hobby for Shandin; now for Jason it was reality. He'd driven long days with his father's approval, year after year, buying, trading, swapping, until they had the Ramahs. A usually dun horse with black points, an average fifteen hands, powerful, long-lived, stocky and strong, but with quick reflexes, eminently trainable, kind-natured, and smart.

Now the last of the gas was almost gone; they were transportation for this and the generations to come. Jason rode one now, a good beast, and he could be proud of the breed. Proud of Stormy's line, too, and proud of all he'd accomplished. The mini-stereo in his saddlebag started playing Bryan Adams singing "18 'til I Die," and Jason grinned. Far away and long ago as that might have been, he still remembered his eighteenth year. His mother's face flashed before him. *Live long and prosper,* she'd said at the last. He'd never been back. It was too far, he'd never bury the Grand's bones, but the land would have taken them by now, of that he had no doubt. They'd rest easy.

He'd buried his mother. That had been the last thing he did before leaving their home. He'd chosen to forget those last few hours. But for some reason, it was in his mind now, as fresh as yesterday. She had been dying while he held her hand. She'd smiled at him, her gray eyes brilliant with love.

"Once it's time, Jase, go and don't look back. It can only get worse and worse still in cities like this one." She'd reached into her bedside cabinet and brought out a single pill, gently scooping up the cat that lay beside her.

"Mom, what..."

"Jase, love, she's almost your age, you can't take her, she won't survive the trip, and she could escape and die alone. Better painlessly now with someone who loves her."

He'd sat on the bed, tears running freely as his mother gave Fluffy the pill. The old cat accepted it graciously, curled purring under their stroking hands, and gradually, her breathing slowed - stopped - and she was gone. His mom looked at him.

"Go and dig a hole now, love. A large one, she can sleep with me."

"But …where…"

"In the back yard, by the roses. Use the quilt I made."

He'd dug the grave, buried them together but not wrapped in that quilt. She'd made it, and it went with him. She lay by the roses, beloved cat curled at her side, both under a quilt his grandmother had made him instead, and he hoped if Gran's spirit knew what he'd done with the quilt she hadn't minded. His mom's quilt was for him, and he'd be buried in that when the time came.

He'd gathered all their favorite music to take with him and been surprised over the years how many others had taken music with them. He smiled at the memories as Bryan segued into *Summer of '69* – Jason had been well into middle-age by that different '69, but he remembered the joy and laughter of his family, the five of the children still young, and his lovely Jaya laughing with them. *He* was stopping near the ranch door, dismounting as his grandchildren ran out, then - blackness flowed over him. He felt himself slipping to the ground as if arms reached out to encircle him, and he relaxed into the warmth and the affection.

They came then, alight with love and welcome, his mom, dad, Stormy, the grands, Jaya; he walked away with them, forgetting the shell that lay behind. Those left would bury him in the quilt and mourn, but they'd also remember a long life well-lived. In time, his trip would become a saga, told and retold, of the wild and fabulous lands, dead cities to the north, and there would be songs made and sung. But he had fought his way home, and here he would lie now and forever, one of them. Jason Waterhawk Trevalen; father, husband, warrior, friend, patriarch, breeder of the Ramah, man of the Diné …

((((((((And one whose tale is done.))))))))

ABOUT THE AUTHOR

Lyn started writing in 1990 and, within a year, had short stories and poems published. In 1993, her first book, a humorous true-life work (*Farming Daze*) about her farm, friends, and animals, appeared, followed by six others in that series. As a joke between them, a longtime friend of Lyn's, Andre Norton, was given a book Lyn had written set in one of Andre's worlds. Andre was impressed with the work and took it to her agents, who sold it to Warner books. This led Lyn to write another six books in Andre's world, published either by Warner or TOR. Lyn has won seven short story Muse Medallions from the (International) Cat Writer's Association and six Sir Julius Vogel Awards for her books. Since the original book, Lyn has seen almost fifty more books appear plus over three hundred short stories and says she has no intention of stopping so long as she can write.

www.ingramcontent.com/pod-product-compliance
Lightning Source LLC
LaVergne TN
LVHW091030080826
845145LV00002B/426

* 9 7 8 1 9 3 7 7 6 9 6 9 7 *